I'LL STAY

Center Point
Large Print

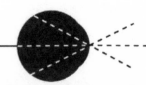

**This Large Print Book carries the
Seal of Approval of N.A.V.H.**

I'LL
STAY

KAREN DAY

CENTER POINT LARGE PRINT
THORNDIKE, MAINE

This Center Point Large Print edition
is published in the year 2018 by arrangement with
Kensington Publishing Corp.

The text of this Large Print edition is unabridged.
In other aspects, this book may vary
from the original edition.
Printed in the United States of America
on permanent paper.
Set in 16-point Times New Roman type.

ISBN: 978-1-68324-707-4

Library of Congress Cataloging-in-Publication Data

Names: Day, Karen, author.
Title: I'll stay / Karen Day.
Description: Large print edition. | Thorndike, Maine :
   Center Point Large Print, 2018.
Identifiers: LCCN 2017057146 | ISBN 9781683247074
   (hardcover : alk. paper)
Subjects: LCSH: Female friendship—Fiction. | Large type books.
Classification: LCC PS3604.A98664 I5 2018 | DDC 813/.6—dc23
LC record available at https://lccn.loc.gov/2017057146

For David, my love

I'LL STAY

PART ONE

1983

CHAPTER 1

We were lost and it was my fault. Again. Less than an hour ago, I was driving north on I-95 instead of south toward Daytona. Finally, I'd gotten off at the right exit but somehow I'd taken a wrong turn, and now we were idling at a stop sign in a dark intersection in a crappy neighborhood with boarded-up buildings and tiny houses with sagging porches and chain-link fences.

I glanced at Lee, sitting next to me in the passenger seat, and then in the rearview mirror. Sarah and Ducky were in the back seat, still talking about the preppy University of Georgia Sigma Chis we'd left at the bar two hours ago. I licked my sunburned lips. Lee looked out the side window. Someone, probably Ducky, opened a beer can and the sound of the pop and fizz seemed to linger in the car.

Why was I so turned around? I'd always thought of myself as being good with directions. I tightened my grip on the steering wheel. Maybe I'd start driving and somehow find Eighty-Sixth Street, and I could pretend that I knew where I was all along. I glanced in the mirror again. If I said that I was lost, I'd have to listen to the grief that Sarah would undoubtedly hurl at me. *Clare, you've been all over the country and yet you can't get us to a stupid house in Daytona Beach?* And Ducky, who had once again had more to drink than the rest of us, would repeat everything Sarah said.

But mostly I didn't want to tell Lee and not because I was worried about grief. Or insults. Quite the opposite. She'd protect me, maybe make an excuse for me, and I was so tired of those things from her that I could scream. I rubbed my temples with my thumb and fingers. If we didn't find this house soon, if we didn't get a place to sleep, maybe a shower, maybe something else to eat, too, I didn't know what I was going to do. I couldn't stay up all night again tonight.

Sarah grabbed my headrest and pulled herself forward. "Oh, my God. What are you doing? Why are we stopped?"

"We're lost!" Ducky shrieked.

"Again?" Sarah asked. "But I told Donny we'd be there an hour ago! What if he left? I'm not sleeping in this car again tonight."

We planned to crash with Donny, Sarah's friend from high school who now lived here in Daytona. He'd been her school's drug dealer. Not bad drugs, she'd said, just regular drugs like pot. And maybe speed, she wasn't sure. But it was only for one night. Then tomorrow we'd make our way to Fort Lauderdale, where we'd stay with friends from our sorority house before heading back north to school on Saturday.

Because of money already spent on the Outer Banks condo we abandoned yesterday, after four days of cold and rain, this was the best we could do. Now we all agreed that we had to be careful and make sure our limited funds lasted the rest of vacation.

"Relax." Lee flipped the switch and bright, bold light flooded the car. She reached for the map and opened it on her lap.

I glanced at Ducky, sitting forward in her seat, her trademark pearls dangling under her chin and her pink sweatshirt just a shade too bright in the car light. She grinned at me, her big blue eyes squinting, and then took a long drink from her beer.

Sarah, whose curly red hair had exploded into a bird's nest with the sudden humidity, barked, "Who would've ever guessed that you were so bad with directions, Clare. I mean, what the hell?"

"It's hard to see in the dark and rain." I shifted in my seat. Sand was stuck to the bottom of my thighs, under my fingernails, between my toes, and the back of my neck was sunburned from when I fell asleep on the beach today.

When Lee turned to me, I frowned and looked away. Our car—a blue Ford Thunderbird that Lee had named "The Travelodge" and that Sarah's mom let us borrow for the week—was filled with empty Miller Lite and Tab cans,

Egg McMuffin wrappers, suitcases, wet towels, backpacks, bathing suits, sleeping bags, pillows, a giant gallon tub of extra crunchy peanut butter, and a large box of two hundred and fifty Fig Newtons that we'd taken from our sorority house commissary before we left.

"Maybe we should've stayed in North Carolina." Sarah sighed. "Even if it was too cold and that condo smelled like cat urine and old people."

"It's not my fault that my aunt's place smelled so bad," Ducky said.

Sarah sighed again. "No one's blaming you—"

"But we couldn't stay there!" Ducky said. "It was going to rain for the rest of the week! I need a tan. We gotta have tans for the end of our senior year."

I couldn't have cared less about tans. I turned off the interior light and stepped on the gas, throwing Ducky and Sarah, gasping, back into their seats. Lee gripped the dashboard with both hands. Water from the puddles slapped the passenger side window as I turned the corner and kept going.

Lee made a circle on the foggy windshield. Then she leaned over and made a circle for me, too, and now I could see a bit better. She said, "You should turn here."

I didn't want to turn. I didn't want *her* to be right. I was still angry about what had happened at the bar, and I wanted her to feel this. She and I had sat in the stairwell of our house too many nights to number, talking about our families. She knew I didn't like people knowing who my mother was. Yet today she introduced me to the Sigma Chis as, "The famous Eleanor Michaels's daughter."

We came to a dead end. Ducky and Sarah groaned.

"Oh, my God, Clare, you're the worst driver!" Ducky said.

"Shut the fuck up!" Lee yelled. "She's doing the best she can!"

Ducky sunk back in her seat. Lee frowned and flipped on the light again. As she tucked her long black hair behind her ears and studied the map, I felt something flip in my stomach. I knew why she did what she did today. Despite sticking up for me just now, she was angry, too. Because I'd pulled away these last couple of months.

But it was our senior year. I didn't want to be so intense. I didn't want to talk endlessly—I was the *only* person she'd *ever* confided in—about how upset she was with her aunt's arrest or what might happen if she didn't get the film internship in New York. And I especially didn't want to keep talking about our friendship.

I rubbed my temples again. For years Lee had been the kind of friend I'd never had. Trustworthy. Earnest. Interesting. And not at all

15

like many of my junior high and high school friends who sucked up to me because of my mother. Where were they all now? I didn't know. I'd flitted from group to group in high school—one foot in, one foot out—so that it was easy to just fall away once I left for college.

I glanced at Lee. Not since junior high had I had a best friend. Lee and I had been nearly inseparable these last four years. But I knew she didn't have the thoughts I'd had lately. That sometimes I didn't want to be around her. That I didn't want to share an apartment with her after we graduated, as we'd loosely planned.

Cool sweat broke out across my upper lip.

"I'm *so* sick of this car," Sarah said.

"I'm *so* sick of it, too," Ducky echoed.

"I think we should go back the way we came." Lee reached up and switched off the light. I nodded—defeated—and turned the car around. As we approached the intersection where a few minutes ago Lee had told me to turn, I sped up and whipped the car around the corner. One block up we saw the sign. Eighty-Sixth Street. I turned and slowed until we pulled up to number twenty-seven. Finally.

"Yea! We're here! Thank God, because we're out of beer. Oh, that rhymed." Ducky laughed, cleaned a small space on her window with her fingers and looked out. "It's kinda small, though. What do you think, Clare? Lee?"

Lee stared at the house. "Something doesn't feel quite right."

"You aren't going to talk about that bullshit karma crap again, are you?" Sarah asked. "You did it, Clare. You got us here. That's what matters."

Lee nodded and said, "Good job, captain."

I cringed. I hadn't done a damn thing. *She'd* gotten us here. Anger boiled up to my cheeks. Stop trying to placate me!

"Maybe this isn't even it." Ducky hiccupped. "Are you sure this is it?"

We stared at the house.

"That's what Donny told me," Sarah said. "Come on. Let's go."

No one moved.

We were parked in front of one of the tiniest, most rundown houses I'd ever seen. It was one level with a wide, full-length window next to the door. On the other side, a single light bulb shone across a yard that was framed with a chain-link fence, broken in several sections. A long piece of gutter hung off the roof. A small kiddie pool was turned on its side and propped against the house under the light. The entire house and yard, which seemed smaller than the kitchen in our sorority house, was just like the dozens of houses that stretched down the street.

I rolled down my window. The rain had slowed to a trickle and the wind had stopped. Under the lone streetlight I watched steam rise from the cement and vanish into the shadows. The cool air smelled heavy and fetid and I shivered.

"The neighborhood looks kinda, I don't know, not that great," Lee said.

"I don't think it looks that bad," I said.

Lee glanced at me.

Ducky sighed. "We coulda stayed at the bar with the Sigma Chis, you know."

"The *Bible* salesmen! That still cracks me up." Sarah laughed and shoved Lee who'd come up with the nickname when we spotted the Sigma Chis in the bar. Dressed in matching beige khaki shorts, Lacoste polo shirts turned up at the collars, brown Top-Siders, and each with coiffed hair—in different shades of blond—the five looked as if they'd leaped off the pages of the Preppy Handbook. "I'm still surprised they talked to us. We looked like hell. We still do."

We were dressed in gym shorts and sweatshirts over bathing suits, layers of dried saltwater, sweat, and baby oil on our skin. After driving all night, we spent the day on the beach. We had no idea what we were doing next until Sarah remembered that Donny was living in Daytona and called him from a pay phone. Before starting to his house, we decided to stop at the bar to have only one beer—we really did have to ration our money—that turned into four or five once we met the Sigma Chis.

None of us had ever done anything like this. Changed plans midweek. Gotten in the car and just taken off. It felt exciting, decadent and reckless, leaving our lovely, if geriatric, Outer Banks condo and living out of The Travelodge.

"Well, I thought they were cute," Ducky said. "And nice. Right? I mean, they paid for everything. When was the last time boys at our school offered to do that?"

"They were boring," Sarah said. "And who dresses like that?"

Lee suddenly turned to them. "The question is, did they plan to dress alike? Or because they live together they just naturally became like each other?"

"Wait, is this conversation going to require me to think?" Ducky asked.

"A girl in my film class is working on this." Lee's voice sped up, as it always did when she talked about films. "There's a theory that women who live together begin having synchronized periods."

Sarah, a biology major who planned to go to medical school, nodded. "That makes sense because it's biological. But how is dressing alike biological?"

Lee shrugged.

"Well, we live together and we don't dress alike." Ducky was the preppiest among us; she rarely went anywhere without her pearls and a

19

pink or blue headband. "Maybe because we're not a typical sorority? We're not skinny and snobby and we have, you know, a lot of variety in our house?"

"We have little variety," Lee said. "There's barely any individualism in the Greek system. It breeds status quo."

"God, Lee, can you be a little more depressing?" My voice was angrier than I meant it to be. I wasn't in the mood for a dissertation on the limitations of Greek life. From the beginning of our pledgeship four years ago, Lee and I had been ambivalent; while fun it had also felt, at times, too exclusive, too one-dimensional, too trite. But this was something we talked about, just the two of us, and I didn't want to sound condescending in front of Sarah and Ducky. They loved the Greek experience, every bit of it, and I loved them for this even if I couldn't completely join in.

"I'm not trying to be," Lee mumbled as she dropped her chin to her chest. I felt her mood darken—my God, I bet I could feel this a mile away—and squeezed the steering wheel so hard that my fingers throbbed. *Stop being so gloomy,* I wanted to scream. I eased my hand off the steering wheel and rubbed my temples again. Either we needed to keep drinking or go to sleep but this in-between state was killing me.

We startled when a car, headlights blazing,

crept up from behind, edged past us, and then slowly turned the corner. From somewhere in the distance a door slammed. A man yelled. A dog barked. And yet the houses around us were dark. No one was out on the street, either. I shivered again as cool, tropical air blew into the car and glanced at Lee, who was frowning as she stared at the house.

Ducky began chewing on a fingernail. Sarah rubbed her chin. I felt a heaviness settle over the car although I wasn't sure why.

"I think there's a light behind the blinds," Lee said. "Do you see it?"

"I don't see anything," Sarah said. Ducky echoed her.

I squinted and couldn't see it, either.

"Well." Ducky tipped her beer can to her mouth but it was empty. She dropped it on the floor. "I just think we shoulda stayed with the Sigma Chis."

"Oh, my God," Sarah said. "Will you stop? I'm so fucking sick of hearing about the Sigma Chis. Sure, we could have stayed and continued to eat their food and drink their beer. But then what? Huh? Where were we going to sleep?"

Lee turned again to look at Ducky. "And if they'd continued to pay for us, did that mean we'd owe them something in return?"

"Not me." Ducky's voice was fast and certain. "We didn't even know them."

"Oh, God, what if they'd lured us into the bathroom, one by one, and had their way with us? The horror!" Sarah threw herself across the middle seat, empty Fig Newton wrappers and beer cans crunching beneath her.

Ducky rolled over her bottom lip into a pout.

"She's kidding," I said. "Except for their preppy clothes, those guys were like the boys we know from school. I hardly think we had anything to worry about."

We turned to the house again. The light bulb next to the door flickered and sputtered but stayed on.

"Wait, Clare, look, it's Ben's pool, under the light," Sarah said.

I squinted. Blue with pink smiley fish, the pool was exactly like the one Ben bought at Target last year. He kept it in his living room and used it to hold his baseball gear. Last spring when the weather got so hot, he put it outside and filled it with water. My own private pool, he'd joked.

I saw his face in my mind, the dimple in his chin and those squinty green eyes, and felt something warm in my chest. I first noticed him in my history class last year. I liked how confident he was and that unlike others he never made fun of our awkward professor. At first we hung out as friends. Recently it had turned into something else although I wasn't sure what it was, even if we'd begun sleeping together. I liked that we were in the same state now—the baseball team spent spring breaks training down the coast—although our worlds couldn't be more opposite. Most likely he was asleep in a dry, warm bed after a hard day of wind sprints and batting practice. Tonight I was sleeping in a house the size of a box.

I felt a twinge of nausea—because of exhaustion or nerves or maybe just the beer and fried mozzarella and tomato sauce—and said, "Maybe one of us should go to the door first."

But no one moved.

Then suddenly someone inside the house rolled up the blind and opened the window. Light from the house poured into the yard. We saw a few legs and torsos and heard music. Bad Company. *In the beginning, I believed every word that you said; Now that you're gone, my world is in shreds.*

Ducky sat forward, her voice an octave higher. "Look, he's having a party!"

"God, we're ridiculous. *I'll* go." When Sarah opened the door, empty beer cans spilled (ping, ping, *ping!*) onto the street. Lee rolled down her window. And then we watched as Sarah opened the gate, stopped on the step, and knocked. The door flew open and a tall guy, barefoot and in striped parachute pants and an open flannel shirt, his chest bare, stood in the light of the doorway. He had long, curly black hair and a huge smile.

Sarah jumped into his arms, laughing, talking, laughing.

"Look! *See?* Everything's fine! This is going to be so fun." Ducky pushed open the car door and ran up the sidewalk toward Sarah.

Now Lee and I were alone for the first time since she told the Sigma Chis about my mother. She turned to me. The lights from the dashboard seemed to exaggerate her high cheekbones and make her smooth and full lips especially shiny. "I'm sorry about today. I shouldn't have said—"

"Can we please not talk about this now?" I asked.

Ducky had started down the sidewalk and soon thrust her head in through the window. "Donny wants you to pull into the driveway and park in front of the shed. Lock the doors, too, because he said there've been lots of break-ins lately."

"Okay," I said. Ducky turned and ran back up to the door.

Lee raised her eyebrows, her lips curved into a partial smile that seemed careful, as if testing me. She said, "Sarah's drug dealer."

I smiled and so did she, a genuine one this time, and a rush of calmness swept over me. Because in just those three ironic words, *Sarah's drug dealer,* Lee was speaking a language, *our* language, that we'd cultivated these past four years. Sarah didn't do drugs, ever, and Lee and I spent many nights speculating as to why and what her dead father, a pharmacist, might have to do with it. Sarah, Ducky, Lisa, Amy—Lee and I discussed them all, not because we were gossipy or mean but because we found them interesting and wanted to understand what made them so.

This was how we usually were. *This* was one of the reasons we were best friends. I turned the car into the driveway and thought about what Sarah had said—*we're living on the wild side!*—less than twenty-four hours ago as we left North Carolina. I smiled at Lee again. Yes, let's have fun. Let's live on the wild side.

In the headlights I saw the shed door hanging by a top hinge and the entire structure leaning precariously to the side. Scrubby grass grew in patches along the driveway. Several palm trees, black with rot, lay stacked on their sides. A ten-speed bicycle, missing its handlebars and front wheel, leaned against a pile of wood.

"Not the best neighborhood," Lee said. "This doesn't feel right."

I'd never known anyone so affected by how surroundings looked and *felt*. But I wanted to keep the conversation light. I didn't want to go back to how I was feeling only a few moments ago. "Hey, we're living on the wild side, right?"

Lee nodded. And for right now, this moment, we were okay.

CHAPTER 2

Donny had friends over. Butch, a tall guy with red frizzy hair and a ZZ-Top beard. Stacy, with hair bleached and teased high on her head, who wore jean cutoffs and a tight white tank top with the word *SEXY* in sparkly green across her chest. A half-dozen girls by the sink whose names I didn't catch. And a group of guys near the refrigerator who were older—maybe twenty-five—and barely looked when Donny introduced us. Last was Smitty, Donny's roommate, who hugged each of us and said we were the most beautiful women he'd ever met.

"Ya'all are college girls, huh?" He wore jean shorts just visible under a tank top that said *This Bud's for You*. His blond hair was shaved above both ears and hung long across the back and top. He had a silver tooth in front, top row, which sparkled when he smiled and caught the light. It matched the chain around his neck.

"Not only are they college girls, but Sarah's gonna be a *doctor*," Donny said.

She punched him in the arm. "Don't jinx it. I gotta get into med school first."

"You will. You girls can do anything you want!" Donny looked at each of us, but stopped at Lee. He grinned, the skin wrinkling in the corners of his mouth. Lee turned away as she took a long pull from her beer.

Guys liked Lee, partly because she acted so indifferent but also because of how she looked. She was tall and thin with olive-colored skin, long, shiny black hair, a small nose and mouth. She wasn't beautiful, Ben said once, but "interesting-looking." Somewhere on her dad's side she had Wampanoag blood and we used to joke about this. My relatives had been in New England for centuries, and maybe our ancestors had had Thanksgiving together. Now I wondered if they fought each other.

"They're *sorority* girls," Donny said.

Smitty raised his eyebrows. "Really? I don't know any sorority girls. But you don't seem the type. And I was meaning that to be a compliment."

Ducky grinned. "See, *Lee?* Thanks. Because we *aren't* typical sorority girls."

Lee shrugged. I wasn't sure why this had become the topic of the day. Maybe we weren't as preppy. Maybe we were bigger partiers and carried around, except for Lee, an extra fifteen pounds more than the average sorority girl. But Lee had been right. There wasn't much variety between the houses and within our own.

And this had ultimately been a disappointment. The first couple of years, I loved coming back to the house each day. It was a huge and intimidating structure, four stories, redbrick with a sloping lawn, able to house eighty girls easily. There was always so much energy and stimulation. After dinner we sat around, sometimes twenty of us, and laughed and talked. It had been a wonderful surprise—so different from the long-drawn-out conversations about books, politics, and war at my parents' house—to find happiness in nonsense conversation and joking around.

Maybe I had patience for this because Lee and I, alone, discussed meatier topics. Our classes. Lee's obsession with Patricia Graceson, the visiting film professor. Our interest in Freud. But by the time school started this year, I'd grown tired of communal living and vapid conversations and Lee wasn't around much; she spent most of her time on her senior film project. And then after winter break, when she *was* around, all she talked about were these worries and how awful she felt.

"Donny, what can we do for these not-typical sorority girls?" Smitty asked.

"Only one thing." Donny grinned. "Get 'em stoned."

He pulled a joint from his pocket and lit it. He passed it to Lee, who took a long drag and gave it to me. I held it between my finger and thumb and let the pungent smoke drift up to my face. Most everyone smoked, even Ben when it wasn't baseball season. I rarely did it because I could never be sure how it would affect me.

29

Ducky, who was on her third beer, was laughing with Smitty. Sarah and Donny were talking about something that had happened in eighth grade. Lee was getting more beers. Across the room, Stacy was drinking shots of tequila with Butch. And the guys by the refrigerator were passing their own joint.

These people couldn't be more different from the Sigma Chis. And this house was unlike any place I'd ever been. Small, just one room, with scummy tiles on the floor—black sludge in the corners—cabinets so grimy that they no longer were white. Low ceilings, dim lights. A giant water heater that jutted out from the wall next to the bathroom. A pale pink phone on the other wall, its dirty cord long and bunched on the floor. A single black La-Z-Boy chair with a floor lamp next to it. We were in a questionable neighborhood. On the wrong side of the tracks.

Not one of our friends was having a spring break experience like this. Julie and Lisa were skiing in Vail. Amy and a group were in Fort Lauderdale. Susie was in Chicago. Which was where my mother was. Or maybe she was in Denver?

What would she think of this place?

I put the joint to my lips, inhaled, and immediately burst out laughing.

Someone turned up the music, Lynyrd Skynyrd's "Sweet Home Alabama," and when

Ducky yelled, "This song is *perfect!* Because that's where we are!" we laughed so hard that Sarah had to cross her legs so she wouldn't pee in her gym shorts.

"We're not in Alabama, sweetie, we're in Florida!" Donny yelled.

After that we kept yelling, "Sweet Home Alabama" and laughing. More people arrived, a girl in a halter top with bleached, feathered hair and a guy with a mullet wearing too-tight jeans. The room was spinning because the pot was so strong and I'd had too many beers and not enough food or sleep.

Outside, it had begun to rain again—we could see it through the huge floor-to-ceiling window—and flashes of lightning lit up the puddles in the muddy lawn. And then suddenly there was another flash and we turned to the window just as a huge naked man leaped into the room from outside, slid on the rain water that had pooled on the floor, and knocked over the halter top girl and the guy with the mullet.

Everyone started screaming at him. When he got to his feet, I saw that he wasn't naked but wearing a tight white Speedo. He had hair everywhere, down his back and legs and arms, and he was at least six feet eight. People seemed to know who he was and eventually went back to what they were doing. Not us. We watched him, even Ducky, who was so drunk that she kept scrunching her nose and forehead, as if trying to focus. He stumbled around the room, bouncing off people, the walls, the water heater. Where were his clothes?

The music was so loud that it was impossible to hear anyone talk. But during a break between songs, I heard Sarah ask Donny what was wrong with him.

"Probably acid," Donny said. "That's his thing."

We glanced at each other. Lee was the only one among us who'd ever done acid. A quick burn started across my chest. It was a nervous, cautionary feeling—one that I recognized from earlier in the car but couldn't name—that told me that maybe this wasn't a good idea. These people were too old, too hardcore. I walked over and dumped my beer into the sink. Someone had to get sober, which would be me, as always. I was the responsible one, the person to count on if you needed a lifeline in the middle of the night, my mother used to say to me.

Ducky, Sarah, and Donny started dancing. Lee bobbed her head as she watched. And when others began to leave and the Speedo giant ran back out the window, as if being chased, I felt a bit silly. I'd overreacted. After all, we had Donny. He and Sarah knew each other not from eighth grade but from fourth. That was a lot longer than I'd known anyone and it made me feel that we had a right, a claim, on Donny, and that we belonged here as much—maybe even more—than anyone else.

We stayed in the corner, listening to music and dancing for another hour. Although we'd found a boost of energy, I felt myself starting to fade again and looked around, wondering how we would sleep. The grimy floor was swimming with spilled beer and cigarette butts. The patch of dry floor near the La-Z-Boy was big enough for only one sleeping bag. And then the music stopped and I heard Lee tell Smitty about her documentary, the one she'd submitted for the film internship.

"Patricia Graceson is this amazing person," she said. "She grew up with nothing, one parent with schizophrenia and the other a drug addict. But she made something of her life. She got her PhD and eventually made a film about malnutrition among children in Africa. My film is about her and her life."

"Whoa! That'd be real interesting, I bet." Smitty was so stoned that his eyes were slits and he swayed from side to side, a persistent grin on his lips.

"But it's not just about what she does," she said. "It's about how she lives. What comes out of the film is this Socratic idea that the unexamined life is not worth living. That's what gives the film its heft and what people can relate to."

Socratic idea? Heft? I cringed.

Smitty scrunched his forehead, as if trying to make sense of what she was saying. Not only had he not gone to college, he probably hadn't graduated high school, either. These were the types of people Lee had grown up with. How could she not notice how uncomfortable this made him? I hated when people, when *anyone,* did this kind of thing. I flinched as sweat broke out on my sunburned neck.

"Wow," Smitty said. "You're gonna be a famous movie director!"

I frowned. It was one thing to produce a twenty-minute short film and another to be a famous movie director. While her film was good, it wasn't perfect. Watching it, I always had the sense that it needed something although I had no idea what that was.

"Not everybody has the luxury to live an examined life," I said. "Some people have to work three jobs to put food on the table. Or they have to take care of sick relatives. They don't have time for anything else."

Lee's smile faded. "I know that."

"Well, don't be so judgmental."

"You don't have to tell me what it's like to worry about putting food on the table." Lee frowned and lowered her eyes.

"Seriously?" Smitty laughed. "I got no fucking idea what you're talking about."

Of course Lee knew what it was like to

struggle. It was one of the things we talked about. And she typically wasn't pretentious or oblivious to people's feelings, either. What was wrong with me? Why was I so frustrated? I walked to the window, my cheeks stinging, and looked out. The lightning had stopped but I heard the rain smacking the puddles. I thought about how sunny it had been when we walked into the bar today. Ducky had started us off after the Sigma Chis moved to our table with their plates of food and pitchers of beer. "I'm Ducky. This is Sarah, Lee and—"

"This is the famous Eleanor Michaels's daughter, Clare," Lee had said.

The boys looked at Lee and then at me. I was so shocked that I felt my mouth fall open. It had been a long time (junior high?) since a friend talked about my mother like this in public in front of me.

"Who's Eleanor Michaels?" the tallest one asked.

"She wrote *Listen, Before You Go*," the blondest one said. "The Vietnam book."

"Never heard of it," the tallest one said.

"I read it," the blondest one said. "In high school, I wrote a paper on it. I talked about the death foreshadowing. At first, you don't realize how much of it there is."

"I didn't get it," the shortest one said. "It was supposed to be about the war but there aren't any battle scenes. I mean, it takes place in, like, Vermont."

"You're joking, right?" the blondest one asked. "That's not really her mom?"

"It's true," Ducky said.

The inevitable onslaught of questions followed. Are the characters based on your family? Are you Phoebe, the heroine of the story? Is her book going to be a movie and will you be in it? Are you a writer? Which was always the worst question because I had no creative abilities. Eventually we stopped talking about my mother and her book but something lingered. A carefulness. A deference that didn't belong to me. A laugh and look from one or two boys that wouldn't have been there otherwise. This was more than enough reason to be angry with Lee. Wasn't it?

"Clare." Lee came up behind me and I turned from the window. "Can we talk? About today? About what I said? I know you're mad."

"Did you notice how they acted after you said that? It changed everything. It always changes everything. I've told you that."

"I know. I'm so sorry," Lee said, her voice just above the music. "I'm sick about it. I don't know why I said it."

Across the room, Sarah was trying to get Ducky to sit in a chair, but she kept standing on it and dancing. Donny lit another joint. Someone turned off the music. I wanted to stay angry with Lee but felt it slipping away. Because really? What she said wasn't the reason we left. That was because the boys were boring, after all, and we were ready for the next exciting, unpredictable thing. But I couldn't let it go.

"I'm just surprised, after everything I've told you about my mother." Well, I hadn't quite told her everything. But almost. Certainly Lee knew how difficult and demanding my mother could be. And how in junior high and high school people had tried to friend me to get to her. "I guess it makes me mad."

Lee's voice was hushed. "But you've been mad at me for months now."

"That's not true," I said. But it was, wasn't it? This problem between us felt complicated and I didn't understand it. Before winter break, we were fine. Normal. Things started to change when we returned to school in January. That first night, we stayed up for hours, talking about her aunt's embezzlement charge and how she'd cut Lee out of her life. Lee was devastated. *Why did she steal from her company? Why won't she answer my letters? Why is she acting like I don't exist?* Every night after that we went over this. It took hours to get Lee to a place where she wasn't so upset, but the next night we had to start again. It was like I had to pull her out of a dark hole.

I felt a jolt of anger that was familiar and utterly

exhausting. "Look, I don't exactly know what's going on—"

"Something's changed between us," she said.

She was right. *She'd* changed. She used to be so strong, intimidating, and mysterious. She'd command attention and respect just by walking into a room. Now she was clingy and needy, always sulking and sad. She kept cornering me, wanting to talk, wanting to dump it on me, and I'd begun finding excuses to avoid her.

I licked my sunburned lips. We were always each other's cheerleader but she was so sensitive now. Would she freak out if I told her how much she'd changed? If I said I didn't want to talk so much about how sad she was? God, it felt daunting. It felt impossible. *She* felt impossible.

But I was the house therapist. Everyone brought problems to me. Why wasn't I more patient with her?

"I know I've been upset about what happened to my aunt." Her voice shook. "I don't get why she can't call. What if I never talk to her again? What if this is it?"

How many times had she said this to me over the last few weeks, twenty? Fifty? I shook my head and said, "That doesn't make sense. She loves you."

"I don't even know if that's true," she mumbled.

"So, now you don't think that she loves you?

Come on, Lee." I glanced into the kitchen where Ducky was doing a shot of something.

"I know. I just feel awful." She slumped against the window.

"I feel bad about what happened to your aunt, too," I said. And I did, even if I couldn't relate to her family. Visiting her farm last year had been a shock. It was so rundown and shabby, unlike anything I'd imagined. That she'd gotten out of there and gone to college, even with help from her benefactor, was incredible. "But like I've said before, you've got to find a way not to let this get you down so much."

"You're right. I don't know why I can't get over this. And I had another one of those dreams last night."

Oh, crap.

"This time you and I were standing in line for a bus and everyone got on and you shut the door on me," she said. "Then the bus took off. You left me behind."

She'd been having these dreams long before I began pulling away. Once, she dreamed that I dumped her and became best friends with Susie. In another, I'd invited her to our cottage on Martha's Vineyard but then ignored her while she was there. I didn't understand these dreams and it didn't seem fair that I was always the bad guy. "That's crazy, Lee. Why would I ever shut a bus door on you?"

She shrugged. "I just feel stressed. I miss our talks. And I worry about us—"

I couldn't stand this. "We're both stressed. It's the end of senior year and neither of us knows what we're doing next. It's a weird time for everyone."

"I know, but something has changed—"

"Stop! We're going through a rough patch. You're still my best friend, okay?"

She nodded. Then the crease in her forehead disappeared and the tightness loosened in her cheeks. Just like that the mood lightened, the thickness between us softened. I held my eyes steady, even though I was confused. Yes, I'd pulled back. But she made it worse by telling me about these dreams and worrying so much.

"Okay. I'm sorry," she said. "You're right. As always."

"I'm not always right. Don't keep saying that. Let's just have fun—"

"What are you guys doing over here?" Sarah came up behind us. "You gotta help me with Ducky. I don't know what to do. She's completely trashed again."

The music started, the Rolling Stones, as we watched Ducky, staggering toward the bathroom and then grabbing the water heater to steady herself.

"I'll go." I hurried over, reached for Ducky's elbow and steered her into the bathroom. When

I flipped on the light, a huge cockroach scurried behind the sink. The room was tight with no windows, a tub with no shower curtain, a toilet and a small pedestal sink that was coated in toothpaste and brown crud.

"I think I'm gonna get sick." Ducky's knees buckled.

"Wait!" I flipped up the toilet seat, pulled a towel off a hook on the wall, and draped it around the dirty rim. I spread a second towel on the floor at the base of the toilet. When Ducky dropped to her knees and leaned forward, her blond hair went with her. I quickly and expertly—like I'd done for my mother that time in New York—pulled her hair behind her and held it while she threw up.

Projectile vomit filled the toilet and fumes leaped into the air. I buried my face in my sweatshirt sleeve and stifled my gags. She finished and tried to stand.

"Hang on." I let go of her hair and flushed the toilet. "Just wait here a second. You don't want to stand too quickly and faint. Try to relax."

She rested her head on the toilet, her white-blond eyebrows quivering. She smelled like vomit, beer, and the Lubriderm lotion she always wore. I reached for a magazine on the floor (*Thrasher*?), rolled it up, and watched for the cockroach. I felt mild disgust for how wasted she'd gotten. Something bad could have happened to her if we weren't here to help.

She peeked at me, and as if hearing my thoughts said, "You can go."

I knew she meant it. She'd never asked me for anything. Never *demanded* anything. I felt myself relax. "It's okay. I won't leave you alone."

"Thanks," she slurred, then grimaced and closed her eyes.

I wasn't as close to Ducky as I was with Lee and Sarah. We didn't have much in common. I was an English major from Boston. She was a business major from the North Shore of Chicago. After we graduated I imagined she'd marry a nice boy from the Midwest, raise four nice kids, and sit by a nice country club pool every summer.

After word was out in the house about my mother (somebody from our sorority's national office told our president), Ducky said, "Gosh! I've never met a real writer before!" Her earnestness was refreshing. She never took herself too seriously. God, I was *so* tired of people taking themselves *so* damn seriously.

"I'm going to get sick!" As she sat up and dry heaved into the toilet, I held her hair again. Then she slumped against the wall and started to whimper. In a few minutes, if she no longer had the dry heaves, I'd make her splash water on her face and wash out her mouth. That might help. That might make her feel better.

That was what I'd done for my mother when

I found her in a heap on the floor in the hotel bathroom before the North American Book Award ceremony. She'd left me at the table with her editor and others I didn't know. I was only eleven and no one was paying attention to me. So, no one noticed when I followed her.

"It's not worth it, this *agony*," she moaned when she saw me in the toilet stall doorway. She was on her knees, her legs splayed behind her, new black patent leather shoes—mine were just like hers but smaller—toe down on the marble floor. I'd never seen her in such a vulnerable position and I was too stunned to move.

I also didn't understand how she could say that it wasn't worth it. *Listen, Before You Go*, narrated by eleven-year-old Phoebe whose older brother, Whit, had just returned from the Vietnam War with a broken leg and damaged soul, was loved by so many people. She loved it, too. Once, I heard her talk for twenty minutes about the importance of the comma in the title. And she'd just won a huge, prestigious literary prize. This was all she'd ever wanted. How many times had I heard her complain when others had won?

"Help me," she'd moaned.

It was a guttural, primal call, and I'd never heard this before, either. All I thought about as I stood in the stall of the swankiest hotel I'd ever been in was that it made no sense. My mother was a college professor, an expert on John Milton.

Her novel was a best seller. She had "saved my life," a woman cried to her one day in Emack & Bolio's ice-cream store. What in the world could *I* do?

Then I thought about Phoebe (I was *sure* this was what she'd do) and with my fingers, pulled my mother's long brown hair out of her face—every strand—while she threw up. She flinched when my fingers grazed her neck. I remembered that. But I saved her hair and the beautiful black dress on which we'd spent so much money.

I leaned toward Ducky and said, "Do you think you can stand up?"

She kept her eyes closed and shook her head. "No, and don't leave!"

"Okay." I was in no hurry to face Lee with her crazy dreams and Socratic references. *The unexamined life is not worth living.* Would Ducky ever examine her life? And if not, who were we—or who was Socrates—to judge whether that life was worthwhile or not? And what did it mean to examine your life, anyway? Keep a diary? Go to the health center and talk to a counselor? Write a book and tell-all?

I stood and washed my hands in the sink as I looked at myself in the mirror. I was totally average; chestnut-colored hair resting on my shoulders, hazel eyes, white teeth and a small nose with freckles. I'd put on weight, but not much. Would Phoebe, if my mother ever wrote about her again, look like me now? Or would I look like her? Phoebe has the same freckles as you, people used to tell me. *Phoebe has the same eyes! You and Phoebe are so good at talking to adults. Why, you're Phoebe!*

I squatted and stared at Ducky, her nose burned from the sun, a roll of pink flesh spilling out over the top of her shorts. She opened her eyes and smiled. After we graduated and she went home to the North Shore and I went back East, I imagined we wouldn't see each other much. This, along with the fact that we were bonding and she was wasted and probably wouldn't remember, made me feel daring. And so I brought up something I'd never discussed with anyone in the house.

"How do you think Lee has been acting?" I asked.

"Like what do you mean?" Ducky squinted at me.

"I don't know, on the trip, I guess. Like with the Sigma Chis."

"Same old Lee." She burped and groaned, but nothing came out. "Sometimes I don't know why she joined the house. She's so different from everyone else."

I nodded. I used to wonder this, too, until one day when Lee, gazing up at the glass chandelier in the foyer, said, "Isn't this house the most beautiful thing you've ever seen? Aren't we so lucky to live here? We're like one big family."

45

If Ducky wondered why I'd joined the house, too, she didn't ask. Which was good because at the moment I wasn't sure I could answer.

She burped again, a sweet, polite one that sounded like the chirp of a baby bird. "I've never told anyone this—Oh! I'm so wasted but that burp kinda made me feel better—and I know you're best friends and all but Lee scares me. She's got all this intense stuff inside of her. Like that thing with the periods. Who thinks of stuff like that? I don't know. She doesn't really talk to me. You know, like talk-talk."

"Do you think she can be, I don't know, insensitive sometimes?" I asked.

"Maybe she doesn't talk to me because she thinks I'm stupid about movies and the world. Which I kinda am. Remember that movie she made sophomore year? How good it was and funny and how she got Mom Tolliver to agree to be in it? Or did you do that? I can't remember. Mom Tolliver likes you two more than she likes me."

"That's not necessarily true."

Ducky grimaced and closed her eyes. Lee's movie, her first, came out of an assignment in a film class. She got so many people in the house involved. Sarah and Amy were gangsters, the dinner cooks hid the gun in the angel food cake batter, and Mom Tolliver, our seventy-year-old house mom, drove the getaway car. Lee showed

46

it one night in the chapter room. It was a huge hit.

Ducky's eyes shot open. "Do you think she'll make a movie about *us?*"

I frowned. Why would anyone want her life on a screen for the world to see? Besides, we'd have to actually *do* something to warrant a movie. Drinking beer, smoking pot, and laughing around a dining room table night after night, year after year, wasn't very productive or interesting. I cringed, thinking about my four years of college. I. Had. Done. Nothing. Zip. Zilch. Nada.

"Wow! I think I *am* feeling better." She sat up and wiped her mouth with the back of her hand. "Wanna hear something funny? I used to think, back when we were pledges, that, you know, you two were, you know. Well. *Together.*"

"You mean, like, lesbians?" I asked.

Ducky put her hand over her mouth. "Yes!"

I frowned. Did anyone else think that? "Why did you think that?"

"Because you were both, like, so intense with each other, you know, huddled in the corner being all intellectual and stuff. But then I got to know you both and now you're with Ben, and I think it's more like you and Lee are, well, I don't know, friendship soul mates or something. Am I talking too much?"

Lee and I *were* intense with each other and it *was* like being in love. I thought back to our nights talking in the stairwell and the trips we took to each other's houses, but I couldn't remember any awkward sexual moments. I'd never felt that way toward her. Had she with me? I doubted it. Lee, who'd lost her virginity when she was fifteen, had slept with many guys. Still, I tried to put into words this feeling between us. Intense. Important. One of a kind. Maybe soul mates.

"I'm so wasted!" Ducky said. "But isn't this fun? What about that bathing suit guy? I can't believe these *people*. And their haircuts. My parents would freak if they knew we were here. Is Donny still a drug dealer? But just pot, right? I can't wait to tell everyone about this. And oh, I just love you. I know you think I'm not respectful because I don't talk to you about your mom's book. But I read it."

"It's okay," I said.

"Don't tell anyone about this, okay?" She started hiccupping. "I mean, that I hurled and everything? Cause I'm so wasted? I think it was the pot."

"And the tequila shots," I said.

"Oh, I'm feeling better! I know you won't tell anyone. Because you don't talk about people. I know what you did for Julie. She told me that you went to the clinic with her and waited until it was over and then drove her home and brought her soup. And you never told anyone, did you? Not even Lee."

Julie's abortion at Planned Parenthood last year. Of course I never told anyone. But I felt my cheeks burn because I'd just gossiped about Lee. But maybe that didn't count since I didn't *say* anything. I just *asked* about her. I tightened my grip on the magazine.

"I have a lot of respect for you," she said. "I know you're an English major but you should do something where you help people. You'd be a great nurse. I'll cry if I talk about it but I can't believe we're graduating in two months. It went so fast!"

Then she started whimpering and I worried that she might have the dry heaves again. "Hey, hey. It's okay. Let's enjoy these last couple of months. Okay?"

She nodded and rested her forehead on the toilet rim.

I'd always planned to teach, but changed my mind after visiting the clinic. The women who helped Julie were so passionate and warm. My plan was to take science courses next fall and then apply to graduate school in nursing or counseling. I didn't know where. Lee and I talked about moving to New York. And one night not long ago, Ben asked if I'd go with him to Philadelphia, where he'd been accepted to law school. I could barely even *think* about that.

You should help people. I smiled. I'd always been good at that (Phoebe and me. Me and

Phoebe). Maybe after working for a while, I'd feel passionate about it, too.

Someone banged on the door. "What the fuck is going on in there?"

"Just a minute." I lowered my voice. "Can you get up?"

Ducky stood and leaned on me as I pulled down the bottom of her sweatshirt and told her to wipe her face. I moved the clasp on her pearls to behind her head and opened the door. The lights were on. Most everyone was gone. Donny and the halter top girl stood next to Sarah and a guy I didn't recognize. It was two a.m.

When the halter top girl slipped her arm through Donny's, I realized why she was still here. Sarah yawned. And Ducky, whose face had turned pale again, stumbled over to the La-Z-Boy chair next to the floor lamp and slumped into it.

"She's a mess," Sarah said.

"Yeah," I said. "Just let her sleep in the chair."

That left only a small, dry spot next to the chair. I glanced at the puddles of beer on the floor and thought about the cockroach in the bathroom.

"This is Charlie," Sarah said. "He said two of us could crash at his place."

"He lives a couple blocks away," Donny said. "It's cool."

Charlie was old, maybe twenty-five, with short dirty blond hair that was thinning across his forehead. He had small black eyes that never seemed to blink and crisscrossing acne scars along his jaw. He was tall with broad shoulders and arms ripped with muscles. I bet he lifted weights like Ben and his friends.

He wedged his fingers into the pockets of his skintight, acid-washed jeans. Now I recognized him. He'd been here all along, one of the guys standing by the refrigerator. Still, we didn't know him. I glanced at Lee, who was studying him, too.

"I'll stay here with Ducky," Sarah said. "You two okay going with Charlie?"

Lee tilted her head. I knew her well enough to see the hesitation. Then she shrugged and licked her lips. "Okay, I guess. We need to get our stuff out of the car."

Charlie nodded.

It was still raining. Lee and I ran across the yard and grabbed our backpacks, sleeping bags, and pillows from The Travelodge. Then we followed Charlie. Most of the streetlights were burned out—it was so dark—and we had to hurry to keep up. How many blocks was it? We were soaked by the time we got to his house. Outside it looked like Donny's and the others on the street, small, one-story, with a big window next to the front door. The inside was like Donny's, too, one tight room with a giant water heater, but nicer. And cleaner. A couch, chair, and floor lamp, the shade with miniature red and blue racecars along the edges, framed an oversized rug in front of the window. A Pioneer stereo and turntable sat on red milk crates in the corner.

"So, you can crash there." Charlie pointed to the rug.

"Thanks," I said. "This is really nice of you."

"Don't matter none to me." And then he walked into a back room and shut the door. But he'd left the lights on in the kitchen area and the back door was open. Had he gone to bed for the night? Should we turn off the lights?

We took turns changing and brushing our teeth in the bathroom. We draped our wet shorts and sweatshirts on the chair next to us. Then I spread my sleeping bag onto the rug and crawled inside. Lee rolled out her bag next to mine and glanced at the back door, then at the window in front of us. "I don't know about this."

"What do you mean?" I asked.

"I don't know."

At least the floor was clean and it was quiet and dry. I was so tired that it hurt to keep my eyes open. I yawned. "It's better than Donny's place."

Lee sat cross-legged on her sleeping bag. Then she got on her knees, reached for her wet clothes, and began stuffing them into her backpack.

"You should pack everything up and sleep with your backpack." She put her flip-flops next to her pillow and shoved her backpack into her sleeping bag. "I know guys like this from home. I'm not sure I trust him."

If she didn't trust Charlie, why did she agree to come here? But she rarely referred to guys from home, only to tell me once—when she was wasted—that she'd slept with some "questionable characters." This was one of several things that we didn't have in common. I'd only slept with Ben.

"What's he going to do, steal our backpacks in the middle of the night?"

"The karma is off," she said. "I just have a weird vibe."

Ben thought Lee was "flaky" when I told him that she believed places gave off vibrations. But part of me felt it here, too. I packed my backpack and pushed it into my sleeping bag. I wiggled in, not sure how I'd sleep with this wet mound.

Lee stood and put her hands on her hips. She wore baggy green Army fatigues, cut off mid-thigh, that she'd bought freshman year at the Army-Navy Surplus store and a tight white tank top, faded to gray. I'd seen this outfit so many times that I could close my eyes and see the uneven hem, the rip on the back pocket, the slight hole below her left shoulder where she'd caught the shirt on the window frame in her room. I thought about how my mother had looked her up and down that first morning on the Vineyard when Lee had walked outside in this outfit.

Later, of course, it didn't matter what Lee wore. My mother was so charmed by her, so impressed by her ambition, her intelligence, her joie de vivre, that Lee could have worn a tent and it would have been *so interesting.*

Lee stepped forward and drummed her fingers on the window frame as she looked out. Then she unclasped the lock and opened the window a few inches. Cool, humid, wet air rushed into the room. Like Donny's window, this one didn't have a screen and now I knew how the cockroaches got in.

"If you're so worried about being robbed, why are you opening the window?"

Lee whipped around, angry, and dropped to her knees in front of me. Her long, dark hair fell over her shoulders and the muscles in her cheeks flexed. But then her dark eyes filled with tears and her thick lips trembled and she brought her hands to her face and cried, "Nothing I say or do is right. Why are you so mean to me?"

"I'm not trying to be mean," I said.

"Then what would you call it?"

"I don't know!" I felt my cheeks redden. No, we absolutely *weren't* going to have another talk about our friendship. Not again.

She slumped forward. "It's my fault. I'm so stressed out and sad and I don't know why. I feel sick all the time. I can't sleep and when I do I have those terrible dreams. That you won't talk to me. That you're ditching me."

"I'm not ditching you," I said.

"It feels so horrible to be so out of sync. You're the only person who really knows me. You're the only person I've ever *really* talked to."

"And that's too much goddam responsibility!" I yelled. "I don't want it!"

My words seemed to hang in the air between us. Outside, car doors slammed. A dog barked. A siren wailed, close and closer, then faded away. And still the rain came down. I couldn't see it but heard it slapping the ground outside the window.

Lee straightened and pulled her hair behind her. She walked over to the counter, turned off the overhead light, turned on a light above the stove, and shut the door. Then she switched off the floor lamp, crawled into her sleeping bag, and faced away from me. The humid yet cool breeze through the window made me shiver. The dim stove light cast long shadows across the room. Across us.

I knew that I was the only person to whom she'd ever confided. She hadn't told anyone about the benefactor from her hometown that paid for her tuition and board, or the boys she'd slept with or her high school track coach's unwanted advances or how insecure she felt about being poor. I'd wanted to hear these things. I liked being her confidant. I'd felt so *honored*. But then she became so demanding, *so difficult,* and wasn't I right that it was too much responsibility? To be the only one? God, I was so frustrated and tired. Maybe I wasn't thinking clearly.

"Lee," I said. Her head was tucked in the crook of her arm and her shoulders seemed to tremble, as if she were quietly crying. I began to worry. Maybe Lee had been seriously depressed this year and I didn't realize it.

Charlie walked out of the bedroom, still dressed in the jeans and wet T-shirt he'd worn earlier. He opened the back door and two guys came in. They stood against the sink, talking. One of them opened the refrigerator, pulled out beers, and handed them around. The cans popped and hissed when opened.

I turned my head and watched Lee slowly roll over. We were face-to-face, but she was looking over my shoulder at the guys. I opened my mouth to say something but she whispered, just loud enough for me to hear, "I think we're in trouble."

CHAPTER 3

One guy was bald and wore jeans and a faded black jean jacket. The other was tall and broad with long, frizzy blond hair. He wore a blue tank top and gym shorts one size too small and he kept shifting his bare feet, bouncing his shoulders, twitching his arms. I thought about the crazy guy from earlier tonight who came through the window wearing only a bathing suit. Was this guy on acid, too?

I tried to listen to what they were saying. Donny. A deal. *Fucking asshole.*

Then the jittery man saw us. When he kept jerking his head back and forth between us and the other two, I felt my heartbeat quicken. I whispered, "Lee?"

"I know." Her voice was soft again but firm.

"Hey, girls." He turned to us, hands on hips. "Wanna party?"

"We're pretty beat," Lee said. "But thanks."

They began whispering again. The guy in the jean jacket tipped his head back and guzzled his beer. Then they walked over and sat, Charlie in the chair, the other two on the couch. Jittery Man's bare feet were inches from my face. Despite being wet from the rain, they were black with dirt and his toenails were long and chipped;

thick, dark, curly hair covered the top of each toe. Never, not even at sleepaway camp, had I seen feet so worn and dirty. I had to keep swallowing so I wouldn't gag.

"Not every day you have girls in your house, Charlie," the bald guy said.

Charlie snickered. Jittery Man sneezed and ran the back of his hand across his nose. Rain dripped from his hair onto his bare shoulders but I didn't think he felt it. His glassy eyes flitted around the room. Did he even know where he was?

Gums throbbing, heart racing, stomach roiling. I sucked in small breaths, trying to control myself. But my senses were wired and alert, *screaming,* as if a fire alarm raged through me. Danger! *Danger!* I knew Lee felt it, too. We stayed quiet and still as if this, somehow, would make them go away. As if this could help us.

"Come on, get up." The bald guy nudged Lee with the tip of his black boot.

"Maybe they don't want to," Charlie said.

"You're a fucking pussy." The bald guy laughed although he wasn't smiling. "You're always a fucking pussy, Charlie."

"Fuck you, Owen!"

"Come on, come on, come on, up, up, up!" Jittery Man took his fingers across his dripping nose, wiped them on the couch cushion and began bouncing.

"What the *hell?*" Charlie yelled. "That's my new couch. You're a fucking idiot."

"Better to be a fucking idiot than a fucking pussy," Owen said.

Jittery Man let loose a long, creepy laugh. "Hhhhhaaaaaaaa!"

Charlie glared at Owen and then leaned forward, elbows on knees, until he was directly over us. "Time to get up, girls."

I just knew that those scars across his jaw were from terrible acne. His face must have been covered in swollen pimples and ugly blackheads and how difficult that was for him, growing up with such a challenge. We all have challenges. That was what I wanted to say. That was what I wanted him to know. Me, Lee. Everyone.

Lee and I scooted close to each other. When Charlie leaned back and told Owen to *fuck himself* again, Lee whispered, "Get your bag. We'll go out the window."

And then we were up, backpacks on our backs, pillows and sleeping bags swooped up in our arms. Lee slipped into her flip-flops.

"Whoa, they're jumping beans!" Jittery Man cried.

"Well, thanks a lot, guys, but we should go see our friends," Lee said.

"You have real pretty hair," Jittery Man said to Lee. "It's so black."

When Lee pushed the window all the way open,

cool air rushed into the room. I was shaking so much that I couldn't get my foot into my flip-flop. Why. Won't. It. Go. *In?* She glanced back at me and then Owen was at the window, blocking our way.

"Now hold on a minute," he said. "Charlie was nice enough to let you stay here. I think there should be some kind of payment. Don't you?"

"I can pay. How much? I don't have a lot but I have some." Forty dollars and my dad's credit card. To be used for an emergency. Surely this was an emergency.

"What do you think, twenty dollars?" Owen asked. Charlie shrugged.

"I wanna party." Jittery Man was bouncing his legs and fluttering his fingers back and forth, as if they'd been asleep and he was trying to get the feeling back. His eyes were so glassy that I couldn't tell what color they were. "With the girls!"

"Let's have some fun, college girls." Owen rubbed his hands together.

"Look, we'll pay you for the time we've been here," Lee said. "But we're not staying any longer. So get out of our way."

"No." Owen shook his head. "Can't do that."

My heart was pounding so hard that I thought it would rip a hole through my chest. I couldn't swallow because something was wrong with my throat. And now I couldn't take deep breaths. Why? And why couldn't I feel my feet?

"You came here for a reason." Owen glanced at Charlie. "They want this."

"No, we came here to sleep." Lee's voice was so steady that I thought I saw Owen flinch. Oh, God, he wasn't going to rape us. Charlie and Jittery Man wouldn't, either. We were okay. Because that terrible thing couldn't happen to us. We were nice girls. And they were nice guys. They had girlfriends, mothers, and sisters.

"This doesn't have to be a big deal," Charlie said. "Let's take this slow."

"You're still a fucking pussy, Charlie," Owen said.

"Fuck you, Owen!" Charlie screamed as he launched out of the chair. Owen pushed him and I thought they were going to start swinging but then they turned to Lee at the same time and when she startled I felt a sob surge into my hot, dry throat.

"I'm done fucking around!" Owen cried. "Who's going first?"

"*No!*" My knees buckled and I burst into hot tears. "No, no, please! I can give you my dad's credit card!"

"Daddy's credit card!" Jittery Man bounced in his seat. "Daddy's credit card! Daddy's credit card!"

"Shut the *fuck* up!" Charlie growled and then

nodded at me. "Hey, Owen. She's a virgin, I bet. The other one's not a virgin, I can tell. Right, Pocahontas?"

Owen's nostrils flared as he looked at me with little black eyes that didn't seem to see me. Sharp stings, with every heartbeat, raced up and down my back.

"Please. *Please!*" I bawled. They didn't have to do this. They could make something of their lives. Why have this on their consciences? This was worse than living an unexamined life. This was the worst thing they could do because they could never take it back. "Please. Please. *Please! No!*"

"Let her go," Lee said. "I'll stay."

Everyone looked at her. What was she doing? What was she suggesting?

"*Right.* Then crybaby goes and calls the cops." Charlie pointed at me.

"There's no problem if I choose to stay." She dropped her sleeping bag and pillow.

I felt that stinging sensation again, this time across the back of my neck. My thick, dry tongue was caught on my teeth. I wanted to argue. I wanted to say no.

The three of them looked at each other. And at that moment, while their attention was off of us, Lee motioned to the window with her eyes and mouthed, *go now*.

The window. Of course! Adrenaline surged

through me. Lee could take care of herself. She'd been on her own for years. *I know guys like this.* Anyone could see the difference between us. She wasn't crying. She wasn't a mess.

When she handed her backpack to Owen, who stepped away from the window to take it, I lunged and dove into the night. My backpack caught the window frame and twisted me around so that I landed with a thud on my side. My head banged against something hard and from somewhere else in my body I felt an explosion of pain. Mud covered my hands and elbows.

"Get her!" Owen said.

I turned just as Jittery Man looked out. Then I pushed off because I had to get far, far away. But after running for blocks (two? Five? Six?), I realized that they weren't coming, they weren't chasing me, and a sickness rushed into my throat. I bent over and threw up in the gutter.

Oh, my God, oh, my God. Lee. *Let her go. I'll stay.* That was what she'd said. That was what she'd done. I had to get help. Where was Donny's house?

Rain came down in fast, cold bullets that pelted my face and bounced in the puddles near me. Something was burning, stinging. My knee? My foot? I whipped around, searching for Donny's house, but couldn't remember from which way I'd just run. Why didn't I pay attention?

Think!

Was it this house? Or that one? They all had big windows. And a single door and tiny yards and look at these giant potholes in the street and why did Lee do that and where was that pain coming from? And where was our car? The Travelodge, oh, God, The Travelodge with the tub of peanut butter and Fig Newtons and sand between my toes and under my fingernails. It was in the back by a shed. I had to go to the bathroom and maybe I already went in my shorts and I was having a heart attack and then I crossed the street and ran back the other way. But what if I went by Charlie's house? What if they were looking for me? Let her go. *Let her go!* I started to sob and I was frustrated and every second mattered.

Get it together! I stopped and bent over, breathing deeply, then straightened. Cold rain stabbed my cheeks and shoulders. Lee. I had to save Lee.

The streetlights. Donny's house had no street-lights in front of it. But neither did Charlie's. Donny had a chain-link fence. So did most of the houses. Then I remembered the kiddie pool, propped against Donny's house. I ran one way for blocks, then turned and ran the other way. Minutes were tick tock ticking. Fifteen minutes. Five minutes. Twenty? Back and forth. Up and down.

We'd turned a corner with Charlie. So, I ran back down the street, turned the corner and ran some more. And suddenly, finally, there was the kiddie pool. I threw open the gate and ran to the door but it was locked. I beat on it with my fists and screamed until finally Donny, dressed only in gym shorts, his eyes slit-like and dreamy, opened it. "What the hell?"

Sarah, our Greek sorority letters blazing across her long sleeve T-shirt, came up behind him, her eyes wide and her red hair springing wildly out of its ponytail. "Oh, my God, Clare, what happened?"

"It's Lee!" I sputtered. "We've got to get her!"

Donny scratched his forehead. "What?"

"We were going to sleep and two guys came in and they made us get up and they were going to make us and said we had to and I got away. But they kept Lee!"

"Oh, *shit!*" Sarah wailed. "Are you *kidding* me?"

"For fuck's sake." Donny turned into the house and returned pulling a T-shirt over his head.

He'd save her. It wasn't too late. I did the right thing, after all. Adrenaline surged through me again and something burned and stung on my leg, but I felt my head clear. Like the time I took Julie to Planned Parenthood. And when I talked my mom up off the marble bathroom floor at the North American Book Award ceremony. Yes, yes, now I knew what to do.

"Get Ducky and your stuff in the car and follow us," I said.

"Take a left, go two blocks, take another left and we'll be up on the right," Donny said. Sarah nodded, and I turned and ran with him.

The rain had finally stopped but the air was still wet and cool. We were quiet as we ran the four blocks—for God's sake, it was right there, all this time—to Charlie's house. The lights were off and the window was closed. Donny banged on the door as he yelled, "Open the door, Charlie. Open up the goddam door!"

A dog began to bark. How much time had passed? Ten minutes? Thirty?

Bang! Bang! *Bang!* "Open the goddam door, Charlie!"

Nothing.

Donny jumped off the step and rushed to the window. He tried to lift it but it was locked. I ran past him to the side door but it was locked, too.

"Are you sure she's in there?" Donny asked.

"Yes!" What if we couldn't get her out? "Donny, do something!"

With his fists he beat on the front door again. Harder. "Open the *door!*"

Sarah pulled up to the curb, headlights blazing, ran toward us, and began beating on the door, too. The headlights lit up the yard and I saw puddles. Cigarette butts. Bottles. Pizza boxes. A sleeping bag, splattered with mud, which couldn't be mine, could it? And a rock the size of a softball. A sharp pain stabbed me somewhere below my right knee. I felt an unbearable weight suddenly settle on my shoulders and I staggered and almost fell against the house.

Sarah and Donny were screaming at each other. About Charlie. About how to get Lee out. About *what-kind-of-people-would-fucking-do-this?*

And then Sarah was at my side. She reached down, picked up the rock, and threw it at the window. The glass shattering sounded like an explosion, a bomb, a cannon. When the lights flipped on in the house, I saw jagged edges of glass, still embedded in the window frame, staring back at me like sharp, angry teeth.

"What the fuck did you do that for?" Donny yelled.

"Somebody had to do something!" Sarah screamed.

The door flew open and Charlie grabbed Donny by the front of his shirt and yanked him into the house like water being sucked through a drain. Donny struggled and then the two of them, pushing, hitting, yelling, stumbled back outside.

"You're gonna pay for the fucking window!" Charlie yelled.

From somewhere in the house I heard Jittery Man scream, "I'm cut, I'm cut, I'm cut! My foot is bleeding!"

When Charlie and Donny staggered back into the house, I ran over to the door and saw

Lee inside, standing against the wall, dressed, backpack at her feet, her head tilted down and her long black hair hanging over her face. One of the straps of her white tank top had slid off her shoulder and rested halfway down her upper arm. And then Sarah was behind me, and when Lee lifted her head, we gasped.

Swollen flesh bubbled out of Lee's sliced open upper lip. She stared at me, her eyes open so wide that I saw tiny red blood vessels to the sides of her pupils.

"*What* did they do to you? *Lee?*" Sarah asked. "We're calling the police!"

Donny, whose forearm was wedged under Charlie's throat and pinning him to the wall, hissed, "You don't call the police, not on these guys. Just get out of here."

Chaos. Confusion. Jittery Man screaming and crying. *My foot. My foot.* Owen telling him to shut up. To sit still. Dog still barking. Siren in the distance. Throbbing pain in my shin. A neighbor yelling. And what was that on Lee's cheek?

"They're not going anywhere." Owen, stepping out of the dark, grabbed Donny around the back of the neck. But Donny turned so quickly that he broke Owen's grip and then punched him in the face. Owen staggered and fell into the wall.

I grabbed Lee's backpack and Sarah took her arm and we ran with her out the door, across the yard, and into the car. Ducky, passed out in the back seat, didn't move as we slammed the doors and Sarah sped down the street. Lee, curled into a ball on her right hip in the passenger seat, dropped her head into her folded arms that rested against the window. I turned in the back seat next to Ducky and watched the house grow smaller and smaller and then it was gone.

"Oh, my God, are we good?" Sarah asked. "Are they coming? Are we good? Are you sure? Are they coming? Are we good?"

"No one's coming," I said. "No one's coming!"

A thick mist hung in the air in front of our headlights. The street was deserted and the houses were dark and quiet, shrouded in fog. Water arched high above the side windows every time Sarah crashed through a puddle. Every so often she took her hand across the windshield, clearing the glass.

"Where are we going?" she asked. "I don't know where I'm going. What the fuck are we doing? What are we going to do? Lee?"

Lee didn't move.

Sarah tossed the map back at me and turned onto a main road, also empty. Stores were closed, metal gates pulled down over the windows and doors. A car, its frame charred, sat abandoned in a parking lot next to the street. Sarah kept asking me over her shoulder, should I turn? Which way? I didn't answer because I couldn't remember. I began to shiver—the air-conditioning was running full blast in the car—and then shake so much that the map bounced on my lap.

And still Lee didn't move. Didn't talk. Barely seemed to be breathing.

"We have to come up with a plan," Sarah said as she turned onto a side street. "We have to do something. Lee should go to the hospital. We should do that first."

"If we go to the hospital, will they call the police?" I asked.

"I don't know," Sarah said. "Lee? Lee, what do you want to do?"

Lee began to weep softly.

Sarah slammed on the brakes—we'd come to a dead end—and began beating the steering wheel with her palms. "Fuck! Where *in the fuck* are we? *Clare?*"

"I don't know!" I yelled. "Just turn around!"

"She's hurt." Sarah spun the car around and glanced at Lee. "Oh, God, Clare, I don't know what to do!"

"I don't either!" I cried.

There were three of them. Three grown men. Three dirty, mean grown men. With needs. And experience. I imagined them on top of her. Behind her. In her mouth. I gripped Sarah's headrest so hard that my fingers burned. I didn't want these thoughts. I couldn't have these thoughts.

Sarah turned the corner and we saw a stop sign ahead. As she sped toward it, she asked, "What happened? I don't understand. What *happened?*"

Lee didn't respond. I sat back in my seat. My stomach was sour and so in knots that I had to talk myself out of throwing up again. And still I shook.

Sarah turned at the stop sign and suddenly we were in a better neighborhood. Single-family houses. Lawns. No trash or burned-out cars on the street. The stores didn't have bars on the windows, either. Up ahead I saw a gas station, lights blazing. Sarah pulled in and Lee buried herself into her arms.

"I'm going to get some ice for your lip," Sarah said.

"Find out how to get to the highway," I said.

When Sarah opened her door, cool, tropic air, mixed with overpowering wafts of gasoline, rushed into the car. I watched Sarah run up to the store, hurry inside, and talk to the attendant behind the counter. Above him on the wall was a portrait of President Reagan next to a sign that read WE'RE FLORIDA AND PROUD OF IT. I glanced at Ducky, asleep next to me.

"I got turned around." My voice felt weak and shaky. "I couldn't find Donny's house. And then it took forever for Charlie to come to the door. I'm so, so sorry."

She didn't say anything.

"What happened, Lee? What did they do?" It hurt to ask this. It hurt my tongue, my teeth, and

71

my cheeks. My shin was throbbing again. Did I hurt it jumping out the window? Then I started to cry because I knew what they did to her, didn't I? I was scared and had a searing headache behind my eyes, like a knife, embedded, that twisted deeper with every blink, every turn of my head.

Still she didn't say anything. She was mad at me. I could feel it. Oh, God, she was mad at me because I left her. How could I do that?

Then Sarah was back in the car. "Okay. We're close to both the hospital and the highway. What do you want to do, Lee? *Lee!*"

Lee sat up, wincing as she brought her hand to shade her eyes from the gas station lights, and turned her head to look at Sarah. "What?"

Sarah handed her a cup filled with ice. Lee stared at it for a moment before slowly reaching out to take it. Then she just held it, arm outstretched. Sarah said, her voice steady and didactic, "Take out a piece of ice and put it on your lip."

But Lee just stared at the cup. I scooted forward, took out a piece of ice and put it up to Lee's face. With her free hand she took it and held it to her cheek.

"No, Lee, put it on your lip," I said. Lee didn't move.

Sarah glanced back at me and I knew we were thinking the same thing: Lee was completely out of it. Sarah shook her head and said, "We should

72

go to the hospital. Lee, you need help. And you need to tell somebody about what happened."

Lee shook her head. "No."

Sarah turned to me, her eyes begging for help.

"Let's find a motel off the highway," I said. "I'll use my dad's credit card. And we can rest and think about what to do. Lee?"

Lee stared at something through the windshield. I wasn't sure she heard me.

Sarah frowned and sighed. Then she pulled onto the road.

We stopped at a motel ten miles outside of Daytona. It was worn out with nicks in the bedside tables, brown carpet worn to the cement below, and curtains so thin they barely kept out the flashing neon lights in the parking lot. But the bathrooms were clean, no sludge in the corners, and it was cheap. I left our backpacks in the room. Then I went back to the car, slung Ducky's arm around my shoulder and walked her up the stairs. Sarah and Lee followed.

Once inside, I dropped Ducky—who was mumbling, eyes open—into a bed where she fell back asleep. Now, lights on, we saw each other more clearly.

"Where's your other flip-flop?" Sarah pointed to my feet.

I looked down. Both feet were covered with dried mud and grass clippings. But I wore only one flip-flop, on my right foot. A bruise, the size of a golf ball, bulged from my shin. Why didn't this hurt? Or did it hurt? Where was my flip-flop?

"Oh, Lee, your lip," Sarah said.

Lee brought her hand to her mouth and winced. She turned, walked into the bathroom, and flipped on the dim light above the sink. Sarah and I stood in the doorway, watching, as Lee leaned across the sink to get a closer look in the mirror. Dried blood crusted in the corners of her mouth. Her upper lip was swollen and bloody. Hands shaking, Lee winced again as she touched a red welt, the size of a strawberry, on her cheek. I glanced at Sarah. What the hell was on Lee's cheek?

Sarah reached inside the room and flicked the switch. Bright white lights flooded the bathroom.

"No!" Lee cried as she slammed her palm on the wall and turned off the light. Sarah and I jumped backward.

"Okay, sorry." Sarah frowned. "But, Lee. Your cheek looks so sore. And your lip looks worse. I think you need stitches. We should go to the emergency room."

"My lip." Lee fingered the swollen mess. "It's my fault."

"Your fault?" Sarah and I said at the same time. We looked at each other.

Sarah shook her head. "How can this be your fault? What the hell, Lee? You should see a doctor. And you should keep ice on your lip. Where's the cup?"

"The cup?" Lee asked.

She was so out of it. My heart pounded and my hands were cold and clammy. The hot and stuffy room smelled nasty, like cigarette smoke and disinfectant. Lee looked at herself in the mirror again. Her face was pale, the muscles in her jaw and neck knotted as if she were doing everything possible to not cry.

"I don't understand what happened. How did Clare get out and you were still inside?" Sarah looked at Lee and then me.

Lee stared into the mirror but I didn't think she really saw herself or us. I reached over her, picked up the plastic ice bucket from the counter near the sink, and handed it to Sarah. She took it, turned, and walked away. Over her shoulder she mouthed to me, *talk to her!* I nodded.

I turned back to Lee. My voice felt pained in my throat. "Lee?"

She touched her lip and winced again. Then she began to cry, not sobs but tiny tears that rushed down her cheeks, one after another, as if relieved to finally escape. She brought her hands to shield her eyes and turned away. In all of our talking and confiding, I'd only seen her cry a few times; two years ago when we found the dying goose on the road. The night we saw Patricia Graceson's movie. And last January, when we sat

75

in the stairwell at the house and she told me that her aunt, the one who'd introduced her to movies and who'd driven her all the way to Boston three summers ago, had been arrested.

"Oh, Lee." I started to cry hot tears that stung my eyes. Lee and I often talked about what Patricia Graceson had said about crying, that it was good, a release and not a weakness, but nothing felt good now.

She began to sob, her body trembling, her face twisted. I felt so repulsed that vomit shot up my throat and into my mouth. When I swallowed, it made me gag. Inside my head I yelled, *Stop crying! Get ahold of yourself, Lee! Don't make me pick you up off the bathroom floor!* I wanted to run, far, far away.

But how could I be like this? Lee sacrificed herself and I repay her by being repulsed? What kind of a person was I? I needed to be patient. Sophomore year I had to ask five or six times, over the course of several weeks, before she told me what her track coach had done. *He touched me. He tried to kiss me. He put my hand on his dick. He fucked with my head.*

Now, I lifted my arms to hug her but she stiffened and backed away. Then she leaned over and turned on the water in the tub.

"I want to do something," I said. "I don't know what to do!"

She adjusted the water. And then she

straightened, lightly pushed me away, shut the door, and locked it. I changed out of my wet clothes and into shorts and a sweatshirt. The moment I sat on the bed, I felt my body release, my muscles relax, and I fell onto my back.

When Sarah returned, ice bucket in her hands, she gasped and said, "What? She's in the shower? She's getting rid of evidence!"

Rape evidence. Sperm. Fingerprints. Ugly, black, curly pubic hairs.

I sat up, my stomach churning. The bed cover, faded blue, cheap polyester, scratched the bottom of my thighs. "I couldn't stop her."

In the other bed Ducky groaned and rolled over. Sarah dropped next to me and handed me the bucket. "Here. Take some. Put it on your leg."

I took the ice bucket but I didn't deserve it. I deserved a bruise. A broken leg. A busted lip.

"She's in shock," Sarah said. "Could she tell you about it? What happened?"

I started to cry again and shook my head. I was so tired that it hurt to breathe. I could only take shallow breaths.

"This must have been awful for you, too." Sarah's voice was calmer, stronger. I imagined her in an emergency room treating gunshot and car crash victims. Rapes, too. She took off the bandana around her neck, filled it with ice from the bucket, then squatted in front of me as she held the ice to my shin. Ah, instant relief. This was how you took care of someone, by tending to her physical ailments. My mother never quite got the hang of this. Cleaning a cut. Taking a temperature. Icing a wound.

And yes, it was awful for me, too.

I told her about how Charlie, Owen, and Jittery Man prodded us and how Lee had a weird vibe and opened the window. They weren't going to let us go without payment so I offered money and my dad's credit card. "But they wanted something else. God, I've never been more scared in my life."

"They raped her," she said.

I nodded.

"*Fuck!* How did you get away?"

"I dove through the window." I started to cry harder, my heart racing again. "And then I got so turned around. I couldn't find Donny's house."

This was my crime, wasn't it? How my seemingly good sense of direction had let me down? Sarah said today—or was it yesterday?—*who would've guessed that you were so bad with directions?*

"It was pouring and the middle of the night," she said. "It could've happened to anyone. You should feel proud. You saved her from being hurt worse."

Maybe if I'd stayed we could have fought them off or talked them out of it. Maybe, together, we could have gone out the window. But I panicked and left her to fend for herself. I abandoned her. How could I be proud of that?

And what would Sarah and Ducky think if they ever heard this?

I'd done something else to Lee, too, although my mind was bouncing around so much—I was so, so wired—that I couldn't remember. *They're like jumping beans*. I cringed and fell back on the bed again.

Sarah went to the bathroom door and knocked. "Lee, are you okay? Lee?"

"Yeah."

She stood at the door for a moment and then came back and sat. "I don't know, Clare. When I was getting ice I thought that we should call her parents. I've never met them. They never come to Mom's or Dad's Weekends, do they?"

"No." I met them last year when Lee and I drove up to her farm. Her dad was quiet, her mom anxious. They were simple, unsophisticated people and right now her family was a mess over her aunt's legal troubles. Even if her parents had money to fly here, which they didn't, I couldn't imagine Lee would want them. *They have no idea who I am,* Lee often told me. I didn't think that we could call her aunt, either. She and Lee hadn't spoken in months. "We can't call without asking her."

Sarah nodded. "I just feel so bad. This would never have happened if we hadn't gone to see

Donny. That was stupid. What was I thinking?"

"This isn't your fault," I said.

"God, it could've been you. Or me. Or Ducky. What if she and I had gone over there instead of you two? And how did you think to jump out the window?"

Let her go. I'll stay.

I should tell Sarah that Lee offered herself if they let me go. And that she distracted them by handing Owen her backpack. And that it was easy to dive out the window. It was easy to leave her. But she'd think I was a terrible person and right now I felt bad enough. I'd tell her after we slept. And ate. And figured out what to do. Relief washed over me for the first time in hours. Oh, God, I *needed* to feel better.

It was still dark outside although I had a sense, by looking at the sky through a hole in the curtain, that the sun would be up soon. I glanced at the clock next to the bed. 5:15. The only other time I'd stayed up all night was sophomore year when Lee and I sat in the stairwell, talking until the breakfast cooks arrived.

I closed my eyes but couldn't sleep. The scene at Charlie's kept replaying in my mind and every time I felt myself relaxing, something would jerk me awake. But I guess I dozed off because suddenly Lee, dressed in sweatpants and T-shirt, was standing at the side of the bed next to me. I started to say something but she shook her head, climbed into the bed next to Ducky, and whispered, "Let's try to sleep."

I must have been out for a longer time because when I woke sunshine was pouring through the windows and Ducky and Sarah were dressed in T-shirts and shorts. The shower was on again, and Lee was missing from the bed. I bolted upright. Sarah was pacing in front of the window. Ducky sat cross-legged on the bed, weeping as she fiddled with her pearls.

"Clare, oh, my God, Clare, you're finally awake, oh, God, I feel so awful!" Huge tears rolled down Ducky's cheeks. "Sarah told me what happened. I'm so upset. I'm so upset! Those *bastards!*"

"Have you talked to her this morning?" I looked at the clock. 9:05.

"I fell asleep for a few minutes and when I woke up she was in the shower again," Sarah said.

"What are we going to do?" Ducky asked. "What are we going to say to her?"

They looked at me.

"I don't know," I said.

"This is Donny's fault," Ducky cried. "Those guys were total creeps. He should never have suggested that you go over there."

"Why's it his fault?" Sarah asked. "We partied all night at his house. He didn't *make* Clare and Lee go."

The shower turned off. We jerked our heads toward the bathroom door but it stayed closed.

"I'm just saying that he had an obligation to us," Ducky whispered.

"Shut up, Ducky," Sarah hissed. "You were so drunk that you don't even remember what happened."

"That's not true. I remember most of it. Except at the end." Her face reddened and then her eyebrows, so blond I could barely see them, dipped into a frown. "If we're assigning blame, then what about you, *Sarah?* We should've never gone there in the first place. They were all low-life, white trash drug addicts!"

"Oh, God, they were not all drug addicts," Sarah said.

"Yes, they were. And Donny's a *drug* dealer!"

"So this is *my* fault?" Sarah yelled. Ducky and I shushed her. "I didn't see anyone forcing you to drink all of those beers, Ducky."

"Stop it, both of you." I'd never heard them argue. Ducky sniffled and with her palm, wiped tears off her face. She began fingering her pearls again and moaning.

Sarah turned to me. "You have to tell us what to do. You know her best."

I was the sounding board. The counselor. The lifeline in the middle of the night. *The only one I've ever talked to.* Now there was so much pressure behind my eyes, thundering in my ears.

I gulped for breaths, a crushing sensation in my chest.

Lee opened the bathroom door. She was dressed in the same sweatpants and T-shirt. A towel wrapped around her hair and rested on top of her head. The swelling had gone down slightly on her lip but the red welt on her cheek was darker, angrier. Was it a rug burn? She walked, gingerly, to a chair but didn't sit.

"This isn't anyone's fault," she said.

"Those fucking bastards!" Ducky cried.

Lee tilted her head and stared at something out the window.

"I still think we should go to the police," Sarah said.

"And say what? Clare and I went there. I stayed. But look, the swelling has already gone down on my lip. See?" Lee's voice was suddenly high-pitched, teary. "And it doesn't hurt as much. It doesn't look so bad? Right? It's okay now, right?"

I stayed. The words stung in my ears. I squeezed my hands into fists, waiting for their questions and condemnations.

"Lee!" Ducky said. "You are not okay!"

Sarah shook her head. "Your lip is still swollen. What do you want to do, Lee? Just tell us."

I glanced at her and then Ducky. Had they not heard what Lee said?

Lee tilted her head and stared at Sarah as if she

suddenly didn't recognize her. Then she said, "What?"

"Oh, Lee." Ducky started to weep loudly again. "I'm so, so sorry!"

"We should go to the hospital," Sarah said.

"No," Lee squeaked.

"If we go to the hospital, will the doctors call the police?" Ducky asked. "Because I seriously hope so. I seriously hope those bastards get arrested."

Sarah and Ducky looked at me. They wanted me to weigh in, maybe convince Lee to go to the hospital, but I was too afraid to speak. What if I didn't sound sincere? What if they saw through me? Because truth was, I didn't want to go to the hospital. I didn't want some doctor questioning us. I didn't want to talk to the police.

"Let's go back to school," I said. "We'll drive north a bit and stay another night in a hotel. I can pay with my dad's credit card again. Then we'll get up tomorrow and finish the drive. The house doesn't open until Sunday but I bet we can get in."

"How will you explain this to your dad?" Ducky asked.

"I'll think of something," I said.

"But what about the hospital?" Sarah asked, her voice less sure now.

"Lee, what do you want to do?" Ducky asked. "Lee?"

Lee was staring out the window again.

"I think she's in shock." Sarah glanced at me and then at Lee. "Clare said that we should go back to school. What do you want to do, Lee?"

Finally, she nodded, unwound the towel, and let her long black hair fall behind her. Then she crawled into the bed and pulled the sheet and blanket up to her neck. But she didn't close her eyes. She stared at the ceiling, barely blinking.

I could do this. Make a decision. A plan. Get people moving. Pay for it. I said, "I'll go get gas in the car and maybe some food. Is anyone hungry?"

"I am," Ducky said. "I'll go with you."

I brushed my teeth and splashed cold water on my face. I'd get something good for us to eat, something healthy. Bananas, apples, maybe pancakes and eggs. And coffee, lots of coffee. Sandwiches for later and cans of Lee's favorite, Diet Dr Pepper. When we filled up the car I'd check the oil, too, and ask about a good town, with a good motel, to stop in tonight.

A warm, gentle breeze floated into the room when I opened the door. Seagulls gathered in the scrubby grass under the palm trees next to the parking lot. Giant puddles speckled the cement. A dumpster, overflowing with garbage, stood next to a small pool enclosed in a chain-link fence. White lounge chairs were scattered along the pool's edges. The sun, climbing in the bright blue sky, danced across the water's surface, making the pool seem as if it were filled with hundreds of small silver flying fish.

Ducky rolled up the sleeves of her sweatshirt, exposing her arms. She said, "Maybe we can eat by the pool."

Her eyes were still bloodshot but she'd stopped crying. She was thinking of her tan. Maybe she wanted to grab a few moments of sun before we left for school.

School. The house. Ben's face flashed before me and I felt something catch in my throat. A lump. A knot. A rock. I imagined telling him about all of this and what I'd done and watching the corners of his mouth fall in disappointment. But I shook my head because there were other things to think about. Ducky and I got into The Travelodge and drove across the service road to the gas station.

CHAPTER 4

We drove all day and through the night, stopping only for gas, food, and bathroom breaks, with an unspoken yet collective desire—I was sure we all felt it—to get back to school as quickly as possible. No one really slept, especially Lee, who rested her head against the passenger side window, her lip puffy and purple, the mark on her cheek red and raw, her eyes fixed in a dreamy, faraway look. We didn't talk or listen to the radio or our boom box. And because one of us stayed with Lee at all times, there was never a chance for Sarah, Ducky, and I to talk alone.

It wasn't until we drove into Bloomington at five thirty in the morning, the streets deserted and sky dark with angry storm clouds, that Lee finally seemed to sleep. Her mouth was open slightly and her chest rose and fell in steady motion. When Sarah pulled into the empty Donut Delite parking lot, we were careful to get out of the car without waking her. Then we stood outside the driver's side, shivering in our sweatshirts and shorts. The air was bitter cold and smelled like sugar and grease. Small piles of snow, scattered across the parking lot, were laced with dirt, ice, Styrofoam cups, paper Donuts Delite bags, cigarette butts, and beer cans.

"I am so totally freaking out!" Ducky said. Sarah shushed her and I peeked in the window but Lee still seemed to be asleep. "I just want to go to sleep and wake up and have this all be a nightmare or something."

"Well, it's not a nightmare and we gotta deal with it." Sarah looked at me. "So you're still good with talking to Mom Tolliver? Because I can't do it. There's no way. She scares the shit out of me."

"And she thinks I'm a space cadet!" Ducky said.

"I said I'd do it." I looked through the Donuts Delite window at a girl, dressed in a pink apron with her hair pulled back in a hairnet, behind the counter. Open twenty-four hours a day, seven days a week, Donuts Delite was where we went for a good dose of grease after a night of drinking. Jelly donuts were also Mom Tolliver's favorite snack, and I needed something like this to give her when I woke her up in a few minutes. She wouldn't be happy. And she wouldn't be happy that we wanted into the house, which didn't officially open until tomorrow, either.

"Just sweet talk her," Ducky said. "Tell her that we drove all night and we want to sleep and that we promise to be quiet."

"Clare can do it," Sarah said. "She knows how to talk to old people. She's got Mom Tolliver wrapped around her finger."

What was that supposed to mean? "No, I don't."

"What are we going to say to everybody?" Ducky asked. "They're gonna ask about our trip. And Julie and those guys will wonder why we were in Florida but didn't go to Fort Lauderdale to see them."

"Shit, you're right," Sarah said.

"We can't tell anyone what happened to Lee," I said.

"I agree," Sarah said. "This is Lee's business. You have to promise, Ducky, that you won't tell anyone. And we fucking mean it."

"I'm not going to tell anyone!" Ducky said. "But what should we say we did?"

"Just be vague," I said. "Say that we had a blast on the Outer Banks. And then ask them about their trip. No one will care about us."

"What if Lee tells someone about Daytona?" Ducky asked.

"She won't tell anyone," Sarah said. We turned when a milk truck, the only vehicle on the road, passed by slowly. "And Clare, you've got to talk to her about explaining her lip and cheek. People are going to ask about it."

I nodded.

"Come on, Ducky," Sarah said. "Let's get some donuts. You want anything?"

"No, thanks." I watched them walk into the store and stand at the counter. Then Sarah stuck her head out and said it would be a few minutes for the coffee to finish percolating. I nodded and leaned against the car. The blinking yellow light threw ominous rays across the empty intersection. Beyond that the limestone buildings of campus stood solid and stately behind leafless trees. Tomorrow the streets would fill with students and cars and the lights would be on in the buildings and everything would be back to normal.

Would anything ever be normal again?

As I watched Ducky, arm linked with Sarah's, pick out donuts from the glass case, I thought about our other friends from the house who would arrive tomorrow. This was my life now. These were my friends.

I glanced through the car window at Lee again and thought about Natalie Smith, my best friend in junior high. Confident, hilarious, and theatrical (tall and skinny with perfectly feathered brown hair and giant chocolate-colored eyes, too), she was the most popular girl in seventh grade, drooled over by every boy, pursued by every girl. She had a way of looking at you, with her eyes *and* her body, that made you feel as if you were the most important person in the room. And one day she set those big chocolate eyes on me.

Her full-court press was flattering: passing notes after class, calling me every night on the phone, shoving others out of the way so I'd sit with her at lunch, insisting I have the coveted sleeping space next to her at slumber parties. I was a quiet kid, more prone to following than leading, but I was liked well enough. I had friends. But Natalie vaulted me to the top of the junior high social hierarchy.

I was no dummy. I knew it was probably too soon to call each other "best friend" after only a few weeks of togetherness. I saw the way she ignored her previous best friend and belittled others. I wondered why someone as dynamic as her would be interested in someone as quiet as me. But then she'd turn to me with that all-engrossing *look* and I'd feel myself being sucked deeper into her orbit. I told her my secrets. My crush on Danny Handley. And how I'd intentionally broken my violin so I wouldn't have to take lessons anymore. In our notes back and forth we made plans. Told inside jokes. Signed off with *your BFF*. It was official.

One day I brought her home after school. For weeks she'd begged to come over. But our apartment was small. My mother worked every afternoon in the living room and didn't want to be interrupted. Natalie and I sat at the kitchen table, the door to the living room closed, and ate popcorn and animal crackers. Every time I suggested we do something—go upstairs to my room, go outside—she said no.

When my mother finally opened the door to the kitchen, Natalie jumped on her like a fly on raw meat. *I love your apartment. I love your kitchen. I love your dress. I love your necklace.* What was going on? But as I watched Natalie settle that familiar, all-encompassing look on my mother, I felt a chill up my spine. Wasn't that the look she reserved for me?

When Natalie began talking about *Listen*, and the screenplay on which my mother was working (an article about it had appeared two months prior in the *Boston Globe*), and then about her own acting ambitions, I realized with razor-sharp clarity what had happened. Natalie had friended me to get to my mother. I was so angry that I left the kitchen and went up to my room.

Soon afterward, Natalie found me and tried to make up. She was no dummy, either, but the damage was done. I stopped sending notes and wouldn't sit with her at lunch. I stayed angry, even after my mother told me that she'd never let Natalie play Phoebe in a movie version of her novel. Natalie was simply too old, "too perky."

Although Natalie was the most popular girl for the rest of junior high, her light faded by high school. Still, she had a lasting effect on me. I was careful when people tried to friend me and dismissive when someone mentioned my mother's books. I became hyperaware of how people looked at me, treated me, talked to me. There were many others who tried to get to my mother through me, especially as she became more and more famous. Eventually I learned to ignore them and by junior year I had several, separate groups of friends. We had fun. We laughed. We never went too deep. And although I was the sounding board whenever someone needed to talk, I always kept a large part of myself in reserve. Just to be safe.

I glanced at Lee again, her hair covering her face as she slept against the window. I'd told her about my mother on one of the many nights we sat up talking in the stairwell of our dorm. It had been a big deal for me to do this. But Lee had simply tilted her head, said she'd never heard of her or *Listen, Before You Go*, and then asked me how it felt to have a famous mother.

No one had ever asked this. And it was a relief to talk about it.

I turned my head and saw the top of my freshman year dorm, rising above the trees. I met Lee on my first day of college. She was late to our floor meeting—our RA had already started talking—and when the doors to the lounge flung open and Lee stood there, the lights from the hallway at her back, it was as if she were making a grand entrance. She looked different from most of the rest of us (so many blondes with blue eyes) with her olive skin, black hair, and dark eyes. But it was her legs that were most noticeable, so long and lean with perfectly sculpted muscles in her thighs and calves. She wore gym shorts, a tank top, and shiny wood clogs. Even I, so unfamiliar with sports, knew she was a runner.

Everyone watched as she walked into the room. She had an immediate presence, an aura, and I imagined that no matter where she went people paid attention to her. She didn't look around, didn't check anyone out, but kept her eyes on our RA. I didn't know if she was stuck up and not interested or if she truly didn't want to miss a word that Brenda said.

"We can form a flag football team, too," Brenda said. "So you see, there are lots of ways the fifth floor can show team spirit. Any questions?"

Sarah, whom I'd met earlier, rolled her eyes at me. The girls on the plastic-covered couches whispered to each other. Several others looked out the window. The room had an institutional feel to it with bare walls and cold linoleum tiles. Except for weekly meetings, we wouldn't spend much time in it.

"Can one of you come up and lead us in a cheer?" Brenda asked.

Someone groaned. Someone snickered. Volunteering was problematic, at best. If you went up there too serious, you'd be called a suck-up. But if you made fun of it, Brenda would be angry. I ducked behind Sarah as Brenda scanned the group.

Then Lee's arm shot up. "I don't know how to be a cheerleader but I'll try."

Brenda clapped, relieved. "Great!"

"That's Lee Sumner," Sarah whispered. "I ran track in high school and she's this amazing runner from up north. She won the mile at the state tournament."

Lee pulled her hair into a ponytail as she walked up and stood next to Brenda. Then her arms dangled at her sides and her eyes darted around the room. She licked her thick lips. "Okay, I *really* don't know what I'm doing."

"That's okay," Brenda said. "What's your name?"

"Lee." She laughed, nervous. Maybe embarrassed. Brenda nudged her and Lee cupped her hands around her mouth and yelled, "Gimme a five!"

"Five!" Brenda and a couple of girls said.

"Give me an F!"

"F!" A few more girls joined in.

"Give me an L!"

"L."

"Give me a double O."

"Double O." The voices began to trail off.

"Give me an R!"

"R?" Brenda tilted her head, confused.

"That spells . . ." Lee grimaced. "Five floor? Okay, that makes no sense."

Everyone burst out laughing and started talking. We were okay now, looser, not so worried about what others were thinking. Lee kept shaking her head and laughing, too, but she'd pulled it off. She'd managed to not look like a suck-up *or* a jerk. And yet as I watched her laughing, arms still dangling at her sides, she seemed so genuine. This made her all the more appealing.

Over the next two months I saw little of Lee. And I began to question my decision to come here. My roommate was a drunk, my classes were fairly easy, and most people I met were friendly but not very interesting. Was I homesick? Maybe. My parents had promised to visit but canceled when my mother got an offer to speak in London. They hadn't rescheduled. Most days I went to class and the library and didn't return to the dorm until dinner. Afterward, I'd brave my room.

One late October morning, my roommate said she was going home for the weekend, and I decided to come back to the dorm early, to enjoy my room for once. I walked up the back stairs, opened the door and ran into Lee, who was sitting on the floor, a book open on her lap and her legs extended across the carpet.

"Hey!" She smiled. "I keep looking for you but you're never around."

I'd seen her in the cafeteria, walking to class, and once at a fraternity party, but she was always surrounded by a group of people. How had she made so many friends already? Of course later I'd realize that one reason people were attracted to her was because she was so unattainable—

she didn't let anyone get too close. But I didn't know that at the time. I was just happy that she'd noticed me.

"I've been around." I squeezed my backpack strap. "Why are you out here?"

Lee nodded toward her door. "My roommate is *busy*. Know what I mean? And I need to study."

She lifted her textbook to show me. Psychology 101. I had the same textbook but Lee must have been in a different section because I hadn't seen her in mine. Of course, two hundred people also took my class. "Me, too. I'm Monday, Wednesday, Friday."

She nodded. "Tuesday, Thursday."

Down the hall two girls came out of a room and yelled hello to Lee before walking away. I shifted my feet. I wanted to keep talking. "Are you a psych major?"

"No, a psych minor. My aunt said I should take psychology to understand people. I'm a film studies major. I'm going to make films." She said this with no hesitation, no self-consciousness, and I felt instantly intrigued.

"I'm a psych minor, too." I hadn't yet decided on a major or a minor, although standing there, I thought, why not? I liked my psych class enough.

"You're the only other psych minor I've met! Everyone seems to be studying business or education." She leaned forward. "Why do you suppose that is?"

I shrugged. "Maybe the world needs a lot of business people? And teachers?"

She nodded. "Yes, it needs a lot of film studies majors, too."

We laughed. I had this feeling that she was going to do exactly as she said and be a big success. Despite her ambition, she seemed surprisingly earnest. Which surprised me. Most ambitious people I knew back home were sort of jerks.

"What films do you like?"

"All kinds," she said. "I like documentaries because I think it's important to be truthful about history. But sometimes they're hard to find on TV and we don't have theaters in my hometown. I have to drive almost an hour to the closest one. And they only show big, commercial films. I like them, too, I guess. Probably my favorite last year was *The Deer Hunter*."

Back against the wall, I slid until I sat on the floor in front of her. The hall was warm, and I felt the heat on my cheeks and back of my neck. *The Deer Hunter* was about three friends, taken prisoner during the Vietnam War and forced to play Russian roulette with their captors. It was good yet disturbing.

It was also a movie about which my parents had talked nonstop. My mother, who was approached several times about making *Listen, Before You Go* into a movie, was never happy with the screenplay drafts she'd written. And my dad didn't think our country was ready for an "honest representation of that travesty perpetuated by our perverse government." So when this movie and *Coming Home*, another gritty, Vietnam-related movie, came out last year, they felt blindsided. For months they refused to see either one. When they finally did, they complained. About everything.

"Yeah, it was good," I said finally.

"Okay, what just happened?" she asked. "You were thinking about something before you answered."

I raised my eyebrows, surprised that she noticed. "Ah, nothing."

"That's such a lie! I saw it on your face. What were you thinking?"

I laughed. No one had ever called me out on this. Should I tell her? But this was months before I'd explain my mother to her and at that moment no one knew I was her daughter. I wanted to keep it that way.

I changed the subject. "What did you like about that movie?"

"Okay, I get it. You're not going to tell me what you were thinking." But she slowly smiled. "So. Three guys are best friends, grow up in the same town, know the same people, go to the same schools. Yet they all react differently to what happened. Why? I think it's because people experience things in their families that other people don't know about. These things make us who we are. And that's why, despite being friends, they all reacted differently."

Down the hall, the elevator opened and a group of girls waved and walked into the lounge. Music blasted from a nearby room and behind Lee's door people argued. In the months I'd been here, I'd talked about my favorite music, what I was thinking about majoring in, and where I came from. Not once had I talked to anyone about anything deeper than that. Had I ever talked like this?

"Where did you grow up?" I asked.

"Up north, near Fort Wayne." She crossed her legs and leaned forward again. "But after I graduate, I'm going east, to New York."

I smiled. "I'm from Boston."

"Brookline. You said that on the first day. I heard you after the meeting."

I kept smiling. I liked that she'd paid attention and remembered.

"I know about Brookline because that's where John F. Kennedy was born." She took a sip from a can of Diet Dr Pepper.

Was she a history buff like my dad? "How do you know that?"

"I love to read about people who've done amazing things. Over the summer I was thinking about presidents, and when you said Brookline

I remembered that that was where Kennedy was born. Although I'm not sure he did anything *truly* amazing."

President Kennedy always seemed incredible to me. "Who would you say has done something truly amazing?"

The arguing in her room grew louder although I couldn't make out the words. Lee was so focused that I didn't know if she heard it. "I like to think about people who've saved others, like Mother Teresa. Or Darwin, who changed how we think. And people like Beethoven, who went deaf, are incredible, too. Can you imagine losing the sense most important to your gift? It'd be like a filmmaker going blind."

I chewed on the inside of my cheek and thought about my mother. When *Listen* was published, reviewers had many reactions—some called her Salinger's heir apparent, especially since her main character shared more in common with Holden's little sister than just a name. Others called her the "Mother of Minimalism" because she'd helped usher in a new type of writing: sparse words, psychologically distant, more reader involvement. My mother was proud of this although she didn't like it when Logan, my brother, turned it around and called her *Minimal Mother*.

"Would you consider any writers amazing people?" I held my breath.

"Maybe. But probably not." She took her

fingers through her long black hair. "I want to do a documentary on an amazing person. *That's* what I'm going to do."

Suddenly her door flew open. A boy, carrying his shoes and coat, hurried into the hall and stumbled over my backpack. His shoes flew out of his arms and bounced down the hall as his knees, then elbows, hit the carpet.

"Oh, my God! You're such an asshole!" Lee's roommate stood in the doorway, her face red and raw and her eyes wild. "Just get out of here!"

He picked up his things and hobbled down the hall. As he pushed open the door to the stairway, he turned and yelled, "Fuck you, *Debby*." Then he was gone.

Debby burst into tears and dropped to the carpet. I'd seen her around the floor but I didn't know her. Still, I felt sorry for her. I had a feeling that this was more than just a fight. I glanced at Lee, who was staring at me, eyes wide with fear.

"Hey, what happened?" I made my voice soft and low.

Her head was between her knees and her hands over her head. The pink polish on her nails was chipped, and she'd drawn little smiley faces on the tops of her hands with a black marker. She sobbed between gasping breaths.

"Tell us," I said. "It might feel better to talk."

Lee looked at Debby, then at me again.

"We've been together since junior year in

high school!" Debby kept her head buried in her knees. "And then we come here and he tells me that he doesn't want to go out anymore. He wants to see other people! I'm so mad!"

"Listen," I said. "I know this girl from back home. The same thing happened when she went to college. Two months later, her boyfriend came back. It's hard to stay together in a new place like this. But it doesn't mean it's forever."

Debby wiped her face across her sleeve. She'd stopped sobbing although tears still rolled down her cheeks.

"You feel awful, don't you?" I asked. "Like your heart is breaking."

"Yes," she wailed. *"Yes!"*

"It's going to be okay," I said. "After a while. You'll see."

She buried her head again.

The door to their room was open. The far side bed was unmade and on top a hot pink comforter, polka dot sheets and pillows tangled in a small pile. The desk was crowded with pictures, books, and notebooks. The other bed, nearest the door, was neatly made, a thin, faded gray blanket on top, a small pillow at the end. The walls and desk were empty. I couldn't imagine that Lee's bed was the one with the hot pink comforter. Later I'd realize that Lee's side of the room was empty because she didn't have any money to fill it with things.

"Oh, no!" Debby hurried into the room and lifted a backpack off the pile on her bed. "John forgot his backpack!" She slid into her shoes, ran to the stairwell door, threw it open, and charged down the stairs. The door slammed behind her.

"Wow," I said. "Poor thing."

"You were amazing with her," Lee said. "I don't think I've ever seen anyone be so good with anyone like that. How did you know what to say?"

"I don't know. It just feels natural." In high school I was everyone's confidant. But I liked that she noticed. I liked that she thought I was good at something. I remembered that feeling very clearly.

Inside Donuts Delite, Ducky was paying the girl behind the counter. I shivered and rammed my hands into my sweatshirt pocket. I was so cold and my head, from lack of sleep, ached and screamed at me. I looked in the car window but still Lee slept. I'd thought a lot over the years about how Lee and I met. Sometimes I wondered if we'd have become so close had I not been so intrigued with her confidence or if she'd not seen how I was able to talk to Debby. But other times I thought it was just inevitable. We'd have found each other, eventually.

When Lee and I parted that day after talking in the dorm hall, I went back to my room, but I couldn't stop thinking about our conversation.

Lee didn't appear to need anything. I'd always thought of myself as not needing anything, either, but that day I had the distinct sense that something was missing. I was happy for the first time since arriving at school. Lee had made me think. And I remembered suddenly feeling as if I'd finally found something even though I hadn't realized that I'd been looking for anything.

Perhaps I had been looking for a friend. A best friend.

Oh, God, what was going to happen to us now?

"Finally!" Ducky said as she bounded across the parking lot toward me. "We got two jelly donuts for Mom Tolliver and chocolate glazed for us."

"And a coffee," Sarah said, coming up behind her.

"Good," I said. "Thanks."

We glanced at the car but none of us moved toward it.

"Okay, we got our story straight?" Sarah asked. Ducky and I nodded.

"I feel so sorry for her," Ducky said. "What's going to happen to her now?"

"Let's go," I said. And then we got into the car and drove to the house.

CHAPTER 5

Spring was late to Bloomington and the last weeks in March were gray and cold. The buds on the trees, which had started to unfurl before we left for break, seemed to hesitate as if unsure whether it was safe to come out. Rain fell nearly every day for two weeks. Then, with only a few weeks left before graduation, the skies cleared and the temperature and humidity soared. In the afternoons we camped out on the sundeck, working on our tans, burning off hangovers. At night we drank in air-conditioned bars, then stumbled home in the early morning hours.

Senior Week, five days of parties, the Little 500 bike race, and events before finals began, was almost here. The baseball team was having a losing season and Ben was in a bad mood. And my mother called one morning—on the house phone in the mailroom because she couldn't remember my room phone number—to ask me where have I been and *why in the world* haven't I called?

I was suffering an epic hangover but felt every inch of my body jerk to attention when I heard her voice. She rarely called and I hadn't realized that she'd paid much attention to when I called her, either (the last time was Sunday, five days ago, at four thirty in the afternoon). What did she want?

"Clare?"

"I've been here and the library. Studying." I cringed with my lie and chastised myself for not calling her. But, no. I *did* call. I haven't done anything wrong. Have I?

"I haven't talked to you in the longest time." Her voice was mildly agitated.

"I called you on Sunday. Remember? You'd just gotten home from your talk with the Harvard undergraduates. At the English department?"

My God, she talked for two hours, she'd said. Just the thought of speaking that long, and to Harvard students, no less, made me shudder. No way could I do that. I rubbed my forehead. My headache was worse by the minute.

"Damn! I can't get the microwave door to open! Why won't it open? Everything is going to pot. I can't count on *anything!*" Her voice was much louder and more agitated. And then something crashed on the counter or the floor.

"Was that the microwave?" I squeezed the receiver. It had been a long time since I'd heard this level of panic in her voice. "Where's Dad?"

"He went out, hours ago!"

I rubbed my forehead again. My brain felt thick and waterlogged—how many beers did I drink last night?—and then suddenly I realized that she wouldn't call simply to complain about the microwave. "Did something happen?"

"Not *one* review has come in yet. Not one!"

Wait, what?

"What am I supposed to do? How can they expect me to wait like this?"

I licked my parched lips. She was talking about reviews of her new novel. But why worry? People loved her other novel. People loved her. Why would this one be any different? I felt a flutter of panic start down my legs. I thought about how afraid I used to be of the dark and reached over and flipped the switch. Light flooded the mailroom but it didn't make me feel better.

I knew what to say, now that it was clear what was wrong. But I was so tired. "Everything's slow in publishing. You know that. I'm sure the reviews will be great."

"You can't be sure." Her voice shook; she was about to cry.

"It's a great book." I had no idea whether her new book was great or not. I'd always begged off reading it when she'd asked. "Everything will be okay."

"But how can you know that?"

"You're a great writer. How many times have I told you that? Don't worry."

She sighed loudly. "You don't know if it's great because you won't read it."

Years ago I'd read part of a different novel she'd begun. But when I gingerly offered a few suggestions, she dismissed each one with a swiftness that left me feeling like an idiot. Because she'd been right. No way was I going through that again. Now the fatigue felt crushing and I blurted, "I'm in the middle of finals!"

"Oh, I know." She sighed. But her voice was beginning to break. I was helping.

"Remember how long it took to get the reviews for *Listen*?" I asked, feeling a bit more energized. "And you know your editor. As soon as she gets a review, she'll send it to you. Don't jump to conclusions. You have so many fans who love you."

"I suppose you're right." She sighed again but I heard the release in her voice. I'd pulled her out of her hole. And although I felt grateful that this time it hadn't taken long, *I* felt worse. Her lack of confidence was baffling.

She cleared her throat. "And I'm sorry to say that we have another problem. I have to be in Denver the night before graduation. It'll be tight."

I felt a whiplash sensation with the sudden change of direction. Did this mean she wasn't upset anymore about the lack of reviews?

Graduation. I swallowed, a slow burn starting across my chest and into my throat. I wanted her here. I didn't want her here. Would she be charming? Difficult? That I didn't know and would have to manage it (was that what I did?)

made me lose my balance. Or maybe it was my hangover. I cradled the receiver between my chin and shoulder and held the counter with both hands. I was shaky, my brain fuzzy, as if someone had stuffed cotton balls in the depths of my ears. I was so saturated with alcohol that I wondered, briefly, if I'd blow up if someone lit a match next to me.

But still. My mother should be here. How would I explain this to Ben, who had never met my parents? "Can you say that I'm graduating from college?"

"Well, of course," she said. "But I'm telling you this because we will most certainly *not* make the dinner the night before. We'll be driving in very late."

The pregraduation dinner with Ben and his parents. Two months ago he'd made reservations at a restaurant in town.

I rubbed my eyes with my thumb and first finger. I shouldn't have had those extra beers. I shouldn't have gone back to Christopher Mansfield's house again. Tonight I'd stay in and work on my English paper. I couldn't keep doing this. I was betraying Ben. I was acting as if I didn't know what I was doing.

Christopher Mansfield. I rolled his name around my mouth and felt my knees weaken and the muscles in my inner thighs tighten.

"Clare? Are you there?" she asked.

"I don't know what I'm doing after I graduate!" I blurted. Maybe we could talk about this? Sarah said she talked to her parents about her plans for medical school. Julie and Amy said they talked to theirs, too. It was normal, talking through things with the very people who'd given birth to you.

"Why, you can do anything you want," she said. "For the first time in history women have all sorts of opportunities. Really, it's extraordinary."

How many times had I heard her say this? It meant nothing to me. It was like saying there were fifty-seven kinds of ice cream. "But I don't know exactly—"

"When I was in school, we had limited options. We could study to be nurses. Chefs. And teachers, of course, but not so much on the collegiate level. There were tenured female professors but certainly no female Miltonists. And then—"

"What do you think of Philadelphia?" I asked.

"Philadelphia?" she cried.

I rubbed my eyes again. I needed something but I didn't know what.

And then I heard commotion in the background, like paper bags being placed on the counter, and my dad's voice. "Why's the microwave in the sink?"

"Clare's on the phone," my mother said, her voice nearly breathless.

"Oh!" he said. "Ask her about Reagan."

I sunk to the floor and put my head between my knees. *Christopher Mansfield. Christopher Mansfield.*

"Your father wants to know what people on campus are saying about Reagan's evil empire speech," she said.

"And the Strategic Defense Initiative proposal," he yelled, his voice closer to the phone. "What a joke! It'll cost billions. And it can't be done!"

The Strategic what? Few people here were as obsessed with politics and current events as my parents. No one I knew read the *New York Review of Books* and only one place, the student union, sold *The New York Times*. Even after I repeatedly explained this to my parents, they couldn't help themselves. Why hasn't Indiana elected a Democratic presidential nominee since 1964? Why did conservatives think a Hollywood B-rated actor would make a good president? What did conservatism mean to them? What were they thinking?

That was the point they always missed. People here weren't thinking about any of it. How many times would I have to tell them this? "Tell Dad that nobody talks about Ronald Reagan. Nobody cares."

"Clare said that nobody cares about Reagan," my mother said. I heard my dad snort. I imagined him in his faded chinos and favorite blue blazer.

"But if they don't care then why did they vote for him?"

I felt anger boil up my neck and explode, hot and throbbing, on my cheeks. "Tens of thousands of people live in this state. I don't know how they all voted. I keep telling you that people here don't care about politics!"

"Well, I don't understand."

Just once I wanted her to say, *I understand.* Or, *of course, you don't know how everyone in the state voted.* Just once I'd like to hear her ask me how *I* was.

But that wasn't nice. If I truly needed her, she'd help me. Probably. Well, maybe. I stretched my legs in front of me and tried to take long, deep breaths. The back of my neck was wet with sweat. Oh, God, I was so hung over.

"But, Clare—"

"Stop! I'm sick of politics! You think I know everything, all of the time, and I just don't!" I was a train, speeding down the tracks, out of control with no brakes.

"Here, talk to your father."

"Clare!" My dad breathed heavily into the phone. "Are you all right?"

No, I wasn't. Tears burned in my eyes as I croaked, "Dad?"

"I imagine you're in the thick of studying. How's it going? How's Lee?"

Lee! I looked at the clock above the closet.

There was still time to meet her, and with coffees from Village Pantry, but I'd have to hurry. "Dad, I gotta—"

"I got your mother into fifteen cities to do book talks. How about that? I don't know why Janice hasn't sent over the *Time* review yet. It's due out today." He called to my mother, "Eleanor, do we have the *Time* review yet?"

"Shush, Dad, don't!"

In the background, I heard my mother moan.

I stood, miniature, silent silver stars bursting in my peripheral vision, and reached for the counter to steady myself again.

"Oh, I forgot to tell you that I talked to Logan and unfortunately he can't come to your graduation," he said. "He can't get away. But he's sorry to miss it."

Logan was in graduate school at the London School of Economics and it was no surprise that he wouldn't be at my graduation. I had seen him only three or four times in the last four years. What would he think of Christopher Mansfield? I knew that they had one thing in common. They both wore boxers, not briefs. I knew this about Logan because I did everyone's laundry last summer when he visited the Vineyard. That I knew this about Christopher was the more troubling surprise.

"I gotta go, bye." I hung up, hurried out of the mailroom, and ran into Sarah, who barely stopped her coffee from spilling down the front of our shirts.

"God, Clare." She switched her cup to her other hand and licked coffee off her wrist. She was pale and doughy and her big, brown-framed glasses made the circles under her eyes darker. Her red hair, unrulier than normal, was pulled back under a blue bandana. We were rooming together but barely saw each other. She was in the library or the lab and not on the sundeck every afternoon or out all night. "What the hell is going on with you?"

"I have to finish a paper today."

"No, I mean, *what* is going on with you?" She leaned in close even though we were alone in the foyer. "Julie told me that you were with Christopher Mansfield, again. Clare! Are you guys, like, an item or something? What about Ben?"

I frowned. I hated this aspect of close living. It wasn't anyone's business what I was doing. Still, I felt my heartbeat quicken. Christopher and I had fun, just innocent fooling around. It wasn't *anything*. I didn't want this getting back to Ben.

"No!" I felt my cheeks sting.

She raised her eyebrows and sighed. "I never see you. You come in late when I'm asleep and you're usually asleep when I get up. I've been wanting to talk to you for days. People are asking me about Lee. You know, what's going on with her."

"Who's asking?"

"Amy said that she never sees her and Julie said that Lee never goes out anymore. And then Susie found her in bed one afternoon in the cold dorm. With all of the lights off. Just staring at the ceiling. I don't know what to say to them. And then I finally saw Lee at dinner the other night, and she looked awful. What does she say about, you know, what happened?"

It had been four weeks since we returned from spring break. In that time, I made sure to find Lee every day. We studied together at the union between classes. And last week, after her first appointment with a counselor at the health center, I surprised her with coffee from Village Pantry. She still hadn't told me what happened that night in Daytona. I'd stopped asking because every time I brought it up she cried or slipped into this awful coma-like stare. Which scared me more than the crying.

People had asked me about Lee, too. And she *did* look awful. I suddenly felt so dizzy again— being hung over was such an awful feeling—and dropped my eyes. It hurt to look at Sarah. "She doesn't talk about it."

"I don't get it," Sarah whispered. "I've been thinking about something else, too. We surprised them by coming back to the house. So, if she was raped, how come she was dressed? And standing there with her stuff? You weren't gone that long, either. What, twenty minutes? A half hour? Have you ever wondered about this?"

"Just look at her! *Something* bad happened, Sarah."

"I'm not saying that something bad didn't happen." She shook her head. "I don't know. She's seeing that counselor again, right?"

I nodded. Forget Village Pantry. I'd get coffee from our kitchen. I started for the stairs. I had to change, grab my backpack, and be out the door in five minutes but I could do it. I *would* do it.

"Maybe you should talk to a counselor, too," Sarah said.

I stopped walking and turned. "But nothing happened to me."

She shrugged, took a sip of her coffee, and stared at me over the rim of her glasses. I whirled around and headed for the stairs.

Fifteen minutes later, I was in the health center office with five minutes to spare, still feeling unsettled after my conversation with my mother. How worried should I be about her? I pulled out the draft of my English paper, but then sighed and put it away. I had the rest of the day to work on it. I'd written about how pathetic fallacy was used to foreshadow the end of Gatsby and Daisy's relationship in *The Great Gatsby*. There wasn't a bit of creativity or originality in this, but the paper was good enough. I had done nothing to distinguish myself on campus, no internships, awards, or club involvement, but I would leave here with good grades. At least I had that.

I hadn't started out this way. I bombed my first English paper. We were asked to write about the role of literature in our society and I'd spouted off this: Readers shouldn't hold up novels to be voices of a generation or believe that they proclaimed any kind of truths about people or our society. Novels were made-up stories, stretched and manipulated by the author (and sometimes borrowed or stolen) in order to provoke some kind of emotion in the reader. Writers, I concluded, were spectacular liars and thieves.

Of course I was speaking about *Listen, Before You Go*, which was proclaimed to be the "Vietnam War novel" of the decade even though my mother had no experience or personal knowledge of what went on in Southeast Asia, whatsoever.

But my teacher, a graduate student who didn't know I was the daughter of Eleanor Michaels, argued that I was wrong. Novels were important statements about society. Novels spoke the truth about the human condition! Back then I was too troubled by the ending of my mother's novel and conflicted with people's assumptions that I was the model for Phoebe to think rationally. Since then I'd learned that I should stick to the basics if I wanted good grades. Identifying metaphors and symbols. Comparing themes in a body of work.

Not ever talking or writing about my mother or *Listen, Before You Go*.

The girl to my right kept glancing at me. When I turned my head to look at her, she shifted her eyes to something over my shoulder. Maybe she was wondering why I was here. Maybe she knew me. When Christopher Mansfield and I were suddenly alone three weeks ago in front of a keg, I'd introduced myself. I'd never talked to him, never been up close—he was such a big man on campus, after all. And he'd grinned and said, "I know who you are. Your mom wrote *Listen, Before You Go*."

And I'd smiled, pleased for once to be acknowledged this way. But for most of my college years I'd lived in relative obscurity.

My mother nearly fainted when I told her I wanted to come here. Not Dartmouth, where my dad and brother had gone, or Sarah Lawrence, where she'd been a star. She put her hand on the kitchen counter to steady herself and said, "Where is it? And just tell me *why?*"

I liked how it looked in the brochures, I'd said, and how large it was. It'd be good to know a different part of our country (it was so far away that I couldn't just pop home for a weekend). Truth was, I'd never heard of Indiana University until one day during the fall of my senior year in high school when I saw my old junior high school librarian, Mrs. Miller, sitting in our living room.

She was attending one of the writing classes that my mother taught in our house.

"Anne Sexton will be nothing more than a footnote," my mother said as she pulled her long hair behind her. "A minor poet at most."

"Oh, I don't care about that," Mrs. Miller said.

A hush fell over the room as I peeked inside. About twenty women were staring at my mother, who sat still and erect in the oversized chair next to the window. You couldn't see out onto the street, it was already dark, and my mother's reflection bounced off the window, making it seem as if there were two of her in the room. The logs in the fireplace hissed, snapped, and popped.

Mrs. Miller sat forward. "I mean, no, she's not in the same league as Milton, of course. But I don't feel anything when I read his poetry. Think of Sexton's poem, 'The Wedding Night,' and those sad last lines. They made me cry when I read them the first time. There's value in that, isn't there?"

My mother's dissertation was on the pastoral elements in Milton's famous poem, "Lycidas," and I'd never heard anyone criticize him in front of her. I'd also never heard anyone challenge her on anything that had to do with writing. I held my breath and waited behind the partially closed pocket door for her response.

The fire snapped and hissed again. Someone coughed.

"Sexton's idea of poetry was to regurgitate every sexual perversion in which she'd partaken and think these worthy of a poem," she said. "She had no scholarly education, no deference to poets who came before her, and certainly no respect for keeping her neurosis where it belonged. *Private*. All that emoting and revealing was self-indulgent, at best."

I cringed and thought about rushing into the room to create a distraction but then Mrs. Miller—her thick blond hair resting on her shoulders and her skin white with patches of pink on both cheeks—smiled. It wasn't an embarrassed or cynical smile. She didn't seem the least bit intimidated or upset.

"Well, I really like that poem," she said. "And I like to think about how Sexton's poems might reflect what was going on in her life. It's interesting."

"Be that as it may," my mother said. "As writers, you want to pay attention to the words, not the author's supposed intentions. I encourage you all to read Welleck and Warren if you need an explanation on the importance of New Criticism."

My mother was in love with Welleck and Warren. Their book, *The Theory of Literature*, had been her bible for as long as I could remember. Ask her what personal stories went into *Listen, Before You Go* and she'd stare, coldly, at you. But ask about the death foreshadowing in Chapter Two, and she could talk forever.

Later, after the class had ended and the women were still milling around, I walked up to Mrs. Miller. She was taller than I'd remembered although everything else was the same. Pink cheeks. Glasses hanging from a chain around her neck. No makeup. I didn't know her well but I'd always liked her. She was different from the adults I knew. Maybe because she smiled a lot and didn't take herself so seriously.

"Clare! Hello!" She grinned. "Nice to see you. What are you now, a junior?"

"No, a senior," I said.

On the far side of the room a group of women crowded around my mother like chicks at a mother hen's feet.

"A senior, my goodness!" She laughed loudly, genuinely. "Have you decided where you're going next year?"

"My parents want me to go to Dartmouth. Logan and my dad went there."

"Excellent school." The corners of her smile dipped. "But maybe not where you want to go?"

It was that obvious? I shrugged. "Where did you go?"

"Indiana University!" She burst into a smile, her white teeth sparkling.

"Did you like it?"

"Loved it! Beautiful campus, great education.

I met my best friend there." She leaned into me, as if she were going to whisper a secret. Her perfume was sweet, flowery and natural, and I leaned in, too. "And I had the *time* of my *life*."

I pulled back, surprised. I'd heard college described many ways—Logan said he'd never worked so hard and my parents said that it was where they became "politically alive." But I'd never heard it described as *the time of my life.*

The next day I went to my school library, checked out a book of poems by Anne Sexton and read "The Wedding Night." It was one of those poems, unlike "Lycidas," where you could actually follow what was going on. Somebody was leaving somebody, and the person being left was sad as she walked down Marlborough Street in Boston (I'd been on that street a hundred times!). I liked it.

Then I looked up Indiana University, copied the address and that night sent away for an application and brochure. The rest was history, a cliché about which my mother would most certainly complain.

The health center door opened and a boy walked in and threw himself on the couch in the corner. Next to me, the girl rubbed her eyes. She was young, maybe a freshman, with feathered brown hair and ruddy cheeks. Maybe someday going to a counselor wouldn't be a big deal but not now, in Indiana, in 1983. People would talk.

A stigma was attached to it. *What was wrong with you?*

Maybe the girl had trouble with her boyfriend. Maybe something terrible happened to her. Maybe she didn't know what she was doing with her life. Maybe she felt guilty. Last night's beers roiled in my stomach and started up my throat.

I swallowed, grimaced, and reached for a magazine on the table next to me. The new issue of *Time*. I flipped through until I saw the review of my mother's new novel. It took up half of a page with her picture—the professional one she'd taken in Back Bay last year—in the middle of the text. With her new short hair, huge eyes and thin lips, the picture screamed *Serious Author* but looked so little like her. Where were the wrinkles in the corners of her mouth and the sagging skin under her chin? Or maybe this picture was how she really looked and I only imagined the flaws.

I felt the familiar, odd convergence of pride and fear. My mother was in *Time*! Oh, no, my mother was in *Time*! I skimmed the article looking for my name and felt relieved, then disappointed, when it wasn't there. Then I began to read. The new novel was a "quieter look at the consequences of war." Set in Saigon before the fall, it was "peculiar in tone and superficial in content. Ultimately, it fails. The minimalist style ushered in with *Listen, Before You Go* feels dated. Michaels needs to dig deeper if she wants her characters to rise above contradictions, clichés, and glibness."

I felt myself melt into the chair—this was very bad—as I read. Toward the end there was a short question and answer. Was the novel autobiographical? "Oh, dear, novels should be talked about in terms of what's on the page." Your husband is your agent? "He handles the business end and is always my first reader." Do you write every day? "Yes." (*When can we open presents?* I'd ask, eyeing my mother's closed door on Christmas mornings.) Yes, it was important work. Yes, she felt an obligation to fans of *Listen* to continue writing, "to keep exploring the damage to our nation's psyche from fighting that needless, senseless war."

I glanced back at the beginning of the review (glibness?) and winced. No wonder her editor hadn't sent this to my parents yet. This was exactly what my mother had worried about and why it had taken her ten years to publish again. She must have asked me a thousand times, how would I top *Listen*? But I always thought that was the wrong question. Why try to top it? Couldn't she just enjoy writing?

I imagined her curled up on the couch, sobbing, when she read the review. She'd been right to worry, after all. Why hadn't I been more sympathetic on the phone? Why had I gone to a school so far from home? After meeting Lee, I should go back to the house and call. *Everything will be okay!* Then I'd tell Dad to make sure there was enough of her favorite tea in the house and that he should remind her of her fans and what about pulling out letters she'd received over the years?

Thank God I wasn't there.

I began rubbing my pounding temples. My enigmatic mother was an expert on a four-hundred-year-old poem and yet her own writing was thoroughly modern. She wrote about war although she'd never been in a single battle. In front of a crowd she was engaging and authoritative but at home she was quiet and distracted. She was an elitist from a middle-class background. She loved to eat but rarely cooked. She loved to drink wine but could go for months without it. She was charming and cold, interested and bored, engaged and distant.

The clinic door opened and I sucked in a quick breath as Lee walked toward me. She wore baggy jeans, a long sleeve, white T-shirt, and brown wood clogs. Her hair, usually down on her shoulders, was pulled back into a loose ponytail. A scab had formed over the welt but had since fallen off, leaving an oblong, off-white patch on her cheek. A thick red scar, like the zipper on my Indiana sweatshirt, stretched down the center of her upper lip. Eventually, the health center doctor told her, the scars would fade. She was thinner, smaller, shorter, so unlike the person who always turned heads—she commanded such presence!—whenever she walked into a room. I felt a sudden urge to run. Instead I stood and, hands shaking, held out her coffee.

"Thanks," she said. If she noticed that it wasn't her favorite coffee from Village Pantry, if she wondered why I hadn't left enough time to go there before coming here, she didn't say.

I pushed open the doors and we started down the sidewalk on Tenth Street. The sun, red-rimmed above the trees, was hot and the air still. It was going to be another scorcher. My head pounded and my hands wouldn't stop shaking. I wasn't going out tonight. What was it now, ten nights in a row? Eleven? I'd go to Ben's practice this afternoon, back to the house for dinner, and to the library to finish my paper. No Christopher Mansfield. Not tonight. Not again.

"How was it?" I shifted my backpack to my other shoulder but it was no use. It was too heavy and I winced as it cut into my shoulder blade.

"Okay."

"Do you think it's helping?"

"Helping with what?"

There it was again! This slight edge in her voice. I heard it the other day when I asked if I could get her a Diet Dr Pepper from Village Pantry, and I heard it the day before that, too. She was angry with me. Yet glancing at her, I wasn't sure. Despite her dark skin, her cheeks were pale, almost ashen, and her swollen eyes seemed more pained than angry. I looked down at my Top-Siders and told myself to put one foot in front of the other.

The first couple of weeks after we got back from Florida, we met in the stairwell or at the student union and I apologized, over and over. *I'm sorry I left you. I'm sorry I couldn't find Donny's house. I'm sorry this happened.* She wouldn't talk about it. She kept saying that she was fine and she'd get this strange, almost dreamy look in her eyes. Lately, I'd tried to talk about normal things. School. Her film. The house. But something was still there between us. I felt it.

"Do you still like this counselor?" I asked.

"I guess. But I don't think she really cares about me. She knows I'll be gone soon and she probably thinks, what's the point?"

I shook my head. "But this is her job."

"I think she got mad at me today."

"What?"

"I kept asking questions, like, do your parents understand your job? Are you close to them? Do you live alone? Do you have lots of friends? She wouldn't answer."

What the hell did these questions have to do with anything? And wasn't Lee the one who was supposed to answer questions?

But I really didn't know what you were or weren't supposed to do with a counselor. Sophomore year when Lee and I were so obsessed with Freud, it was because of our fascination, and horror, with the Rat Man case and because Freud had made such a valuable contribution to civilization. He was one of her great people in history. Eventually we decided that talking to a counselor was good. But until Lee began going, I didn't know anyone who'd actually been to one, except my mother, but she hadn't gone for long.

"Maybe you should stick to talking about, you know, the thing." My voice stung in my throat. "The thing. You know. That happened."

We crossed the street and now the sun was out of the trees and I felt the rays burn my skin, sear into my headache, tighten my breath. Beads of sweat broke out across my upper lip and forehead. Water. I needed a water fountain.

"We don't talk about that," Lee mumbled.

When I stopped walking, Lee stopped, too. I blurted, "You told her, right?"

Lee was staring at something over my shoulder. She had that strange look on her face again, forehead slightly wrinkled, lips parted, eyes wide and unblinking. She was here but not here. Was she thinking about what happened?

"Lee? Did you tell her?"

"What?" she asked.

Was she still in shock? I asked again, "Lee, *what* do you talk about?"

"I don't know." She frowned and we started to walk again.

Oh, God, did she talk about me? But if she hadn't told the counselor about what happened, what did she say? Maybe she told her that I was a lousy friend. I felt the heat burn across my chest. This weather and hangover were *killing* me.

Then we were in front of the union where Lee would break off to go to class and I'd go inside to work on my paper. Tears filled my eyes and I lowered them because it was so hard to keep looking at her. The other day I also found her in bed in the cold dorm—it was only two o'clock in the afternoon—just staring at the wall and the day before that she was nowhere to be found for the senior speeches. The senior speeches, for God's sake. No one ever misses that. Finally, I looked at her.

She lifted her eyebrows and this time seemed to see me. "What happened to you last night? I looked for you. Julie said you went out with her but then stayed."

I hadn't told her about Christopher. He was a frat boy, the type she hated. *Too good looking*, she'd say, *too full of himself. Vapid. Entitled.* Would she think that I was compromising myself? Selling my soul? Or some other reason?

But then I thought about Christopher's lips, full

and meaty yet disciplined. I felt a tingling in my thighs. Could lips be disciplined?

"I came back late." My heart raced with too much caffeine. And I was clammy and hot and not at all myself.

And then, just like that, it was as if she didn't see me anymore. As if she were drifting away again, like the smoke from Christopher's cigarette. I thought about an early chapter in *Listen, Before You Go*, when Phoebe describes Whit, who'd just gotten home from the Army hospital, as "fading away in mid-sentence." Lee did the same thing, didn't she? She faded away. She zoned out.

"Oh, Lee," I sobbed. "I'm so worried."

Lee pressed her lips together in a frown and shook her head rapidly. Her voice was loud and agitated. "I'm fine. Stop it! Stop *crying!*"

Then she turned and walked away.

I hurried up the steps of the union, through the doors, and around the corner to the South Lounge. Hardly anyone was here—it was too early—and I dropped into a leather couch near the piano. My heartbeat and breathing began to slow. No more gulping. No more feeling as if my lungs were caving in. The lounge was cool, quiet, and dark. This was what I needed. My problem was the sudden heat outside and too much drinking and not enough sleep. Maybe I'd just rest for a moment.

CHAPTER 6

That night at Nick's, the bar we'd monopolized this past month, we took a table on the second floor, at the top of the stairs, with enough seats for others who were coming later. Julie ordered pitchers of beer and popcorn as I squeezed onto the bench next to Lynn. The music was loud, the room stuffy and hot. I was staying for one beer. Lee went to dinner with her film class, the first night she'd been out since we got back from spring break. She'd agreed to meet me here afterward and then we'd walk back to the house. Before bed I'd call Ben, as I'd promised today, to wish him luck. Tomorrow he and the team were leaving for a three-game series in Michigan, the last of his regular season college baseball career.

I'd met up with him today at his practice. Afterward, while hurrying across the field, he said, "I called you last night. No one answered."

"I wasn't in my room yet," I said. "And Sarah can sleep through anything."

He nodded and pushed his glasses up his nose. Black framed and sturdy, they looked like the glasses my dad wore and were so out of fashion that people often gave him a double look. Even if he noticed, which I didn't think he did, he didn't care. Ben was practical. Because of astigmatism he couldn't wear contact lenses and he needed something solid, *dependable,* he said, while playing baseball.

At five feet ten, Ben was thick and solid with sturdy legs and strong arms. His dirty blond hair was so short that it didn't move as we jogged across the field. It took all my energy to keep up with him. When we reached the weight room door, he turned and grabbed my arm. I was so used to his spring routine—hurry up, baseball, study, no time, gotta go, baseball, study—that I gasped. This campus had thirty thousand students. Surely he didn't know anything about last night.

"Are you okay?" He let go of my arm.

I'd taken a nap in the South Lounge this morning and woke, feeling a little better, to a crowded room and a girl playing the piano. But I wasn't okay. I was out of shape and sweating and I was deceiving him. I was a bad person. I cringed and nodded. "What about you? How are you feeling about the Michigan games?"

He sighed. "I'm in *such* a hitting slump and I missed that big play at second in the Purdue game. Coach doesn't want to pull me because I'm a senior. But I told him to do it. Put in Kelsey. He's got so much promise and he's a better shortstop than I am. Kills me, but it's true. And it's going to kill me sitting in the dugout and watching him play, too. But it was the right thing to do. The team's more important than me."

"Oh, Ben, you're so good," I croaked. And he was. He loved baseball. How many other people would work as hard as he does and then give it up for the team? I felt something sour—last night's beer and tuna casserole—churn in my stomach.

"I'm not *that* good," he said. "My batting average sucks."

"No, that's not what I meant." I could barely get the words out. I felt myself growing smaller and smaller as I stood there, looking up at him. And then I turned to the line of trees along the far side of the field. On the top of a giant maple a few leaves flapped frantically back and forth, like the leaves are having a nervous breakdown, Lee used to say, looking up at the trees. Maybe I was having a nervous breakdown. I started to cry. Again.

Ben sucked in a breath and reared back. I'd only cried in front of him a few times, and each had left him dumbstruck. He pushed his glasses up the bridge of his nose and reached out and rubbed my arm slowly, then faster and then slowly again. He quickly dropped his hand, scratched his forehead, and asked, in a timid voice that I imagined was afraid of the answer, "What's wrong?"

"I'm so tired," I blubbered. "And you're in a slump. And I just feel so bad."

"About my slump?"

Ben and I gave each other a lot of freedom. We didn't need to be with each other all the time or find each other at the end of a drunken night. We were practical. He needed his sleep. He needed baseball and to maintain his straight-A average. And I needed, well, what did I need?

"I don't know!" I cried.

"Come here." He reached for me and I fell against him. He smelled like sweat and fresh dirt, and something in his pocket poked my ribs. His arms were loose around me, not taking my breath away. Not as if his life depended on it. Not as if my life depended on it.

"Ben, let's go!" Coach opened the door.

"I gotta hit the weight room," Ben said. "Look, you don't have anything to feel bad about, okay? This is just happening to us because of baseball season."

Something was happening to us.

I poured myself a second beer. Amy was telling a story about a party. Lisa ordered another pitcher. The music was Aerosmith, then Zeppelin. *You need coolin', baby I'm not foolin'.*

Something *was* happening to us. Ben's comment before break, *why don't you come to Philadelphia with me,* was a shock. Because this meant something different, something more serious. I respected him. Other than my mother and Lee, he was the hardest working person I knew. But to go from a few *I think you're beautiful* to *come to Philadelphia,* well, that was a big leap. How was I supposed to take that? I'd blurted, "let's just see how it goes," and hurried to the bathroom to give myself time to think. And we hadn't talked about it since then.

On the stairs in front of me I saw heads, then shoulders, and I leaned forward, my heart hammering in my chest. But it was just Ducky, pearls bold and white against her tan neck and pink Lacoste shirt, and a few others from the house. I watched Ducky's blue eyes flicker as she glanced around the table, hoping to squeeze in somewhere, anywhere, except next to me. But Tracey pushed her forward and she had no choice but to slide onto the bench and scoot next to me until our shoulders and thighs touched.

She smelled like Lubriderm lotion and I remembered—I could still see—how at Donny's house she'd hugged the toilet seat as I held her hair. I glanced at the tiny green alligator on her shirt and imagined it jumping off her chest, blowing up to life size, and swallowing me whole. I shuddered, reached for the pitcher, and poured another beer. When had I drunk the previous one? Ducky and I had barely seen each other since we got back. I felt a prickly sensation on the back of my neck. Maybe she felt it, too, because she kept shifting in her seat. She drank her beer in two giant gulps and poured another.

The cockroach in Donny's bathroom. The bass

137

of the music thumping in my chest. The window. Jittery Man's corroded toes. And Lee's face, white as a sheet. I cringed. Such a cliché. What would my mother say? White as milk. White as a cloud. Maybe she wouldn't even say white. Maybe she'd say alabaster. Pallid. Snowy.

"How's Lee?" Ducky whispered. "She's never around. Have you noticed that? How she never goes out with us anymore?"

"She's out tonight," I said. "She's meeting me here in a little while."

Ducky nodded and fiddled with her pearls. The others were busy planning our graduation party at the house and not paying attention to us. I looked around the table. We were red and swollen from too much time on the sundeck, too much beer, too much cheese strata and starchy potato casserole. We were giant tomatoes, bursting on the vine, ready for picking.

"Did she tell you what happened?" Ducky whispered.

"We know what happened." I shifted in my seat.

"She finally told you?" Ducky sucked in a breath. The corners of her mouth turned up slightly, and I knew that she hoped it wasn't as bad as she imagined.

"Ducky, something bad happened to her," I said. "We know this."

She slumped forward, her pearls dangling under

her chin, her blond feathered bangs falling into her eyes. "I feel so awful. It could've happened to you or Sarah. Or *me*. That's all I keep thinking about." She leaned back. Her big blue eyes filled with tears and her white eyebrows began to tremble.

I shushed her. We'd made a promise, after all, not to tell anyone. Not a soul.

"Is it all you think about, too?" She didn't wait for me to respond. "And I can't stand to see her. I know this is awful, but I can't help it. The other day when she came into the dining room, I ran up the back stairs so I wouldn't have to talk to her. Isn't that terrible? At least that thing on her cheek is gone. Oh, but her lip! Are people still asking her what happened to it?"

I nodded. *I tripped.* That was what I heard her tell Susie. *I tripped and didn't break my fall.*

"I've hardly talked to her," Ducky cried. "I feel *so* bad."

See? We were all bad. I wasn't the only one who wanted to run away.

"Sometimes I feel so thankful, you know, that it wasn't me," she said. "It could've been me and I was so drunk and I wouldn't have even known. Or maybe I would have. But then I feel so guilty for thinking that way." Giant tears, as big as her pearls, rolled down her tan cheeks.

"For Christ's sake, Ducky, why are you crying?" Amy asked. Everyone looked at Ducky.

"Tell me you aren't talking about how sad you are to leave college. *Again.*"

"And you're not sad?" Lynn asked. "I'm so sad that I feel sick."

"Well, of course I'm sad, but Ducky's like a water faucet," Amy said.

Ducky tried to smile but her puffy bottom lip rolled over into a pout. They went on to something else, everyone talking at once, everyone wanting to be heard.

Let her go. I'll stay.

I gripped the table and thought of my mother, before she hit it big, when she wasn't so pre-occupied and needy, when we were still in the apartment on Dean Street and she wrote late into the night, every night, at her desk in the living room. My dad, who hadn't yet left his teaching position at the business school to be her agent, always said, "Shush! She needs space and quiet!" He felt a reverence for her writing; we both did, we helped cultivate it. Many nights I made her favorite tea, tiptoed to her desk and set it in the corner, close enough to reach but far away from the typewriter return. Most times she didn't look up. But sometimes she said, "Thanks, Clare, you're a lifeline in the middle of the night!"

When I was younger, I looked up lifeline in the dictionary: Salvation. Help. Support. Sustenance. I thought about what Logan called me, *Clare-taker,* when I'd screen phone calls while our mother wrote. But did these words truly describe me?

Look around this table! I helped Ducky that night at Donny's. I drove Julie to Planned Parenthood. I comforted Amy when her boyfriend broke up with her and listened to Lynn when she dropped out of the nursing program because she flunked chemistry. I knew these secrets because I was discreet, able to tolerate uncomfortable emotions and could be trusted to listen and give advice. I was a shoulder to lean on. A confidant. A person who brought tea with honey. A lifeline.

And yet how could this be? Maybe together Lee and I could have fought off those guys, maybe even talked them out of it. Instead, I'd panicked and bolted.

I watched Julie's throat move up and down as she drank her beer and Amy's lips stretch into a smile. I felt the heat from Ducky's thigh. I imagined their hair and fingernails growing, millimeter by millimeter. They were alive and evolving yet somehow I was suddenly frozen in time, suspended in midair, stuck.

Because I wasn't the person they thought I was. I wasn't the person *I* thought I was, either, and this made me feel sick. I needed to go home. I needed something.

More heads on the stairs and then there he was, Christopher Mansfield, with his friends. Tall, broad, his hands large and strong—the size of dinner plates—piercing blue eyes, wavy brown hair, long, thick arms that wrapped around and squeezed me. Looking at him, I couldn't breathe. His eyebrows rose slightly when he saw me, and then he grinned as he led his friends up the ramp to the back room.

"Woo-hoo, Clare, there he is!" Amy sang. "Did you see how he looked at you?"

"What's going on?" Susie asked. "Did you break up with Ben? I don't get it."

"Senioritis," someone else said.

I put my hand over my heart. Could they hear the thundering and wanting in my chest? They watched me, waiting for an answer, an explanation, but I didn't have one. I looked down at my glass, empty again. How many beers had I had, two? Four?

"He's a sexy man," Amy said.

"Be careful, Clare," Susie said.

"Be careful of *what*?" Lisa asked.

"He's just a pretty boy," someone said. "Ladies' man to the max."

"The ultimate *bad boy!*" someone else said.

I poured another beer. Because I'd started to shake and maybe this would help with my nerves. I was going home. Soon. When Lee got here.

An hour later, maybe two, Christopher was waiting for me as I came out of the bathroom. He wore tight blue jeans and a white polo shirt, snug against his chest, collar turned up. A few hairs leapt out above the buttons. More hair, curly, brown, and hidden under his shirt, stretched down to his navel. I felt that familiar tingling in my thighs.

"Come with me," he said in that rich, deep voice.

If he was the ultimate bad boy, did that make me a bad girl?

"I have to go home tonight." I straightened. I'd done it. I'd stood up to him.

He laughed. "We're not leaving. Just outside for a smoke."

"Oh." Maybe he didn't want me to go home with him. Maybe he wanted to tell me that it was over, whatever this was. I was dizzy, my eyes blurring under the lights, the music too loud in my ears. He reached for my hand—as if he could see or feel my unsteadiness—and held it as we started for the stairs.

It was still too early in the year for the hot days to extend into the nights. Outside, the air was cool and damp and felt as if at any moment rain would pour from the sky. Students were everywhere. Across the street the lights were blazing in the Daily Grind, the coffee house where Lee and I had gone to a few poetry readings. A muscle car, engine revving, charged up to the stop sign near us. I waited for it to gun across the intersection, but it just sat there, its engine grating on my nerves. Just go already!

Christopher lit a cigarette, inhaled, and then exhaled out of the side of his mouth. The smoke drifted away from us, from me. I'd told him that I didn't like the smell. I hadn't told him how sexy he looked as he smoked. He rolled the cigarette between his finger and thumb and leaned against the brick wall. The streetlights and glow from the store windows and bars that lined the street threw patches of day-like light across the sidewalk.

I felt a nervous flutter in my chest. Would this feeling ever go away? I thought about what Julie or Amy had said in the bar. *He's a pretty boy.* Was that all there was? No, I'd seen the books on the desk in his room. Economics. History of Europe, 1750-1820. And *Slaughterhouse Five* for his Modern American Prose class.

"Did you decide on a book for your English paper?" Oh, God, I sounded desperate. But at one point we'd talked seriously. Last night? The night before that? This wasn't all a joke, was it?

He laughed. "Maybe your mom's book? Seems appropriate, considering how intimately involved I am with her daughter. Maybe you could give me some insight."

I rolled my eyes. He was joking, flirting, teasing. This was what we did.

"Seriously," he said. "I might write about her book. By the way, I saw it coming, Whit killing himself at the end. But what I want to know is, who committed suicide in your family?"

I startled. He was serious. But I didn't want to talk about my family with him. "Just because she wrote about suicide doesn't mean she experienced it."

He straightened. "Bullshit. Give it up, Miss Vagueness. Who was it?"

Miss Vagueness? I swallowed. "Well, her grandfather."

Christopher crossed his arms and leaned back against the wall again. I looked across the street where a group of girls were laughing as they walked into the Daily Grind. Over the years my mother had talked to us about her grandfather. He was her favorite relative and introduced her to poetry. On her annual summer visits, which she shared with her cousins (including her favorite cousin, Oliver), she read to her grandfather while he mucked the stables. She was crushed when he killed himself.

"So why Vietnam?" he asked. "Wasn't he too old for that?"

I shrugged. He'd been in Europe during the First World War and came back a "changed man," my mother had said. She believed he was traumatized by what he'd seen, and especially by what he'd had to do, although he rarely spoke of it. She never talked about this in public and she'd probably deny the connection but I knew she was thinking of him when she wrote about Whit's suicide.

But Christopher didn't need to know any of this.

He took a long drag, blew the smoke over my shoulder, and grinned. "Know what I was thinking about today? That I liked how flustered you get when I'm taking off your shirt. I hope you're still like that after we're married."

Ah, now we were back in familiar territory. I rolled my eyes again. "*Big flirt* should be written in black ink across your forehead."

He laughed. "You flirt with me, too."

Flirt. Tease. Kiss. Touch. But this wasn't really me. I wasn't like this in Brookline or in any of the last four years. This was because we were leaving soon and we'd never see each other again. Most of us would never see each other again. And this was good because I barely recognized myself. I might even hate myself.

"And I was also thinking that tonight is the night." He winked at me.

A group of girls I didn't know walked toward us. *Hi, Christopher! Hey, Chris!* He nodded but kept his eyes on me. I felt dizzy and the pavement seemed to shift under me. I needed to stop drinking. Or maybe I needed one more beer to steady myself.

"Yes, indeed, tonight's the night." He leaned into me, his chin close to my cheek but not touching. Grab me! Hold me! A line of sweat rolled down my back.

"No," I said. As long as we didn't go all the way, I wasn't really betraying Ben. Because this was flirting and touching, not real sex. Christopher and I weren't having real sex.

He leaned away from me, flicked the ashes behind him, and looked out across the street. "Of course, we have to figure out what to do about your boyfriend."

I sucked in a hot breath. "How do you know about him?"

"I have my ways." He pulsed his eyebrows at me but didn't smile.

I slumped against the wall next to him. Ben was my boyfriend, even if we hadn't officially defined our relationship, and this was a betrayal. I was desperate now. "Yeah, well, tell me about your girlfriends?"

"You have this way of avoiding things by asking questions."

Lee was the only other person to call attention to this. It was a habit. All I had to do was pick out pieces of what people said, even if I had no idea what they meant, and ask questions. *What was Paris like after the war? What is it about Milton's* Paradise Lost *that you like?* People were interesting and I learned a lot when I listened. But he was right. This was my way of avoiding personal questions.

"When we get married, you're going to *have* to talk to me," he said. "You'll be so satisfied with how I take care of you that you'll never *look* at another man."

How I take care of you. Has anyone ever taken care of me?

What a silly thought. My parents took care of me. There was always enough food and money and the orthodontist and hairdresser and did my mother ever take me to the doctor? Did she ever go to a parent-teacher conference? Surely she did because what mother doesn't take an interest in her daughter's health and education? I should ask her about this. I should know how many trips to the dentist she made with me.

I rubbed my neck, my fingers shockingly cold against my hot skin. What did this have to do with anything? Something was wrong with me.

Suddenly we were in the light of an oncoming car. Christopher's lips were pressed together and his blue eyes were staring at me so hard that I thought they'd see into my soul. Then he'd know, too, that I wasn't the person he thought I was. I hadn't told him about Florida. But I did tell Ben.

We were talking in bed one night after spring break and the heaviness of the secret (I'd told no one) felt as if it were strangling me until I couldn't breathe. I wanted relief, I wanted closeness, I wanted him to tell me that I'd done the right thing. As I explained what happened, he tightened his grip until his solid, warm body felt like a cocoon around me. When I finished he said, "For God's sake, what the hell were you two thinking? You could have gotten killed!"

I started to cry because he was right. What was I thinking? I felt awful. Why did I tell him?

Then he began shushing me. "It's okay. You're safe now, it's over. Be thankful it didn't happen to you. You did the right thing."

Yes, I did the right thing. I was safe. Be thankful! Did it matter that I hadn't told Ben the whole story? That I left some parts out?

I glanced at Christopher. That heaviness was still there in my chest and head and stomach and up and down my back. I shook out the hair in my eyes and said, "We can't get married because I'm not staying in the Midwest."

He dropped his cigarette, stepped on it with the toe of his brown Top-Sider, and ground it firmly into the cement. "Me, neither. I got a job in Washington."

Ask me to come with you.

But he didn't. Nor did he say anything about when we are married or how he'd take care of me or how beautiful I was with my clothes off, lying across his bed with the olive-green comforter and lava lamp on the bureau. Then I was horrified with myself and with what we were doing, with the neediness of wanting this playboy, this fraternity boy, this Big Man on Campus.

Don't ask me to go home with you again tonight. I can't do this.

Ask me, please, ask me.

Christopher bent over me, his lips next to my cheek and his eyes on my mouth. With his finger he traced a line up my arm and to my clavicle. He let it linger, drawing circles on the bone. I tried to swallow but my mouth was dry, my tongue stuck to my teeth.

This was passion. Yes! Lee and I talked about this a lot, where passion came from, how it couldn't be taught. How she and my mother had it and others didn't. It was relentless, she said about her film passion, this desire to *explain* and *show* what she sees and feels. How ironic and pathetic that I, after all this time, finally found a passion that had absolutely nothing to do with any redeeming talents of my own.

"Let's drink a few more beers," he said as he started for the door.

No kiss, no crushing hug, no talk of going back to his place. Tears stung my eyes. Silly girl. He was toying with me. Flirting. Keeping me on my toes.

I started after him but when I heard my name, I turned to see Lee walking toward me. Her hair was down on her shoulders and she wore the long, flowered skirt she'd bought at a street fair last year. As she got closer and I saw her feet in sandals—not those God forsaken worn-out wood clogs—I felt my spirits rise. Look at her, dressed and out of the house. She looked good and, well, normal. Mostly. I glanced back at Christopher but he'd already gone inside.

"Hey!" I heard the exuberance and relief in my voice. "How was dinner?"

"Okay." She took the tip of her tongue over her scar. I knew by how her eyelids drooped that she'd been drinking or smoking. Did she have fun? Maybe she was feeling better. Oh, God, I wanted her to feel better. I would have given *anything,* right then, to have her back to the way she was before this mess.

"I have something to tell you." Her mouth drooped into a frown. "Finally."

Then, just like that, I felt sick in my stomach. This was it. We were going to talk about that night. She was going to yell at me for leaving her.

"I just found out," she said, "that I got the internship."

"What?"

"The internship. I got it."

Before spring break she'd submitted her film about Patricia. With all that had happened, I'd forgotten about it. I felt my mouth open and paused. "Oh. Great!"

She did it. She was going to New York on a prestigious internship with one of the best documentary filmmakers in the country. She'd probably be great at it because she had real talent. I felt a familiar ping in my chest—what the hell was *I* going to do?—but no, I wouldn't dwell on that now.

She told me that Dr. Hannigan, her advisor, announced it at dinner. "He said they loved my film. The offer is in the mail."

But she wasn't smiling nor did she seem very excited. She kept batting her eyes, as if she had something in them, and shifting her feet and flicking the side of her skirt with the fingers of her right hand. I thought about earlier today when she'd shouted *I'm fine!* I said, "Oh, Lee. Well, congratulations."

We turned as a noisy truck pulled up to the stop sign across the street, its high beams shining on us. Lee turned away so abruptly that she stumbled. I raised my hand to shield the light but then the truck turned and roared past us, leaving a stench of gasoline and a plume of exhaust.

"When do you start?" Surely this would turn things around for her?

She stopped flicking her skirt and wrinkled her forehead as she looked over my shoulder. I looked, too, but I had no idea what she saw.

"Lee? When do you start?" I asked again.

"The pay is bad. I don't know how I'll do it. They offered me a room in university housing. It'll be cheaper. I don't know. I don't know what to do."

"You don't know what to do about what?"

"The internship. I won't know anyone."

Since when had *that* stopped her from doing anything? "Lee, you gotta do this. And you should take the room. This is what you've always wanted."

"What do you think you'll do?"

I had a plan. I was going to apply to graduate school. I would help people. But help people do *what?* What could I do? That terrible sensation I felt earlier in Nick's seized me again. Suspended in midair. Stuck. "I don't know."

"I'm so tired. But I can't sleep. What if I can't ever sleep again?" She covered her face with her hands. "Can I do this alone?"

"Oh, Lee." Then it was gone, all the hope I'd seen in her skirt, sandals, and hair. And I wasn't sure what she was even asking.

I thought about a scene in *Listen* when Whit and Phoebe were in the parking lot outside of a restaurant discussing how lambs are led to slaughter. What they were really talking about, my mother said in speech after speech, was the danger of blind trust in our government during times of war. When I first heard her say this during her speech at the North American Book Award ceremony, I was shocked. If that was what she intended, if the scene was really about war, why didn't she just write it that way? Why did it have to be hidden in this other scene? At age eleven, I wanted people to be direct, to say and do what they wanted.

I still wanted that. I bet Phoebe wanted that, too, despite being a hero. In charge of keeping her brother alive, she was the only person he trusted. What an amazing, precocious little girl, people said. Was I supposed to be her? Did my mother model me on her, or vice versa?

One day when I was twelve, I snuck a copy of *Listen* into my bedroom and read it in one sitting. I was so surprised at the things my mother lifted from my life and put in the book (did Phoebe *really* have to throw up on the hairdresser, *too?*) and horrified at the ending, at what Whit did to himself, that I threw the book across the room. After that I didn't always want the comparisons and expectations. I wasn't Phoebe. But now, staring at Lee, I felt a horrible plummeting sensation in my chest. Phoebe and I truly *did* have something in common, after all. We'd both let down the people who had trusted us most. Phoebe wasn't a hero, after all, and neither was I.

I brought my hand to the side of my face. I knew what Lee was asking. But how could she still want me to help her after what I'd done? "Oh, Lee. I feel so bad."

She ran her tongue over her scar again. Her voice was full of anguish as she whispered, "The other day Ducky ran away from me."

A sob filled my chest. "We all feel so bad about what happened."

"You don't have to feel that way."

"But we do. *I* do. Something terrible happened to you, Lee. And I—"

She shook her head. "But I asked for it. I stayed and—"

"Don't say that! This isn't your fault!" I said. What was she insinuating? "I shouldn't have left you. Together maybe we could have—"

"I told you to go. I don't blame you for that."

Her eyebrows dipped into a frown and something foul settled in the back of my throat. I said, "But you blame me for something."

She stared at me with her head pulled back and her face muscles taut. But then her shoulders fell forward and her lips began to tremble and there was so much pain etched in her cheekbones and eyes that I suddenly felt as if I couldn't breathe again. Lee was my closest friend. Meeting her was one of the best things that had ever happened to me. And now look at us.

"I don't know what I did. I don't know what's wrong with me. I can't stand feeling like this!" I burst into tears.

Lee's lips stopped quivering and her face relaxed but as she stared at me I didn't think she really saw me. She was zoning out again, floating, like a piece of driftwood in the water. Like a boat untethered from the dock. Finally, she said, her voice a monotone and a whisper, "Can we not fight anymore? And can we never fight again? Because it's so lonely. I just need to know where you'll be."

"Okay," I sputtered. I hadn't realized that we'd been fighting.

I flinched when two cars began honking at each other. Next to me the cool breeze sent a loose leaf of paper—someone's homework, someone's exam—fluttering in the air and then settling in the gutter. Outside the Daily Grind a group of girls began singing. And still, Lee seemed to be floating.

When I heard a low rumble of thunder in the distance and felt the first drops of cold rain on my bare, sunburned arms, I knew that I couldn't abandon her again. Maybe what she needed was to move on from this terrible place she was in. She needed to move forward, and not look back, and by God I had to help her with that.

PART TWO

1986

CHAPTER 7

The scones were dry again. I knew before I even peeled back the cellophane and lifted one of the neatly arranged scones out of the box that Donna hadn't fixed the problem. Dry and grainy, they were worse than the batch she'd delivered on Tuesday. I tried to ease one off the waxed paper, but it crumbled in my fingers. I picked up the pieces and carried them into the back room where Lorenzo was sitting in front of a long wood table that he used for a desk.

He looked up from his notebook and calculator. "What now?"

When I'd interviewed for the job last year, Lorenzo told me that he wanted to make his new coffeehouse a "destination where students and young professionals gather to enjoy fancy coffee drinks and upscale breakfast foods." No bad coffee served out of cheap white cups. Lorenzo saw the future: two-dollar cups of coffee, comfy couches, eclectic music, and scones. So far, the future was still the future.

"What do you mean, what now?" I asked. This was part of our daily routine. Pushing, pulling, arguing, accusing, teasing, and laughing. We both loved it.

"You were in here an hour ago complaining about how I make cappuccinos."

"The customer thought the milk tasted sour," I said. He threw up his hands to complain. "Lorenzo, we have to make customers happy or they won't come back. This won't make anyone happy, either." I set the scone pieces on the desk.

Lorenzo stared at them for a moment before putting one of the pieces in his mouth. He tilted his head as he chewed and grimaced as he swallowed. "It's dry."

I nodded. "I thought you were going to talk to Donna."

"I did!" At thirty-five, he was only ten years older than me, but already his black hair was streaked with gray. Women flirted with him, especially when they heard his Italian accent. At first I thought he must have a girlfriend because he seemed so uninterested. "Don't say that we should serve croissants. Damn French."

"I won't." I picked up the scone pieces. "But we need to have better scones."

"But it will cost me?" He arched his right eyebrow and then picked up his pencil. I knew this sign—our conversation was nearing the end for now. Lorenzo lived in Back Bay, drove an old BMW, and wore Cole Haan loafers. This wasn't the first business he'd started. He might be a good businessman but he had a blind spot when it came to food quality.

But I smiled. Lorenzo was a good person. Open, too. He kept a business card for his therapist (*she's like a mother*) taped to the wall above his desk and recently he'd started confiding in me about his boyfriend. But he never dumped anything on me or expected me to fix his problems. He didn't need encouragement, either. He was strong and just wanted me to listen. I so appreciated that.

"You remember that I'm leaving today and will be gone until Monday," I said.

He shook his head. "I am quite sure that we will not survive without you."

I laughed. "You'll survive."

Just as I started into the front room, he called my name. He always drew out the last letter so that it sounded as if he were saying Clara instead of Clare. "Claraaa. You should learn to bake delicious scones. That would solve our problem."

I laughed and thought about my recent cooking attempts. Chicken that tasted like rubber. Grilled pork chops with charred edges. Yet I'd made a solid spaghetti sauce last night for Ben and my parents and everyone loved my sugar cookies.

I glanced at my watch. Four hours until my train left. I felt a twist in my stomach, but I didn't have time to worry about my trip now.

I wet a rag and worked through the front room, wiping down tables, straightening chairs and couch cushions, and organizing newspapers on the giant coffee table. After sweeping the floor and organizing the counter, I surveyed the room. Not bad. It was ten, past the breakfast rush. The rest of the day would be spotty with people looking for a place to study and hang out, but no big crowds.

I'd been working the same shift, Tuesday through Friday, six to eleven, for the last six months. I loved smelling that first pot of coffee and greeting the regulars—the dog walker, the sociology professor who took a latte to go, and the French students who practiced conversing at the far table. I always felt a letdown at the end of the morning, especially on days like today when I had to hurry to my college's English department's writing center where I tutored three afternoons a week.

I stepped behind the counter and opened my book. I was a year away from finishing my master's degree in English literature, and this summer I was taking a class on D. H. Lawrence. My mother thought Lawrence was one of the world's greatest authors and that *Sons and Lovers* was a masterpiece for the way Lawrence's themes infiltrated the text. She called it "thematic penetration," which always felt so overtly sexual that it made me cringe. So far, I thought Lawrence was overrated.

I began to read, but after a few sentences glanced at the remaining scones in the box on the counter. Donna owned a bakery in Brighton and had promised scones and muffins—no croissants—delivered by six every other morning. That she was four hours late today was only part of the problem. I'd never tasted a good scone, but Elise, Logan's girlfriend, loved them and once described them to me. Flaky but not dry. Sweet but not too sweet. And best served warm out of the oven. I glanced at our industrial stove next to the counter. I didn't think it had ever been used.

The bell on the door rang, and I looked up to see a woman and a young girl take their usual table in front of the huge window. I frowned. The other day I had to scrub the window to get the girl's grimy fingerprints off the glass. The floor-to-ceiling glass was twice as wide as my outstretched arms and let in light even when it was cloudy outside. It was the most important part of the room.

"What can I get for you?" I shoved my hands into my back pockets.

The woman didn't look at me as she tied her daughter's sneaker. "Earl Grey tea, an apple juice, and a blueberry muffin. That's all."

No smile. No please or thank you. The woman screamed privilege with her massive diamond ring and big Coach bag. I didn't move. I wanted her to know that I wasn't just a coffeehouse waitress, still living at home with my parents. I was somebody, too. But instead the girl looked at me. She couldn't have been more than five years old. She had a roll of fat around each wrist and stubby fingers speckled with brown. I imagined those fingers on my window and when I frowned again, she lifted her arm and gave me the finger. I was so surprised that I stumbled backward. The woman finally looked up.

"Anything else?" I grabbed onto a chair to steady myself.

"I said that was all."

I felt a jolt of anger. What kind of mother *was* she? But oh, no, I'd be nice. And good. I'd be good even if it killed me. I marched back to the counter. But my hand wouldn't stop shaking as I poured hot water into a mug.

Three hours until my train left.

My problem was that I was nervous about my trip. I was going to New York to help Lee move yet again, her fifth place in three years. I didn't understand how she kept getting herself into these situations—bad roommates, bad landlords, bad apartments. Tomorrow she was moving into a two-bedroom apartment in a much safer neighborhood with new roommates. Anyone would be better than her current ones, Tina and her rude boyfriend, Markus.

But it was the second part of the trip that made me nervous. On Friday, Lee and I were flying to Chicago. Amy was getting married and nearly everyone in our pledge class would be there.

Over the years I'd hardly seen college friends; just Sarah, who came through here last year, and Lee, of course. This would be the first time since graduating three years ago that we'd all be together.

Everyone was disappointed that Lee and I hadn't gone back for football games or birthday parties. But traveling was expensive and I was saving to move into my own apartment. Which would happen, finally, in August when Ben, who was living with us for the summer, went back to Philly for his last year of law school.

"Of course, Clare, you can do whatever you want. But everyone I knew lived at home for a while after college," my mother said when I told her that I was the only one of my friends not to have an apartment. It wasn't 1960, I'd said, and times had changed. But in the end, it didn't make sense to move out. Even Sarah, who scoffed when I told her I was still at home, agreed. My parents traveled or were on the Vineyard three quarters of the year. Why rent an apartment when our house, completely furnished and with a new alarm system, sat empty and the utilities paid?

Still, I worried what people would think. Everyone was doing amazing things. Sarah was in medical school. Amy was in the marketing department at Kraft Foods. Lynn worked for an ad agency in Dallas. And who would have thought that Ducky would be running half-marathons and selling commercial real estate in Chicago?

I was almost finished with graduate school and looking into PhD programs. That was what I'd say. Not that I still slept in the bed I'd had since I was twelve, thought D. H. Lawrence was boring, didn't like tutoring, and worried about a giant window in a coffeehouse that sold two-dollar cappuccinos. Oh, God, I felt my nerves churning through my stomach like water boiling on the stove.

I carried the tea, muffin, and juice over to the woman's table. The door opened and a tall brunette walked toward us. The women hugged and then the brunette smiled at me and ordered a cappuccino. She even said please.

See? It was easy to be nice. It didn't take much.

I made the woman's cappuccino and retreated behind the counter. I could tell by how they leaned toward each other, how they smiled and laughed so easily, that they were old friends, maybe college friends, like Lee and me. We were still close, despite living in different states. I called her every day to listen, cheer her up, and offer advice. *Try adding beans to rice, for protein. Tell the asshole Markus to get his own laundry detergent! Maybe the next job will work out!* Last night she said that she needed to tell me about an awful conversation she'd had with her mom regarding her twelve-year-old twin siblings, whom Lee called The Miracles. Maybe this time I'd be helpful. Knowing what to say about her family was often a challenge.

"I wanna go to the zoo!" the girl squealed. I glanced up from my book, her words landing like cement in my stomach. *Take her to the zoo,* for God's sake. Go!

The mother was too busy to respond. The girl frowned as she scooted behind the table. She plucked a blueberry from the muffin, squished it, and took her finger across the window, leaving a foot-long streak. I glared at the woman. Why bring your daughter just to ignore her? Pay attention! Love her! Get her away from my window!

I licked my dry lips.

It would be a jam-packed weekend. By coincidence my parents and Logan were going to be in Chicago, too. Logan, who was bringing Elise, had a meeting, and my mother was speaking at a conference. Lee and I were joining them for dinner when we arrived tomorrow; afterward, we'd meet up with our friends.

Ducky was selling commercial real estate?

You should learn to bake delicious scones.

I glanced at the stove again. I had this sudden urge to pour sugar into a bowl and unwrap sticks of cold, slippery butter and knead the dough— was this how to make scones? I'd ask Elise and when I got back next week, I'd make a batch.

Maybe they'd be better than Donna's. Maybe they'd be good enough to sell. I felt excited, suddenly, and hopeful. Yes, hope was a wonderful feeling.

The bell on the door rang and I grinned. Ben. The law office where he was interning was only a mile away but he rarely left his desk. Not for lunch. Hardly for dinner, either. Leaner than he was in college, he wore an old suit, charcoal gray, with a white shirt and blue tie. By the end of the day his shirt would be untucked and his eyes blurry from reading. When he got back late to the house every night, he was often too tired to do anything but sit on the couch and watch baseball on TV.

"This is a surprise," I said. Ben wasn't going to Chicago with me. He barely knew Amy or Dougy, her fiancé, and hardly anyone was bringing dates. Besides, he wanted to work all weekend. I straightened and smoothed the front of my apron. Then I made sure my earrings were straight and tucked my hair behind my ears. We'd broken up for a few years after college and had recently gotten back together. At first we were a little careful around each other. Sometimes I still felt that way, especially now that he was living with us at the house.

"I've been calling." He sucked in quick breaths. "Is the phone off the hook?"

His cheeks were flushed and sweat dripped

down the sides of his face. I reached up and flicked off a few drops. I asked, "Wait, did you *run* here?"

"Yeah. I couldn't find a cab. And I had to hurry."

I glanced at his black dress shoes and imagined his feet, hot and sweaty, swimming in his socks. I pulled him over to the counter and poured a glass of water.

He drank and then pointed to the scones. "What are those?"

"Scones. Here, taste this." I handed him one of the pieces.

He turned it over in his hand and popped it in his mouth. He chewed and then shrugged. "It's bland."

"I know, right? I've got this idea. I'm going to start making really, really good scones. And maybe sell them here."

"I thought you were going to quit this place and try to get more hours at the writing center," he said as he took the back of his hand across his forehead.

"I know . . ." I shifted my feet. He was right. I'd said that. I glanced at the scones. Butter, flour, baking soda. Yes, scones were made with baking soda. But maybe not.

"I've got to get back. I came to tell you that your mom called. She's been trying to reach you. You left your credit card at the house. You'll need it to travel."

How had that happened? Then I remembered being on the phone the other night with the airline and paying for Lee's ticket to Chicago, and I must not have put the credit card back in my wallet. I shifted my feet again. I didn't want Ben to think that I was irresponsible with money. "Oh, no."

"Your mom didn't have time to run it down here to you, so I told her that I'd get ahold of you. She was pretty relieved."

Of course she didn't have time to run it down here. I was surprised she even knew the phone number. Neither parent had visited me here yet. I wasn't surprised, however, that she called Ben. My parents loved him. He was, as my dad liked to say, "a practical person who got things done." And I was happy, for the most part, that they felt this way about him. "Thank you."

"Are you going to have time to get it before you leave?" he asked.

I'd planned to go straight to the airport after tutoring this afternoon. But I could stop at home, if I hurried. I nodded.

"Oh, and as I was leaving the house this morning, you got a call from Joel."

Joel was the director of the writing center and had hired me a few months ago to work as a tutor. It was a good deal. I received a small stipend and could take graduate classes for free. But Joel's perpetually bloodshot eyes (broken blood vessels, someone told me) and grouchy personality made me so on edge that I avoided him as much as possible. "What did he say?"

"Something about some woman you worked with yesterday. He wanted to talk to you about her. He sounded concerned. Did something happen?"

My last appointment of the day. The woman was older than me, heavy with shoulder-length, curly black hair and a nasty scowl. She walked in, threw herself into the chair, and told me that if she failed her next paper she'd fail the class. She wouldn't get her degree. *You have to help me,* she'd demanded.

"This woman was so angry," I said. "And her paper was a mess."

Ben dipped his eyebrows into a slight frown. "Were you able to help her?"

"Yes." I shifted my feet. Actually, no. She was supposed to compare a novel and film and yet she'd come in with only a weak, scattered analysis of *To Kill a Mockingbird*. Her sentences were long and incomprehensible and at the end, when our time was up, she burst into a tirade of obscenities at the school, her professor, and me. Then she stormed out of my cubicle. "I'll see him this afternoon."

Ben shook his head. "He said he'll only be in this morning."

"I'll call him on Monday."

"Maybe you should call him now?"

"But—"

"Clare, you said yourself that only a few grad students get tapped for these positions. You don't want to mess it up. It'll help with PhD applications. Right?"

I glanced at the window. Yes, PhD applications. I should tell Ben that the only reason I got the tutoring job was because Joel realized I was Eleanor Michaels's daughter. He was so dismissive when I interviewed (*you went to college where?*). When he called later to offer me the job, he was much nicer as he added, "Maybe you could ask your mom to speak to our undergraduates?"

Why had I *ever* decided to get a master's degree in English literature?

I should also tell Ben that I was a terrible tutor and wasn't sure I should go for my PhD. But that was what I'd said *(I'd make a terrible nurse!)* when I'd finished my science courses two years ago and decided against pursuing nursing or counseling. I needed a career where I could work without disappointing anyone.

Ben lifted his hand and touched my cheek. It both surprised me, he wasn't much for affection in public, and made me soften. I felt, suddenly, overwhelmed. Maybe it was the trip ahead. Or the woman and the call from Joel. Or D. H. Lawrence and his thematic penetration. It most definitely had to do with getting that window clean before I left. I bit my lower lip, trying to hold back tears.

"Is something wrong?" he asked. I glanced at the woman, ignoring her daughter, and the blueberry streaks on the window. "You okay going without me?"

I nodded. He leaned over and kissed me, lightly, quickly, on the cheek. I had a sudden urge to grab him in a bear hug and plant a wet, passionate kiss on his lips, one that would cause the women to stop talking and gape at us. He glanced at his watch and turned to go. I reached for his hand and squeezed.

He grinned. "Call me when you get to Lee's. Okay?"

I nodded again and watched him leave. Ben wasn't sentimental or overly romantic. He didn't talk subjects to death or play manipulative games. I was happy we were back together and I loved him even if sometimes I wished for something. But I didn't know what that was, and I certainly didn't think it was very nice to wish or yearn for someone or something when Ben and I were living together this summer. This feeling reminded me of how out of control I felt senior year of college.

I'd tried not to think about that crazy time and what had happened to Lee. When I caught her zoning out, which she still did, or when she called, crying over something innocuous *(the homeless woman on the corner is blind!),* I wondered if she was remembering, somehow, what had happened. But she rarely talked about it nor had she ever told me what happened that night.

Sometimes I had nightmares about it although I never told Lee. They were always the same. I was trying to run from Charlie's house but my legs wouldn't move. I never saw the men but felt them behind me. I'd wake—heart pounding—and go over that night as I stared at the ceiling. I was always angry with myself and imagined behaving differently. I would have stood up to Owen and the other two; I wouldn't have left Lee. I would have been the hero.

"Excuse me!" the mother yelled at me from her chair next to the window.

I gave them the bill. When they left, I took out the Windex and paper towels and cleaned the streaks. Then I looked up and down the street. It was quiet, only a woman walking with her head down. I tried to remember why I'd been excited about baking scones. Maybe I was trying to remember the feeling of being excited.

Excited. Excitement. Exhilaration. Joy. These were words Lee always used to describe her passion back in college. *I just want to make films. That's all I want to do. I can't imagine any greater joy!* She must've said that to me a million times. This often led to a conversation about the origins of passion. Was it something you were born with or could you learn it? Who had it and who didn't?

The sunlight shifted and now I saw a big smudge on the glass that I hadn't seen before. I took my paper towel over it, scrubbing until it was gone.

Lately Lee hadn't talked much about film-making. This was what happened. The college years were for dreams and idealism but the world made demands. Rent, food, clothing. Look at my brother. All those years of studying to be an economist and what did he do? Went to work at a London hedge fund, whatever that was.

Lee had changed although I didn't think it had anything to do with idealism or demands. Ever since that night in Florida, she was different. Less sure of herself. Slow to make decisions. Easily intimidated. Take, for example, the time she house-sat in Scarsdale last year. It was a beautiful house and she planned to spend her time writing a screenplay. But at the end of two months, when the couple who'd hired her returned, they reneged on their offer to pay. They said the house stay was "payment enough." The old Lee would have never put up with this. The new Lee cowered and walked away without a fight.

When I pushed her on this, she said, "But they were so nice to let me stay. And I wasn't very productive. I couldn't even finish the first act."

As if that were some kind of justification for not paying her.

I stepped back from the glass. There, now it was clean. A couple, arms linked, walked into the coffeehouse.

"Someone'll be right with you," I said. In the back room Diana, who was working the next shift, was tying on her apron while Lorenzo filled his briefcase. The back door to the alley was propped open and warm air wafted into the room.

"Clarraaa is leaving us," he said. "But she says we will survive without her."

Diana laughed and rolled her eyes. She liked working here, too. I motioned toward the front room, *we have customers,* and she nodded and hurried by me.

Lorenzo stopped shoving papers into his briefcase and looked at me. "You seem a little tense, my friend. Pretravel anxiety, perhaps?"

"Just a little nervous." Last week I'd told him about Amy's wedding and that I hadn't seen my college friends in a long time but I didn't go into detail.

"Ah, yes, it could be wonderful. Or a disaster! May I give you some advice?"

"Because you are so much older and wiser than I am?" I grinned.

"Yes, yes! Old enough to be your older brother." He tilted his head back and laughed. Then he swept his hair off his forehead, folded his arms, and I knew he was going to be serious. "If I were you, I'd spend my travel time remembering who these people were when you knew them. Because now everyone will try to impress each other with their jobs and lives. Do not be fooled. It is very difficult to change."

"Thanks for the advice." I shook my head. "But that's really cynical."

"It is human nature." He shook his finger at me.

"So, you really don't think people are capable of changing?" I asked.

"That is not what I said." He reached for his sunglasses. "It is easy to change apartments. It is not so easy to change the inside. I should know. I spend hundreds of dollars every month trying to do that. Now I am off to see her to try yet again."

He nodded at his therapist's card on the wall. We smiled at each other and then he was gone. I sat in his chair, still warm, and thought that college seemed, suddenly, so far away. I wasn't like Ducky who dressed in our school colors for her annual Christmas card or Susie who once told me that she rarely missed a home football game. I never ran into people from school—Boston wasn't a popular post-graduation destination— and most people here knew nothing about it.

I put the phone on the cradle—it *had* been off the hook—and twirled the cord between my fingers. Lorenzo was wrong. Like Lee, I'd changed over the last three years, too. I was more patient with my mother and Lee, happy to be back with Ben, and I always tried to be a good person. But were these changes natural or because of what happened in Florida?

I jumped when the phone rang and then picked it up.

"What the hell, Clare? I've been trying to reach you for *days*. Doesn't anyone answer the phone at your house? Why don't you have an answering machine yet?"

Sarah. I sat back in the chair. "Well, nice to talk to you, too, Sarah."

She laughed. "Okay, sorry. It's just that you're impossible to get ahold of. I've been calling this number for the last three hours! Just tell me that you're still coming and bringing Lee. Tell me that you two aren't bagging out."

"Of course we're not bagging out," I said. "Why would we do that?"

"You know why. You never come back. And it's not the same without you guys." She sighed. "Okay, listen, so you know that Ducky got us a block of rooms at the hotel? You, me, Lee, and Lisa are sharing one. You okay with that?"

"Of course. Thank you."

"And you'll both be there tomorrow night?"

"Yes."

She sighed again. "Oh, God, we're going to

have a blast. Everyone's gonna be there! Even Lynn. She's flying in from Dallas."

In my mind I saw Lynn's freckles, Sarah's frizzy red hair, and Ducky's pearls. Sarah was right. These were old friends and we *always* had fun together. No one would care that I was living at home and working in a coffeehouse. Right?

"How's Lee? I heard she has another job, like at CBS or something?"

"ABC." My dad, who knew a programming director, got her the job six months ago. It was a relief because now, at least, she had a real job with health insurance.

"Well, does she like it? I mean, anything's better than that stupid internship, right? Didn't she hate that?"

"Yeah, it didn't work out," I said. And neither had the other jobs. The NYU library. The wedding photographer's assistant.

"But is she, like, *okay?*" Sarah asked. "You know, about everything?"

I felt the hairs stand up on the back of my neck. Sarah always brought up Florida, even in roundabout ways, whenever we talked. "Yeah, she's all right."

"Okay, good," she said. "Listen, Clare? The real reason I called is because . . ."

I heard a familiar hesitation in her voice and sat up. "What?"

"Well, Amy told Lisa, who called me. Not that it'll matter because I know you and Ben are back together, but we thought you should know so you'll be, you know, prepared. Christopher Mansfield will be at the wedding. Apparently he and Dougy were friends through intramural basketball or something. Who knew?"

"Oh." I felt goose bumps race up and down my arms. I'd had no contact, nor had I heard anything about him, since we graduated. He seemed to have disappeared much like I had. "Oh."

"Yup, that's all there is to say about this, *huh?*" She laughed slightly.

In my mind I saw Christopher's big eyes and those huge hands. I put my head on Lorenzo's desk, the wood cool against my forehead. I couldn't decide if I was happy or afraid, excited or worried.

"Clare? Hello?"

"I'm here. Wow. Thanks for telling me. Do you know what he's been doing?"

"Politics or something. He lives in Washington, D.C. Anyway, I have to go. See you *tomorrow night!*"

After we hung up, I pushed out of the chair and went to the open door. In front of me, I saw the dark alley with the garbage barrels and trash bins against the redbrick wall, and yet my mind was flooded with other images. The scrubby yard behind Christopher's house, the tables in our sorority's dining room, and the beautiful, tree-lined walk through campus to classes.

I thought about Christopher's breath on my neck and how he traced my collarbone with his finger. But I had no time to dwell on this now. I had to be at the writing center in a half hour. I reached for my bags and hurried into the alley.

CHAPTER 8

Ben was right. Joel's office was dark as I passed by on my way to my cubicle. Grateful that I didn't have to talk to him today, I pushed my duffle bag and backpack under my table, sat, and looked at my schedule. I was booked for the next two hours with four half-hour appointments. But thank goodness the angry woman who called Joel to complain wasn't one of them. I sighed and looked out the window. Maybe someone wouldn't show and then I'd have time to read or think about what I should write for next week's paper in my D. H. Lawrence class. At the moment, I had no idea.

I reached up and took my fingers along my collarbone. Did Christopher still smoke? Would the chemistry still be there between us?

The tutor in the next cubicle sneezed.

"Bless you," I said.

"Thanks," he mumbled. I thought about asking him how long he'd been here and if he'd had any no-shows. But I didn't know him well. I didn't know most of the tutors. We had biweekly meetings where we gathered to talk about clients, problems, and strategies but for the most part we were on our own, stuck in these cubicles with our heads down while students brought in a myriad of problems that we tried to help them fix. We hadn't had any formal training. Simply being an English major and interviewing had been enough.

"Excuse me, are you Clare Michaels?"

A woman stood in the doorway of my cubicle, a notebook clutched to her chest and a giant, scuffed-up black pocketbook hanging from her shoulder. She was older than me, maybe in her thirties, with short, curly blond hair (she reminded me of a sunflower) and dark eyes so wide, maybe frightened, that I wondered if she'd seen something horrific, a car accident or assault, on the sidewalk outside.

"Yes, I am, come in." I motioned to the other chair. "Are you okay?"

She didn't move from the doorway but stared at me with a look that suddenly morphed into something else. Anger or disappointment. I tried to remember if I'd seen her before, if I'd messed up a paper and she was coming back to complain, but she didn't look familiar. I glanced at her name on my signup sheet, Lucy Weslawski, but didn't recognize that, either.

She slowly walked into the cubicle and sank into the chair, the notebook still pressed to her chest. She wore a blue and white striped sundress, faded from so many washes and with a slight tear along the right shoulder. She had long fingers with perfectly painted red nails that didn't match the shabbiness of her dress. Was she a full-time student? Part time?

She lowered her notebook to her lap and placed her hands on top and now I saw that they were shaking slightly. And her eyes, which had seemed so big, were smaller under hooded eyelids. Maybe she *did* see something awful. Or maybe she was just a nervous person. I felt uncomfortable in a way that was becoming all too familiar in here. What if I couldn't help her with her paper, either?

"So, what can I help you with today?" I glanced at her notebook.

"Your mother is Eleanor Michaels." This wasn't a question. I nodded. I wasn't sure how many people here knew this. I'd only talked about my mother with Joel. "When I saw your name on the tutor list, I thought of an article I'd read in which your mother said she had a daughter named Clare who liked to read. I took a guess that you were her daughter and asked someone and she confirmed it was you."

Who confirmed this? I shifted in my chair. She kept batting her eyes every few seconds in a way that was making me nervous, too.

"My name is Lucy Weslawski. I know your mother. Or at least I used to know her. Years ago when I was an undergrad, I took her Milton class. She was quite a teacher. Everyone was terrified of her. But not me. Because I realized early on that she wasn't interested in nonsense and mediocrity. She respected hard work. I liked that. And I respected her. She was so strong and capable."

Well, yes, some of the time. But what about when I was expected to be the strong and capable one? I cleared my throat. "What did you bring to work on today?"

Lucy pulled her shoulders back and laughed. "I'm quite able to write an argument or analytical paper. I could do what you do with my eyes closed."

Something was wrong. I gripped the sides of my chair and sat up.

"Look." She licked her lips and sighed. "I'm not here to argue with you. You seem like a nice enough person. I'm here because I want you to give this to Eleanor." She reached into her bag, pulled out a white envelope, and pushed it across the desk toward me. *Eleanor Michaels* was written in black cursive letters across the front.

I frowned. This had happened to me many times before. Most things I passed along were simple fan letters. But a few were something else: a high school teacher who wanted my mother to read her five-hundred-page novel. People who asked for signed books or her time or presence at fundraising events. One who threatened to "track you down" if she didn't write back. I always felt responsible for these letters I gave to my mother, especially when she chose not to answer. Which was most of the time.

"My mother is busy and it's hard for her to respond to letters she receives," I said. "I'm happy to give it to her, but know that you probably won't hear from her."

"I'm used to her not responding. I just want her to know that I'm still here. And I'm still wondering. And I'm not going away."

This didn't sound so good. Was she a crazed fan, like some of the others?

Yet her face, with her droopy eyelids and pout across her thin lips, made me feel more curious, and a little worried for her, than afraid. Somehow, she'd been terribly wronged or mistreated. The world had not been kind to her. I glanced at her hands, still trembling in her lap, and said in my softest voice, "I don't understand."

"I know you don't. And you don't need to know. I wouldn't ask you to do this if she'd answered my letters. And if her publisher hadn't referred me to its legal department. All I want is for her to answer questions about what she did."

And all I had to do was thank her, take the letter, and say that I'd deliver it. Then she'd be gone because clearly she wasn't here for help with a paper. But I wanted to know what she was talking about. I needed to take care of this before it went any further, to Joel, to a newspaper, to

God knows where else. "Maybe I can help you with this. What do you think she did?"

Lucy shook her head. "No, no, you're making a distinction that just isn't there. This isn't about what I *thought* she did. This is about what she *did*. Plain and simple."

I was starting to feel impatient and thought about a woman who kept calling our apartment on Dean Street, just after *Listen* was published, demanding to talk to my mother. *She has to change the ending,* the woman screamed at me on the fourth call. *Whit can't die. Whit can't die!* We got an unlisted phone number after this.

"Okay," I said. "What did she do?"

"You really want to know?" she asked. I nodded. "Phoebe and Whit, and their *entire story,* are mine. Your mother stole it from me."

I felt my mouth fall open—to my knowledge no one had ever accused her of this—and quickly closed it. Writers borrowed and stole from each other all the time. But I had a hard time believing that my mother (you had to be tough, resourceful, and smart to be a female *Miltonist,* my dad once said) would stoop to stealing Phoebe and Whit's *entire story* from this woman. "How did she steal it from you?"

I started to shake and stuck my hands under my thighs. I didn't want this woman to think that she'd unnerved me.

She studied me for a moment before speaking.

"Your mother was, well, my savior. For a while. If it weren't for her, because I was having such a terrible time, I probably wouldn't have stayed in school that year. One day I took a short story I'd written into her office hours—I was always going to her office hours—and asked if she'd read it and give me feedback. She agreed."

Wait, my mother was her *savior?* I pulled my hands out from under me. Every part of my body felt at attention.

"The next week, I went to office hours again, and she told me that my story would never be published because a young narrator wouldn't work in an adult story," she continued. "I said, 'but there are plenty of adult stories told from a young person's point of view.' She shook her head and said that it didn't matter. It wouldn't work. I'd never get published. I wasn't *good enough*. I didn't *have* what it *takes*."

My cheeks had grown warm and my heart was beginning to beat faster. This woman was making an outrageous claim. Yet at the same time, I felt a sudden sliver of doubt—could it be possible?—that I didn't like or want. "So, you're saying that my mother stole Phoebe and Whit from a short story you wrote."

Lucy seemed not to hear me. "That day I went back to my dorm, devastated. I'd expected criticism. I hadn't expected humiliation. Two weeks later, I went home for Thanksgiving,

189

put the story away in a box under my bed and forgot about it *and* writing. I even switched out of English. That's how much I believed your mother, that I was no good as a writer. So, imagine my surprise, years later, when I read in the news about your mother's book. And imagine my anger when I actually read it and saw what she'd stolen."

My mother was many things but not a thief of this caliber. I shook my head. "These are serious allegations. Why didn't you contact the publisher's legal department if you were so sure about this?"

"I'd never shown the story to anyone else. And when I went looking for it at my parents' house, I realized that it had been tossed out with the rest of my papers from college. Which was so typical of my family. Let's erase anything Lucy ever did! Let's erase Lucy! *Christ!* Anyway, it was essentially Eleanor's word against mine. You don't believe me, do you? You probably think your mother is above this."

I wasn't sure what I believed but I certainly didn't want her to know this. I thought of another woman who burst out crying in the grocery store when she told my mother that she'd found her father hanging from a rafter in the garage when she came home from school one day. *Please write about this,* she'd cried.

"You can't believe the claims people have

made on her." I glanced at the envelope. I wanted her to leave and folded my arms across my chest again. "So, what do you want?"

She sat forward, her sad eyes opening wide again. "I want to talk to her. I want to know why she stole my story. And I especially want to know why she turned against me, after she said that she'd help. I want to hear these answers from her."

I felt sudden, sharp needles race up and down my back. They were warning signs, telling me that something wasn't right. Something was *off*. I was beginning to feel angry, too, although I didn't know why. "My mom is working and doesn't meet with people very often. If you think I can talk her into meeting you, you're wrong."

"You don't believe me."

She was making me angry. I shook my head. "I'm sorry that you think she stole your story. But I can't imagine her doing that. I'll give her the letter, however, and maybe she'll write you back."

Her nose flared and then her eyes seemed to shrink—she was skeptical—as she stood and hoisted her big bag on her shoulder. Then she was gone.

I sank back in my chair. What the hell? I imagined Logan, if I told him about this, saying, *She's lying! She's after our cash!*

I rubbed my forehead.

My mother had always been mum on the origins of Phoebe and Whit. I assumed she took a little from my life, a little from her own life and a whole lot of imagination to come up with the story. I held the sealed envelope up to the light but couldn't see through it. I imagined telling my parents about this and both of them shaking their heads and saying, *not again. That poor woman!* I slipped the envelope into my backpack. I wasn't going to worry about this. In two hours I'd be at the house, picking up my credit card, and I'd hand the letter to my mother and ask about Lucy's accusations. And then I'd know who was lying and who was telling the truth.

CHAPTER 9

I hopped off the T, walked across the street, through the Feldmans' backyard, and then up the steps to the back door of our house. When I was a freshman in high school, my parents moved from our apartment on Dean Street to this much larger house off Washington Square. A Georgian colonial with floor-to-ceiling windows and a large winding staircase to the second story, the house was charming, old, and creaky. Too hot in the summer and too cold in the winter, it was "an uncomfortable nightmare," according to Logan. I didn't know if he believed this or just no longer felt welcomed. When we moved, our parents got rid of his bed and bureau and when he came home, which he did less and less, he had to sleep in the guest room. Which now Ben had taken over for the summer.

I let myself in with my key. I glanced at Ben's running shoes that he'd placed next to the door on a perfectly folded sports section of the Boston Globe and then up at the kitchen counter. I wouldn't find his empty oatmeal bowl in the sink with the other dirty breakfast dishes. Ben, so neat and organized, always put his bowl in the dishwasher.

"Are you sure?" Ben asked when I told him

that my parents were fine about him living with us for the summer while he interned at the law firm. Originally, he planned to be with us only a few weeks. But then his sublet fell through and rent was so expensive, so I said, why not stay here? "Your parents are a lot more liberal about this kind of thing than mine."

My parents were liberal Democrats, to be sure, but I didn't think liberalism was behind their decision to condone our living arrangement. Actually, I didn't know what was behind it. All I knew was that on the days they were here, which weren't often, they didn't ask questions or even seem to notice that Ben woke every morning in my bed (and *not* in the guest room bed).

"Hello?" I dropped my backpack and duffel bag on the kitchen table. The house was quiet and stuffy, the smell of onions and tomatoes from the sauce I'd made last night still hung in the air. I listened for my dad's familiar voice and the carriage return on my mother's typewriter. Nothing. I glanced at my watch—my train was leaving soon and I had to hurry. I pulled Lucy's letter out of my backpack. The wood floor creaked under me as I peeked into my mother's empty writing room and then walked to the living room.

The heavy burgundy curtains were pulled across the floor-to-ceiling windows and it was so dark—my God, it was a bright, sunny day outside—that I barely saw my mother on the couch.

"Clare?"

This wasn't the voice she normally used. I felt the back of my throat tingle and my cheeks sting. I squinted, my eyes slowly adjusting to the dark, and saw her sprawled on the couch against the window, papers spread around her.

"Clare!"

Anguish. That was what I heard in her thin, shaky voice. Not whining or complaining; not asking—not demanding—anything. For a moment I felt dizzy and disoriented and then suddenly I was eleven, when I'd first heard and seen her this way, and we were back in the hotel bathroom and she was on the checkered tiles in her Halston dress and black patent leather shoes, her head in the toilet. But that was then and this was now and yet I couldn't remember why I was here. All I thought about was that I was scared and *had* to do something to help her.

Outside, a siren shrieked and came so close that I squeezed my hands into fists and waited for it to crash through the window. Soon it faded. I reached for the light and turned it on. My mother moaned and covered her eyes with her arm. I saw my credit card on the antique wood coffee table in front of her and remembered that yes, that was why I was here. All I had to do was walk over, pick it up, and leave.

Finally, I looked at her. Black smudges from where her mascara had run formed half-moons under her eyes. She wore no lipstick, no cover up, and red blotches peppered her cheeks and neck. Outside, behind the curtains and the closed windows, I heard the faint sound of birds chirping. Where was Dad?

"It's not worth it." She buried her face in her hands. "I've got to end this."

End writing? Or her life? I'd always feared, even though I'd never articulated it until now, that she'd kill herself just as Whit had killed himself. Just as her grandfather had killed himself. I didn't care how much she or Welleck and Warren insisted that a novel leads an independent life. Writers wrote about what they knew.

She didn't say these things to her fans or her students or news reporters. I was sure she didn't do this to Logan, either; she never let him see this *chaos*. Yes, that was the perfect word. I wasn't even sure Dad saw it in the same way I did.

My breath seemed to catch in my throat and my body seized. I tried to move but couldn't. I felt myself reaching back for something, anything, to steady myself. I saw glimpses of afternoons at Lucy Vincent Beach, walks through our neighborhood and dinners in the kitchen. Her hair was longer and fuller and her body plumper, more sensual. But I couldn't see her face. Surely she was happier and less anxious back then.

Because these problems, this crushing insecurity and fear, began with the success of *Listen*. Right?

When my mother shifted and knocked a stack of papers off the couch, the top sheet fluttered toward me before resting on the rug. I was too far away to read it but recognized the letterhead. My mother's publisher. Something had happened. Something had set her off.

"What's wrong?" I asked.

"Janice hated it," she said. "She said that it didn't feel like 1920 Europe. That she didn't believe the voice. That the war scenes were *unrealized*."

My mother's new novel. Why did she always write about war? But no way would I engage her in a conversation about what she should or shouldn't write. Too many times I'd seen her defensive over this question. I shifted my feet and then something came over me and I slowly felt revived. Or maybe I just knew what to do. I put Lucy's letter in my back pocket, walked behind the couch, and pulled the curtains. I unlatched the lock and lifted a window. Warm air and noises—birds, cars, dogs barking, the T from down the street—blew into the room. I breathed in the freshly cut grass and put my hand on the glass and felt the coolness travel up my fingers and into my wrist and forearm.

"Ah, it's too bright," she moaned.

But we were on the other side. I felt it. I turned

from the window, put my credit card in my front pocket, squatted, and began picking up her manuscript; pages and pages, red lines drawn through entire paragraphs, thick red words in the margins. *Not clear here. Where did this come from? Need to show this.*

"I'm never going to get another book published," she said.

"Don't say that. You're a great writer."

"Nothing will ever be as good as *Listen, Before You Go.*"

"That's ridiculous." I dropped the stack on the coffee table. "Where's Dad?"

"I don't know!"

"Have you eaten today?" I asked. She shook her head. "I'll make you something and then I have to go."

"No, don't *leave* me!"

I frowned. "I'll just be in the kitchen. I'm not leaving yet."

In the kitchen I filled the kettle and put it on the stove. I loaded a plate with sausage pieces, cheese, crackers, and a few digestive biscuits I found in the pantry. And then I waited for the water to boil.

Was she safe to leave? I'd gotten fairly used to these fits of insecurity—they were happening more and more—but it had been a while since she'd scared me. I thought about three years ago when she cried for a week when the reviews of her second book, one after the other, had been so harsh. And last year when she couldn't get out of bed after the Broadway people backed out of the *Listen* theater deal. But not since the awards ceremony in New York had she said, *I've got to end this*.

I heard the lock in the back door turn and my dad walked in, his sturdy arms filled with grocery bags. His cheeks were rosy, but his hair, streaked with gray, swept every which way across his forehead and over the top of his collar. I should remind him that he needed a haircut. "Clare! What are you doing here?"

I took the bags and set them on the counter. "I forgot my credit card and Mom called Ben, who came to the coffeehouse to tell me."

"So nice!" Dad beamed, the wrinkles in the corners of his eyes multiplying, and pulled a tea box from the grocery bag. "This'll go with those dynamite sugar cookies you made. Which Ben and I fight over. Where'd you hide them?"

"Dad?"

He nodded toward my mother's office. "She's not working?"

"She's in the living room. She heard from Janice and it's not good."

He frowned, dropped the tea on the counter, and walked past me. I poured the boiling water, dunked a tea bag, and set the cup on the tray with the food. Then I carried everything into the living room. My mother was at one end of the couch, curled into a fetal position, her bangs pulled off her forehead and exposing her gray roots. My dad was at the other end, elbows on his knees and the fingers of his right hand lost in his hair as he read Janice's letter. When he looked up at me, face pleading, I felt a rush of anger. How could he let this go to her editor before it was ready? Why did he allow her moods to run our lives?

It was true. How many times had I walked in the door, nervous about how she'd be? Nervous about how *I* should be because of her and what I'd have to do to make her feel better? Her moods and state of mind had gotten worse with each book. *I'm not good enough. What am I going to do? Help me, Clare!* Why put us through this? Why didn't Dad stop it? Well, I wouldn't put up with it anymore.

I dropped the tray on the table, the biscuits bouncing off the plate and the tea sloshing over the rim of the cup. Then I turned for the foyer and stomped up the stairs to my room. Sheets and blankets, piled on my bed, were just where I'd left them this morning. Clothes, towels, shoes, books, an empty Doritos bag, and a bowl of curdled milk and bloated Lucky Charms (the oats, not the stars and moons, because who would ever leave the candy?) covered the floor. Everything I planned to take on my trip was packed and waiting downstairs. Yet I crossed the room and opened my closet. Hanging in the back, behind my ski parka, was the dress I'd bought last month with Elise. I pulled it out.

The dress was cherry red with spaghetti straps and a plunging neckline that rested low on my chest. It was made of soft, stretchy material that fit so snug against my hips and stomach it almost hurt to breathe when I wore it. Sexy and revealing, so unlike anything I'd ever owned, the dress had been a joke—a challenge by Elise—to simply try on. That I'd bought it was even harder to believe.

I walked out into the hallway and stopped at the top of the stairs.

"I have no idea what to do," my mother said from below.

"That's not true." My dad's voice was slow and steady. "We'll go through these comments, point by point. You said yourself that the plot was problematic."

"But this isn't fair!"

"Fair, Eleanor? What does fairness have to do with it? Your editor had problems with what you wrote and gave you specific revision recommendations. I suggest you think hard about them and get back to work."

My mother sighed loudly but I heard the resignation and maybe a bit of relief. Dad was taking control. And he said the magic words. *Get back to work.*

I walked to my room and pulled the letter out of my pocket. My mother was much too upset to deal with this. That didn't mean I believed Lucy's accusations. Because a few things had occurred to me while on the T coming over here. Why would my mother steal from an undergrad with no writing experience? Wasn't it a little too convenient that Lucy's short story was lost and no one else had read it? And if she wanted to be a writer, why let one negative critique ruin her dream?

I slipped the letter into my desk drawer. I'd give it to my mother when we returned from Chicago. Then I stood in front of the mirror and held the dress against me. I looked good in it. It put me, as Elise said, *out of your comfort zone* and there was nothing wrong with that. Why not take it to Chicago? I wouldn't wear the dress just because of Christopher.

Would I?

My relationship with him had been so flimsy that we hadn't even said goodbye. He'd probably had dozens of girls since then and maybe he was even engaged or married. It would be nice to talk to him. That was all.

Because Ben and I were solid now. At least I thought we were. Well, maybe we weren't quite solid yet but things between us were certainly better than when he started law school and I went down there that first October. Staying with him for three days in his tiny apartment, I'd been overwhelmed by his dedication and goodness. The rice and vegetable dinner he'd tried to make but burned that first night. The groceries he'd carried up four flights for his elderly neighbor. His focus, day and night, on his studies. I sat there watching him, trying to study, too, and feeling smaller and smaller—so small, in fact, that I was terrified that I'd disappear altogether— until finally I picked a stupid fight that sent me home a day early. We broke up over the phone, angry and yelling at each other, the following week.

Over the next two years, I went out with a few guys including John from my biology class who I slept with a number of times. But that didn't work out and I began to miss Ben and his predictability, his confidence, the way he was so certain about how he felt about me. We began sending postcards and letters, followed by lengthy phone calls, and so by the time we saw each other last Christmas, we were ready to get back together.

I turned from one side to the next. The dress fabric fell across my jeans and my blouse, clinging to my body. No, I'd bring this dress not for Christopher, but for me. As a confidence booster. I flung it over my arm, took the back stairs to the kitchen, and put it into my bag. I hurried to the living room, where my parents were exactly as I'd left them. I felt angry again, that they hadn't budged, hadn't even crossed a leg.

"I'm leaving." My voice was sharp and certain.

"Oh!" Dad said. "How are you getting to the station?"

"The T." If he offered to take me, I'd refuse. He needed to stay here.

I turned to the fireplace mantel, where a first edition of *Listen* rested against the wood. Everything in this house was always about my mother and her writing and legacy and that goddam book. I *hated* it for what it had done to her.

"I'll see you tomorrow," I said, although I wanted to add that Lee and I might not show up for dinner. But I wanted to see Elise, who was coming with Logan, and when I looked at my mother I felt a slight sting in my chest. She looked so small curled up like that, her bony hand gripping my dad's thigh, the folds of skin on her neck hanging like an unfurled flag. Why wasn't I more sympathetic and patient? Why was I so angry? Why was I so *bad?*

My dad followed me into the foyer. After I put on my backpack and slung my bag over my shoulder, he cupped my face in his hands and kissed my forehead, just as he used to do when I left for school each morning. "Travel safely, my dear."

I pulled away. I wasn't a child and wanted to stay angry. But as I glanced back at the living room again, I wondered how I could leave her. What was I doing? I whispered, "She was a mess when I got here. She was saying crazy things."

When he raised his bushy eyebrows, his entire face seemed to rise with them. How many times in my life had I seen him angry with her, twice? Three times? He took care of her. He covered for her and made excuses, too.

I should let it go. But how awful if one day she hurt herself and he could have stopped her if only I'd said something. Maybe this was it, the moment I'd tell him about *ending it* and explain what happened at the North American Book Award ceremony. I didn't know why I hadn't told him about it. I hadn't told anyone.

"Yes, crazy things," I said. "That it wasn't worth it and she might end it and—"

"Your mom's upset." He shook his head. "She'll get back to writing and everything will be fine."

"She scared me," I said.

"Don't let it bother you. We'll get a revision plan in order. And tomorrow we'll meet and have a whale of a dinner. With good wine, too. You've turned into quite a fretter, Clare. You don't have to worry so much."

I worried too much or he avoided real conversations about her?

"You're a good daughter. I know she counts on you."

I grimaced. Yes, she counted on me. I made food and tea and told her she was a great writer. But if it came down to something life threatening, if I had to save her, could she count on me? This all felt so confusing. "But how am I—"

"Have fun!" he said as he reached for the door. "Go on, I'll stay with her."

Let her go, I'll stay.

I stumbled down the steps outside and felt that familiar yet awful sense of paralysis. It was as if I were suspended over the sidewalk—tethered to the trees and held in place—not growing or changing, not moving forward or backward. Cars and people rushed by. The T trolley at the end of the street rumbled over the tracks. Put one foot in front of the other and breathe. In and out, in and out. Yes, now I was moving away from the house. But it wasn't until I got onto the T that I began to relax. My dad would make dinner and reread Janice's comments. Those were the kinds of practical things he always did for her. I could count on this.

"Saint Anders," my dad's sister, Aunt Denise, called him. Growing up, he looked after his siblings while their dad went wandering and their mom succumbed to MS at a ridiculously young age. Dad took us to visit her while she was still alive. Logan barely said hello before bolting for the nursing home lounge. But not me. I stayed at my dad's side. Despite being terrified of her shriveled body that someone had stuffed into a wheelchair for our visits, I was in awe of him. He was patient and kind as he talked to her, held her hand and wiped drool from her chin.

By God, I wanted to be that good, too.

I thought of Lorenzo and his advice: Use this travel time to think of the past. Remember who people were. But I just wanted to try to remember who I was.

CHAPTER 10

After the train cut through Providence, it hugged the coast of Connecticut before approaching New York. I liked the views of Long Island Sound and the marshy shoreline, birds and herons. It was beautiful and peaceful, although I often thought of it as the calm before the storm. Because later, as the train made that sharp turn and the marshes had changed to apartment buildings and industry and the New York skyline stretched miles across the horizon, my heartbeat quickened and I pulled my bags closer. The city was dangerous. You had to be ready.

I didn't always feel this way. When I was younger my parents often brought Logan and me down here to Christmas shop or see a show. It was fun. I sometimes felt this way with Lee, too. Over the years we'd done so much together; explored new neighborhoods and browsed through thrift shops and bookstores. One night last summer, drinking beer on the Circle Line, we laughed so hard at the man on the loudspeaker with his New York accent that the entire upper deck stared at us.

I smiled, thinking about Lee's crooked grin and how her shoulders shook as she laughed. It was in these moments (how about that time at the diner in Chelsea? Or the comedy club in the West Village? Or drinking beer that cold Saturday with the cute guys we'd met at the Red Sox game?) when I knew we were free and neither of us thinking about what happened in Florida. Sometimes this ease, this *not remembering,* lasted an entire weekend. And then I'd let myself imagine that we were on our way. Everything would be better from then on.

But it never lasted for long. Despite these reprieves, what happened was always lurking, even if we didn't talk about it. For Lee, remembering didn't seem to be triggered by anything predictable or specific. But I knew when she stared into space, or cried at random, inexplicable moments or her mood darkened that she was remembering. Then I'd remember, too.

I didn't want to keep remembering.

The train slowed as it approached the tunnel that would take us under the city and into Penn Station. The man next to me snickered and turned the page of his magazine. I closed *Sons and Lovers* and looked out the window. The sun had gone down but it wasn't dark enough for streetlights. Instead the sky was a strange mix of light and dark, day and night. As if it couldn't make up its mind which way to go.

Years ago when my mother and I had traveled here for the North American Book Award ceremony, she'd turned to me as we entered this tunnel and said, "Hold on tightly to your bag. You don't want to lose your shoes."

That was the last thing I wanted to do. The week before we'd gone shopping on Newbery Street—usually it was too expensive—and bought black patent leather shoes for each of us. Mine were shiny and stiff, no heel, and a half size too small although I didn't admit this because the store didn't have a larger size. My mother also bought an expensive black dress, no sleeves and low across the front, made by someone named Halston. Altogether, we spent a fortune.

My dad was angry when we got home—it was one of the few times I heard my parents argue—but my mother insisted, "I have to play the part." I was never sure what this meant. Successful author? Glamorous author?

I couldn't wait for the trip. My mother never took Logan or me with her to author events, but this was special, she'd said. She promised a visit to the Central Park Zoo (this was during my animal phase) and a carriage ride.

But back to those amazing shoes. After school I walked around my room, trying to break them in. They were too tight to wear socks and so my bare toes and heel rubbed against the leather until I'd formed blisters. I didn't care. With my peach-colored dress, the one we'd bought for Logan's eighth-grade graduation the year before,

I liked how I looked. I'd play a part, too. Famous Author's Daughter.

The lights in the train car flickered and suddenly we were in the dark as the train lurched into the tunnel. I squeezed my bags against my thigh.

How was my mother now? I imagined she and my dad would spend the rest of today devising a revision plan, preparing for her book talk, looking forward, not backward. I should do that, too. I didn't want to worry about her. But she'd scared me, and now I couldn't help but think about what had happened years ago.

Standing in the toilet stall doorway and seeing my mother on the marble floor in her expensive Halston dress and new shoes, her head in the toilet, I knew she didn't have the flu or food poisoning. I knew when she moaned, "it's not worth it, this agony," that she was talking about something graver. Was it intuition, a Phoebe-like knowledge of the world that led me to believe this?

It certainly wasn't Phoebe-like to pee myself. I just stood there, terrified, as warm urine streamed down my legs, stung the blisters on my heels, and pooled in the arches of my new shoes. After I got my mother cleaned up, I poured out the pee, wiped my shoes and feet with toilet paper, and wadded my underwear into a fancy cloth hand towel. Back at the table, I kicked the towel under our table and prayed that people wouldn't see that I was naked under my dress.

But it was excruciating, my dress tickling my bottom and my legs stinging from dried pee. As I watched my mother walk to the podium, I made a desperate plea: Please, Dad, magically appear! Help me! But I kept my face and body still. I showed no emotion. This ability to appear one way when I felt another taught me a valuable skill that day: how to hide my true feelings, especially from my mother.

And by the way, she gave her speech *(Phoebe's innocence was a metaphor for our nation's)* just fine.

Once home, I put my shoes, which had begun to smell, in a bag and buried it in the back of my closet. Weeks later I came home from school one day to find all the closets in our house neat and rearranged. My mother had gone on a cleaning frenzy, something she did when she had writer's block. The shoes were gone.

I was so afraid that I wouldn't allow myself to be angry with her for going through my closet. After a while, when nothing had been said, I wondered if she'd thrown the shoes away by accident. Later, I realized that the shoes were just part of the entire experience about which we were never to speak.

My mother's denial began immediately. After her speech that day, and after the congratulations, book signing, wine, and whispering about how great she was, how brave Phoebe was, how important her book was, we rode the elevator to our room in silence. Once inside, she called Dad, who'd stayed behind with Logan, who was in the hospital. As I watched her, phone to her ear, black dress spotless, ink stains on the callus on her right middle finger, I relaxed. Surely she'd tell Dad about those crazy things she'd said and how she couldn't get off the bathroom floor. And then she'd tell him how I'd helped her.

I listened. I heard every word. But after she told him about the shrimp cocktail, the seventy-seven books signed, and how Mailer had been so welcoming, she hung up. Then she turned to me with a warning look that I might have missed had I not been paying attention.

I could have told this story to my dad. But he'd been so angry when we bought the shoes that I didn't want to admit what had happened to them. And I must have known, as I saw today, that he didn't want to hear negative things about my mother. That he wanted to always look forward, too.

Let her go, I'll stay.

I stretched my palm on the cool window and tried to see the tunnel walls but it was too dark. I closed my eyes and saw Ducky with her pearls and Sarah's sunburned nose and Lee standing in the bathroom, her bloody lip, her cheek with the strawberry-sized rug burn, her vacant eyes. I felt something grind in my stomach and just knew that Sarah would bring this up over the weekend and maybe Ducky, too, and what in the hell would I say? What would they expect from me?

Ben and I sometimes talked about this. What happened to Lee was a tragedy, he always said; most people in my situation wouldn't have been able to handle it differently. "People like to think they'll be heroes. But in truth, they'll save themselves. The will to live is a basic biological instinct."

Oh, I loved him. He was so smart and practical and good and it was okay that I'd left out a piece of the story, wasn't it? That I'd still not told him what Lee did? Because when he talked about this logically and insisted that only one person at a time could have possibly gotten through the window and that I was lucky to be the first one, it made sense. Even had Lee tried to follow, Owen would've grabbed her after I escaped. It was in these small, rare moments that I felt a glimmer of peace.

The train slowed and then the lights were on outside and I saw the platform. When the train stopped and the doors opened, people rushed, trying to beat the crowd. I gathered my things and was one of the last off the train. I lingered, pausing to read the signs above the tracks and the headlines from a newspaper thrown on the ground. My feet felt heavy as I slowly climbed the empty stairs to the lobby.

I saw Lee before she saw me. She stood in front of the Hudson News Stand where we always met. Dressed in jeans, brown clogs, and a simple white button-down, she'd barely changed her wardrobe since college. Her skin was pale—she said she was never in the sun—and her long black hair had fallen across one side of her face. She seemed to be watching an older woman who stood near her. When we were younger, Lee might have spent the next hour talking about her. What was she doing? Who was she meeting? *Let's follow her!*

I stopped so suddenly that a man from behind ran into me. I apologized but didn't move. An oppressive feeling settled in my chest and I fought an urge to run the other way. But then Lee looked up, waved, and smiled. She hurried across the walkway and we hugged. She felt thinner, almost frail, and I cried, "Don't tell me that you're not eating again because you don't have enough money!"

She pulled away and shrugged. "It's so expensive living here, you know that, and then the deposit on the new apartment was more than I thought and—"

"We're getting dinner. I'll pay. And we're *not* going to some dive again." We'd eat something substantial, like steak or roasted chicken. Mashed potatoes and creamed corn, too. Comfort food. I felt very certain with the task ahead.

She shook her head. "You're paying for my flight. And tomorrow night we're meeting your parents for dinner. I won't let you pay for everything."

"I'm not. Tomorrow night my parents are buying dinner. And I'm loaning you money for the flight. Right? You can pay me back when you have the money."

"Did you tell Ben about this?"

"No!" I laughed, to show her that I was independent. I didn't need his opinion or approval. She didn't need to know how much I worried about disappointing him.

"Okay. Thanks." She gripped the strap of her backpack—the same backpack she'd had in college—with both hands and began chewing on the inside of her cheek. Then she sighed, her voice soft and slow. "We're going back to see everyone."

I nodded. But when I saw her eyes flicker and felt her mood darken, I grabbed her arm. No way. This wasn't going to be one of *those* visits. We weren't going to sit in some gloomy basement bar, the air thick with her sadness and confusion as we mulled over something that had happened at work or with her roommates. Or worse, I didn't want to sit there while she zoned out, struggling to answer my questions or simply not speaking at all. No, we were going to have a *fun* couple of days. We'd laugh and keep it light. "Come on, I'm completely starving."

We took the subway south to Christopher Street and then walked on West Fourth Street, past NYU and up to Astor Place. It was late June but the night air was cool and damp. People were standing on street corners, gathering in restaurants, hurrying by us. It was a different crowd and neighborhood from what I knew in Boston; less provincial, less student-oriented. More sophisticated, worldly, darker somehow. I walked with my backpack across both shoulders and my bag tight at my stomach.

We stopped at a burrito place, small and not what I had in mind, but at least it wasn't too dark and Lee insisted it was good and served big portions. We sat at a table next to the window and ordered beers. Through the glass I watched a woman, her hair dyed an outrageous pink, walk by. The crowd at the surrounding tables was young, in jeans and T-shirts, like us.

The entire way here, Lee had been talking about her job. Her boss told her that her job was to make *his* job easier. If that meant getting coffee for him or making squash court reservations, so be it. The list of menial jobs went on and on. She was nothing more than a secretary. But unlike other times when I'd heard her complain about jobs, she wasn't in tears. She mostly seemed annoyed.

"Did you tell him that making his squash court reservation isn't in your job description?" I asked. When our waitress set our beers on the table, I smiled at her and said *thank you* but she simply shrugged and hurried off.

"Well, no, he's my boss."

I took a sip of beer. Ben had to put up with a lot at work, too; it was what you did to get ahead, he said. But something about this felt different. I didn't understand why she kept working for bosses who took advantage of her. It was like this at her last job, too. And the film director for whom she interned was the worst.

"What do you think I should do?" Lee pulled off the label on her beer bottle, folded it several times and then wedged it into a crack in the wood table.

My God, it was a stable job with a guaranteed salary, vacation time, and health benefits. So many people would love to have this opportunity. "You want to get into the business of videos and TV. This is a good stepping stone. Right?"

She tried to pull out the label but it was stuck in the crack. "But I haven't touched a camera, and I don't get to see a studio unless I sneak into one. Do you think I should, you know, ask to do more?"

"Maybe you have to be patient and work your way up."

"Maybe it's not a good fit for me?" She sunk her head into her hand.

Maybe *she* wasn't a good fit for them. Maybe she should think about getting rid of the clogs and start wearing makeup and doing something with her hair instead of letting it hang in her face. I imagined that she fit right in down here—another woman with colored hair just walked by the window—but a place like ABC had standards. Maybe they didn't appreciate her sulking around, either.

I put my hand on my chest, surprised at how angry I felt. But God, could she sulk. It took months to get her out of the funk she was in after the internship ended. Every night on the phone she cried while I listened and tried to talk her down. *You didn't know he was a drunk. A boss should never call you a bitch. This isn't your fault. You aren't a failure!*

She took everything so personally. Like the time she was let go from the library. It wasn't her fault that the school eliminated her position. I sighed and glanced out the window. What was wrong with me? Why wasn't I more patient? I lowered my voice, trying to make it sound gentle. "Look, this isn't easy. You're in a really competitive field. You're lucky to have gotten in the door at a place like ABC."

"And I'm grateful. I know I'm complaining a lot, but I'm working really hard. I know your dad had to pull some strings to get this for me."

"It's okay. He made a couple of calls. I just

think that you have to learn to play the game," I said. Ben always talked about this. Jockeying for positions. Placating your boss. It was like a chess game.

Lee scrunched her forehead, as if she had no idea what I was talking about, and fiddled with the label again. Then she drained her beer and sat back in her seat. "Ah, forget it. How are you? And the writing center?"

I could tell her about Lucy's accusations or Joel's phone call but I didn't want to get into all of that. "Oh, Lee, I wish you liked your job."

She sighed. "I don't know what's wrong with me. I *know* I'm lucky to be here. It's just that I hoped, you know, to be doing something else."

"Filmmaking?"

She nodded, slow and methodical and not at all convincing.

The beer had gone to my head or maybe I was just hungry—I hadn't eaten since before work this morning—and so I wasn't as careful as I usually was. I said, "Maybe you don't want to make films anymore?"

Her lips parted as she turned her head toward the window. And then she barely seemed to move or breathe. She was stunned and I didn't know if this was because I'd said out loud what she'd been feeling or because she hadn't quite let herself know this yet. Or maybe I was wrong? But I began to worry because she still wasn't moving and I hadn't meant to upset her—this wasn't at all how I wanted the evening to go— and so I leaned forward. "Hey, sorry. I shouldn't have said that."

She shook her head and mumbled, "It's okay."

"Have you thought any more about graduate school?" I asked.

"I don't see how I can pull that off. Financially."

Outside the window two men were arguing although we couldn't hear through the glass what they were saying. Then the shorter one punched the bigger one, who fell back against the window with a thud that shook the restaurant. People turned to look and I gasped and gripped the edges of the table. The men continued shoving and arguing as they walked down the street.

"Oh, my God, what was that about?" I asked.

The waitress, who'd walked over to see what had happened, leaned into the window and watched the men disappear down the street. Her dirty blond hair was pulled behind her in a sloppy bun and she had four earrings that ran up the sides of both ears. She hissed, "Assholes."

After she walked away, I turned to Lee, who was staring at her beer bottle. She hadn't even flinched. Did she *see* what happened? Random acts of violence occurred every day in this city and you had to be prepared. You couldn't just *zone out* like she always did. Where was she? Maybe she was still thinking about what I'd said.

I'd upset her, damn it, and now it was my job to make her feel better.

"Listen, I've seen what my mother has gone through." I didn't want to think about how I left her today in the living room. "It's hard to be an artist. It's hard to choose that life."

Lee startled. "You think it's a choice?"

And suddenly there they were, the most magnificent burritos I'd ever seen. Huge and warm, bulging with grilled vegetables, black beans, chunks of chicken, and gooey, melted cheese. As we ordered more beer and dove into our food, I felt the mood lift. We ate and drank as if it had been weeks, months, since our last meal.

When we finally finished, Lee pushed her empty plate away and rested her elbows on the table. The color was back in her cheeks from the food and the beer. No wonder. She was on her third bottle.

"I'm glad we're meeting your parents tomorrow night," she said. "You're so lucky that they like to do fun stuff. I wish my parents were like that."

Over the years she'd said this kind of thing to me a lot. I asked, "So, you said on the phone that something happened with your mom?"

"Yeah, I called on Sunday and told her that I was thinking about coming home for The Miracles' thirteenth birthdays. And she said, 'just give us the money you'd spend on an airplane ticket. If you can afford to fly around the country any time you feel like celebrating someone's birthday, then you must be doing a whole lot better than you've been telling us.' And then she laughed."

I took a sip of my beer, now warm. "She didn't mean that. Right?"

Lee shrugged. "She thinks everyone in New York is rich. I should have never told her about the house-sitting I did. She didn't get why someone would hire me to stay in a house as nice as that. She thought it was where I lived, permanently. If I thought she'd use the money to pay bills or buy The Miracles some presents, I'd find a way to get it to her. But she'd probably just spend it on herself."

I reached for Lee's label, still stuck in the crack in the table, but I couldn't remove it, either. I didn't know what to say about her family. "Oh, Lee."

"I know. It's kind of pathetic. I wasn't even going to fly back home. I was going to take a bus. Anyway, it's just confirmation that I've done the right thing, you know? Coming out here? Trying to make it work? What do you think? I mean, what would you do if your mom said something like that to you?"

Our mothers are nothing alike, I nearly blurted. I looked down at the label again and thought about my visit to Lee's farm junior year. When meeting me, her aunt Gail compared my mother to Lee's mom, and I'd been offended.

"I know, I'd be bummed out, too." I reached for the label again, this time pulling as hard as I could, but no use. It was stuck.

"I shouldn't be surprised or anything." She sighed and stood. "I'm going to the bathroom. Order me another beer, okay?"

I finished my beer and ordered two more. And then I turned to the window.

It was March of junior year when we visited her farm, but still very much winter. Dirty, porous mounds of snow lined the two-lane highway and on both sides flat, empty fields stretched for as far as I could see. We passed one tiny, depressing town after another, many with boarded-up storefronts, pawnshops, and giant grain silos that stood next to farm feed stores and taverns.

Finally, we turned down a long driveway and at the end I saw a one-story house with dirty yellow siding, standing alone in a field and attached to a small barn. Cars, some without wheels and doors, were scattered across the dirt yard. A rope swing hung from a lone tree off to the right. A scrawny dog, tied to a stake, was barking at us as it ran back and forth, nearly hanging itself with each lunge.

"Now why'd they do that to Barney?" Lee stopped the car and hurried over to the dog. She tried to hold him but he was still frantic as he tried to escape.

The skies had darkened and I watched small, grainy snowflakes bounce off the windshield. This was no longer a working farm, Lee had told me, and they had little money. But I hadn't known, exactly, what that meant. My God, the house was tiny—like a trailer, really—and the yard so bare. No bushes, no flowerbeds. I couldn't move, not even when the door to the house opened and two kids—Pammy and Billy, The Miracles—ran across the dirt and knocked Lee over.

Lee told me about the help she'd gotten over the years—encouragement from teachers, financial help from her benefactor, emotional support from her aunt. But as I watched her wrestle with The Miracles, I thought how truly difficult it must have been for Lee to get out of here. How was she able to hold on to such big dreams?

Inside, the house was smaller than it seemed. The dark paneled living room had a low ceiling, only two windows, a giant sectional couch, and a TV. When The Miracles jumped on the couch, it slid and banged against the wall, shaking the house. Lee let Barney go and he scampered into the next room, his nails clicking on the linoleum.

"Why's it such a mess?" Lee began picking up clothes and straightening piles of blankets. I didn't see books, magazines, or newspapers. "It's not usually like this."

"Who let the dog in?" A woman stood in the

doorway. She didn't introduce herself nor did she look at me. She was dressed in a deep purple, velour warm-up suit, her bleached hair piled in a bun on top of her head. Her lips were painted red and sparkled in the dim light.

"I did. He was miserable tied up like that." Lee, her cheeks red and eyes wild, hurried around the room. I'd never seen her like this.

"Hello, nice to see you, too, *Lee Ann,*" she said. Lee told me that her family still called her by her formal name, even though she didn't like it, but it was startling to hear it. "I can't control that dog. He won't listen."

"But why tie him up?" Lee piled glasses and plates into the pizza box.

"I can't have him running away!"

"It'd be better than having him freeze to death! Why's it a mess in here?"

"You think I got time to do anything with these two around?" She nodded at The Miracles and put her hands on her hips. "I'm sorry we don't live in a mansion or a new fancy condominium. But at least we pay our bills!"

I didn't know what to make of this. Nor did I know what to do, so I turned to the TV. As I watched the Road Runner speed down a dirt road, kicking up dust behind him, I felt a plummeting sensation in my stomach. Now I knew why Lee didn't put photos of her family and farm on the walls of her room and why she wouldn't invite her mom to Mom's Weekend. She was embarrassed. This was what she wanted to leave behind.

I smiled and held out my hand. "I'm Clare. Thanks for having me."

"Oh! Here we are blabbing away." She smiled and shook my hand, loosely, limply. "Clare this, Clare that. You're all Lee Ann ever talks about!"

Lee still wouldn't look at me but at least she'd stopped cleaning.

After that, we went into the kitchen. I did most of the talking, asking Lee's mom about her tomato plants on the window ledge and how she'd liked growing up here. She answered everything in sweeping paragraphs that included multiple layers of information with a little hostility. "There's not a darn thing wrong with living here. These are good people. I just said yesterday that we're blessed to have this farm. Lee Ann and the twins have a roof over their heads, plenty to eat, and loads of family for as far as the eye can see. Everything you'd ever want is right here."

I smiled and said, "That's nice."

Lee's dad was tall and thin, like Lee, with black hair and small black eyes. He nodded when he came in the back door and Lee introduced us, nodded when her mom told him to clean up, and didn't say a word until midway through dinner when he turned to Lee and said, "Does the Chevy need an oil change?"

"Nah, I did it the other day," she said.

I glanced at her, surprised. "I didn't know that you could do that."

"She's a girl of many talents," her mom said. "Did you know that she was the champion state miler and president of her class and editor of the yearbook, too?"

"Mom," Lee mumbled.

"It's true! She can do anything. People think so highly of her around here."

Lee's mom hadn't touched her dinner. Little beads of sweat dotted her forehead and two giant red circles colored her cheeks. Over the years, Lee had told me many stories about her. That she'd barely graduated from high school. That while pregnant with the twins she nearly lost them a dozen times and had to be on complete bed rest until they were born. That she was insanely jealous of her more successful sister. Watching her fan her face with her hand, I felt sorry for her. She was trying so hard. I wanted to ask something else, but I'd run out of questions.

"You gonna make movies, too?" Billy turned to me.

"No, I'm an English major." I glanced at Lee's dad, hunched over his food and so quiet you didn't even know he was here. He's shy, Lee told me, but I also felt a somberness that made me think he was deeply worried. Or unhappy.

Lee's mom laughed, nervous. "Lee Ann says you

have books all over your house. My goodness. She gave me a copy of your mom's book but I haven't had time to read it yet. I will though. I know how famous it is. I hear it's real good. You must be real, real proud of your mom." She licked her lips and wrinkled her forehead and looked at me as if she were so uncomfortable that she might launch out of her chair.

"I am proud of her," I said. "But she's not perfect or anything."

Mrs. Sumner relaxed her forehead, relieved for a moment.

After we finished dinner Lee and I met her aunt Gail at a bar in town. Gail looked a lot like Lee's mom (they were only fifteen months apart) but her hair wasn't as bleached and her lipstick not as red. She wore gold hoop earrings, a gold necklace, and dozens of gold bangles. A Coach pocketbook hung from the back of the stool. She looked both at home in the bar and completely misplaced.

Gail and Lee's mom had a love-hate relationship, Lee told me, and at the moment they weren't speaking. Which was why she wasn't invited to dinner.

"So, you're the famous Clare." Gail put her hands on her big hips and tilted her head back. "I read your mom's book. I didn't care for it."

I felt my lips part and glanced at Lee. I had no idea what to say.

"Ah, I'm kidding! Call me Gail. No Miss or Ms." When she laughed a little too loudly, two guys at the bar turned to look at us. I smiled although I wasn't sure how to take her. I glanced at Lee again but she was smiling at Gail. "Come on, let's get some drinks! I'm paying. The night's on me!"

We walked to the back and sat next to a pool table, the green edges worn to the wood. Above us, beat-up Indiana license plates were nailed to the wood between posters for Schlitz and Budweiser. The ceilings were low. So were the lights.

"Good lord, what are you wearing?" Gail asked as Lee draped her coat over the back of her chair. It was an oversized brown military trench coat that she'd recently bought at the Army-Navy Surplus store for a marked down price of only seventeen dollars. It was lined with wool, had huge, deep pockets, and a circular tear on the chest that Lee told everyone was a bullet hole.

"It's my officer's coat." Lee grinned. "It's the warmest coat I've ever had. And my pockets hold everything—money, keys, and up to six cans of beer, each."

Gail burst out laughing, squeezed her shoulder, and said, "Oh, I've missed you! Tell me, what's going on back at the farm?"

Lee told her about finding Barney tied to a stake outside and then how her mom had made a spaghetti dinner that we all ate at the kitchen table.

"And you actually sat at the table?" Gail asked. "Like civilized people?"

Lee glanced over at the bar where the two guys were laughing quietly. On the way here, Lee had told me that she wouldn't talk to Gail about her mom. I saw the annoyance on Lee's face as she took a long drink of her beer.

Gail must have seen it, too, because she leaned toward Lee, as if she didn't want to miss a single word, and asked, "How's your film coming along?"

Lee broke into a huge grin as she talked about Patricia Graceson and the video camera she'd brought home. She wanted to film down by the river before we went back to school tomorrow. I'd heard Lee talk about her film so much that I could repeat everything, verbatim. Gail smiled, her eyes not leaving Lee's face.

After that we played pool and drank more beer and laughed a lot. Lee loved Gail and looked up to her—she was the manager of an insurance company in Fort Wayne—and I wanted to like her, too. But something didn't feel right.

After a while, Lee went off to the bathroom and Gail and I were alone. She scooted her chair so close to mine that our thighs touched. She said, "So tell me, Clare Michaels. Is Lee doing good down at school?"

I nodded. "She's doing great."

Gail smiled a little too wide and leaned a little too close. It would be a grave insult to back up and so I held my breath and didn't move. She didn't like me. Maybe she was jealous because she knew how close Lee and I were.

"And the other girls at that sorority house, they're nice to her?" she asked.

I tilted my head, unsure what she was asking. "Sure. Everyone loves Lee."

"Good. Lee was a star in high school. Unique and talented. Honorable, too. But she was a target. Kids were jealous and mean. She protected herself by not having many close friends. And she's *never* had a best friend before."

I felt myself stiffen. Was she threatening me? "I haven't had too many best friends, either. But I wasn't a star or anything. I'm pretty average."

Gail burst out laughing. "Well, you're honest. That's good."

I took a sip of beer and felt unsettled in a way that I couldn't describe. Maybe this was some kind of test?

"Lee and I are close," she said. "I know how much she looks up to me. And boy, when she latches onto something—and let me tell you, it doesn't happen very often—she can't let go. It's her tragic flaw and I hope it doesn't dog her all her life."

Another warning? I cleared my throat. "Well, you're like a mother to her."

"My sister doesn't get her. She thinks Lee oughta come back here. But Lee's like a bird. She has to be free to fly on her own." She looked over the room and then snapped her head back at me so quickly that I startled. "Gotta admit that I wasn't sure about you. I mean, what could you two possibly have in common? The only thing I could think of was that you both have mothers who are too wrapped up in themselves to pay attention to either of you. But you're okay."

At the time, I was so surprised that I couldn't respond. I couldn't think of two people more different than my mother and Lee's mom.

I watched our waitress hurry by with two plates of steaming burritos and thought about my mother on the couch today, completely done in by her editor's comments. My mother had always been too *wrapped up* in herself.

Lee walked toward me, her shoulders slumped and her head tilted down so that I couldn't see her eyes. I thought about Sarah packing for the weekend and Ducky setting up the hotel rooms and Lynn flying in from Dallas. I felt my stomach seize and wished, suddenly, that I'd had a conflict so I didn't have to go this weekend.

Lee sat and we drank our beers and then I paid the bill. Outside, the air was chilly and the street busy. We wound through the crowds and turned down a side street. Tonight we were staying at her apartment and moving her things in the morning.

Then we were leaving on an afternoon flight for Chicago.

The street was lined with brownstones and buildings in various degrees of disrepair. Several had crumbling cement stairs. Another had wood boards covering the windows. The one to our left had no stairs at all, just a giant hole beneath a picture window. Empty plastic cups and Styrofoam containers, cigarette butts and beer cans littered the sidewalk. From somewhere nearby, a car alarm blared. I kept looking over my shoulder—it was dark and I had a foreboding sense that someone was following us—as we walked.

"What makes you most nervous about going back?" Lee asked, her eyes on the sidewalk in front of her as we walked.

"I don't know," I said. "What about you?"

When she didn't answer, I glanced at her. We were under a streetlight and she was staring at me as we walked.

"What?" I asked.

"Every time I ask a question, you answer with asking a question," she said. "I don't get it. Why can't you talk about yourself?"

"That's not true," I said. "I answer questions."

"Not really. It's been happening for a long time now."

I stopped walking. "Okay, ask me a question."

"What makes you most nervous about going back?"

Just the other day, we were all sitting around the table at the house, laughing about some party the night before. Now Ducky was selling real estate in downtown Chicago and Sarah was in medical school. Amy was working in marketing and Christopher was in politics. I was a bored graduate student, a mediocre waitress, and a lousy tutor. Our friends were going to be so disappointed in me.

"Everyone has great jobs." I used to know what I wanted. I used to be certain. Right?

"You're in graduate school and you're going for your doctorate and that's big," she said. "And you're a good friend."

What did it mean to be good?

We turned the corner and up ahead I saw her apartment—her shitty, dark, two-bedroom apartment that she shared with Tina, a copyeditor at *The New York Times* who worked all night and slept all day, and her creepy boyfriend Markus, a pot-smoking guitar player who used Lee's laundry detergent and ate her Cheerios.

I wanted to go home. But Ben was most certainly working late and I couldn't imagine sitting with my parents as they plotted revision strategies.

"Know what I'm nervous about?" Lee's voice was so soft it was almost a whisper. "That Ducky and Sarah will want to talk about Florida."

I glanced over my shoulder again but no one

was there. When I turned back around, I saw a light turn on in her apartment and then someone was in the window. Markus? But surely he'd gone out by this time.

"Do they ever talk to you about it?" she asked.

If I told Lee that they never asked, she might think they didn't care. But if I told her that Sarah asked about her every damn time we talked—and that she always wanted to know if Lee had ever told me what, *exactly,* had happened that night—would that make her feel worse?

"I hardly ever talk to Ducky," I said. "And Sarah is busy with school so I don't talk to her much, either. But she always asks how you are. She always does."

Lee nodded.

In the window again, a dark figure moved in and out of the light. The last time I was here Markus sat at the kitchen table smoking, drinking beer, and smirking at me as he made up stupid, creepy songs about princesses and prostitutes. Thank God Lee was moving in the morning and wouldn't have to put up with him anymore.

"So, do you think they *don't* want to talk abou Florida?" she asked.

I glanced at her. The scar on her lip was not so noticeable in the dim glow of the streetlight. In our first year out of college, she cried a lot on the phone about nightmares, problems with the internship, and crazy things that kept happening (*the lights are getting brighter in my bathroom! There are noises in the closet!*) but never about what happened that night. Since then, we'd talked about it. Although now, trying to remember what was said and when, I couldn't come up with anything.

"Nobody knows what to say," I said.

She nodded and raised her hand to the side of her face. "Sometimes I feel like it's all I ever think about. Do you have that feeling, too? That it's always here?"

A wave of heat roared up my throat and burst into my cheeks. I *didn't* always think about it. Not anymore. It was like something you took off the shelf and put away in a drawer. Where it belonged. But this analogy didn't feel quite right.

I looked up at the window again. Markus! See? I'd been right. How could I concentrate on anything Lee was saying with him standing there?

CHAPTER 11

Markus sat at the tiny wood table next to the bathtub that was next to the water heater that was next to the front door. I was on the couch across from him, pretending to sleep but with one eye open just enough to watch him. It was early the next morning, a little after six, and he'd just gotten home. He stared at the wall, his eyes glassy, his head bobbing side to side. I didn't know if he was wasted or just tired from being up all night. Lee insisted that he was harmless, just filled with a lot of disappointment and hot air, but I wasn't taking any chances. If he even took one step toward me, I'd scream. I didn't care if I woke up the entire block.

He tipped his head back and closed his eyes, his mouth falling open. He had a scruffy black beard, mustache, and dark, curly hair that covered his head, the tops of each hand and knuckle. He wore heavy, scuffed black boots with a dark green bandana tied around his right ankle, a tight white T-shirt, and a brown blazer, ragged around the cuffs and collar.

I could tell by the way his chest rose and fell that he'd fallen asleep. Ben could easily fall asleep like that, too. But this was all they had in common.

I glanced at the small window above the sink. A thin streak of light shone through it, puncturing the air in the middle of the room and falling across the baseboard on the far wall. Even in the middle of the day it was always so dark in here. Would more windows help? The apartment needed everything—paint, carpet, and appliances. The furniture was old and falling apart—holes in the cushions and chairs missing backs. How many times had Lee found cockroaches in her shoes?

At least she was getting out. Today. In a few hours. I'd been hounding her to leave for months, since the last time they were burglarized. She'd lost three hundred dollars—why hadn't she taken that money to the bank?—and a new Walkman. I didn't know how she found her new apartment, maybe the same way she found the others. Through friends of friends of friends. Lee wasn't excited about it, she kept saying the new place was too sterile, but anything was better than this.

Lee walked out of her bedroom, dressed in running shorts and a T-shirt, both I recognized from college. Her legs were skinny and bird-like; the muscles had shrunk. It was too hard to run in the city, she always said. Thank God she wore flip-flops. Who knew what she'd catch walking barefoot on this floor.

Markus jerked awake and slapped his hands on the table. He watched as Lee walked to the sink and filled a glass of water. Last night, on his way down when we met him on the stairs, he smirked at me and said, "The princess has arrived."

Such a jerk.

"So this is it," Markus said. "You're leaving."

"Yep," she said. "In two hours."

"There's still time for you to kiss me," he said. "Tina isn't home yet and Princess over there is still asleep."

My heartbeat quickened but I didn't move.

Lee drank the water, washed the glass with a sponge and soap, and put it back in the cabinet. Her actions were slow and steady, as if she hadn't heard him. Or maybe she was used to it. Maybe he said this kind of thing all too often.

"That bedroom better be clean before you go," he said. "I think I'll do the white glove treatment. You know, if a speck of dust shows up on my glove you have to clean all over again."

"You don't own a white glove," Lee said.

"The bathroom, too," he said.

"I've cleaned the bathroom the last four times," she said.

"I don't remember that. The kitchen needs cleaning, too."

Lee turned to the sink and filled it with soapy water. Then she began washing the dirty plates and glasses that were stacked on the counter. This wasn't her mess—she'd told me this last night—so what was she doing?

"You're sexy when you clean," he said. "It

counters that awkward tomboy look. Maybe you should try a little harder. Buy a push-up bra. I could help. I—"

I sat up.

"She's awake!" Markus reached for a pill bottle, opened it, and pulled out a joint. He lit it and passed it to Lee. She hesitated and glanced at me before shaking her head. He arched his eyebrows in surprise and handed it to me. "You need it, sweetie. It'll help loosen you up."

"You're such an asshole." I pulled the sheet across my lap and folded my arms. He was a loser, too; a bouncer in a bar in Chelsea? What kind of future was there in that?

He grunted, tipped back in the chair, and took a drag on the joint. I frowned at Lee. Why didn't she tell him off? Was she getting high with him in the mornings? And why was she doing their dishes?

I heard footsteps in the hall, a key in the lock, and then Tina opened the door. She was tall with thick hips, long, kinky brown hair, and giant, round glasses that sat on the tip of her nose. She was homely and attractive at the same time and I was so intimidated that I could barely speak around her. I flinched when she threw her bag onto a chair and kicked her sandals into her bedroom.

"Really, Markus? This early?" She pointed to the joint.

He shrugged. "It helps me sleep."

She grunted at me and turned to Lee, who was rubbing her soapy hands along the sides of her running shorts. Half of the clean dishes sat upside down on a dishtowel next to the sink. The other half was still in the sink. Tina began counting on her fingers. "You've got the deposit, you've put in a change of address form, and you'll leave the keys when you finish moving out."

Lee nodded. "I think we're all set."

The room was so small and tight that I felt high just breathing the air. Or maybe I was still a little unnerved by Markus. And Lee's lack of reaction to him.

"How was work?" Lee asked.

"I spent two fucking hours working on an article about Benazir Bhutto that was riddled with errors and then they pulled it at the last minute. But thank you for asking." She shook her hair out of her face and loosened the belt around her waist.

"Benazir who?" Markus asked.

"Possibly Pakistan's next prime minister," Lee said. "The first woman."

I looked at her. How did she know that?

"At least Lee reads the paper every day." Tina glared at Markus, picked up her bag, and walked into her bedroom. Then she stuck her head back out. "Good luck, Lee. Markus, are you coming?"

"In a minute." He held the joint between his

lips and folded his arms. He was trying to prove something by staying, either to Tina or Lee or possibly to me. But I was no longer quite so afraid of him. Lee was right. He was full of hot air. I couldn't imagine why Tina kept him around.

"Let's get breakfast," Lee said to me. "Jimmy won't be here until eight thirty."

"Sure," I said.

"What about me? Do I get to have breakfast, too?" Markus took the joint out of his mouth and blew a smoke ring above him.

"Goodbye, Markus," Lee said. "Have a nice life."

I was fairly certain that she was sincere.

"Markus! *Fucking* get in here!" Tina screamed from behind her door.

He frowned as he jammed the end of the joint into a flowered saucer, chipped along the rim, on the table. Then he stood, pulled down the sleeves of his blazer, and slipped into the room. The door clicked when he shut it, then locked. Sex could be the only reason Tina wanted him and that felt completely repulsive to me.

Lee turned back to the sink and stuck her hands in the soapy water.

"What are you *doing?*" I jumped off the couch and hurried over to her. "Let's just go. They're both jerks, especially him. Don't do their dishes."

"It's okay," she said. "I don't mind."

"Well, you *should* mind!" I hissed. "He treats

244

you like shit. What was all of that crap about kissing him? Does he say that to you all the time?"

"Don't be so loud," she said. "They'll hear you. And it's not a big deal. He's just kidding around."

"I don't care if they hear me!" I said. "He has a *girlfriend*. And it's abusive the way he treats you. How can you not see that?"

Her hands were hidden in the suds and her arms weren't moving. She turned to me, her lips parting. Three long worry lines stretched across her forehead.

"Abusive?" she whispered finally.

"Yes." I nodded.

"Sometimes I don't know what's real and what's not real," she said. "Like I'm living in a dream and I see what's going on around me but I can't react. Or maybe it's that I don't feel anything. I don't know. It's like I'm still there. But not there."

Still where, in the dream? I stared at the faint purple scar that ran down the middle of her upper lip. The health center doctor said it would heal and the scar would eventually disappear but he'd been wrong. Dead wrong. I hated when she talked about living in a dream because I didn't understand it. And it scared me. Lee was better, wasn't she? She wasn't *still there,* wherever there was. We were in New York. We were going to breakfast. And this afternoon we were going to Chicago.

"You're not doing their dishes." I pulled her hands from the sink and handed her a napkin. A fresh towel would have been better but this was the best her apartment could offer. "Come on."

CHAPTER 12

The back of the old station wagon Jimmy drove was filled with his boss's tools and we weren't supposed to move them. That left only a small space for Lee's things. But the car had a roof rack and so we were able to tie Lee's twin box springs and mattress on top. Aside from this and a small bureau, Lee didn't own any furniture. No bed frame or headboard. No tables, chairs, or desk. She had several duffle bags filled with clothes, wood boxes that held her albums, a turntable and speakers, piles of blankets, sheets and pillows, and several boxes of books. Last night when we got back from dinner, it only took a half hour to pack.

"You still have this book?" I asked. Lee and I were in her room, deciding which things would make the first trip to her new apartment. Jimmy was waiting outside with the car. I lifted the textbook off the top of the stack. It was from our Abnormal Psychology class, junior year.

Lee zipped up a duffle bag. "I kept all my books. Didn't you?"

"I think so." But I didn't remember seeing my Abnormal Psych book on the shelf in my room. Where had it gone? I put the book back in the box. My mother never got rid of books, either.

They were stacked on the kitchen table, along the walls, in the bathrooms, two rows deep on the shelves in the den and her office. Your mother's books are her best friends, my dad always said. I used to feel that way about my books, too, although not so much anymore.

"We should get going." With her head, Lee motioned to the door. I picked up a box and followed.

Jimmy took Lee's things from us and stuffed them into the car and then we made another trip up and down before squeezing into the front seat for the short drive to her new apartment. Jimmy drove with one hand on the wheel and the other stretched across the top of the seat behind us. He was big with dirty blond hair that was thinning on his forehead but fell long down his back in a ponytail. His eyes were glassy and red—he was either stoned or had been up all night, too—and after our experience with Markus, I wasn't taking any chances. I watched Jimmy closely. I didn't care that Lee said he was nice and a brilliant cameraman.

Jimmy turned off Houston and took a sharp right, then left. I was so turned around that I didn't know where we were. East Side? West Side? It was close to nine thirty and people were hurrying down the sidewalks, dressed for work. I was sure that Ben, after running his usual four miles, had already been at his desk for an hour.

Finally, Jimmy slowed in front of a tall white stucco building. It was at least fifteen stories high with thin, long windows evenly placed across the facade. I didn't see a doorman in the glass-door entrance but still it felt safe to me. And clean. The white stucco sparkled in the sunlight.

"So, this is it?" Jimmy turned to Lee, who nodded.

"It looks like a prison," Lee said. Jimmy snickered. "Don't you think, Clare?"

"I think it looks safe," I said.

Rachel, one of Lee's three new roommates, met us at the elevator when we got off on the tenth floor. She wore blue and white checkered pajama bottoms and a tank top the same shade of blue as her bottoms. Even her blue and white slippers matched. She had a long face and big blue eyes and her lips barely moved when she talked. I liked how neat and organized she was; she seemed like the kind of person who wouldn't steal from you or expect you to do her dishes.

Rachel opened the door to the apartment and we followed her into the living room. Sunshine poured through the windows that lined the far wall and the furniture—lots of white wood and white wicker—looked new and barely used. Two lamps, blazing on either side of the couch, made the room bright, cheerful. Even the giant plant in the corner looked happy. I felt a wave of relief and turned to Lee.

She'd begun shifting her weight from one foot to the other while she opened and closed her hands. Her nose flared, as if she smelled something she didn't like, and her eyes darted around the room. And then suddenly she rushed across the rug to the window, looked out, and said, "It's so different from last time."

Rachel glanced at me and then at Lee. "What?"

"It wasn't as bright," Lee said.

"Well, you were here at night, I guess?" Rachel scrunched her nose in concern, or maybe worry, and I knew I had to do something. I didn't want her to think that something was wrong with Lee. I didn't want her to change her mind about letting her move in.

"You know filmmakers, always in touch with their surroundings." I laughed and turned to Rachel. "This is great. Can you show me the rest of the apartment?"

Rachel licked her bottom lip as she watched Lee and then shrugged and started down the hallway. To Lee I mouthed, *stop it* and motioned for her to follow.

In addition to the living room and galley kitchen, there were two bedrooms. Lee would share a room with Monica, who worked at Swiss Bank. Rachel, who was in graduate school at Columbia, shared the other room with Laura, who worked for an accounting firm. Rachel's father owned the apartment and rented to the girls.

I glanced at the half-dozen framed pictures on the table in the hall. Graduation. Formal dances. Pool parties. The girls wore big smiles that matched their big eyes as they posed with handsome boys dressed in suits and ties. These were normal girls who worked normal jobs and had normal friends. They could have been people we knew in college.

I leaned into Lee and whispered, "This is good. Don't you think?"

Lee ran her tongue across her scar as she glanced at the picture frames. She continued to open and close her hands until finally I grabbed her right hand, when Rachel turned to open a closet, and yanked it.

"Where did you go to undergrad?" I asked.

"Boston College." Rachel shut the closet door and turned to us. She'd been carrying a magazine that she now hugged to her chest with both arms.

"I live in Boston," I said.

"Really?" Rachel asked. "My grandparents live in Brookline. I love it there."

"I live in Brookline." I felt my voice raise an octave. "I grew up there."

"Do you know my grandparents, the Feiths? They live on Dean Street."

"No, but I grew up on Dean Street!"

We smiled at each other. To think that I'd be talking about Dean Street here in New York. This apartment was safe and clean and these were

251

good girls. They'd take care of Lee. Watch out for her. Not that I didn't want to do it anymore. But sometimes I felt, well, it was a challenge to help her keep her head above water. Yes, that was what it was like. It was as if she were treading water, and I had to keep yelling, kick your legs! Move your arms! And breathe!

Lee and I didn't talk on our way to the elevator. We still had to bring up the bed and things from the car and then make another trip back to her old apartment.

"What the hell?" I said when the doors closed and the elevator started down. "Why did you do that in the living room? You freaked her out."

"It was just so white everywhere. It wasn't like that when I saw it a couple of weeks ago. I'd have remembered."

"Well, maybe they painted. So what?"

"It's so high up. What if something happens? Like a fire?"

"Well, at least you don't have to worry about anyone breaking in through a fire escape," I said. "It's nice and bright and clean, Lee. You should be happy."

"I know. But—"

"But, what?" I asked.

"The karma's off. And there are hardly any outlets in the bedrooms. And the place smelled funny and there were no screens on the windows and the plant in the corner was fake and there were five lamps in the living room. Why so many?"

I glanced at her. How had she had time to notice all that? I watched a thin line of sweat start from her temple and trickle down her pale cheek. I couldn't remember the last time I saw her so worked up like this.

"And did you see what she was reading?" she asked. "*People* magazine."

"What's wrong with that? Every time I go to the dentist I read *People*."

"Yeah, but it's one thing to read it in the dentist's office and another to buy it."

"You don't know that she bought it," I said. "Maybe she found it. Or maybe she *took* it from the dentist's office. Who cares?"

The elevator doors opened and through the window we saw Jimmy, idling at the curb. These girls were welcoming Lee into their home, trusting her when they didn't know her. Maybe Rachel had been up all night working on a paper and needed downtime. Maybe she'd just taken an exam. Maybe she had to read "Lycidas," for God's sake.

"Not everyone has time to read *The New York Times*." I didn't care that my voice sounded angry. How could she be so critical? How could I read the paper every day when I had to read D. H. Lawrence?

"I know."

"It's safe, Lee."

"You don't have to be so protective all of the time, you know," she said.

"And you don't have to be so reckless. I'm just trying to be a good friend."

"I know. Thank you."

On our next trip, Lee wasn't as fidgety or critical and even smiled when I pointed to the dishwasher. Jimmy thought the apartment was great, too. After we dropped the box spring and mattress in the corner of the bedroom, he took the back of his hand across his forehead and said, "Lucky. You got air-conditioning."

On the way back to her old apartment, I rolled up the window and watched the city through tinted glass. People—a homeless man with his shopping cart, a woman walking a dog—flashed before me and disappeared. A cab raced by. A black limo turned sharply and nearly cut us off. Jimmy slammed on the brakes, yelled, "Dick!" and then sped up. I tightened my seatbelt. Maybe Lee's new roommates weren't as interesting or creative as her old ones. Maybe the neighborhood was less "cutting edge." But you needed to make compromises to live here safely.

Lee stared out the window, too, but her dark eyes had that distant, faraway look that always made me nervous. I nudged her. "You okay?" She twitched—I'd startled her—and nodded.

Jimmy turned the car and we wound around

Washington Square and then he turned right, and left and right again, and we were on Lee's street. He pulled up to her apartment and double-parked.

"You wanna stay with the car and I'll go up with Lee?" he asked.

"Thanks," I said. "But I'll go. We only have a few boxes left."

I followed Lee out of the car and up to the door. Once inside, we climbed the stairs. Someone on the second floor was cooking with onions and garlic. A baby cried behind one of the doors on the third floor. On the fourth floor, we let ourselves into her apartment. Tina and Markus's door was still closed and I didn't hear voices. Lee told me that they usually slept until late in the afternoon.

We carried the last of Lee's boxes from the bedroom into the living room.

"Want to take one last look around?" I whispered. Lee nodded and went back into her bedroom, then into the bathroom, and finally returned to the living room area. Which took all of twenty seconds, that was how small the apartment was.

We both jumped when the phone rang. Lee glanced at Tina's door, picked up the receiver before the second ring, and said hello. I watched her eyes widen and her lips part. Then she straightened, her whole body rigid. "Hello! It's so nice to talk to you again. How did you find me?"

"Who is it?" I leaned against the counter. The room still smelled like pot. The soapy water had turned to dull gray and I saw knives and plates at the bottom of the sink. From somewhere down the street I heard a siren.

Lee kept nodding and finally mouthed, *Patricia Graceson.*

How long had it been since Lee talked to her? Patricia had been her mentor, the subject of her documentary, and the one who helped get her the internship. But when that went bad, Lee had been too embarrassed to tell her. Finally, a year after she was let go, Lee wrote Patricia to explain but Patricia never wrote back.

"So, are you looking to compare with what you found in Africa?" Lee began twirling the phone cord around her finger.

Patricia was one of the most successful documentary filmmakers in the country and yet she wanted something from Lee. I saw it all over her face. Lee began to pace, the phone pressed to her ear, her forehead furrowed as she concentrated.

My God. Patricia Graceson. We were sophomores when she arrived on campus for a two-year stint as a guest lecturer. One night a group of students gathered in Lee's theater to watch Patricia's new documentary and Lee asked me to go with her. It was an uncomfortable night for me. I remembered that clearly.

"There's Dr. Hannigan," Lee said as we found seats among the thirty or so students who were there. She pointed to a man on the stage and then nodded at a boy with red hair who was sitting in the front row. "That's Rodney. Just, I don't know, see what you can see."

Rodney was Dr. Hannigan's assistant and Lee didn't understand why he'd been giving her a hard time. Part of the reason she wanted me to come with her was to see if I could figure him out. As I settled in my seat and watched Lee start down the aisle, I noticed how people turned to look at her. She had a presence here, too.

When Lee approached Dr. Hannigan, Rodney jumped on the stage and worked his way between them. It was obvious what he was doing, yet Lee seemed oblivious. She just kept talking and smiling.

A few moments later when she sat next to me, I whispered, "He's threatened by you. Can you not see that?"

"Maybe I'll sleep with him and really fuck with his head," she said. I must have looked horrified because she laughed. "I'm kidding! God, Clare, you're so spooked by sex."

"No, I'm not—"

The crowd began to clap and Lee said, "There she is! That's Patricia!"

Patricia Graceson climbed the stairs to the stage. She didn't wear a sleek pantsuit or black dress or patent leather pumps. Nor did she have long red-painted nails or perfect hair. She reminded me of the women who came to my mother's writing classes, not someone famous. She had big, round glasses, short gray hair, and she wore a yellow cardigan that was too long in the sleeves and covered her hands. She wore no lipstick, no eye shadow. I'm not even sure she combed her hair. She grinned and waved as she scanned the group. When her eyes reached us, Lee sat forward and waved back.

Once she started to talk, I thought she had a warm voice and a nice smile. Did she have children? She seemed so open and friendly, and I imagined she was a mom who gave bone-squeezing hugs and listened when her children talked. But if she was so successful, wasn't she married to her work?

Then the lights dimmed and the film began. As I watched the opening, a landscape pockmarked with dried riverbeds and tumble brush, blistering blue skies, and dead cattle carcasses, I started to think about the sorority house. I imagined everyone was still sitting at the table in the dining room, talking and laughing. I stifled a yawn and felt my eyelids droop. The film was very dry, very academic.

Everyone but me seemed mesmerized. And I remembered thinking, as I sat there, that I was a *pretend* intellectual. I could spit back what the professor wanted to hear and make lame, generic connections. But my mother was a true intellectual. Maybe Lee, too. They were talented and passionate and believed in what they were doing. They thought about things, *pondered* them, *wrestled* with them.

I glanced at Lee, who was watching the screen, her lips slightly parted, her dark eyes barely blinking, her hands gripping the arms of her chair. She was passionate not just about film-making but about *many things*—the way bare tree branches crisscrossed the sky on a bright winter day or the first cup of coffee in the morning. I didn't feel things in the same way and I suddenly wished so much that I did. I'd settle for one passion, just *one* thing that got me excited.

Patricia Graceson's voice boomed through the room. Drought, starvation, epidemic. On screen there were poor, starving children with distended stomachs, fly-infested wounds, and runny eyes. Where were the parents? Why couldn't they keep their children safe? Were they not *paying attention?*

Crude farming techniques. Vicious circles of malnutrition and lack of education and oppor-tunities. Years of oppression and war. Many parents died before their children. Many died trying to feed their children before themselves.

Oh.

I sat back in my seat. From listening to my

parents talk so much about war, I knew that no one really anticipated how horrible it would be. What was wrong with me? My mind was turning to silly putty. I needed to have something important in my life. A passion. Maybe a career counselor could help me find this.

An hour later, the documentary ended and Patricia took the stage again.

"I think your work is inspiring," a girl said from the back row. "Your use of lighting is both symbolic yet functional, utilitarian and yet transformative."

Oh, God, she sounded like the pretentious women who went to my mother's book signings. I sighed loudly. The girl in front of me turned and frowned.

"I appreciate your insights but we were filming in the desert," Patricia said. "I wasn't thinking about symbolism or transformation. I was trying to get the shot."

Ha! The questions went on, about style, lighting, government restrictions, securing visas and making sure that you aren't liable for filming subjects without written permission. When Lee's hand shot up, Patricia smiled and pointed to her.

"What advice can you give someone who's starting out?" Lee asked.

Patricia nodded. "Excellent question. So, here it is. We simply can't judge others—and let's face it, that's what we do regardless of how much we insist that we're objective—until we have judged ourselves. As Socrates said, and this is something I firmly believe, 'the unexamined life is not worth living.' For your life and sanity and especially for your art, you must learn about yourself."

No one said anything. From the surprise on everyone's faces, I imagined that this wasn't something taught in Film 101. I sat up. Learn about yourself for art's sake? Had my mother done that?

"But if we're filming something that doesn't have anything to do with us, why is it important to know yourself?" Rodney asked. "Shouldn't we forget ourselves?"

"Your unconscious runs everything you do, from what you decide to eat to how you pick your subject matter," she said. "The sooner you understand what your story is, the better you'll be at recognizing when it gets in the way of creating something authentic and true to your subject. Learn about yourself."

Usually when my mother talked about her writing process, she referred to research techniques like how to get the librarians at the Harvard library to thread the microfiche. I didn't think I'd ever heard her utter the words unconscious or authentic. My mother, a New Critic as she often reminded people, thought conversations about the author were "indulgent and superfluous."

Lee raised her hand again. "What did you learn about yourself?"

Rodney whirled around and glared, as if to say, *how dare you be so personal?* The two girls in front of us turned to look as well.

Patricia folded her arms and nodded. "That's fair, that's okay. Well, I grew up in a small town in Kentucky, in a house with dirt floors and an outhouse in the back. My father drank himself to death and my mother suffered from severe depression. I got myself out of there, to college and eventually on to do my doctorate. Along the way I sought out mentors and mental health counselors."

The room was so quiet that from far behind me I heard someone softly burp.

"I learned that I have a temper and am prone to depression. That I'm happiest when working. That I have trouble with authority figures. And that my interest in the African crisis is both a response to the devastation but also due to a need, based on my background, to help children in a way that I didn't receive."

I'd never heard anyone talk like this. Wasn't she embarrassed? Wasn't she worried what people would think? I couldn't imagine being this open. I couldn't imagine my mother doing it, either.

Later as we started back to the house, Lee was twitching, bouncing, turning to me—so excited, so animated—in a way I'd never seen from her before. "Can you believe her, growing up without a bathroom? What do you do in the winter? How could she afford college and graduate school? She's not just a good filmmaker. She's great. And she's so nice!"

"She's so nice," I echoed.

"I couldn't believe how much she talked about her life. I wonder if she sees her mom much and if she's supportive of her filmmaking or not. And what do you think about what she said about the unexamined life is not worth living?"

I flinched because I'd briefly examined my life during the film and didn't like what I'd found. "It's probably good advice."

"This whole night wasn't what I expected. I thought we'd talk about the film. I didn't think she'd talk about her *life*. Don't you think that was interesting? She had lots of help, don't you think? Scholarships. Loans. Maybe she had a benefactor, too."

Suddenly I had a thought that surprised me so much that I stopped walking. Lee stopped, too. We were under a streetlight on the path back to the house and the night was so cold that we could see our breaths.

"You always talk about making a film about a great person who changed our world," I said. "But maybe that's too big. Maybe you should do a film about someone who has changed her life. Like Patricia. That's equally important. Right?"

Lee brought her hands to her face and sank until she sat cross-legged on the pavement. Had I said something wrong? I didn't know what to do, so I squatted next to her. Her hands were still on her face, but tears rolled down her cheeks. I sucked in a breath. I'd never seen her cry before.

She dropped her hands and started laughing while still crying. "I'm just so . . . It's fantastic, your idea. It's absolutely what I should do. It's perfect! This is so helpful. I want to do this, make a film, *so badly*. I'm so, I don't know, grateful. Because you think about me. You know me. You. Know. Me! People don't really know me."

What had just happened? It was like a flood or a tornado had suddenly unleashed within her. I said, "But people know you. Your family. Your aunt."

She shook her head. "I've tried talking to my parents, but they have no idea who I really am. My aunt is great but she's about fun and success and only gets, like, one side of me. You know all sides of me because you listen. You're so good at that."

I *was* good at listening and that was a talent, wasn't it? I suddenly felt proud and satisfied. Lee wiped her sleeve across her wet face. Which was the same sleeve of the same gray sweatshirt that she'd worn nearly every day this spring. As I watched the tears soak into the fabric, I thought that I loved her. And she loved me. With

Lee, maybe for the first time in my life, I felt like I could be the person I was supposed to be. I imagined us years from now, living near each other and married to men who were best friends. We'd talk all day. Lee would make movies. And I would help people by listening to them. But what, exactly, did that mean?

"I wish I was passionate and sure about what I wanted to do." I felt a sudden panic and fear as the words rushed out of me. I'd never told anyone this before. I'd never allowed it. I felt petrified.

Lee looked at me. "If you can find what you want, and believe in yourself, you'll be great. Your main problem is that you doubt yourself too much. Before you even get started with anything."

This was true. Oh, God, she really knew me, too. But I bit my lip. Even with her, my best friend, I felt little needles of shame. I wanted to tell her more—about how I didn't have tornadoes or floods within me—but revealing these things, actually, revealing *anything,* seemed so unnatural, almost excruciatingly difficult. How could she do it so easily with me?

I sat next to her on the pavement and then we both started laughing. And crying, too. And laughing. It was crazy. I didn't even know what was so funny or sad.

Outside the kitchen window, I heard a car alarm and then a siren. I glanced at Lee, who was still nodding, phone pressed to her ear, as she listened to Patricia. Finally, Lee said, "Wow, this is incredible. So, you think it's at least eight months?"

"Eight months of what?" I whispered.

"Yes, I know I'd have to quit. You're right. I'll think about it over the weekend and call you Monday. I'm really interested. Thank you for thinking of me." Lee reached for a pen on the table and wrote a phone number on the back of a napkin. After she hung up, she pulled out a chair and fell into it.

"What did she say?" I asked.

Lee didn't take her eyes off the napkin. "She wants me to go to Southeast Asia with her to shoot a documentary. For eight months."

"Eight months!"

"Her assistant just told her that she's pregnant and can't go. So, she thought of me. She can't pay much, hardly anything, but she'll take care of airfare, lodging, food, and all expenses. What do you think?"

"But what about your new apartment? And your job?"

"I'd have to let go of everything. Quit my job. Put my stuff in storage."

"God, Lee. This is a huge decision."

"She's going to Thailand and Cambodia to look at childhood malnutrition." Lee's voice sped up. "She got all sorts of grants and funding. Did you know that in the last couple of years Thailand has seen a reduction in the severity of malnutrition in children? Why is that? And why haven't other countries in the region been able to do that? Patricia wants to look at that. Doesn't that sound so interesting?"

I lowered myself into the chair across from her, tears springing to my eyes. Because I'd miss her. And because she had the courage to do something that I'd never do. And mostly because I'd have no way to take care of her if she was halfway around the world. What if she had terrible roommates who took advantage of her? What if Patricia turned out to be a horrible boss who made her fetch coffee and make stupid squash court reservations? Oh, I was being ridiculous. There were no squash courts where she was going.

"Oh, Clare, you're worried that it's too dangerous?"

I nodded. This was risky. A gamble. You don't quit your life and go halfway around the world without getting paid adequately and with someone who wasn't dependable.

"I'm just shocked," she said. "I can't believe she called me after all of these years. I mean, I guess she hasn't forgotten me, after all."

"You don't have to decide right this minute."

Lee nodded again, scooted the saucer toward her, and lit the joint. She inhaled deeply and then turned slightly so the light from the window caught her eyes and made them flicker. Then she smiled. Something about this reminded me of when we went to her movie theater in college and the lights dimmed and she'd lean forward in her seat, excited for the first five minutes (*the most important minutes of a movie!*) even though she might have seen it a dozen times already.

She took another drag on the joint and held it out to me. I shook my head. It was only ten on a Friday morning, and we had hours of plane and subway travel ahead. God knows what would happen to us if I got stoned and freaked out.

Outside, a car horn honked.

"That's Jimmy. We better go." She stubbed out the joint, put it in her pocket and picked up a box. When she hurried for the door, I followed.

CHAPTER 13

The restaurant in downtown Chicago was typical for my parents—dark paneled walls, white tablecloths, heavy silver, oversized menus handed to us in thick, leather-bound covers, and barely anyone—including the waitstaff—under the age of forty. We sat at a table in the middle of the room, two empty seats between my mother and me, and looked at our menus. I was starving and a little frazzled—the L train from the airport had taken so long—but not nearly as frazzled as my mother.

The airline had lost her luggage and had no idea if it would arrive before morning when she had to give her talk. She wasn't happy with the new outfit she'd bought today. The hotel had run out of umbrellas and it was pouring outside. The concierge at the hotel had no idea who she was. Neither had the maître d'. And now Logan and Elise were going to be late. She told us this in one breath when Lee and I met her and Dad in the lobby. And then we were seated at our table.

Lee sat across from me, hugging her arms to her chest as she looked around the room. I was fairly certain that she'd never been in a place so staid and expensive. When she looked at the ceiling I looked, too, half expecting to see a dark cloud. Even though my dad had whispered to me that my mother had figured out a revision plan, that she was *just fine,* I wasn't so sure.

My mother's makeup was perfect and her short hair styled and hiding the gray. But she sat forward in her chair, her right elbow on the table and her fingers massaging her forehead. The muscles around her mouth sagged in a kind of perpetual pout. I had no idea where she was, but didn't think she was here.

Was she thinking about Janice's letter? Was she worried about tomorrow's talk? Dad, who was a marketing professor before managing my mother, came up with the Book Talk concept when *Listen* was published. He'd contact a bookstore or library and offer an intimate talk with my mother with one stipulation: participants had to purchase the novel. It was a "win-win," as my dad liked to say, for everyone.

"Did you see the lilies in the lobby?" I leaned across the empty seats toward her. Lilies were my mother's favorite flower. "Aren't they beautiful?"

"So fragrant, too!" my dad said. My mother sighed.

"Don't worry about your outfit tomorrow. You always look great." I watched her, waiting for a smile, a sparkle in her eye, anything to tell me that she was feeling better. God, sometimes it took everything I tried to make her happy.

I glanced at Lee, who was staring at me,

eyebrows raised as if to ask, *what's going on?* She'd been with my parents a dozen times over the years and had mostly seen the charming side of my mother's personality. But I'd told her about my mother's moods. I'd told her a thousand times.

"Shouldn't we have waited to be seated?" I saw the waiters near the bar, watching us. "What if Logan and Elise don't get here for another hour?"

"We have every right to sit here and wait," my mother said.

People came into the coffeehouse all the time to sit and wait. We were a destination, a hangout. But this was an expensive restaurant, on the first floor of my parents' expensive hotel, and it made money by turning over tables. I felt so entitled, sitting here and waiting. I turned to my dad, who was reading the wine list.

"They have a Chateau Montelena," he said.

"Is that expensive?" I asked.

He nodded. Good. The restaurant was less likely to be angry with us if we sat here and waited with an expensive bottle of wine.

"Of course, we could get a Chablis," he said.

"Just order the Chateau Montelena!" my mother said a bit too loudly, her thin lips pinched in a straight, flat line. I cringed and looked around but no one was paying attention to us.

My dad signaled for a waiter. He wore his favorite blue blazer and a white button-down.

271

His hair—he hadn't had time to get it cut—was at least combed back off his face. The wrinkles in the corners of his eyes were deeper and more pronounced than normal, and I imagined he'd been up late last night with my mother. But he smiled as he turned to Lee and said, in his most energetic, earnest voice, "How fortunate that we get to see you, too! How is New York? How is ABC?"

Lee glanced at me. All afternoon during the cab ride, the wait at the airport, the flight, and on the L, we talked about Patricia's offer. One minute Lee was going, the next she wasn't. The difficulties of the logistics had settled in. For example, as I said to her, how would she reestablish herself in New York when she came back? Would ABC give her a reference if she quit her job so soon after starting?

"Everything's going pretty well," Lee said. "Thanks for having me tonight."

"Of course, our pleasure! You're seeing college friends this weekend. My goodness, you'll have a good time. Nothing like college friends."

I saw Lee's head drop slightly and her eyes flutter and I felt a pinch in my stomach. If we'd gone back for a football game or one of the many get-togethers, maybe this weekend wouldn't seem so loaded.

"It's supposed to rain all morning tomorrow," my mother said.

"People will still show up for your talk," my dad said. "They always do."

"What's your talk about?" Lee asked.

My mother looked at Lee over the top of her reading glasses, perched on the end of her nose. "Minimalism and what the success of *Listen, Before You Go* was like. It's the only thing people ever want to hear about."

"It's a great book," Lee said.

"Yes, well, it may very well be my only great book."

"You've published two well-received novels," Dad said. "There'll be more."

"*Saigon* was not well received," she said.

I pointed to the menu. "Look, they have chicken marbella. Isn't that what you had last year when you spoke in London? That you liked so much?"

My mother sat up as she scanned the menu. "Yes, you're right; well, look at that, I didn't see it at first. Anders, remember that dinner?"

"Yes, wonderful meal," Dad said.

She smiled, finally, and settled back in her chair. It was easy to distract her. I should have thought of this yesterday when she was on the couch and talking about *ending it*. Was she really okay?

I glanced at my watch as the waiter poured the Chateau Montelena. Logan and Elise should be here soon. That I was looking forward to seeing her more than my brother was no surprise. Elise was wonderful. One night last summer, during a visit to the Vineyard, she and I sat on a stone wall overlooking the field that stretched down to the ocean and talked for hours. She was an academic but she didn't act like one. She liked to talk about feelings. *How does it feel to be three years out of college? How does it feel to have a famous mother?* She and Lee were the only people who'd ever asked me this question.

I looked up from my menu as a couple about my parents' ages walked past the table and sat at the bar off to our left. The woman wore a white linen dress, the man was in a suit and tie, and the tops of their heads and shoulders were wet from the rain. The woman took a cocktail napkin and dabbed the back of her neck. When she caught me looking, she smiled and shrugged. I smiled, too, and looked away. At least she had a sense of humor about it.

I glanced at my watch again. Ducky had rented a suite at the hotel in Evanston where we were all staying. A party room, she'd called it. Everyone should be arriving there soon.

"I've never had luck with rain," my mother said. "People stay home."

"Your fans love you," I said. "They'll come out."

My dad winked at me. "Clare's right. My goodness, we have ninety-seven people signed up for this talk. Ninety-seven!"

"Think about the positive stuff," I said.

My mother nodded and glanced around. Book Talks and speaking engagements helped pay the bills. It was a coordinated effort orchestrated by my dad. Plane tickets supplied by the publisher. Additional books sold and signed. An article about my mother guaranteed in the hosting city's newspaper. But I wondered if my mother also liked to do them because they kept her in the spotlight.

"The last time I spoke here was three years ago," she said. "I remember because a gentleman asked if I was going to write a sequel to *Listen, Before You Go*."

"I thought everyone asked you that." I glanced at the bar where the man and woman were laughing with the bartender.

"Not the way he asked. Remember, Anders, what he said?"

Dad looked up from the wine he was swirling in his glass. "Yes, he said, 'I want to know what happens to the little girl after her brother blows out his brains on the garage wall.'"

My mother winced. "I'd never heard it asked quite like that."

She'd never told me this. But what was so surprising about what he'd asked? *Blowing his brains out.* It was, after all, how she wrote about what Whit did. But she was still wincing, even as she sipped her wine, and I wanted to make her feel better.

"You *should* write a sequel," I said. Part of me didn't care if I ever read about Phoebe and her crazy family again. The other part wondered if Phoebe, as an adult, would be like me.

Lee, who'd been staring at my mother, turned her head and looked at me.

My mother shuddered. "For Heaven's sake. I can't imagine writing about those characters. They're stuck in time. I never think about what happens to them."

"There he is!" Dad stood, grabbed Logan's arm, and slapped him on the back. My mother smiled as Logan bent over and briefly hugged her. He pulled away, dropped into the seat next to me, squeezed my shoulder, and nodded at Lee.

"Bloody taxi took forever." Logan was a swimmer when he was younger and still had the body for it—tall and broad shouldered with a narrow waist. Usually he dressed in expensive handmade Italian suits and three-hundred-dollar silk ties (he liked to show me price tags). Today he looked disheveled; chinos with wrinkles across the front and the shoulders of his blue button-down speckled with rain. His light brown hair was longer than I'd seen it in years and fell across his forehead, obscuring his eyes.

"Where's Elise?" I asked.

"Couldn't come." He reached for the bottle of Chateau Montelena and held it in front of his face, reading the label. He poured some into his water glass and took a big gulp. Then he swept his hair out of his eyes, licked his lips, and nodded. "Not bad. Pedestrian but not bad."

"We were looking forward to seeing her," Dad said.

"Yeah, well." Logan took another gulp of wine, then rested his elbows on the table and looked around. "Seems typical that you'd pick the stodgiest place you could find in this bloody city. It looks like a funeral home."

Something was wrong. Logan was sarcastic and certainly distant—my God, when was the last time he was home for Christmas?—but he normally wasn't quite so rude. My mother shifted in her seat and my dad sat back and crossed his arms. Lee stared at me. I had to do something. "How was your flight?"

I could count to ten in the time it took him to turn his head toward me. He curled his upper lip into a snarl. "Jesus, Clare. Who the fuck cares about that?"

Dad leaned forward. "That's just about enough, Logan. What's this all about?"

"Nothing," he mumbled as the waiter handed him a menu. He opened it and began reading. Dad asked for another bottle of wine.

Something was wrong between Elise and him. I pushed away my wineglass and sat back in my seat. They'd broken up several times before but they'd always gotten back together. Maybe this was like those times. Maybe they'd had an argument. A *row,* as Elise would say. I glanced at the bar. The woman in the white linen dress was smiling at me. Then I realized that she wasn't looking at me but at my mother. She recognized her.

"Is everything okay with work?" my mother asked.

Logan waved his hand at her. "Sure. I'm going to make a shitload of money again this year."

Logan was drunk. He rarely swore and he was slurring his words. Had I ever seen him like this? Usually he was so much in control. Lee was watching him, too. She'd only been around him a few times, the latest two years ago on the Vineyard when he breezed in for a three-day visit with Elise.

The waiter came back to the table with the wine and took our orders. After he left, Dad said, "I thought you two would announce an engagement soon."

Logan snorted. "That would require us actually being together. We're done, this time for good. She's in love with someone else." He gulped his wine again.

"Oh, Logan, I'm sorry," my mother said. Dad groaned. Tears sprang to my eyes, and I held my hand to my chest.

"She said she got tired of waiting around for me," he said.

"You should've asked her to marry you when you had the chance," Dad said.

"I did! Last Christmas in her parents' living room! I even had a ring."

"I don't understand," my mother said.

"She said she was tired of waiting for me to get my shit together. She said she wanted someone with not so much *baggage*. She went after one of those touchy-feely blokes. You know, the kind who's been on a couch for the last twenty years."

It took me a few seconds but I knew what Logan meant by on a couch. Freud. Therapy. As I watched him, I thought about something Elise had said that night on the stone wall. She was talking about how family members inadvertently "assign" roles for each other and then she'd turned to me and said, "I know that your mum's fame has been hard for Logan." Was this what she meant by baggage?

My mother folded her arms and sat forward in her seat. "We all have baggage, Logan. I'm not sure that wallowing in it is any way to live."

"Wallowing?" He shook his head. "We don't wallow. In fact, we don't even talk. According to Elise."

"Ah!" Dad grunted. "That's where she's wrong. We talk all the time."

"She meant that we don't talk about emotional things," I said. Everyone looked at me. Logan raised his eyebrows, as if impressed, but I

279

didn't trust him. Had I ever seen him this drunk and angry? I didn't want him to pounce on me again.

"I think my friends and business associates consider me a very friendly and open person," Dad said. "Your mom and I have not shied away from our opinions."

"That's the truth," Logan mumbled. He signaled the waiter and ordered a Dewar's on the rocks.

"I think you've had enough to drink," my mother said.

"I'm just getting started," he said.

Dad kept turning his knife over next to his plate. Lee sat stiff and straight and stared at something on the table. My mother's thin lips were pinched into a frown again. When she began rocking, I picked up the breadbasket and passed it to her. I passed her the butter plate, too, and said, "Maybe you should eat something."

She took it from me but didn't eat anything.

I frowned at Logan. I *had* seen him angry like this, years ago, when I visited him in the hospital after he'd had his appendix out. He was angry with our mother for leaving him behind while we went to New York for the award ceremony. Now he was mad at Elise for leaving him. Or at our parents because they didn't talk about emotions. Or at me because I'd asked about his flight. Maybe he wasn't mad but upset. I wasn't sure about anything because staring at the way his lids drooped over his eyes and how the freckles on his cheek looked like a star—why hadn't I ever noticed this?—I realized that I didn't know my brother that well. How could this be?

Lee raised her eyebrows at me again, and I began bouncing my leg.

"What was she referring to, Logan, with your baggage?" Dad asked. "The way you were raised? Your heritage?"

"My heritage? Ah, you mean our relatives. We know all about your family, Dad. Your father, the engineer who bolted, and your poor mum." Logan pointed his drink at our mother. "But this one's family is a mystery. Maybe they were all bloody, gun-toting murderers."

"Logan!" I glared at him. How insensitive could he be? He knew as well as I did how our great-grandfather had died.

For a moment my mother looked stricken. But then her cheeks colored and she shook her head. "There's no mystery. What do you want to know?"

"Why didn't we ever meet anyone?" Logan began weaving side to side.

"Who was there to meet, Logan? You met my mother. I had no siblings. My father died when you were a baby. My cousins are scattered all over the globe. You're trying to make me feel guilty or responsible or something. But it's not my fault that I had such a small family. And it's not my fault that Elise left you."

"Oh, Chrriiissttttt," he slurred. "You don't get it!"

"You're drunk, Logan." My mother sat back in her chair and nodded at Lee. "And I'm sorry, Lee, that you have to witness this."

"Witness what?" Logan hissed. "What are you sorry about?"

Then the waiters swooped down on our table, delivering chicken marbella for my mother and me, steak for my dad and Lee, and fish for Logan. A bouquet of roasted garlic, butter, and lemons surged into the air above the table, but no one seemed hungry. Staring at my plate, I was no longer glad that Lee was here. This dinner was embarrassing, and I was furious with Logan for treating our mother so poorly. The sooner we ate, the sooner we'd leave.

"Excuse me." A voice, soft and unsure.

I looked up to see the woman in the white linen dress standing next to my mother and wringing her hands in front of her. She said, "I'm sorry to interrupt. We're on our way to our table but I wanted to say how much I loved *Listen, Before You Go*. I reread it every couple of years. Phoebe is such an interesting character, and she had to deal with so much at such a young age. I saw in the paper that you were in town and I just, well, want to thank you for writing it."

"Oh, my goodness, thank you." My mother turned her entire upper body toward the woman. And then she beamed, as if they were old friends who hadn't seen each other in a while.

"I always wondered how you came up with the story," she said. "You know, where you got the idea."

I watched my mother blink rapidly—as if she'd been caught in a car's high beams—before dropping her eyes. Normally I wouldn't spend time thinking about this, but now, remembering Lucy's accusations, I wondered. Why *was* it so hard for her to talk about this? Where *had* the story come from?

I glanced at my dad but he was swirling his wine and smiling at the woman. Finally, my mother looked up and smiled slightly, too. Then she pointed to her head and shrugged.

"I've read both your books. I liked *Saigon,* too, but *Listen* is my favorite. I think that's because, well, I had an uncle who killed himself. And you wrote about this so well. How the family suffers. Anyway, sorry again for interrupting." She nodded at my mother, smiled at the rest of us, and walked to the back of the room.

"That was nice," my mother said, her big brown eyes widening. "After all this time to still be recognized. And how lovely that she liked *Saigon,* too."

People didn't often mention her second novel.

Relief seemed to wash over her. The other day Dad showed me an article he'd kept hidden from her. The writer questioned the "merit and future of minimalism" and suggested that *Listen, Before You Go* may not hold up to scrutiny in coming years. I was glad that he'd kept it from her, especially now that her editor didn't like her new book.

"Of course you're still recognized," I said. "You should remember this the next time you start doubting yourself."

My mother nodded.

When Logan slapped the table with his palm, I jumped and the couple at the table next to us turned to look. He said, "That's it! Our heritage! That's where we came from, good ole Phoebe and Whit!"

"That book put you through Dartmouth," my mother said.

"That's right," Dad said.

Logan drained his drink. "Well, fuck Dartmouth. And fuck Phoebe and Whit." He was weaving so much that I thought he might fall off his chair.

"Stop raising your voice and stop using that language," my mother growled. "It's rude and people know me here."

"Oh, Christ, people know you," he sputtered. "That's *always* how it's been. Your books and image have always been more important than anything else. What, you don't think I know this? Think about how you left me to die while you went off and got your award for that goddam book."

"What are you talking about?" Dad asked.

"When Clare and I went to the book award ceremony?" my mother asked. "Logan, you weren't dying. You had appendicitis."

What kind of sick joke was this?

"How was the zoo, Clare?" he asked. "Pet any elephants?"

What the hell was he talking about?

He laughed. "*Phoebe and Whit.* Well, maybe Phoebe and Whit aren't so good for us, after all. Just think about how much they've fucked up Clare. She can't decide if she should be Phoebe or your mother. They're basically one and the same."

"I am not fucked up!" I felt a rush in my cheeks and then a hot pulsing.

"Really? You can honestly say that you don't think you're supposed to be Phoebe?" He turned to Lee. "Did you know that she thinks she's supposed to be Phoebe? And that we've always called her 'Claretaker'? Jesus, Elise loved to talk about this crap."

"That's enough!" Dad roared.

The tables around us went silent, and then it was so quiet that I heard the bartender pour ice into a glass across the room. My mother dropped

285

her head into her hand. Logan reached for the wine bottle. I had a sense that everyone was looking at us, although when I glanced around, all heads were down. I was so angry that my entire body shook. Me, fucked up? I wasn't the one so drunk that I could barely sit in my chair. Ever since I could remember, Logan thought he was smarter than everyone else. The way he'd breeze in and out with no thought to helping her, helping anyone.

Logan, eyes closed, began weaving again. My dad stood, threw his napkin on his chair, and walked behind Logan. He ripped the bottle out of his hand, reached under his elbows, and helped him up. Then my dad put his arm around Logan's waist, guided him around the table, and said, "I'll get him settled and be back."

After they'd gone, my mother waved both of her hands in front of her and said, "Let's eat, you two. Don't let it get cold. Go on, eat!"

But she wasn't eating and I certainly had no appetite. Lee held her knife in her hand, but she kept looking at me, then at my mother, unsure what to do.

My mother was hurt—I felt it and saw it in the way the corners of her mouth sagged and her nose flared—and this made me even angrier. How could Logan treat her like this? How could he be so ungrateful?

"Logan's a jerk. He shouldn't have said those

things to you. They weren't true." I reached across the empty seats, picked up her fork, and held it out to her.

My mother sighed and took the fork, staring at it as if she had no idea what to do. She watched as I cut into my chicken and put a piece in my mouth. It was tasteless as I chewed. Lee, still holding her steak knife, had a surprised look on her face, as if she'd just remembered something important. I tapped my watch—we had to go soon—and she nodded and started to eat, too.

The people at the next table began to talk again. But the silence at our table was excruciating.

As my mother started to eat, Lee continued to glance at me and then at her. Finally, she said, "Mrs. Michaels, I know you're familiar with Southeast Asia because you wrote about Vietnam. But have you ever been to Thailand?"

"No. Why do you ask?"

"Just wondering what you knew about it."

Then my mother began a long explanation of the history of Southeast Asia, starting with the French colonization of Vietnam in the 1800s. I was pretty sure that this wasn't what Lee was asking, but I was grateful for the help with my mother.

I sat back, rubbed my chin, and thought about a scene in *Listen* when Whit and Phoebe drove to the lake. The night before, Whit woke from a nightmare and Phoebe read to him until he fell back asleep. But it was an unsettled sleep and Whit was exhausted. Phoebe hoped a walk in the woods would "pep him up."

Once at the lake she ran ahead as she spotted a bunch of wildflowers that she wanted to pick. As she got closer, she saw a deer lying on its side in the flowers, half of its right flank torn to the bloody bone. She was fascinated by the juxtaposition of the deer's peaceful, beautiful body among the flowers and its gruesome, fatal injury. She was able, I heard my mother once explain, to tolerate such graphic images of death. Then Phoebe, thinking quickly and knowing a scene like this could unhinge her increasingly despondent brother, gently guided him away. He never saw it.

When I was younger, I thought about that scene a lot. I imagined that I'd have been just as strong had I found the deer. For a while I even found myself saying, when something challenging happened at school, what would Phoebe do? She was so helpful, such a lofty model to emulate. I hadn't meant for this to happen. Over the years, others had pointed out my connection to Phoebe, but there was something mortifying about Logan acknowledging it so publicly tonight.

I glanced at my mother, who was now into the late 1800s in her Southeast Asia dissertation. Did it mean something that she'd dropped her eyes and wouldn't answer when the woman asked about *Listen's* origins? I rubbed my eyes and looked at my watch. It was almost nine. Everyone would be expecting us soon.

"Well, that was a disaster." My dad kissed my mother on the cheek and sat. He took a long drink from his wine and began cutting his steak. "I don't think I've ever seen Logan like that."

"Where is he?" my mother asked.

"In our room, passed out in the bed next to ours," he said, mouth full of steak. "He'll sleep it off and be fine. Nasty hangover tomorrow, I'm afraid."

"Logan was totally obnoxious tonight," I said.

"Logan is very drunk and very heartbroken," he said. "I can't imagine that he believed anything he said."

"And so that excuses him?" I asked.

My dad sighed. He'd had a lot to drink, too. Maybe in the morning they'd all blame this on a night with too much alcohol and we'd never speak of it again. If there was one thing I could count on in my family, it was that we didn't dwell on conflict. We didn't discuss bad behavior. My mother set a good example for that.

It didn't take Dad long to finish eating. Now that Lee and I were done, too, I wanted to go. Nothing we were facing tonight could be as awkward as this dinner.

"Thank you," Lee said as we stood. "Dinner was really good."

"We could have done without the fireworks." My dad pulled out his wallet and handed me a twenty-dollar bill. "Here, take a cab up north, not the subway."

"Thanks," I said.

"Good luck tomorrow morning," Lee said to my mother.

"Thank you," she said. "Nice to see you again, Lee."

I kissed my mother on the cheek and we were off.

Outside, the rain had stopped and a damp, humid smell rose up from the concrete. A foggy mist hung so low that we couldn't see the tops of the buildings. The hotel concierge told us that he'd call a taxi, but I wanted to walk for a bit. Maybe it would help clear my head and settle my stomach.

The lights from the hotel cast long shadows across the pavement as we walked toward Michigan Avenue. Then Lee asked, "What was *that* about?"

"Logan was drunk," I said.

"No, I know that. I meant, what was going on with your mom?"

I felt a cold ripple in my chest. "Logan hurt her feelings."

"No, before he arrived," she said. "Your mom was so, I don't know. I've seen her be really opinionated and all. And you've always talked about how much her writing means to her. But I've never seen . . . well . . ."

"Well, *what?*" What was she trying to say? What had she seen?

"She seemed so different tonight." Lee's voice was slower, careful. "She was so, well, almost like . . . well, needy, maybe that's it? And she reminded me . . . Well, I guess I just haven't ever seen her like that. It kinda surprised me. That's all."

"I've told you that she's moody." I spoke quickly, sharply. "I've told you that for years."

"I know, I know," Lee said. "I don't know what I'm saying. I'm sorry."

An ominous feeling had followed me out of the hotel and I wanted it to go away. I didn't want to be in a bad mood. Not now.

"I guess you really take care of her, don't you?" she asked.

"We all take care of her, *Lee,* not just me."

"Okay."

Michigan Avenue was filled with people walking, cars and taxis rushing, and storefront lights blazing. A few blocks over I knew Lake Michigan waited, huge and silent, like a sleeping bear. When we flew over this afternoon, I couldn't take my eyes off it. A lake that size in the middle of the country?

A sudden weightiness settled in my chest. I imagined the lake rising and raging and then barreling down Michigan Avenue, flooding the stores and sweeping away cars and taxis. Sweeping me under, too, until I drowned. And if I were to be opened up afterward in an autopsy under bright, unforgiving lights, what would the doctors find? Maybe nothing. I would be the empty girl with no organs, no identity, no convictions, no courage, no passion.

Stop this!

I shivered. "Let's get a ride."

We flagged down a taxi. In the back seat we were quiet as we headed north along Lake Shore Drive. The lake was on our right—the lights reflected off the water near the shore—and beyond that was a huge, black, endless nothing.

"Are you okay?" Lee asked. "Do you want to talk about what Logan said?"

"No."

How embarrassing and humiliating. I *hated* this attention from Logan, from Lee. I hated it more than anything. I belonged on the other end, listening. I tried to think of something to ask Lee. I tried to think of something to ask the taxi driver.

"I guess you have to consider the source," Lee said. "You've told me a hundred times that you and Logan aren't close. What did he mean that he was dying? And what was that about a zoo?"

"Logan was just being dramatic." I leaned forward and looked at the identification and picture tacked to the glove compartment.

Ebrahim Jahandar. Interesting. "Excuse me, sir. Where are you from?"

"Iran."

The revolution was less than eight years old. My parents and their friends spent countless dinners poring over what had happened with the hostages and President Carter's attempts to free them (we must not go to war over this, my mother always insisted). I started asking questions. Why did you leave Iran? Where is your family? How do you feel about the revolution? For the rest of the way to Evanston, as we listened to this man's story, I began to feel better.

CHAPTER 14

It had been a ripple effect. First Susie said she wasn't bringing her boyfriend and when I said I wasn't bringing Ben, the others with boyfriends decided to come alone, too. There were sixteen of us at the hotel, out of the original twenty-two who had pledged together, and so from the beginning, the weekend felt more like a reunion than a wedding.

Only three years out of college, we easily fell back into old patterns, especially after a few drinks. It was nice to see everyone and within minutes, I wasn't sure why I'd been so ambivalent. The first night we were up until two, closing down the hotel bar and laughing in the suite. Because there were so many of us, and because it was the first time we'd all been together since graduation, there wasn't much time for in-depth conversations. Everyone seemed to be on hyper mode, screaming when someone new arrived, flitting from topic to topic.

Still, by the next afternoon I'd learned a lot. Ducky was by far the most changed. The weight she'd lost—more than twenty pounds—made her cheekbones stand out and her neck long and lean. She was still the same bubbly girl with the blond eyebrows, but she'd traded in her pearls and pink sweatshirts for expensive pocketbooks and trendy skirts. Everyone had jobs, selling office equipment or working in human resources for big companies. I thought about Lorenzo's comment that people don't change, but to me everyone looked more stylish, more successful, and more mature than we'd been in college.

Now it was late afternoon on Saturday and Sarah, Lee, Julie, and I had just returned from a long lunch. A group of us were drinking in our room and when we'd polished off the last beers, Sarah said to me, "Let's go on a liquor run."

Outside, the skies were overcast but the rain had held off. I had no idea if people would come out for my mother's talk no matter the weather. Had Logan, who was supposed to be in town until Tuesday, gone to it? I hoped so. I also hoped he had a horrible hangover although I was beginning to feel something I'd overlooked last night. He wasn't the only one who would miss Elise.

Mary Poppins. I smiled, thinking about Lee's nickname for Elise. It was perfect, not only because Elise was English but mostly because, like Mary, she made things better whenever she was around. Logan was nicer. My parents were relaxed. She treated me as if I were a peer, a sister. And I loved her observations about our family because they were so insightful and on target. *Logan likes to make money to prove to your mum that he's successful. Your dad enjoys taking care of your mum. You will be a great mum someday.*

How did she know so much?

But now Elise was in love with someone else. Did this mean I'd never see her again? Would it be okay to write to her? Would she want to hear from me?

We started down the street.

"Amy said that most of Dougy's friends are staying at the Hilton across town," Sarah said. "I'm glad. It's fun just being with all of us."

"Agree," I said. Had Christopher arrived? Was he staying across town, too? I imagined catching his eye in the church, and how he'd smile, surprised to see me dressed in something so out of character. Would we flirt? Would there be sparks?

Sarah walked quickly, her short legs taking long strides. She wore her curly red hair longer now and I thought she had unusually large circles under her eyes but otherwise she hadn't changed much. She asked, "How's Ben?"

"Good." I stared at my feet as I walked. I felt guilty at how excited I was to see Christopher, and I didn't want to think about Ben right now.

"Are you guys going to get engaged or what?" she asked.

I shrugged. We turned the corner and up ahead I saw a liquor store.

"You don't know or you're just being

mysterious about it?" she asked. "Because that would be right in character with you."

"Shut up." I laughed. "I honestly don't know. We don't talk about it."

She sighed. "I wish I could find someone. Meeting people is impossible. And med school's so hard."

"Yeah, but you're going to be a great doctor," I said.

"If I get through school. God, it was tough just getting away for a weekend. Speaking of that, how did you get Lee to come?"

I felt the muscles tense across my back. "She wanted to come. We couldn't miss Amy's wedding."

"Well, it's good to see her," she said. "Last year, I planned a trip to New York and called her, like, three months ahead of time but she couldn't meet me. I've called her so many times but she's worse than you are. She hardly ever calls back."

I glanced at Sarah, surprised. Lee had never told me this.

"No one else talks to her anymore, either," Sarah said. "And I'm worried."

"I talk to her every day." I was a good friend to Lee. I called and went to see her. A lot. Sarah should *know* this. Then maybe she wouldn't be so worried. But I cringed as I looked at my feet. Why was it so important that Sarah know this?

"Well, what's going on with her?" She didn't

wait for an answer. "She's too thin and not excited about her job. She told me that she's a goddam secretary and makes her boss's squash court reservations. What the hell is that?"

"She has to start at the bottom." I held open the liquor store door and Sarah walked in ahead of me. Frigid air from the air-conditioning unit above the door blasted us and raised the hairs on the back of my neck and arms. The store smelled as if someone had spilled from a keg two years ago and forgot to clean up. We walked to the back, pulled out three six-packs, and then went to the checkout.

"She wanted to make movies." Sarah put the beer on the counter and glanced at me. "That's all she talked about. And now she's some asshole's secretary?"

"It's a hard industry to break into."

We paid for the beer and walked outside. The sky was lighter with patches of blue between gray clouds. This should make Amy, whose reception tonight was outside on the lake, happy. I should be happy, too. I had my new dress. I was glad to be here. But I was beginning to feel miserable in a deep-in-my-bones kind of way.

"She told me about Thailand," Sarah said. "What do you think about that?"

"It's risky," I said.

"It sounds more interesting than making squash court reservations."

I shifted the beer to my other arm. Sarah was a lot like Ben. They both assessed a situation and made a decision. But Sarah didn't know how unpredictable Lee was or the many bad decisions she'd made over the last three years. I glanced at her as we turned the corner. She was frowning as we walked. Goddam it. Why did she do this to me every time we talked? Why was she so judgmental? Why ask a million questions? I made a mental list of the things I'd done to help Lee. I said, "Last year she joined a running club in New York that I found for her. And—"

"What does she say about what happened?" Sarah asked. "In Florida."

I stared at my feet again, concentrating on putting one foot in front of the other. "She doesn't talk about it."

"We really screwed up that night. We should've insisted that she go to the hospital. She should've been checked out and not just for her lip. For *everything*."

"She didn't want to go," I said. "Remember? She wanted to leave Daytona."

"She didn't know what she wanted. She was a mess! The whole thing was a mess. And remember how she asked me if there was something wrong with her eyes? She should've had her eyes checked out, too."

"What?" I startled. "I don't remember that."

"You don't? Really? You don't remember how she asked me to check them? I couldn't see anything but then I worried that when I broke the window a glass shard had gotten into one of her eyes or something."

"I don't remember that," I said.

Sarah shrugged. "Maybe that happened when you and Ducky went to get food? I don't know. The whole night was such a fucking mess."

How could I not remember this? I cringed, thinking that I'd somehow either forgotten or wasn't privy, which was worse, to this detail.

"And I still don't understand why she was standing there in her clothes, with her backpack at her feet. If Lee was raped, which I have no doubt that she was, when did she get dressed? How had that happened?"

I couldn't breathe. I began gulping breaths.

Sarah sighed. "Has she ever, you know, told you about what happened?"

"No," I squeaked.

"I don't know, Clare." Sarah shook her head. "She doesn't look so good."

Tears sprang into my eyes and my heart began pounding and I had this terrible sense that I was running but couldn't catch whatever I was chasing. I didn't want Sarah or Ducky to think that I'd failed. That I hadn't kept Lee safe. I just wanted—more than anything—for them to forgive me.

I startled. But how could they forgive me when they didn't even know what I'd done?

A car sped up behind us, screaming voices piercing the air. Ducky slowed her little red convertible and Julie leaned out the passenger window and said, "Get in! We're going to get more beer!"

I held up the bag. "We've already got some."

"Okay, well, we're off to get more," Ducky said. "Be back in a minute!"

Sarah chuckled as Ducky pulled away. "Can you believe her? Who would've ever thought?"

But I couldn't think about Ducky. I was trying to talk myself out of crying.

More than a dozen people were squeezed into our room. I ducked into the bathroom, washed my face, and waited until I'd calmed. Then I went back out with everyone. By this time, Ducky and Julie had joined us, too. The noise was deafening as everyone talked and laughed. Then Julie stood on the bed, put her fingers in her mouth, and whistled so loudly that everyone groaned but finally quieted.

"Remember when we went behind the house and got high in that stranger's car?" she asked. Everyone started screaming and laughing again. I turned to Lee, who watched from across the room, arms crossed as she leaned against the wall. *She doesn't look so good.* But she looked the way she always did, didn't she?

I thought about the time a few years ago when I took the train down to see her. We met at Penn Station and bought bagels and a slab of cheddar cheese from a convenience store on Sixth Avenue. It was a warm spring day, the buds popping out on the trees and the sky brilliant blue, and we walked all over Manhattan. She was quiet and gloomy—I couldn't remember what the problem was that time. I *did* remember how I felt her intensity sucking the life out of everything. But I got her going. I got her laughing. By the time we stopped for dinner in Chinatown, she was happier. That was the thing that no one, not Sarah or Ducky or Ben or Patricia Graceson knew about her. That her intensity could suck the life out of everything and that she looked to me, and only me, to help her get out of it.

"And remember how the owner of the car opened his door and said, 'What's going on?'" Julie yelled over the shrieks and laughter.

Everyone screamed again. And I let myself smile and even laugh a little because I remembered this funny story and didn't want to keep worrying.

And then there was another story and one after that. I passed out beers and popped one open for myself. Soon, Lynn and her group left. Ducky went to the suite and came back. The phone rang. Someone was screaming in the hall. More people left. Others arrived. I went to the bathroom again and when I walked back into the room, I saw that almost everyone had gone. I stretched out on the bed. Soon we'd have to get ready for the wedding.

Lee was talking to Lisa and Susie. I rolled onto my side, away from them, and listened to Sarah and Ducky, who were sitting on the floor by the window. And then suddenly Ducky, in mid-sentence, stopped talking. Sarah lowered her beer from her mouth in slow motion. I rolled over. Susie and Lisa had gone and now it was just the four of us—Ducky, Sarah, Lee, and me—alone in the room. No one had to say anything. I was quite sure we were all thinking the same thing, that this was the first time we'd been alone together since our spring break trip. That we were in a hotel room made the moment even more pronounced.

Lee was still dressed in her running clothes from the morning, the same blue shorts and white T-shirt that I'd seen her wear hundreds of times. She stared at Ducky, waiting for her to finish what she was saying, a slight smile on her lips. But when Ducky and Sarah dropped their eyes, Lee's smile faded and she looked at me. My breath caught in my throat—I tried to cover it up by coughing—but I didn't fool her. She lowered herself onto the edge of the bed.

"You guys are acting like somebody died," she said. "Come on."

Ducky glanced at me and then at Lee. This was

why I hadn't come back to visit. I didn't want to do *this*. I didn't want to talk with Ducky and Sarah about what had happened in Florida.

"So many times I thought about our spring break trip, Lee." Ducky's voice was serious in a way that wasn't familiar. "Sometimes it was all I thought about. Did you get those messages I left for you?"

I looked at Lee. She hadn't told me that Ducky had called her, either.

Lee nodded. "I called you back. Right?"

"You called me back once," she said. "I left a bunch of messages. I wanted to know if you were okay."

Sarah and Ducky exchanged looks again. Lee licked her lips and said, "Yeah, I'm okay. I'm sorry. I'm really sorry."

"You don't have to apologize," Ducky said. "I just feel bad. About everything. And that we never really, like, talked about it when we got back to school."

"Oh." Lee's voice was soft, hesitant. "Don't feel bad, Ducky. It's okay. I had a rough couple of years but I'm okay." She glanced at me, mouth parted as if trying to call for help but couldn't get the words out.

My heart had started to throb and I was suddenly light-headed, dizzy. I pulled myself up until I was sitting against the headboard, my legs crossed under me. I felt so much pressure on my chest and in my lungs. I felt as if I could barely breathe.

"Do you not want to talk about it?" Sarah asked.

"Talk about it?" Lee said.

"We talk about it." My voice sounded to me as if it belonged to someone else. Lee shot a look at me.

"Well, I'm glad about that." Sarah shook her head. "But I'm sorry. I still don't understand what happened that night. Everything feels mixed up. Like, how did Clare get away and you didn't?"

I felt ringing in my ears that seemed to pierce my eardrums and vibrate through my head. Someone was screaming. *I* was screaming, only it was inside of me and I didn't think anyone could hear it. No! Don't talk about this! Because I led everyone to believe that I was lucky to have gotten away and Lee was unlucky. That it was a fluke, maybe even that I'd been smarter, slyer, faster. I was the one who knew what to do and what to say.

Lee stared at Ducky—she didn't look at me—but I saw the muscles in her jaw tighten and her eyes blink. I knew that look. I saw it on Logan's face last night at the restaurant and I'd seen it on my mother's, too. It was the look of heartbreak, when you realized that something wasn't as it seemed.

"Clare was just quicker." Lee's voice was a whisper. "I guess."

I started to cry. Everything about this was wrong. Lee just saved me the embarrassment of having to admit that I let them believe I'd gotten away on my own merit and not because she'd sacrificed herself for me. Just saying this made me sick. I was a phony. Tell them!

"I've been talking to a resident in emergency room medicine, not about you but about this topic," Sarah said. "It's complicated. Have you seen a counselor? There are support groups, too. What happened can impact you for a long time."

Lee nodded and still wouldn't look at me. I felt tears stream down my face and pool in the corners of my mouth.

"God, Clare, are you okay?" Ducky asked.

"It affected the rest of us, too," Sarah said. "Clare was there."

If only you knew. If only I wasn't such a coward.

"You look really tired," Sarah said to Lee. "And too skinny."

All eyes were on Lee, just like in the old days when she walked into a room and heads turned to see what she was doing or to listen to what she was saying. I felt a jab in my stomach as I cried. I was a flood, a faucet. I couldn't stop.

"Work isn't so great," Lee said.

"What about going to Thailand?" Sarah asked.

Lee's elbows were on her knees and she turned her hands over, palms up, and stared at them. "I don't know. It's kinda risky."

"But you'd be getting back to filmmaking, what you love, right?" Sarah asked.

Lee nodded.

"Jesus Christ, Clare." Sarah frowned at me. She was disappointed. Maybe guilt was stamped all over my face. I wiped my wet cheeks with the back of my hand.

No one said anything for a moment.

"Look, I'm just going to say this," Ducky began. "What happened to you was a tragedy, there's no way around it. But I've always admired you, Lee. You were the only person I knew who was excited and sure about what you were going to do with your life. I guess I never told you this because I was such a screwup and so intimidated by you. But don't let what happened stop you from reaching your dream. You deserve to go for your dream, Lee. Am I making sense?"

"Amen." Sarah raised her beer bottle.

Then Julie bounded into the room, telling us that we only had forty minutes to get ready. I stood, went into the bathroom, and closed the door. And then I sat on the toilet and sobbed. I barely knew what I was crying about anymore. I just knew that I couldn't stop.

CHAPTER 15

I saw Christopher before he saw me. We'd gotten to the church early and I'd turned in the pew to watch the others entering at the back and suddenly there he was, behind a group, taller than I'd remembered and better looking. His wavy brown hair was short on the sides and long in front—a trend I'd seen a lot of lately. And yet unlike other men, who announced their new locks every five seconds by flipping their hair out of their faces, Christopher seemed at ease. He smiled as he talked to a man next to him, and in my mind I saw him walking down the halls of Congress, confident in what he was saying. Confident in his hair. I imagined introducing him to my parents and not caring if he told them he was a Republican.

"Clare!" Susie squealed from the pew behind me. "Now I know why you're wearing that sexy red dress. *Look!*"

The others turned. A few gasped and laughed. Some, who hadn't known, whispered, "What are you talking about? Who?"

I felt my cheeks redden and turned to face the front. I still felt a little sick about what happened earlier in the hotel room. I didn't feel so good in my dress, either. It was too tight. Too revealing. Too much the same color as a fire truck.

I glanced at Lee, who sat several people over at the end of the pew. She wore a simple blue peasant dress that made her look thin, almost concave, across her chest and shoulders. She stared at the altar, dark eyes not blinking and her face still. She'd barely spoken to me, barely even looked at me, since this afternoon. *Clare was just quicker, I guess.* Of course she was angry with me, for leaving her that night, for not telling our friends the truth. I needed to apologize. And I needed to apologize soon.

Once the ceremony started, I didn't turn around to find Christopher and yet I kept thinking about him. I went over our time together, the excitement I felt seeing him in Nick's, the anticipation of going home with him, the late nights across his bed, and those wonderful hands and thick lips. But I decided that when I saw him at the reception, I wouldn't talk about this. I'd ask questions about his job. We'd catch up, like old friends. I wouldn't betray Ben if this was all we did.

The service was quick, a few Bible verses, a few funny anecdotes, a long, passionate kiss and then they were pronounced husband and wife. I didn't see Christopher again until we were outside on the steps. His arm was lightly touching a woman's back as the two of them walked toward the parking lot.

Oh. Of course. Just because I'd come here

single, didn't mean he did. Had I forgotten the dance pictures in his bedroom? The way every girl on campus seemed to know his name?

When Ducky yelled, "Who's riding with me," I followed.

Amy's parents' house was a small, two-story Colonial—nice, but not fancy. The yard, however, was spectacular. Long and wide, it sat high on a ledge with sweeping views of Lake Michigan. Dozens of tables, chairs, and a small dance floor were dwarfed under the biggest tent I'd ever seen. It was a large wedding, maybe two hundred people, and all around me there were cheers, laughter, excitement, and drinking. People were in the mood to celebrate.

Five of us—including Lee—had squished into Ducky's back seat on the way here, everyone talking and music blaring. Sitting next to Lee, I'd complimented her on her dress and asked if she'd talked to Susie, who was thinking of moving to New York. She answered with one-word responses. Now I turned to her. She stared at the lake, seemingly oblivious to the people around her, a distant, familiar look in her eyes. I could feel her heaviness seep into my skin.

Ducky, at the bar at the edge of the tent, called us over.

"Come on, let's get a drink," I said.

Lee turned, walked across the grass to the edge of the yard, and stopped, hugging her arms to her chest as she stared at the lake. If I hurried over, took her arm and dragged her to the bar—made her laugh and got her to talk—I could pull her out of her gloomy mood. I knew how to do this.

"*Clare!*" Ducky called.

But God, I needed a drink first. And so I turned and walked toward Ducky.

Later, after dinner had been served and the band was setting up next to the cake table, I ran into Christopher, who was alone, as I came out of the bathroom in the house. I gasped and brought my hand to my chest.

"We have to stop meeting like this." He grinned. It was so good to see him up close again. I tried not to stare at his lips or think about how wonderful his hands felt on my body. I straightened and pulled down the sides of my dress. "You're avoiding me. You kept running away during cocktail hour."

"I did?" But he was right. As I watched him and his girlfriend work their way toward me in the crowd—God, she was beautiful with her long brown hair and high cheekbones—I stayed a step ahead. I had no interest in meeting her.

"Ah, you're still Miss Vagueness." He laughed and leaned over me, wiggling his eyebrows.

I was a little drunk, the waiter kept filling my glass and the Chardonnay was so good, but not enough to be fooled. I was suddenly glad that he'd brought a date, a girlfriend—whatever she was—because it gave me cover. "And *you're* still a big flirt."

He laughed again and took a long drink from his wine. I glanced down the hall where I heard voices in the kitchen, dishes being stacked, water running in the sink and then back at Christopher, who was staring at me. He said, "So, it's been a while. How are you?"

"Good. And you? You're still in Washington?"

He nodded and took another sip of wine.

"What are you doing there?"

"A little of this. A little of that." He drained his wine and smiled. Then he reached down, took my left hand, and raised it to eye level. "Not engaged to the baseball player yet? I thought that was a done deal."

"He's in Philadelphia and I'm in Boston. So . . ." I felt my cheeks redden and pulled my hand away. Why did I say that? "Looks like you're doing okay for yourself. You're serious enough to bring your girlfriend with you today."

He wrinkled his nose, laughed, and shook his head. "She's not my girlfriend."

"Right."

We both moved against the wall when a waiter, carrying a tray of dirty dishes, walked past us. Christopher slipped his empty glass onto the tray and then turned to me and crossed his arms. "I grew up not far from here and so I'm staying with my parents this weekend. Kim's a friend from high school. That's all."

"I'm sure that's true." I laughed. He didn't smile but shrugged and looked over my shoulder down the hall. I straightened and chided myself for having so much wine. Don't make a fool of yourself!

"You look great," he said. "You're beautiful. I still don't think you know that."

My cheeks began to throb. "Thanks. You look pretty great yourself."

"Thanks." He reached out to touch the strap of my dress. "This dress isn't like you. You were always so, let's see, au naturel. You know, the T-shirt and jeans girl."

I knew it. I looked like an imposter. I was bloated from the wine and bread and butter and chicken Kiev and suddenly felt as if my dress were strangling my stomach and intestines. This dress belonged on someone like, well, his date. "Sorry to disappoint you."

"No, no! I like the dress. It looks good on you." He lowered his hand. "You left school without saying goodbye."

"You didn't say goodbye to me, either." I squeezed my hands into fists. I felt my head spin—it was the wine and the conversation—and I wanted to be in control.

He shrugged. "I was at Nick's on graduation night. And you weren't."

It was true. I hadn't gone there that last night. After saying goodbye to my parents, I'd helped Lee pack and then had gone over and helped Ben pack, too. And what did I do afterward? Did I promise to meet him and forgot?

He burst out laughing. "I'm kidding! I was long gone after graduation."

I shifted my feet, unsure what to think. Then I smelled the smoke from his cigarette and the taste of all those beers. What would have happened if I'd gone with him to Washington? Would we still be together? People began to crowd the hall, some wanting the bathroom and others looking for more to drink. Sarah and Susie walked in and told me that it was almost time for the father-daughter dance.

As I turned to say goodbye to Christopher, he leaned over again and whispered, "We have unfinished business, don't you think?"

Then there was a big cheer as Dougy, his bowtie undone and hanging down his chest, walked into the hallway, a bottle of champagne clutched in his hand. I hurried out into the night behind Sarah. I felt as if I'd been sucked back into a head-spinning time warp. Partying with college friends. Worrying that Lee was angry with me. Unsure what to think about Christopher.

"I couldn't tell if you needed rescuing or not," Sarah said.

I didn't know, either. "Thanks." We walked

to our table under the tent. Band members were milling around, talking and tuning instruments.

"Oh, God, look at Ducky," Sarah said. Although there wasn't any music yet, she'd run onto the parquet and started dancing with a tall, good-looking guy with short hair and a thick, square jaw. She wore a strapless, light blue dress like the other bridesmaids, but on her the dress was perfect. Her hair was short and her skin tanned golden brown. She smiled as her partner swung her out and then yanked her back to his chest. Everyone began laughing and clapping. Ducky waved to the crowd, beaming, as if she were having the time of her life.

"You know, that night in Florida completely freaked me out," she'd whispered to me a few hours ago while we stood in line for the bathroom. "After college when I moved downtown, I was terrified. If I was out late, I worried I was being followed. I thought every man I met wanted to attack me. I had two bolt locks installed on my apartment door. It was awful! Then one day I decided that I couldn't live like that."

"What did you do?" I leaned closer so I wouldn't miss a word.

"I signed up for a self-defense class at a gym. And that led me to an aerobics class that led me to running. I started feeling stronger, physically, which made me feel stronger all over, I guess. I'm not the deepest person in the world. I know that doesn't surprise you! But that night made me afraid of everything. It *changed* me. And so I had to change, too. Do you ever think about what that night did to you?"

If only she knew. That night changed everything. I nodded.

"I know how upsetting this is. You cried so hard today in the hotel room." Ducky wrinkled her forehead in concern. "But I'm glad you've been a good friend to Lee. This morning she told me that you call her every day and see her, like, once a month. I hope this doesn't sound corny, but that just warms my heart. I'm not surprised. You were always good at helping people. You were the house therapist."

Her compliments made me so uneasy that I couldn't look into her eyes. I had to stare at her white eyebrows. Then it was her turn to use the bathroom and after that I lost her in the crowd and we never picked up the conversation. But now, watching her dance, I wished I'd said this to her: that night completely messed me up, too. Because it proved that I wasn't good at helping people, after all. No wonder Lee was a mess. I was good at saving myself.

Ducky, giggling, bowed to her partner and they walked off the floor. Then the music began, a soft, sappy tune that brought out Amy and her dad. I drank my wine and held out my glass so the waiter could fill it again. I glanced at Lee, who stood with two older women—somebody's mothers—as they watched Amy and her dad. Then she turned, smiled at the women, and said something that made them laugh. All night I'd watched her, animated and talkative with others.

I thought about the weekend last year when she drove up to Boston with Phillip, a guy she was kind of seeing. The three of us had gone to the Head of the Charles. It was cold and snowy and the flakes were giant, the size of quarters. Lee and I glanced at each other and without speaking, without planning, began running through the crowd along the river, trying to catch flakes on our tongues. I remembered being happy in a complete kind of way, as I often felt with Lee before everything went bad. Later, drinking beers at a bar, I imagined that one day I'd marry Ben and Lee would marry Phillip and we'd live in the same town and raise our children together. When I told this to Lee, we both burst out laughing.

But there was a difference between Lee's laughing then and now. Because at the moment she was barely talking to me.

When the band broke into a loud disco song, "Stayin' Alive," most everyone jumped up to dance. I looked for Christopher but couldn't find him. Instead, I saw Lee slip away from the crowd and out through the back of the tent. Her flight to New York in the morning was much earlier than my flight to Boston. This was it. I chugged my wine and fortified with Chardonnay, I somehow found the courage.

I followed her as she walked on the narrow, sandy path and then down the wood stairs. I paused while she took off her shoes and disappeared into the darkness. At the bottom of the stairs, I slipped out of my sandals and walked across the cool, hard sand to the water. Millions of stars stretched across the sky and gentle waves lapped the shore. I fought a nervous urge to run back to the reception, to the safety of lights, people, and happiness. As I walked toward her, the voices and music faded and a breeze pulled my hair across my face.

In the moonlight her dress looked white and her dark eyes seemed to melt into the shadows on her face. She turned to the lake and opened her palms in front of her. "Have you ever seen anything like this? It's *beautiful*."

I startled. I hadn't expected her to talk about beauty.

"Look at how the moonlight and stars change the color of the water," she said. "It looks black and then the light makes it look silver. Water reflects what's around it. Right? Water's funny like that, don't you think, how it changes?"

She didn't wait for my answer but tilted back her head and took a deep breath. I shifted my feet and looked up, too. I tried to see what she saw, tried to feel what she felt, but I was too anxious.

Underneath this talk of beauty, I knew she was still angry with me.

"I don't mind being in the dark," she said. "Sometimes, if it's too bright, you can't see anything. You know? But if it's darker, you somehow can. That was such a revelation to me just now."

I had no idea what she was talking about. "Lee."

"Know what I was thinking about today?" she asked. "The Rat Man case. Remember how we spent weeks, months, talking about it? Remember how at first we were horrified that the guy had to experience it, and then we wondered how the torturer had come up with such a thing? Remember what we decided?"

Of course I remembered. It was one of Freud's most famous studies; in it, a patient talks about a torture method he'd heard from a military officer whereby a rat would eat its way into the anus of a victim. It freaked us out. It still freaked me out. But what did this have to do with anything? Still, I didn't want to upset her. "We wondered if the torturer had had this done to him, too."

"Right! That's what we decided. I wonder if we could ever find this out. You know, so we would know for sure."

The breeze blew my hair across my face again, and I felt my hand tremble against my cheek as I pulled it away. I was fairly certain that she was talking about more than the Rat Man case. "I feel horrible about today and not telling Sarah and Ducky that you, well, you know, that you told me to go that night. That you'd stay. I don't blame you for being mad."

She kept her face tilted away from me. "I'm not mad at you for not telling them. And I'm not mad at you for leaving. I told you to go."

"But you're mad about something."

She glanced at me. "You know what was odd today? You told them that we talk a lot about what happened."

"We talk every day."

"But not about what happened. I hardly ever bring it up but when I do, you cry or get defensive. Then I feel bad because you feel terrible about everything."

Wait, *I* cry? *I* get defensive?

"You know what?" Her voice was suddenly so soft that I had to lean into her to hear. "I think I've been depressed all these years and just going through the motions of living."

"But you've been okay, too, right?" I stammered. "I know you don't like your job but you've got a new apartment now and—"

"Remember how we used to talk about our psychology classes and Patricia and everything? It was so much fun. It made me feel so *alive*. I don't think we do that much anymore because what happened gets in the way. It shuts us down or something. We don't talk about anything meaningful anymore."

I shook my head. I didn't feel shut down. And I wasn't fucked up, either. "What do you mean we don't talk about anything meaningful?"

"It's all about jobs and logistics." She sighed loudly. "I've been so stuck."

"We can still talk about all of that," I said.

I didn't think she heard me. She'd turned toward the water and her voice was dreamy and distant. "It was *something* today when Ducky said that I deserved my dream. The good dream, the happy dream. I want to figure out how to get back to that. Honestly, I don't know what I've been doing the last three years."

"Living in New York. That was always part of your dream, too, you know."

"I want to make films." Lee's voice choked with tears. "It's the only thing I've ever really wanted. I can't let my life slip away. That's what's been happening, you know. I've got to do something. Now. I've got to take some risks."

"Risks, like going to Thailand?" I asked.

"Maybe. Other risks, too. Like, thinking about things, you know? What am I doing? What's important? What kind of filmmaker do I want to be? What kind of person? Is this a life worth living?" She paused. "Maybe you should ask yourself some questions, too."

I felt myself stiffen. "I'm happy with the way I am."

"Really?" Her voice was abrupt and tinged with anger. "You can truly say that you have no questions about yourself? Nothing you want to rethink? No regrets?"

I frowned. "Other than leaving you in that hellhole? No."

But I wasn't so sure. She'd surprised me with this talk and I wasn't reacting well. Something was growing inside her, excitement over getting back to her dream, or maybe anger.

"You introduced me to this kind of thinking and talking," she said.

"In college? For God's sake, we were all experimenting and testing things out back then," I said. "But I can't live with that kind of chaos. It's too hard to keep asking questions and *evolving*. People are counting on me. At some point, you accept things and live with them."

"We're only twenty-five!" she cried. "Don't you *die* if you stop growing?"

"Lee—"

She burst into tears. "I don't want to die. And that'll happen if I stay like this. I know it. You know it, too. We have to change. We both do! We can't die!"

She was scaring me. I felt the muscles seize in my lower back and I stepped back. "I just want to be happy."

"Please don't be defensive, Clare," she cried. "*Please!*"

"I don't understand what we're even talking about! Why does everything have to be such a big drama all the time?"

"Because that's how it feels to me! And I bet it would happen to you if you'd just let yourself feel, too," she said.

"You think I don't *feel?*"

We were yelling at each other now, our voices echoing off the water.

"I have no idea *what* you feel sometimes," she yelled. "Last night as we were leaving the restaurant and you were upset, I thought, okay, here we go. You were exposed and hurting and I thought I could help. But you can't stand to feel that way. You can't be open and *vulnerable* with me. Or anyone!"

"My brother was being a complete jerk to me and my mother!" I yelled.

"And that's another thing," she said. "I never realized how much you take care of her. I was shocked! You never told me that! You keep everything so close to the vest, especially with your family. *God!* I'm an idiot. I look to you *way* too much. How are you supposed to help me when you don't even know what *you* feel?"

"That's so mean."

"Mean? It's truthful."

"It's *mean!*" I was screaming so much that I sprayed saliva down the front of me.

"Me, *mean?*" Lee yelled. "How can you say that? After what *you* did?"

The words sent a shudder down my back. "I knew it! You say you're not mad at me for leaving, but you are. You had those premonitions and dreams before we left for spring break about how I was going to leave you. Then you made it happen. *You're* the martyr and yet you're pissed at me!"

I'd never screamed at anyone like this. I barely knew what I was saying and wasn't sure I even meant it. Premonitions? *Martyr?*

"You have no idea what you did on the Florida trip, do you?" She was still angry but her voice wasn't as loud.

"Other than leave you? No. Tell me!"

"You *fucking* figure it out." And then she turned and walked back up the beach to the stairs.

I started to cry again—why was I always crying?—as I watched her go. I began to shiver although I wasn't cold and I didn't want to think about Florida but I couldn't help it. I turned to face the water. The cold rain on the Outer Banks. Sleeping in Sarah's car. The Sigma Chis. Donny's house. Charlie's house. The Jittery Man. The window. Let her go, I'll stay. Glass shattering. Hurry. *Hurry!* So many things had gone wrong on that trip. How was I supposed to *fucking figure it out?*

"Clare! Clare, where are you?" Sarah yelled. I saw her silhouette at the top of the stairs. "Clare?"

"Yeah," I said.

"Come on! You're missing everything. We're just about to take a picture of all of us. From the house."

I turned back to the water. What had I done that was worse than leave her or not tell the truth to the others? How was I supposed to figure this out?

"Clare, come on," Sarah yelled. "We need you!"

I cringed. So many people needed me. It was unfair, that people asked so much of me. But I shook my head because this made no sense. Sarah needed me only for a picture. Get it together! I wiped my face, turned, and walked up the stairs.

I was drunk and not myself and after the picture—Lee and I had stood on opposite ends of the group—I plopped down in my chair and stared so hard that I saw two flower centerpieces, not one. I wasn't there for more than a minute when Christopher leaned over from behind and asked me to dance.

I followed him to the floor. Everyone around us was dancing wildly, but Christopher put his arms around my waist and I reached behind his neck and then he drew me close. The heat from our bodies caused my cheeks to flush. I wanted to close my eyes and drift—maybe even sleep—but I was suddenly wired, my heart thundering in my chest.

"This is a surprise," he said. Hair fell over his eyes but he didn't swing it away.

I didn't know what he meant; was it a surprise that we were here together, that my heart still beat madly for him, that I was wearing a dress meant for someone more confident, sexier? I felt my knees begin to wobble and I wanted him to kiss me and why didn't I feel this way with Ben? He didn't take my breath away or make my skin beg. *This* was passion. Was this love, too?

"I'm full of surprises." Then I stumbled, my sandal catching on something, I didn't know what, and Christopher tightened his grip on my waist.

"And full of alcohol," he said. "Which seems to be our routine."

It was true, I was drunk. And I didn't know what I was doing and you fucking figure it out and Sarah and Ducky would be so disappointed in me if they knew and then I rested my head on Christopher's chest. Why hadn't I taken more risks? My God, I lived at home with my college boyfriend. *Live* a little. Take chances. Don't keep everything so close to the vest. Be vulnerable. Let her go, I'll stay.

When the song was over, Christopher dropped

his arms and stepped away from me. His eyes weren't playful and he no longer had that sly grin on his lips. I remembered that somewhere, maybe over near the bar, was a date. A friend.

"What time is your flight tomorrow?" he asked.

"One."

"I'll meet you in the hotel lobby at nine," he said. "We'll get coffee and spend some time together. We'll see if anything's really there."

Did I want to do this? "Are you sure you'll remember?"

"I never forget anything. And I'm never late."

"Right." I laughed, nervous, still unsure.

He reached inside his jacket, pulled out a pen, and wrote *nine a.m.* in black ink on the inside of his palm. And then he wrote it on the inside of my palm, too.

"Okay." I nodded, squeezing my palm closed. He put his pen back, winked, and then walked to the bar. I stumbled over to our table and slid into my chair. At my place was a slice of wedding cake, the white frosting curled into waves on the edges and little red roses so intricate, so perfect in their dimensions, that they looked real. Were they real? Why couldn't I tell?

Sarah, her cheeks rosy and a layer of shimmery sweat across her forehead, plopped down next to me. "This is a blast. I'm so goddam happy to see everyone."

I nodded. But it was too much, this thing with

Christopher, my fight with Lee, and seeing everyone again. And I didn't like balancing on the edge of being very, versus moderately, drunk, either. I kept my fist in my lap, and with my other hand, I took a long drink of water. Across the way Ducky laughed with the handsome square-jawed boy while Susie and Lynn crowded around Amy. I looked for Lee and when I didn't see her, I had to admit that I felt relieved.

CHAPTER 16

At 9:03 the next morning, I stood on the second floor of the hotel and peered over the railing to the lobby. I saw a family with two small children, dressed in swimsuits, walking to the doors leading to the pool. An older couple, sipping coffee, sat at a table next to a giant plant while a younger couple, arms around each other, stared at a map shared between them. Two women, dressed in matching beige shirts with shiny silver nametags, talked quietly behind the counter. I scanned the room again, in case I'd missed him, and found the same results. No Christopher.

I rubbed my screaming temples. A shower hadn't helped my hangover nor had the aspirin I took. I needed coffee. As I started down, I held my hand to my forehead, shielding my eyes from the sunlight that pierced the windows lining the stairs. Next to the concierge desk, I found a coffee urn and poured a cup. I shuddered. Lukewarm, weak, tasteless. No way would Lorenzo serve something this bad.

I looked at my palm. The shower water hadn't erased the bold, sharp letters, *nine a.m.* But now my watch read 9:07. Of course Christopher might be late. He said he was staying with his parents, who lived nearby. Which could mean anything.

Nearby in Evanston. Nearby somewhere on the North Shore. I took another sip, walked to the front of the lobby, and looked out the revolving door. Then I hurried away, not wanting to seem too eager if he suddenly appeared. I felt a sheet of cold sweat on my forehead and wiped it away with my palm. I sat on a couch, hidden behind the plant.

We'd gone to bed by one o'clock but I hadn't slept well. My mind kept spinning from the wine and all that had happened. I felt anxious around Lee and didn't know what to think about Christopher. Would he show? Why was I here? But I knew why. I was still attracted to him. I needed to see if something was there, too.

Lee left early this morning. I heard her wake and shower but I pretended to be asleep until she'd gone. *You fucking figure it out*. Every time I said those words, I tensed and last night's argument began playing in my mind.

The revolving doors turned and I sat up and peered through the plant leaves, but it was only an older man, dressed in a suit and wearing a fedora.

Christopher and I were meeting for coffee, in daylight with people around us. We would see if anything was there. I opened my palm again and stared at the letters. This wasn't a joke.

I moved to the far end of the couch and kept my head down when I saw two of Dougy's friends stop at the front desk and then walk out the door. Suddenly Ben's face flashed in my mind but no, no, no, I wasn't doing anything wrong and couldn't think of him now. I lunged for a newspaper next to me on the couch. I tried to read but couldn't concentrate and when I looked at my watch again, it was nine twenty-five. I walked the length of the lobby, empty now except for the two behind the counter, and stood to the side. A half hour was more than fashionably late. I'd give him five more minutes and then leave. But when nine thirty came and went, I was still there.

What if this *was* a joke? Maybe he'd meant it at the time but had since forgotten. Maybe he was in bed with his friend who was actually his fiancée. Maybe he wrote nine a.m. on several girls' palms last night.

I checked the front desk to see if a message had been left for me. And as the minutes ticked by, I felt a prickly, hot sensation on my neck that began creeping into my cheeks and up to my ears. Even if he arrived now, what did it mean that he was forty minutes late? And that I was still waiting?

I threw my coffee cup into the trash. He wasn't coming. Maybe he wasn't ever coming. I felt so angry and flustered that I had to get out of there before anyone saw me and wondered what I was doing. I hurried up the stairs but instead of shading my eyes again, I looked out the window and saw Christopher strolling across the street toward the hotel. He stopped on the sidewalk below, next to a very pretty woman in a flowered sundress.

I gripped the railing. So, he'd come, after all. Had he been delayed by car trouble? An alarm that didn't work? The woman, her blond hair pulled back in a tight ponytail, was talking and Christopher, a slight smile on his lips, seemed to be listening, attentively. Perhaps she was lost and explaining where she wanted to go? Maybe they knew each other. Any moment now he'd excuse himself—he was forty minutes late, for God's sake—and run into the lobby. Maybe I'd let him wait before I came down. Just so he wouldn't think that I'd been standing there, looking for him, all this time.

But Christopher didn't seem to be in a hurry. Not once did he look up at the hotel or begin to move away. Instead, he leaned over the woman, as I'd seen him do so many times, and smiled as his hair fell into his eyes. When he reached up and tossed it back—how often I'd seen those pretentious Back Bay businessmen do the same thing—I felt last night's overindulgences rumble in my stomach and start up my throat. I gagged and took the back of my hand across my damp forehead.

I imagined our life together, the parties where I'd always wonder about every female he greeted.

The nights I'd be home, worrying about why he was late and who he was with. The flirting that would inevitably dissipate between us and turn into something else. Boredom? Hostility? Or worse, indifference? I deserved this, didn't I? To be with someone unreliable who didn't treat me well, who disappointed me?

No. Maybe I didn't quite deserve Ben, but I didn't deserve this, either.

I hurried up the stairs before I could change my mind.

I got home from Chicago two hours before Ben was due back from work. I let myself in the back door and stood in the kitchen, eyeing the empty tray on which I'd carried my mother's tea and food just three days before. My parents were still in Chicago and tomorrow would go straight to the Vineyard where they'd spend the rest of the summer. Ben and I would have the house to ourselves again.

I perked up. Why not make dinner? I might not be very good at this yet but he always appreciated my effort. I imagined him walking through the door, his tie hanging limply from his neck and his shirt untucked, and smiling as he smelled the meal. I'd set the table with candles and our good china, too.

I felt giddy and fortunate and took the stairs two at a time, unpacked (the red dress went to the back of my closet) and cleaned my room until it was as tidy as Ben's. Downstairs, I washed the dishes in the sink, swept the floor, and then opened the refrigerator. Not much here except yogurt, lox, and the spaghetti sauce I'd made. I opened the container and tasted it; much better than when I'd served it the other night.

I walked to the market where I picked up bread, lettuce, fresh pasta (it cost twice as much as the boxed), and a chunk of expensive Parmesan cheese. Back at the house, I turned on the radio, opened the windows, and got everything together. I didn't mind when Ben called to say that his boss, Patrick, was keeping him later. Because it was so considerate of him to call and because I knew where he was. At his desk. His nose in a book. I could count on this.

Finally, when I heard the front door open two hours later, I rushed through the house and threw myself into Ben's arms. He dropped his backpack and caught me. I kissed him hard on the lips and then lifted his big, brown-framed glasses and kissed his eyelids, too.

"This is a nice surprise." His white button-down, rumpled along the bottom, had three large yellow spots (mustard?) that fell in a perfect line down the front. His cheeks were stubbly from not shaving and his hair, still so short, was streaked with something blue. I touched it with my finger. Was it chalk?

"I missed you," I said.

He grinned. "I missed you, too. How was it?"

I picked up his backpack. "Come on. I'm making dinner."

He followed me into the kitchen and grinned when he saw the table. I handed him a bottle of Budweiser and then stirred the sauce simmering in a pan on the stove. He leaned against the counter, took a drink, and smacked his lips. "I'm psyched that you made dinner! I had cereal both nights because I worked so late."

"Well, my dinners haven't been so great lately," I said.

"Are you kidding? I always love what you make."

See? He appreciated me. And he needed someone to take care of him. I bet I could even get the mustard stains out of his shirt although I'd have to ask someone how to do it. This was the kind of thing Elise might know. I felt a twist in my stomach when I saw her face in my mind. But now was not the time to miss her. Or anyone.

"So, tell me about it." Ben sat at the table.

I wasn't going to think about Christopher again—I planned to put that way, way behind me—and I wasn't ready to talk about Lee or my mother, either. "It was good. But tell me why you worked all weekend."

"It's been *incredible*." Ben sat up, put his elbows on the table, and leaned forward. "Last week this mid-level associate, Johansson, was fired. Patrick called him into his office and the next thing you know he's escorted out of the building. Todd said he lied about work he was doing on Patrick's class action lawsuit. Someone else said he just didn't *do* the work. I think he probably lied and that's why he got canned. You can't do that. Lying ruins your credibility, forever. You know?"

I leaned into the counter until the sharp edge caused a hot burst of pain in my hip. I winced but didn't move and nodded slightly.

"So, now they're desperate," he said. "And get this. Patrick asked *me* to fill in. This never happens to interns. It's a once in a lifetime opportunity."

"Wow." I straightened. "What do you have to do?"

"Can't talk about the lawsuit, it's confidential, but I *can* say that I'm becoming an expert on chemical wood preservation. Did you know that wood preservatives account for the single largest pesticide use in the United States? Take this nasty preservative, chromated copper arsenate. The arsenic in CCA is a known carcinogen. It damages the nervous system and a recent study linked it to birth defects. And yet it's found in all this shit we use. Picnic tables, fences, decks, playground equipment."

He was talking so fast that his sentences ran

into each other. I pointed to his empty beer bottle—did he want another?—but he shook his head.

"You'd think, well, find another preservative that's not toxic. But it's not that simple. Billions of dollars are at stake. The whole thing is fascinating. Know what I kept thinking all weekend? That I'm going to love this. I'm going to love taking on new cases, researching, learning, arguing. God, the weekend flew by. And I brought home more reading to do tonight."

Just look at him, so passionate about his work. It was both comforting and familiar to see him so excited even if I couldn't shake the sting I felt in my chest. Lying ruins your credibility. Yes, it did.

I drained the pasta, mixed it with the sauce, and then carried everything over to the table. He smiled and squeezed my thigh and I thought that maybe tonight we'd go to bed early and I'd rub his back before we fooled around. Or maybe we'd sweep the dishes off the table and do it right here, right now, like in the movies.

"So, you had a fun time?" he asked.

"Well," I said. "I'm happy to be back."

He lifted a forkful of pasta, shoved it into his mouth, and stared at me as he chewed. I had nowhere to go now. I had to talk. I started with Logan and Elise breaking up and how drunk and obnoxious my brother had been during dinner.

"He yelled at my mom about *Listen* and said the restaurant looked like a funeral home, and he bit off my head when I asked about his flight. Then he had the nerve to tell everyone that Phoebe messed me up. Can you believe that?"

I put my fork down, turned my head, and watched him.

"*What?*" Ben asked. "What does a fictional character that your mom dreamed up twenty years ago have to do with you?"

"I know, right?" I laughed even though I felt a rush of disappointment. But it wasn't his fault that he didn't understand. Over the years I'd told him about people comparing me to Phoebe, but I'd always done so in a flippant way and then laughed. Besides, how could he truly understand my mixed up feelings about this when I didn't understand them?

I told him about the wedding and the reception on the lake, Ducky's makeover and Sarah's hours in med school. And then I told him that Lee and I had gotten into a big fight. Just saying her name made my stomach seize.

He stopped chewing, scrunched his forehead—in mock concern—and then grinned. "Does this mean your lesbian love affair is over?"

Usually when he said things like this I punched him in the arm or teased him back. But I was in no mood to laugh. I sighed, suddenly exhausted, put my elbow on the table, and rested my chin on my palm. My hand smelled like the soap I'd used to scrub off the black-inked *nine a.m.*

He cleared his throat. "Okay, what happened?"

"On Saturday, Ducky, Sarah, Lee, and I were in our room," I said. "It was the first time the four of us were alone together since Florida. So of course we started talking about what happened. I don't know, Lee got mad and we had a fight."

"Wait a minute. Why did she get mad?"

I dropped my hands into my lap and then squeezed the sides of my chair until my fingers ached. I shook my head. "It had to be about Florida. I got out and took forever to get back with help. But she said she wasn't mad about that."

You fucking figure it out. I cringed and looked away.

He nodded and shoved another forkful into his mouth. Still chewing, he said, "Look, you did nothing wrong. You escaped and went for help. It's a shame what happened to Lee, but it's not your fault that you got away and she didn't."

I'd never told him the entire story of what happened that night nor was I telling him the full truth about the argument. The smell of this realization seemed to permeate the air like a pan of burned brownies.

The phone rang. Lee! She was calling to apologize or tell me about her new roommates or to say that I didn't need to figure out anything.

Ben stood and walked toward the phone. Then he turned, after the second ring, and as he walked, said, "You called back Joel, right? About the writing center?"

Joel. The writing center. I hadn't called. What if he was on the phone now, calling to yell at me for messing up that woman's paper? Ben would be angry. This would spoil our night.

"You called, right?" Ben reached for the phone.

"Yeah." Something thick and heavy turned over in my stomach and I thought, one lie begets another lie that begets another lie that begets another. I was sliding into something very dark and murky and sticky, and I didn't like it.

Ben picked up the phone and then straightened and said, "Patrick! No, you're not interrupting anything important." He stretched the phone cord—it was so long that once I sat on the driveway while talking to Lee—and went into the dining room.

I pushed away my uneaten plate of pasta and stared at the flame of the candle in the middle of the table. All the energy and giddiness I felt when I first got home had suddenly crashed. I'd just lied to Ben. Tomorrow I had to face Joel with his bloodshot, beady eyes. On the plane, I'd slept instead of worked on my D. H. Lawrence paper. And Lee and I had a big fight.

You fucking figure it out.

Figure out what? What I wanted to do with my

life? Why I didn't take risks? Why I took care of my mother? Why I left Lee with three grown men? I thought about the vision I had of myself in Chicago, the drowned woman whose autopsy revealed nothing inside.

It was a crime not to know who you are. What was it that Patricia told us during the lecture back in college and then again in Lee's film? Life is. Life isn't. It was something about how a life should be lived.

That terrible night in Florida was the problem. Since then, nothing had been the same for Lee and me. Nothing! It was like a roadblock with no detour sign. The proverbial elephant that sat in the room, sucking the oxygen. I'd give anything, *anything at all,* to go back and undo what happened.

"You're not going to believe it!" Ben charged into the kitchen and then stopped and pushed his glasses up the bridge of his nose. "Oh, no. What's wrong?"

I turned in my seat and cried, "Am I a good person?"

"What?" He sat and scooted his chair until our knees were pressed into each other. "What are you talking about? What's wrong?"

"Am I a good person or am I mean?" I began to cry. "I just want to be a good person. I want to be as good as you."

"Clare! You're the nicest person I know. You're

kind. You always ask people about themselves. Is this about your fight with Lee?"

He was so earnest in his mustard-stained shirt and chalk-streaked hair, a spot of spaghetti sauce in the corner of his mouth and smudges on his glasses, and I realized, suddenly, with heartbreaking clarity, that there would always be a part of me that he'd never know.

"What are we doing?" I blurted, terrified. "It's like we're playing house."

Ben scrunched his forehead and looked away, so serious that I wondered if he was thinking about some chemical wood preservation fact. But then he turned to me and said, "We're trying things out, I guess. Right?"

"But what does it mean?" I asked.

Ben, flustered, sat back in his seat and took his hand through his hair. "Look, you're the one who doesn't want to ever talk about us. You keep saying, let's just see how it goes. You've always been like that. Since college."

I sucked in a hot breath. Last night Lee had said, *you keep everything so close to the vest. You can't be open and vulnerable with me. Or anyone!* But I was trying now to be more open, more vulnerable, wasn't I?

"I love you," I said. "I know I do."

He leaned forward, elbows on his knees, and took my hands. They felt soft and warm. He grinned. "I love you, too. You're a good person.

And I've got some amazing news. That was Patrick. He said the partners are thrilled with my work and they're going to offer me a job. They're not going to wait until the end of summer."

A job here in Boston. "That's great. Congratulations."

"It's a great firm and it'll mean so much work. Late nights, weekends. But I can't think of anything more interesting." He squeezed my hands. "We should get an apartment together and think about, you know, getting married or something."

Was this a proposal? I felt a burst of panic in my chest but nodded.

He squeezed my hands again. "This is what I've always wanted. An amazing job like this. And you! This is what I've been hoping for."

And I finally felt relieved because he was so happy and because this was what he always wanted and because just as I felt myself getting smaller and smaller, he pulled me into the safety of his arms.

CHAPTER 17

At the writing center on Tuesday, I had four students, each scheduled for half hour sessions. My first two appointments came on time and both wanted help writing personal essays for comp classes. The third wanted to talk over a sociology essay and the last needed me to proofread his resume. These tasks were fairly straightforward and I felt confident that I'd been reasonably helpful. Packing up, I heard Joel's voice and felt a lump grow in my throat. This was it.

He was on the phone but when he saw me standing in his doorway, he hung up and motioned me in. Leaning back in his chair, he began rubbing his chin. I tried not to look into his bloodshot eyes.

"I'm sorry I didn't call you back," I said. "I was out of town for the weekend."

He lifted his hand from his chin and waved, dismissing my apology. Then he frowned. "Tell me about the student you saw last week."

"I couldn't seem to explain how to support her thesis," I said. "I got flustered. It was my fault. I should have been more patient. I feel terrible that I didn't help her."

He began rubbing his chin again. Behind him a floor-to-ceiling bookcase, jammed with paper

347

and books, reminded me of my mother's office at home. I wasn't a patient person anymore, I decided. I panicked. If I'd been able to take home the woman's paper, where I could slowly and quietly work, where I had time and people weren't staring at me and expecting so much, then maybe I'd have been able to save her. I mean help her. Little dots of sweat broke out across my upper lip.

"I appreciate your willingness to take responsibility," he said. "Students come here seeking help for a variety of reasons. They want a fresh set of eyes or a quick fix. Others have some kind of writing block or disability. In other words, it's not always the tutor's fault for not being able to help."

"Oh." I hadn't thought of this.

"I suggest trying to keep your composure. You can also bring up this case at a writing center meeting. Others might have suggestions. Okay?"

"Thank you."

I stumbled out of his office, down the stairs, and out onto the street. Then I leaned against the building and sighed loudly. The air was damp and heavy and the sun was hidden behind soupy gray clouds. I felt the heat rise up through the pavement and into my feet and the sweat gather under my arms and in the small of my back. And yet I felt cooler somehow, maybe because I was done with the writing center for today. And because I was relieved that Joel hadn't yelled at me. I didn't know why I always assumed I was wrong, but I was grateful for the confidence boost. I'd need it. I was on my way to a private tutoring session that Mr. Donahue, my dad's best friend, had asked me to do, and I wasn't looking forward to it.

I straightened and began to walk but stopped and turned when I heard my name. Lucy, her big black bag swinging on her shoulder, hurried toward me.

"I thought that was you." She stopped in front of me, her droopy eyes squinting and her yellow curls extra frizzy in the humidity. "I'm glad I ran into you. So, did you give my letter to your mom? What did she say?"

It had only been five days since she gave me the letter. No normal person would expect a response this soon. "I was out of town for the weekend and haven't seen her yet."

Lucy's lips dipped into a frown. "There's no urgency if I'm not threatening legal action. Am I right?"

"She was out of town, too," I said. "You know, people can read into things and believe that there's something there when there isn't and—"

"This is *my* story." Her voice was louder, more forceful. "My brother came home from Vietnam completely shattered and I tried to help him. I

349

read to him. I took him on walks. That girl in the story? Phoebe? That was me!"

I felt my nostrils flare and a pain shoot down my jaw from where I was clenching my teeth so tightly. No, *I'm* Phoebe!

I took a deep breath. Thank God I didn't say this out loud. I needed to get it together and not let her confuse and anger me. I needed to think about what to do.

"It's all in the letter," she said. "You should read it. If you still have it."

"Of course I still have it. But my parents are traveling and I don't know when I'll see them again. It might be weeks."

I forced myself to hold her glare. Then she nodded as her shoulders fell and her mouth curved again, this time into a pout, and she looked every bit like a wilted sunflower. I felt myself soften, embarrassed that I'd reacted so poorly to her comments about Phoebe. I should dismiss her as an opportunist who merely wanted something—like the others—from my mother. But there was such sadness about her. And when I thought of my mother's hesitation the other night in Chicago and her reluctance to ever offer any background information on *Listen*, I felt uneasy.

"Why didn't you ask someone else's opinion about your story?" I asked. "Why did you let my mother's reaction stop you from writing?"

"Your mom meant everything to me! And she

liked me, too. I had entire passages of *Paradise Lost* memorized and she said I was the only student ever to do this. When I told her about how terrible my family was being to me, she said she'd help. No other teacher was that nice! I used to think how lucky I'd be to have an actual mother like her. You know, so smart but also warm and nice."

Were we talking about the same person? Just how close were they? Did they see each other outside of class and office hours? What did they do and talk about? I'd never heard anyone describe my mother this way. I felt anger building as I stood there, trying to make sense of it all.

"And then she stole my story." Lucy pushed her yellow hair out of her face and frowned. "So, you'll give her the letter?"

"Yes!"

I started for the T, in the opposite direction, anger pulsing in my cheeks. I knew my mother better than anyone did. I didn't care how much of *Paradise Lost* Lucy had memorized; my mother wouldn't friend students nor did she steal this woman's story. But I stopped in the middle of the sidewalk. Because if I knew my mother so well, why didn't I know where the story of *Listen* came from?

Marta Volkov was a brown-haired, green-eyed fourth grader who lived with her dad, the superintendent of Mr. Donahue's building, her mom, her sister, and about thirty other people. At least it seemed that way when I stood in the entrance to their cramped, windowless, basement apartment. The people, who seemed to be stuffed into every crevice of the room, were watching *The Price Is Right* on a small TV resting on cardboard boxes in the corner.

As Mr. Volkov, a big, hulking man with a thick accent told me we could work in the girls' bedroom at the back of the apartment, I stole a glance at his daughter. Two red circles burned into Marta's cheeks, her eyes glued to the floor in front of me. I felt her embarrassment and immediately liked her.

"Please make sure you tell them that I'm not an elementary school teacher," I'd told Mr. Donahue when he called to ask if I'd help. Marta was falling behind, struggling with reading and writing, and her parents—newly arrived from Russia—couldn't afford tutors. I didn't want to do this. What did I know about teaching fourth graders? But when Mr. Donahue, who lived on the sixth floor of the building, said that *he'd* pay me, the situation was that desperate, I agreed to give it a try—but only on the condition that I do it for free.

I followed Marta to her bedroom and closed the door behind us. I could still hear voices from the TV and smell whatever was cooking on the stove (cabbage?) but at least it was private. The room was sparsely furnished and everything, from the skimpy pillows to the pockmarked bureau, felt second or thirdhand. Marta sat on the bed, her pudgy legs dangling over the edge and her head hung. Her little sister grinned at me as she bounced around the room and showed me her new Barbie, her latest drawing, and her Blowpop lollipop that she'd won at the second-grade spelling bee that day.

I put my backpack on the floor and sat in a folding chair near Marta. I was sweaty and still bothered by my conversation with Lucy. But I had to get through the next hour. As I watched the two girls, so different in looks as well as personality, I instantly saw the dynamic between them.

"So, Anna, that's your name, right?" I asked the grinning sister. She nodded and giggled. "You want to go out to the other room so Marta and I can work?"

"No." She shrugged. "Mamma and Poppa say I get to be here."

Great. I glanced at Marta, who still wouldn't look at me. "So, Marta, did you bring home work we can look at?"

She shrugged. Anna giggled and I shot her a look that she completely ignored.

"Did you bring home any books?"

She shook her head.

"How about any assignments?"

She shook her head again.

I sighed and looked around. I had to take a different approach. "So, do all those people out there live here, too?"

"No!" Anna giggled.

"Really? I thought they did. I thought maybe they all slept in the living room, you know, stacked on top of each other like Pringles potato chips."

Anna burst out laughing. Marta smiled, although cautious, and looked up at me. She had a mouthful of white teeth and a nice smile. I grinned back at her.

I glanced at a plastic pink backpack, covered in pictures of Dalmatians, on the linoleum in the corner. "How come you guys don't have a dog?"

"We want one!" Marta said, her voice quick. "But our parents won't let us."

"We're not responsible enough!" Anna cried.

I shook my head. "Keep working on it. I had a dog. She was the best friend I ever had. I used to dress her up in doll clothes and pretend we were in the circus."

Now both girls laughed. It didn't matter that I was lying—my mother was afraid of dogs and would never allow one—because I was on my way. When I pulled out a book I'd found on the T last week, *The BFG,* by Roald Dahl, they settled into the bed and stared at me as if I'd just promised them a dog if only they'd listen.

Later, after I finished a few chapters and Marta was able to answer the questions I asked, I realized that she *was* smart. Next time, I said to her, I'd read more and then maybe we'd work on her homework together. She nodded. By the time I walked into the dark living room, the light of the TV providing a path to the door, I felt better than when I'd arrived.

As I walked to the T, I thought about my fourth-grade year. I remembered it well, maybe better than almost any other time, because it was the year my mother was in between. She'd taken a sabbatical from the university and *Listen* had been written, although not yet published, and she was more relaxed, more calm and pleasant to be around, than at any other time I could remember. The four of us ate dinner every night in the dining room. We watched TV and read by the fire. And that spring, my mother and I began walking all over town every night after dinner and sometimes stopping for ice cream on our way home.

I liked that year not only because the craziness with *Listen* had yet to begin. It was also a magical time, as I saw with Marta, when you're not yet jaded or worried about boys or friends or whether you're a good person or not. You just are. You got excited by a dog or a lollipop. You could lose yourself in a novel.

Maybe I shouldn't be tutoring adults but teaching children.

But I cringed, thinking how my mother might respond. And what would I say to Ben (oh, God, we hadn't talked at all about the marriage thing he brought up the other night)? Maybe I'd just blurt it out. Guess what? I'd decided to change careers.

Yet again.

CHAPTER 18

"You should've asked Lee to come up, too," my dad said.

It was a month later and we were sitting in the kitchen of the Vineyard cottage, the warm air blowing through the screens. I had come out two days earlier, ahead of Ben, and now I was cradling a mug of coffee and watching my dad heap strawberry jam on a thick slice of bread cut from the loaf I'd made the day before. The newspapers were spread before us. I glanced at a paperback, *The Portable Milton,* which propped open the window, and then at my mother, dressed in a casual black dress that I'd never seen before, who was working at the picnic table on the patio. Later today their friends, the Donahues, were coming for a barbecue.

I tried to straighten the book—the weight of the window was collapsing the spine—and then wiped my dusty fingers on my napkin. My parents referred to this place as a house, but it was nothing more than a summer cottage; no insulation, a leaky roof, wood floors that squeaked when you walked on them, and a kitchen, with the tin sink and dishes and plates stacked on open wood shelves, that resembled the camp I attended as a kid. For years Logan had been urging our parents to remodel, that Vineyard real estate would hold its value, but so far they'd done nothing.

"Don't you think, Clare, that it would've been nice for her to come up?"

"She's pretty busy," I said.

He smiled. "Ah, ABC is working her hard."

I nodded and looked out the window again. Truth was, I didn't know what Lee was doing today. I hadn't spoken to her since returning from Chicago four weeks earlier. I glanced at the clock above the stove. Ben should be calling soon from the dock. He promised to be on the eight o'clock ferry.

"I still feel awful that she had to witness Logan's meltdown in Chicago," he said. "He was mortified the next day."

My dad continued lathering his bread. This was the fifth or sixth time he'd told me how mortified Logan was. I'd yet to talk to my brother. I was in no hurry to call him and he, obviously, was in no hurry to call me, either.

"Did he at least apologize?" I asked.

"Well, of course!" he said. "These things happen from time to time."

He set his knife on the table and wiped his fingers on his napkin. It occurred to me, as I watched him, that I'd never heard him criticize Logan. I didn't remember his ever criticizing me, either. His style of parenting was to let us go through our lives with a little encouragement and a total lack of condemnation. And did my mother have a parenting style? I glanced out the window again. Tap, tap, tap, *slam!*

"She's a good girl, that Lee." He lifted the bread to his mouth.

The first few weeks after I returned, I startled when the phone rang and held my breath when going through the mail. But she hadn't called or written. Sometimes I composed letters to her in my head while on the T but once home I never followed through. It was confusing, all the emotions I felt.

"Delicious," he said, chewing. "You've become quite a good cook, my dear."

"Thank you." I'd tried over the last couple of weeks to make scones but so far they were as dry as Donna's. But my breads were improving and I was a good cookie maker, too. "I'm thinking about selling my cookies at the coffeehouse."

"The sugar cookies?" he asked. I nodded. I didn't talk much about the coffeehouse. Usually when he asked about work, he was referring to my graduate studies. He screwed up his forehead and tilted his head. "But don't you have to have some kind of permit to sell food products for profit?"

"How would I do that?"

"Might be more bother than it's worth." He put his bread down and placed both hands on the table. "*So,* I want to tell you, I read that letter you gave me."

I'd been fiddling with the Milton book in the window again but with this, I pulled my hands across the table and into my lap. I'd given Lucy's letter to my dad last week, the first I'd seen him or my mother since Chicago. "And?"

"They're claims anyone could make," he said. "The world is full of people who are envious or sick or unhappy. Remember the woman who accosted your mother in the grocery store and wanted her to write a book about her father?"

"Sure, I do. So, you don't think it's true?" I asked. When he shook his head I nodded toward the window. "What did she think about it?"

"Not much. She read the letter and put it aside."

"Without saying anything?"

"What was there to say? The woman accused your mother of stealing her story. But she had no proof. And frankly, all the things she cited were things anyone could claim. I think she's a troubled woman."

"Did she remember having her as a student?" I asked.

"We didn't talk about that." He shrugged. I frowned and shook my head. "What's wrong, Clare? Do you think there's some truth to all this?"

I glanced at the clock. Why hadn't Ben called? I turned back to him. "I don't know. The woman just seemed like she might be telling the truth."

Your mother was so warm and nice. I'd met a few of my mother's students over the years at book signings and several times on the street while we were walking, and they'd all acted fairly stunned and mute in her presence. But Lucy, at least in the beginning, had thought of her differently. What had she seen in my mother that others hadn't? What had she seen that I'd missed?

I glanced out the window at my mother, chewing on the stem of her glasses as she stared at her typewriter. "I know she calls herself a New Critic. But don't you think it's a little odd that she never talks about where *Listen* came from?"

He chuckled. "I heard her say once that only readers cared about where a story came from. Writers cared about understanding how a novel is put together."

"What do you remember about where it came from?" I asked.

With the side of his hand, he began scooting breadcrumbs into a pile next to his newspaper. But he wasn't very thorough and left small trails all over the table. "I remember her talking about an idea of a man coming home from war altered from all he'd seen and done. I know she tried a couple versions from his point of view. I don't remember how she settled on Phoebe's voice. But once she did, the writing seemed to fly out of her."

Had she stolen Lucy's story? It would explain why her novel sounded so different from her academic writing and why she was reluctant to speak of it. And yet I still had a hard time believing my mother would do this. She was so capable in this part of her life. Why steal?

"You should ask her about it," he said.

When the phone rang, I jumped up and hurried to answer it. The moment I heard Ben's voice I knew he wasn't coming.

"I'm at the office again," he said. "I was here until midnight last night. I can't swing it. I'm sorry. I gotta be here all day today."

"But you've been working every day for the last three weeks," I said.

"I know, but this is unusual. They're counting on me. I don't know what else to do. I've got to put all my research into a document by the end of today."

I imagined poor, innocent children dying as they went down poisonous slides and Wellesley couples keeling over after barbecuing on their contaminated decks. Yes, it was important work. But still.

I glanced at my dad, who was cutting another piece of bread. "All right. I'll see you later tonight." I put the phone back in the cradle and sat at the table.

My dad looked at me over the top of his glasses, his knife poised above the strawberry jam. "You and I are surrounded by workaholics. Your brother, your mother, Ben." He smiled and smeared his bread with jam.

Last week when I gave him Lucy's letter, I'd told them about Ben's job offer. I didn't tell them about our marriage conversation. It was too soon and besides, Ben and I hadn't talked about it since that night. Truth was, we'd barely seen each other. I glanced at my mother, whose hands flew over the typewriter keys. My dad had done most everything when I was growing up—cooked, cleaned, paid the bills, took me to the park, put Band-Aids on scraped knees.

"Don't you wish that you could do what you want to do?" I asked.

He put his knife on the table. "What I want to do?"

"Yeah, I mean when you were a kid you took care of everything and now you're still taking care of everything." I wasn't sure where I was going with this.

"What I did as a kid has nothing to do with what I'm doing now." He slapped the table with his palm. "Listen, I have an idea. You should stay and have dinner with us tonight. We'd love to have you. Take the ferry back tomorrow."

"Well—"

"You could help me cook. The Donahues would love to see you." He chuckled. "Walt said to me the other day, 'Sure would be nice to see

Clare.' He reminded me of the dinner parties we had when you'd toddle in, pull up two stools, one for Ellie and one for you, and listen and ask questions. So precocious! Everyone loved you."

I smiled, remembering the giant stuffed elephant that my mother's cousin Oliver had given me when I was young. For several years Ellie, who was nearly as big as I was, went everywhere with me. On planes. To the beach. Even to the grocery store. People chuckled when they saw us coming but I didn't care. No, I didn't care at all until I read about Ellie in *Listen*. Couldn't my mother have given Phoebe something else, a giant bunny? A kangaroo. A shark?

I glanced out the window. Phoebe looked like me and I looked like Phoebe.

"Some children, once they have adults' attention, get silly," he said. "Or try to perform or impress. But you never boasted about anything. You were genuinely curious about others. And confident! You were wise beyond your years, Clare."

But that was then and now I didn't feel so wise. I didn't feel curious, confident, or precocious, either. You fucking figure it out.

I stood, walked to the counter and poured more coffee. If we had a different relationship, I'd tell him about how much I loved the coffeehouse and reading to Marta on Tuesdays and how much I hated tutoring. I'd tell him about missing Ben and the fight with Lee and what had happened in Florida. But that would require me to be honest and emotional (vulnerable, as Lee had said) and tell him things he didn't want to hear. Besides, there was value in perpetuating this myth of confidence and precociousness. Because at least this way I was good at something.

The whistle on the teakettle pierced the air and my dad walked over and lifted it off the stove. He poured boiling water into a mug waiting on the counter. Then he dunked a tea bag, cut another piece of bread and slipped it into the toaster. I thought about how I'd begun making lunches for Ben to take to work. I'd learned this from my dad. I felt, suddenly, tender toward him. He was starting to gray along his temples and his strong arms were dotted with small brown aging spots. We'd spent so much time together over the years, and yet we knew little about how the other truly felt. Why wasn't he furious with Logan? Did he ever feel oppressed by my mother? Why didn't we talk about these things?

"This D. H. Lawrence class is killing me," I said.

He laughed. "Don't tell your mother. She loves Lawrence."

"What about you, do you love Lawrence?" I asked.

"Sure!"

I wanted something from him, an acknowledgment or confession or maybe just a nod, a wink, collusion over something meaningful. "Ben's so passionate about his job. He told me that he loves the law because it's so exact. I think he also loves always trying to be right."

"It's good to be passionate about what you do," he said. We were standing so close that my shoulder was touching the middle part of his upper arm. He raised his brows and glanced at me. "Passion is what keeps your mother going."

Yes, passion and love of words made my mother write every day. Although when I remembered how I'd found her on the living room couch last month, despondent over Janice's letter, I wondered if it was worth it.

"Do you feel passionate about anything?" I wanted him to say *no,* not everyone feels so much. People like us are worker bees, the soldiers who support those who burn up the world with their ambitions, desires, and appetites.

He put the tea, toast, and a miniature container of milk on a tray. "Sure I do. I feel passionate about my family and work. I wake up every day thinking about how best to market your mother's books. Passion keeps us alive. Now, do you want to take this out to her?"

I sighed, took the tray, opened the screen door with my hip, and walked onto the porch. The brisk air was warm and fragrant, the tops of my dad's tomato plants next to the shed swaying, the leaves on the birch trees clustered in the lawn fluttering. My mother nodded as I set the tray on the picnic table. It was a good writing day. I could tell.

"Thank you." She reached for her tea without looking at me.

"Ben just called," I said. "He can't come. He has to work."

She nodded, as if this made sense, and stared at her typewriter.

I turned to go—she wanted to work—but stopped and stepped in front of her. My shadow fell across her typewriter and notebooks and when she looked up at me and frowned, I felt my heartbeat speed up. What a funny thing. When my mother was lying on the bathroom floor or strung out on the couch, when she needed me to take care of her, I was welcomed. Now, when she was stronger and feeling better, not so much. I thought about last December, sitting in Ben's parents' kitchen and watching his mother, dressed in a pink cashmere cardigan and a plaid skirt, a white apron tied at her waist, making dinner, while her husband sat in the living room nursing a gin martini. Somehow the traditional parental roles were converted in our family. My mother was more like Ben's dad—the primary breadwinner whose work in the world was so important, so revered, that little was required of him once he got home. I still had no idea who he really was.

"Did you want something, Clare?" she asked.

Where did she get that black dress? It was new and so were her earrings and the clip in her hair and yes, I did want something. I began fiddling with the spoon on the tray. I wasn't sure this would go over very well.

"Dad said you read the letter that that woman gave me in the writing center," I said. "And I just want to know what you thought of it."

She nodded slightly as she looked at the paper in her typewriter. "People are constantly inferring things about that novel. It's a lightning rod for attention."

"But I'm wondering about the things she said."

She wouldn't look at me. She was concentrating on the paper, her lips moving as she read what she'd written. And this made me angry. Because Lucy would be back in my cubicle any day now, and I didn't want her to accuse me of not delivering the letter or tell me more about how close she'd been to my mother.

But I couldn't ask if she stole the story. I didn't know why it felt so hard to form the words. But I wanted to know. *Now.* "Mom?"

"Do you honestly believe that poor woman's story?" she asked.

"That's what I'm asking. You never talk about this."

She took off her glasses and tossed them onto the picnic table. "I never talk about it because it's uninteresting. Who cares? The characters and plot in a novel come from a variety of places but once they go through the mill of an author's mind and end up on the page, it's all fiction. It's all the author's creation."

She wasn't answering the question. My arms hung heavy at my sides, and I began drumming my fingers against my thighs. Finally, I blurted, because I couldn't stand it anymore, "Do you remember having her in class? Did you take her story?"

She picked up her glasses, put them on her face, and readjusted the paper in her typewriter. "I do remember her. She was a troubled, unfortunate person. And no, I didn't steal her short story. I don't even *remember* a short story."

Something about the way she said *I don't even remember,* as if Lucy wasn't worth her time, as if she couldn't be bothered, landed like a giant thud in my stomach. I wanted to believe her. But as I stood there, arms at my sides, and still she wouldn't look up, I felt a cold sweat across the back of my neck and anger seep into every pore of my body. Goddam it. My mother was lying.

CHAPTER 19

The next day when I came home from the Vineyard I found a letter waiting for me from Lee. My heartbeat surged as I stared at the familiar handwriting. Lately I'd felt better—I hadn't cried in weeks and my head wasn't muddled—and wasn't sure I wanted to open the letter. But staring at the handwriting, I suddenly missed her so much that I felt as if I couldn't breathe.

I glanced down at Ben's running shoes on the newspaper next to the door and then into the kitchen that he'd kept so clean while I was away. I turned the letter over in my hand. I didn't have to read it, at least not yet. I stuffed it into my backpack, changed clothes, and hurried out the door.

At the coffeehouse, Diana was behind the counter. She looked up when she heard the bell on the door and smiled. "You're back! How was it?"

I slipped my apron over my head and tied it behind my back. Sometime over the last year Diana and I had settled into undeclared yet set roles. She was the talker, I was the listener. "Great. How are you?"

She closed her crossword puzzle book. "Terrible! I haven't had a customer in four hours.

Four hours! And the last two days were worse."

"People are away. It's summer."

She shook her head. "I heard Lorenzo on the phone the day before yesterday. He was telling the landlord that he couldn't afford a rent increase. And he's worried about this new coffee place, two blocks over. It's part of a chain called Starbucks."

I smoothed the front of my apron. No, this was too great a place to be in trouble. We should work harder. Why hadn't I found a good scone recipe? And maybe we needed to advertise. "Where is he?"

She took off her apron. "He said he had an appointment and that he'd be gone for a couple of hours. If we go under, I'm in trouble. I need the money. I can't survive on just the salary from my other job."

I would be okay, seeing that I didn't pay rent to my parents. But I worried about Diana and Lorenzo, if we closed, and I didn't want tutoring to be my only job.

What did Lee write in her letter?

After Diana left I swept the floor, wiped down the chairs and tables, rearranged the sitting area—the couch looked better against the wall, not floating in the middle of the room—scrubbed the counter and sink, and cleaned the window. And still no customers. I put my backpack on the counter and pulled out my books. I opened *Lady*

Chatterley's Lover and tried to read but kept thinking about Lee's letter.

Had she yelled at me?

I went back to my book. Focus! It was fairly scandalous when it was published, and my professor practically salivated when he introduced it in class. But what turned me off was not the abundance of sex, language, and long diatribes about class differences. I was tired of reading yet another book about men returning, damaged and broken, from war. My mother, when asked once why she wrote so much about this topic, said, "It's a horrific task we ask men to do. In killing a human being, man is essentially killing a part of himself." But when is enough enough?

In the novel, Constance Chatterley's husband, Clifford, returns from war paralyzed from the waist down. He can no longer satisfy his wife, sexually or emotionally, and she slips into an affair with the gamekeeper. She can barely contain herself, that's how good the sex is, but it gets her into trouble—pregnancy, scandal, and divorce.

I'd never say this in class, but I thought the bliss Constance got from sex with the gamekeeper was unrealistic. Was it really *that* great? Or was Lawrence writing about his own fantasies? Sometimes I thought books, and male writers, made sex out to be better than it truly was. I glanced at the window as a couple hurried by on the sidewalk and remembered Christopher as he traced my collarbone with his finger. Fooling around with him *had* been blissful. But Ben was so hardworking, loyal, and good. That I didn't feel irrepressible passion with him was a small price to pay, wasn't it?

The bell on the back of the door rang and I looked up to see two young girls hurry to the counter. They ordered iced teas to go. As I made their drinks, I listened to them giggle and talk. They were going to meet the tall one's boyfriend and his friend. It was a setup for the other girl. They were older than Marta, maybe just out of middle school, and their bodies looked it. Chipped pink polish on their fingernails. Long, gangly legs under baggy jean shorts. Freckles. Thin lines of sunburn on their shoulders from where they'd missed applying sunscreen.

I watched as they began to whisper, their heads touching and their tan arms intertwined, and I turned away to give them privacy. But they weren't paying the slightest bit of attention to me. They were too engrossed with each other.

Like Lee and me. I thought about one night—there were so many like this—when I was asleep in the cold dorm on the third floor of the sorority house and Lee woke me in the middle of the night. The shades on the windows were closed and the room was so dark that you couldn't see the fifty beds lined up, one after the other. But somehow I knew it was Lee shaking my arm. I woke instantly.

"OhmyGod!OhmyGod!" she said. I smelled coffee on her breath and felt the electricity charging through her. "I've been thinking about you all night! Remember the guy with the beard at the lecture last week who kept asking tough questions and we couldn't figure out what his story was?"

I leaned on my elbow, trying to find her in the dark. In the bed next to me, Amy moaned and rolled over. I whispered, "Of course."

She was talking about the panel on Soviet and US relations, sponsored by the sociology department. Lee and I had started attending random lectures around campus—sometimes the subject matter was so dense that we had no idea what the speaker was talking about—because we worried about how myopic Greek life could be (*our minds are turning to mush!*). During the panel discussion, an old, white-bearded man who spoke with an accent kept harassing the Soviet expert. Afterward, Lee and I talked about him for hours. She thought he might be a turned Soviet spy. But I saw incredible sadness on his face and speculated that something terrible had happened to him and his family.

"I met him tonight!"

"What? Where?" I whispered.

"He came to the theater," she said. "He sat

by himself in the back. I saw him from the production room upstairs."

"What did he see?" I asked. Amy moaned again.

"Star Trek."

"*Star Trek*?" I said. "I wouldn't have imagined him seeing that—"

"Shush!" Someone from a bed across the room sighed loudly.

"My shift ended when the movie was over and so I followed him." Lee lowered her voice. I groaned. "I know, I know! But it's okay. So, listen. I followed him over to Kirkwood and into the square, and then suddenly he turned and stormed back to me and demanded to know why I was following him."

"Oh, God, Lee! Why would you follow a stranger—"

"Shush!"

Lee lowered her voice further. "I told him about seeing him at the panel discussion and that I imagined he'd escaped from the Soviet Union or that he was a spy. I think I really caught him off guard because he relaxed, and we went and got coffee at Donuts Delite and he told me his story. Oh, my God, Clare! You were right. Stalin wiped out his whole family. And he was sent to a labor camp!"

"Who the hell is talking?" An angry voice boomed from across the room. "Lee and Clare *again?* Is that you? What time is it?"

"I'll tell you more tomorrow," she whispered. And then I felt her move away.

Whatever happened to that man? And did Lee still think about him, too? I stared down at the iced teas in front of me. Sometimes when I remembered things, like now, they felt so far away. From a different time. When I was a different person.

"Excuse me!" A voice from behind me. "Are the drinks almost ready?"

I turned to the girls with their drinks and felt such an urge to warn them about something although I didn't know what. Not until they opened the door and the warm July air swept into the room did I know what I wanted to say. Be careful! The world is dangerous. Men are dangerous. And most of all, be careful with each other. Don't let anything, not a boy or a bad decision, come between you.

The door slammed, and as I watched them pass in front of the window, I felt an unbearable pull inside of me. I glanced back at the counter. And then I walked over to my backpack, took out the letter and started for the back room. I sat at Lorenzo's desk and opened it.

Dear Clare,
Every time I think about Amy's wedding or see something on the news about Chicago or Lake Michigan, I think about

that night on the beach. I'm sorry that we're in a bad place now but I'm not sorry that we argued. I think it was a long time coming. I think our friendship will survive it.

I'm writing to tell you that I'm leaving for Thailand on August 1. My last day of work will be July 28. This is a big risk and I know you're worried about it. But I'll tell you that I've been asleep these last couple years and I've finally woken up. I want this more than anything.

You can reach me at the address at the bottom of the page after August 5. Patricia says that mail takes a while but it's reliable.

Life is too short. I don't want to be so afraid anymore. I don't want to be afraid of anything. If we don't take chances with our lives, then what's the point of living? I meant what I said about finding answers.

I'd love to see you or talk to you before I go. I'll miss you, Clare. I miss you so much right now. Please call or write back. Okay?

Love, Lee

I read the letter again, then twice more and each time I felt sick to my stomach. She was, to put it in Ducky's words, *following her dream*. I was so angry or envious or sad—maybe all of them at once—that I started to cry again.

For the next couple of weeks, I thought about calling Lee but couldn't. I started several letters but never finished. I had trouble sleeping and couldn't eat. Every day I cried. Sometimes it happened when I was on the T, sometimes while in class. I couldn't tell anyone, especially Ben, and not just because he was so busy. He'd told me that I was the nicest person he knew. And what I'd done wasn't so nice.

Then one day at work, studying at Lorenzo's desk while the coffeehouse was quiet, I thought about something my professor had said, how D. H. Lawrence was "hamstrung" by his mother and how it showed up in all his work, especially *Sons and Lovers*. This kind of biographical analysis always made me suspicious. After all, I'd grown up with the mother of minimalism who always had a mouthful on this topic: *What did the author's experience have to do with the quality of the work?*

But then I sat back in the chair and thought about that word, hamstrung. I knew what it meant. To be crippled or limited, in some way, from doing something. That was when I thought of Lee and me. Maybe we hamstrung each other. Maybe we were bad for each other. Maybe we shouldn't be friends.

I needed to talk to someone about this. All of it. Before I went crazy.

I glanced at the calendar tacked to the bulletin board in front of me. Friday, July 29. In three days, Lee was leaving. I should call to say goodbye. I still had time.

I picked up the phone. But instead of calling Lee, I called Lorenzo's therapist, Dr. Houseman, whose name and number were on the card next to the phone. I left a message and not more than fifteen minutes later she called back. Then it was set. Tuesday afternoon, three o'clock, at her office on Marlborough Street. I'd barely had time to think about it and it was done.

CHAPTER 20

On Tuesday, I was packing up after my writing center sessions—it was a tough day with three students all working on essays whose subjects were nearly incomprehensible to me—when Lucy appeared in my doorway. She stood there, silent, her black bag on her shoulder and her yellow hair looking longer and unrulier. She wore a different sundress, this one with red and yellow flowers.

I hadn't seen her since early last month. For a while after her last visit, I looked for her whenever I was on campus. But when I didn't see her, I hoped she'd given up or had moved on to something else. I put my notebook into my backpack and zipped it up. I didn't want to deal with her today.

"I've been away," she said. "But now I'm back and wondering if you gave my letter to Eleanor."

"I did."

"What did she say? Will she write me back? Did you talk to her about it?"

I was done with this. I pulled my backpack across my shoulder and stood to face her. She wore no makeup and her face was blotchy red. Maybe I should feel kind toward her—after all,

I was almost sure that my mother had wronged her—but I was embarrassed and angry and tired of being in the middle of this.

"I gave her the letter and she said that it wasn't true," I said. "I doubt she'll write you back. I'm sorry but there's really nothing else I can say or do about this."

"Haven't you ever wondered why *Listen, Before You Go* is so different from her other novel?" Her voice was gruff and defiant and she seemed to stand taller.

"It's not so different. She always writes about war." This wasn't entirely true. *Listen* had a young narrator, a simple sentence structure, and a freshness about it that was missing from her other work. I shifted my feet. I felt strangely protective of my mother. "She's got a lot going on. I'm sorry. But I have to go."

Lucy bit her lower lip as she squinted at me. I couldn't tell if she was about to cry or rip my head off. She said, "She's ashamed, that's why she won't talk about it. She's ashamed because she lied about what she did."

Who was she to blame my mother? And *she* wasn't the model for Phoebe, either. I blurted, "I'm not delivering any more letters or messages. I'm sorry this didn't work out but please leave me alone."

I had to get out of here before I said something I'd regret. Before I made a mistake. I ripped my sweater off the back of my chair and started out of the cubicle.

She stepped in front of me. "Okay. I won't come back. But if I were you, I wouldn't forget this."

"You aren't me." And then I blew by her.

Outside, the hot and humid air was thick with moisture. I began walking as fast as I could, my sandals slapping the pavement and my arms swinging at my sides. I walked for blocks, Lucy's words pounding in my ears and her wild hair and hooded eyes, her tacky dress and big black purse, in my mind. I kept looking over my shoulder, worrying that she'd followed me. I expected to see her in the windows of the shops I passed and opening the door of a taxi and sitting in an outdoor café. Then I stepped into traffic and when a car, charging down the street, swerved to avoid me, the driver yelled out of the window. "Get your head out of your ass!"

I jumped back onto the curb. How had I gotten here? But it woke me up. I was still blocks away from my appointment and going to be late if I didn't hurry.

Dr. Houseman was tall with shoulder-length gray hair and small, dark reading glasses that sat on the end of her nose. I didn't like how her lips pinched together into a frown, as if she'd somehow gotten a glimpse inside of me and didn't like what she saw. But then she smiled and extended her long arm for a shake, and I thought her hand was soft and her voice kind.

We sat facing each other. Despite the air-conditioning, sweat poured down my back and the sides of my face. I took a tissue from the box on the floor next to me and wiped my cheeks and forehead. Then I glanced around her office. It was small with an enormous desk, a floor-to-ceiling bookcase stuffed with books, a wood filing cabinet, and a round coffee table between us. On the walls were framed diplomas and a painting of a coastline. Two small windows above her desk were frosted over; they let light in but I couldn't see out. I began searching for my mother's books in her bookcase and wasn't sure that it was good or bad that they weren't here. When I saw several books by Freud, I realized that all titles were related to psychology. I bet she knew the Rat Man case. Should I talk to her about that?

"Why don't you tell me why you're here." She wore a white blouse, gray pants, and black, open-toed sandals. My mother rarely left the house in anything other than a skirt or dress. Hose, too. A large, spiral notebook sat on her lap, a ballpoint pen poised in her right hand. She was old, about my mother's age. Maybe they went to school together. Maybe they knew each other. That I didn't know this made me squeeze the sides of my chair with my hands.

I could tell her that a crazy woman who reminded me of a sunflower was stalking me. But I didn't know what that had to do with anything. Then I remembered why I'd made the appointment. I said, "I can't stop crying."

She wrote something in her notebook. Then she stopped but didn't look at me. "When did it start?"

When I was eleven, I almost said. But why start there? I didn't remember crying much when I was a kid. "Three years ago. Well, I mean, I haven't been crying continuously for three years. Kind of off and on. But then since June, a lot more."

She nodded and kept her head down. "What happened three years ago?"

I should start with how I jumped out the window and how it took me thirty long minutes to find Donny's house. But then I'd have to tell her about what Lee said, *Let her go, I'll stay,* and I wasn't ready to do that. I didn't want her to think I was a bad person. Maybe I should start at the beginning, when we decided to leave the Outer Banks. But was that the beginning? The beginning of what? Suddenly, the idea of telling this story with all its complexities and unknowns seemed so daunting, so exhausting, that I felt completely deflated. I started to cry. I was a faucet, a waterfall. Minutes passed.

She looked up at me. "Do you want to talk about what happened in June?"

"Okay." I reached for a tissue and blew my nose. "I went to a wedding of a college friend. It was the first time we were all together since college. And my best friend, Lee, and I got into an argument and now she's going to Thailand. And then my brother accused me. But that was before, at dinner . . ."

See? How could I talk about the argument without first talking about spring break? I had never told the entire story to anyone. Would she think I was a terrible friend? Maybe she'd be shocked that I didn't stay to help. Maybe, like Ben, she'd think the need to save oneself was stronger than any other desire. But maybe she'd think Lee was a martyr for staying.

Why did Lee do that? Because I was so sexually inexperienced? Because I was scared and couldn't stop crying? And what did she want me to figure out?

The doctor wasn't saying anything. Wasn't she supposed to help me?

I thought about my mother's experience in therapy, how she said that it didn't do much good. Did she talk about her feelings? Did she divulge family secrets? I didn't know if our family even had secrets.

The silence was excruciating. Why was she just sitting there, waiting?

I glanced at the diploma behind her. "How long have you been a therapist?"

"Thirty-five years."

"Do you like it?"

She paused. "Ah, yes."

I stared at the little black clock on the coffee table. One minute passed. Then two. Then four. It was becoming clear that she wasn't going to say anything else.

"Have you ever read *Listen, Before You Go?*" I crossed my legs.

She paused again. "Yes, years ago. Why do you ask?"

"My mother wrote it." A flicker in her eyes, a slight grimace or smile or wrinkle of her forehead would tell me what she thought, whether she was impressed or didn't like it. But she simply nodded, the muscles in her face still, her eyes on me. I felt nauseated and my head ached from crying. I didn't understand how Lorenzo did this every week. What did he talk about?

I felt a sob rise from my chest and into my throat. "I'm not usually like this!"

"Like what?" she asked.

"I don't know!"

"Do you want to tell me what you're usually like?"

All I thought about was what I wasn't. I wasn't passionate. I wasn't a writer. I didn't feel the beauty in a stone wall or a sky full of stars. I wasn't really brave or the lifeline you called in the middle of the night. And despite what Logan had accused me of at dinner that night in Chicago, I wasn't Phoebe, either. I wanted to tell her that I was confused about my mother and that I didn't always tell my boyfriend the truth and that I'd let my best friend sacrifice herself for me.

Instead I sat there and cried, minute after long minute. Finally, with only a short time remaining, I told her about one of the first times someone talked to me about Phoebe. *Listen, Before You Go* had just been published, and I was in the music room at elementary school, practicing "Hot Cross Buns" on my violin, when the new art teacher poked her head into the room and called to me. I'd never spoken to her. I hadn't realized that she knew my name.

"She said, 'Clare, I thought of you as I read your mom's book over the weekend. Phoebe looks just like you! Isn't that something, to be the inspiration behind your mom's main character?' My parents' friend, Mr. Donahue, had said nearly the same thing to me the day before. But this shocked me, maybe because I didn't know the new art teacher. I wasn't even sure it was true. But then everyone in the class looked at me and I liked it. It was like *I'd* done something important.

"It started happening a lot, people saying that I was Phoebe and asking me questions. Did you help your mom write the book? Did those things happen to you? I began paying attention when people talked about her. I knew the book was about a guy coming home from Vietnam, but I didn't know much else about it. Everyone loved Phoebe. She's a hero, sort of. Well, she's a great listener. She saved her brother, everyone said. Although at first I didn't know what she saved him from."

Dr. Houseman was writing frantically, her expression unchanged. Was I making sense? What did she think of this crying?

"I started asking myself, when things happened at school or when my mother was depressed, what would Phoebe do? Then I read the book and it was so, I don't know. I mean, she put a lot of my life in there. My stuffed elephant. The throwing up thing. But it was confusing. Phoebe was smart and a good listener but she doesn't save her brother. She watched while he put the gun in his mouth. She didn't try to stop him before he pulled the trigger. I don't know why I'm telling you this. It doesn't have anything to do with what happened three years ago or the wedding. Isn't it so embarrassing that I'd make myself into a fictional character?"

I closed my eyes and dropped my head into my hands. I felt completely spent, like the time Lee and I rode in this crazy fifty-mile bike race during junior year and we could barely climb the stairs when we returned to the house.

"It seems that others were awfully invested in this myth, too," Dr. Houseman said. These were the most words she'd strung together since I'd arrived, and I didn't know how to respond so I said nothing and kept my eyes closed. We were quiet for another minute and then she asked, "Why was your mother depressed?"

I'd finally stopped crying but my eyes felt swollen and dry and hurt when I opened them. I shook my head. "I'm sorry. What?"

She glanced at her notebook. "You said that you started asking yourself, when your mother was depressed, what would Phoebe do? And so I wondered, why was your mother depressed?"

Had I said that? I crossed my legs again and glanced at the clock. "I meant to say upset. She got upset about things, like with her writing."

"So, she wasn't depressed?" she asked.

"I don't know." Sometimes I used this word—depressed—about my mother but I hadn't given it much thought. Was she depressed? Why? And why were we talking about her, anyway? I wasn't here to do that. I didn't know why I was here.

We were quiet for another minute and then she cleared her throat. "We have to stop for today. Same time next week? The week after that I'm away, but I'll be here for the rest of the month and most of the fall."

"Oh," I squeaked. "Okay."

Outside, the sun was big, bold, and hot as it burned through the trees. The air was still and smelled like overripe garbage. I started walking, not sure where I was going, my legs heavy and my head foggy, and feeling as if I were drunk or hung over or just awake from a deep, unsettled sleep. With every step I felt the hot air burn into my lungs.

I thought Dr. Houseman and I would talk about Amy's wedding and the argument. I thought she might help me call Lee to say goodbye. Instead, she'd barely said a word. And what did she mean that she'd be here most of the fall? I hadn't planned to see her more than once or twice. It was expensive. I hadn't told Ben about it, either. I didn't want him to worry that there was something wrong with me.

A therapist was supposed to make you feel better. But nothing about today felt good, not the worrying I did—in anticipation of coming—not the sobbing or the headache and exhausted way I felt now. How embarrassing that I only managed to talk about Phoebe. And what other people were invested in this myth?

I missed Lee and how we were before everything happened. She knew me better than anyone. She'd have something funny or enlightening to say about my meeting with Dr. Houseman. But then I remembered what she said to me that night we argued, that I couldn't be vulnerable, and I felt a flash of anger. Well, excuse me for not wanting to be so needy and demanding.

I crossed Arlington Street, entered the Public Garden and walked along the path until I came to the pond. And then I sat on a bench. The air was so still that the leaves on the trees didn't move. In front of me, several swan boats, loaded with tourists and families, slowly paddled by.

I came here a lot when I was younger, mostly with friends and their parents and sometimes with my dad. Once when I was seven or eight, I remembered riding a crowded boat with him on a hot summer afternoon, just like today. Suddenly, a man jumped off the back. He wasn't in danger—the water was mucky and not deep—but there was a lot of yelling and pointing as he waded through the water to the shore. My dad said to me, "I've lived here my entire adult life and have never seen that!"

For some reason, maybe because I'd never seen anything like this, either, I couldn't wait to tell my mother. I kept saying this to him as we finished the ride, as we walked through the gardens, as we stopped for lunch. "Let's go home. Let's go tell Mom about that man jumping off the swan boat!"

He took his time, walking slowly, looking in store windows and leading me down side streets. I didn't understand why he wasn't in a hurry. I'd convinced myself that my mother would love this story. I hardly ever said anything to her that she thought interesting, that surprised her or made her hungry for more. But *this!* Surely this was something that she'd never heard or seen.

It was close to four when we finally got home. I had to use the toilet so badly that I burst through the door and ran down the hall to the bathroom. Sitting there, I went over the story and how I'd tell her. But as I finished, I heard my mother say, "I told you to keep her away until after five. You've wrecked my concentration."

"What a terrible thing to say," my dad had said. "She's your daughter."

I was glad he'd said that to her. But I was so worried about wrecking more of her concentration that I went to my room, got into bed, and read until I fell asleep. The next morning, I woke early and went to her office. The door was closed but behind it I heard her fingers on her typewriter. Tap, tap, tap, *slam!* Later, when we finally met up in the kitchen, I realized that the story no longer held the same interest and excitement for me. I wasn't sure that I ever told her about it.

A mother with two small children walked to the water's edge. The little girl was dressed in a sundress and sandals, the boy in shorts and a T-shirt. They were squealing and clapping as they watched the ducks swimming in front of them. The mom reached into her bag and pulled out a loaf of bread. She tore off pieces and handed them out and the children squatted and tossed the bread in the water. Every time a duck grabbed a piece, the children turned to their mom and giggled. As if this were the best thing they'd ever seen. As if they were having the time of their lives.

What a pleasure to watch. And their mom was so good with them.

Occasionally my mother did fun things with me when I was younger. On the Vineyard we went to the beach and the fair. On weekends in Boston, we sometimes went to museums and movies. But there was usually a diversion in these activities (*we'll just stop by the bookstore on our way to the park*) and she was always distracted, always a bit *not there*. I knew, even as a child, that she would rather be home writing. It was her reason for being. It was the most important thing in her life. As I watched the ducks circling in front of the children, I wondered—and this wasn't the first time—why writing was so important that she'd choose it over me?

But no, I didn't want to think like this. My mother was an important author. She touched the lives of millions of readers. And she was a good enough mother, just, maybe, unconventional. Right?

I closed my eyes and breathed in the hot summer air. When I heard the children squeal again, I opened my eyes and saw the little girl wrap her arms around her mom's neck and pull her face toward hers. The mom smiled and laughed, her eyes never leaving her. Maybe she was having the time of her life, too.

When I became a mother, I'd be like this woman. I didn't want my children to worry about wrecking my concentration or growing up with impossible expectations. This woman wasn't writing books or taking risks or chasing dreams. She was here. She was present.

I didn't know how long I watched, but when I glanced at my watch again, it was after five. Something had lifted from my shoulders and chest. Tonight when Ben came home, I'd tell him how cute the mom and the two children were. I'd tell him about the ducks and the bread. And I'd tell him that maybe it *was* time to find an apartment together. And to get married.

Tomorrow Lee was leaving. People needed breaks from each other from time to time. I'd been okay this last month because I didn't have to call every day and try so damn hard to keep up her spirits. She'd made her choice. She was going to Thailand. I would write in a few weeks or months. Or maybe I wouldn't write at all.

When I got back to the apartment I'd call Dr. Houseman and say that I'd decided not to come back. I wasn't ready and couldn't afford it. Or better yet, I'd leave a message on her answering machine so I wouldn't have to talk to her. Then I'd make something light for dinner, a salad that

I could keep in the refrigerator and give to Ben when he got home at ten.

I would not have another day like today or another month like this past month. Life was too short to spend it crying and feeling guilty and trying to make up for things that happened three years ago. It was better to live for today and the simple things in life. Like watching children throw bread at the ducks. Like smelling the hot humid air. Like baking bread and making the perfect spaghetti sauce.

I stood and started for home.

PART THREE

1991

PART THREE

CHAPTER 21

My fourth-grade classroom overlooked the playground, and as I stood at the window, on my tiptoes with my hand on the chalkboard to balance, I searched for the two of them. Would they be together? Had their recent classroom bonding extended to the playground? Part of me wanted to see them off by themselves, heads bowed, examining an anthill or looking for four-leaf clovers or simply sitting in the grass, talking. Another part of me felt a twinge of foreboding.

Sophia and Talia. Talia and Sophia.

Before school started earlier this month, the third-grade teachers prepped me. Jonah, they said, had a temper. Abby was the most popular girl while Max, the athlete. And sweet Sophia (she's like a little mother, one of the teachers said) was the receptacle of everyone's secrets. Over the weeks as I watched her share her colored markers with Jonah and stay in during recess to read to Randall, who was confined to a wheelchair with a broken leg, I couldn't help but see a little of how I must have been as a kid. She even looked like me. Freckles. Shoulder-length brown hair. Big, dark eyes. She became my favorite, just like that.

But no one had told me about Talia. She

arrived only ten days ago, her mother dropping her off at the front desk with barely a wave as she hustled back to her car. Later, Kitty, one of the fourth-grade teachers, told me about the drop off (a dump off, if you ask me, she'd said) and that rumors pegged Talia as a scholarship student, accepted after a second grader abruptly left. I didn't know if this was true nor did I care because there was more to Talia than this. She had a presence. Whenever she walked in the room, attention instantly swung her way.

"Excuse me," she'd said that first day she'd arrived in class. Many of the kids had been staring at her, some doing goofy things to show off, but with this everyone jerked to attention. It was after lunch and we'd gathered on the rug by the window for read aloud. "Why are most of the adults always so bad in Roald Dahl's books?"

I marked the page with my finger and closed *Matilda*. She was right, of course. But new kids were notoriously shy and I was surprised that she'd spoken. She was tall with long dirty blond hair, small, squinty eyes, and unforgiving, severe eyebrows. Was this a rhetorical question, asked so she could show off by answering? Was she challenging me? I didn't know. Her question seemed genuine.

"That's a good question," I said. "Does anyone have an answer?" I glanced at Sophia, our class's most well-read student, but she stiffened and dropped her eyes and I knew not to call on her. Others began shifting, uncomfortable, too, when I met their eyes. No one seemed to know which way this was going to go.

"They're always so *mean*." Talia scrunched her nose in concern.

I nodded. "Yes, that's right. Do you have any idea why?"

With fingers from both hands, Talia tucked her hair behind her ears. And then she shrugged, her nose still scrunched, and said, "I have no idea!"

I felt the collective sigh as everyone nodded. Yes, the new girl didn't know, either, and wasn't afraid to say it. Randall, who had an answer for everything even if he was wrong, stared at her. Sophia turned her entire upper body to look. And with this Talia became an instant magnet, the unspoken leader, the girl with the power. This was something most kids, and a lot of adults, didn't understand: people were often most attractive when they admitted they didn't know.

Sophia slowly raised her hand, and when I nodded at her, she said, "Maybe Roald Dahl knew a lot of mean adults when he was growing up?"

"That's stupid," Max whispered to Jonah.

"Max, that's not nice," I'd said. He shrugged and hung his head.

Several girls began whispering. Paolo picked at the loose rubber on the heel of his sneaker. And I remembered, very clearly, how Talia had turned to Sophia. The two of them stared at each other in a kind of solemn and silent way that signaled something profound had just occurred.

I strained my neck, my hand still on the chalkboard, trying to see the far edge of the playground, but I couldn't find either of them. I knew that by putting Sophia and Talia at the same table, and in the same reading group, I was encouraging a friendship. And I was quite sure this was not a priority with the other teachers. Even though Meadows Academy wasn't as intense as some of the local private schools, such as Winsor or Belmont Hill, and championed the "whole child," most everyone—teachers, administration, parents—were focused on one thing. Performance.

"Look at you, watching your flock from your window. Do you see mine down there, too?" Kitty, hands on her big hips, grinned from my doorway. She charged into the room and threw herself into my chair. Cheeks flushing, I stepped away from the window. Even though she was only a few years older than me, Kitty was already jaded. Perhaps someday I'd be that way, too, but so far this was new to me. I was only in my second year of teaching and terrified that my students, moving to fifth grade next year, would do so without learning enough from me.

"Thank God we've got the day off tomorrow,"

she said. "I love these random holidays. I *need* a three-day weekend. It's been such a bear here so far."

"We've only been in school three weeks, Kitty," I said.

"I know." She sighed as she laid her torso across my desk and began fiddling with a pile of paperclips. Pasty white flesh spilled over the top of her chinos and her feathered brown hair spread across her shoulders. She reminded me so much of Ducky that I felt a soft spot for her, even when she annoyed me.

I also felt grateful. I'd learned a lot as her assistant for two years before getting my own class. She was one of the best teachers in the school. I cleared my throat and asked, "Think you could help me with another student? I can't figure out what's not working with Max's writing. I don't think he's got executive functioning issues. But I don't know what to do. He's such a smart, articulate kid. But he was all over the place in his last essay."

She rolled her head on her arms and looked at me. "The what-I-did-over-summer-vacation essay?"

I nodded. "He wrote about visiting his cousins in Maine."

"Maybe the question was too open ended. Tell him to write about the three best things about visiting his cousins. Make him list them, one per paragraph, and tell him to elaborate. Sometimes you gotta lead them a bit."

Of course. Why didn't I think of that? I felt the same way last week when she helped me with a science lesson. Teaching was not intuitive. Yet.

She sat up. "Did you hear we're getting a new gym teacher? Someone says he's coming over from Concord Academy. Do you know?"

I shook my head. I tried to stay out of the gossip mill as much as possible.

"Well, I hope he's young and hot and single," she said.

"It's a terrible idea to date someone you work with." I laughed and glanced out the window. My student teacher, Eileen, was lining up the kids on the blacktop. Recess was almost over.

"I know, but I'm feeling desperate," she said. I rolled my eyes. "I am! You have no idea how hard it is to meet nice, eligible men. By the way, we're all still waiting to meet your husband. We're beginning to wonder if he even exists." She laughed.

"Ha, ha, real funny," I said.

"Seriously, Clare. Does Ben really work all those hours?"

"He does. It's insane." Ben and I had been married for three years, and I could count on two hands the weeknights he was home before nine. But this wasn't the only reason I'd not introduced him to the group. I liked Kitty and the other teachers but I wasn't anxious to become best friends with them.

"So, come out with us," she said. "After book group next Friday night. We're going to that bar over in Brighton. You know, the one with the karaoke."

I felt a flutter in my chest. But then I remembered what we had planned (how could I have forgotten?) and was relieved that I had an actual conflict this time. I shook my head. "I can't. I'm headed to the Vineyard for the weekend."

"You're going to miss book group *again?*" she asked. I nodded. "What are you doing out on the Vineyard? God, Clare, you're so, I don't know, hard to pin down."

I liked Kitty and didn't want to be hard to pin down or elusive or anything else. I wished I'd never said yes to her book group. One meeting had been enough. All those women in one room, yakking and drinking wine, had made me so anxious. "Remember that my mother died last summer? It's a little late, but we're having her memorial service next weekend."

"Oh." Kitty's lips parted. "I'm such a jerk. I'm so sorry. I didn't know."

Suddenly dozens of little voices erupted at the far end of the hall, and I felt their energy blow into the room like a sudden gust of wind.

I stiffened, as I always did before class resumed. Would I ever feel completely confident here?

"It's okay, Kitty," I said. "How would you have known? Most people have memorial services right afterward, not a year later."

"Losing your mom, oh! That must be awful." She shook her head. "I'm never going to survive my mom dying. She's my best friend."

The kids charged into the room, their faces flushed and sweaty. Kitty stood, started toward the door, and tapped each kid on the head as she said, "I know you and you, and I know you." The kids giggled as they watched her. Everyone loved Kitty. Maybe someday I could be like that, too, so loose and comfortable and funny.

As she waved goodbye and blew kisses, I imagined Kitty and her mother having coffee over the breakfast table and talking on the phone.

My mother had been many things but not my best friend.

As the last of the kids filed in, I went over my lesson plan; math and lunch and then a long afternoon of reading, science, and social studies. Did I have enough material to hold everyone's attention? Sophia and Talia rushed by, talking about a sleepover, and stopped at their social studies project at the back table. We were beginning a unit on location and their group was assigned the Pacific Northwest. I watched them bend over their map, talking intently, excitedly, while the other kids, unfocused and uninterested, milled around them.

Lee and I had been like that. We knew each class and each professor that we both had and at night we discussed them all. How many times had we been shushed after waking each other up in the cold dorm? How many times had we obsessed over someone or something—the Rat Man case, Patricia Graceson, the old Russian man—and turned them inside out by talking about them?

I glanced at the window again. The sun, at a different angle now, cast a thick streak through the glass that crossed the center of the blue and red reading rug. Lee and I had not spoken since Amy's wedding, five years earlier. In the beginning she'd written me several short, terse letters that were filled with traces of anger (*well, I've been back from Thailand for three months and happy to tell you about it if only you'd write me back*). But except for a short condolence card after my mother died, she hadn't written in the last couple of years. I always meant to write back. Truth was, my life was calmer with her not in it. Sometimes I went for days without thinking of her or what happened.

"Ms. Michaels?" Paolo stood in front of me, his cowlick sticking out above his right ear and his face twisted in worry. He was a fragile, cautious boy, intimidated by authority. After meeting his father at parent night last week, I could see why.

I knelt in front of him and smiled. "Is everything okay?"

He bit his lip, trying to hold back his tears. "I can't find my mitt."

"Do you remember where you had it last?"

He slapped his hands to his face, hiding his eyes. I watched with alarm as his shoulders began to quiver and knew how embarrassed he'd be if others realized he was crying.

"Think," I said, my voice low and gentle. "Did you leave it on the playground?"

He shrugged, his hands covering his eyes. They were little boy hands, fingers hairless and pudgy, dirt and God knows what else wedged under ragged nails.

I glanced back at Sophia and Talia and watched as Abby, who'd not been happy being usurped by the new girl, maneuvered her way between them. When Abby began talking to Talia, I saw Sophia wilt and wanted to shout to her, "Don't let this happen! Don't let anyone come between you two!"

I licked my dry lips. "How about Sophia goes with you to look for it?"

He nodded and I called Sophia over. After explaining the task, I saw her shoulders rise. She grabbed Paolo's elbow and they hurried out.

I turned to my desk. I needed to get a grip. These were fourth graders. They had their own lives. My job was to teach them, not control or manipulate their friendships or worry about them in this way.

I reached for my math lesson plan.

After school I drove to my parents' house and let myself in the back door with my key. My dad, who'd been devastated when my mother died, had recently begun to feel a bit better. He was taking an antidepressant and getting out of the house for walks and movies and an occasional dinner. But I worried that after the memorial service next week he'd slip back into that quasi-functioning state he'd been in right after she died.

"Dad?" I said. The kitchen was just as I'd left it three days ago—the tin of crackers next to the bowl of apples and oranges, the pile of clean dishtowels next to the stove. Had he eaten the chicken salad I'd made? Did the milk spoil in the refrigerator again? "Dad? Where are you?"

"In here," he called.

I found him at the dining room table, hunched over a piece of paper. *The Boston Globe* and *The New York Times* sat at his elbow. Dozens of copies of *Listen, Before You Go* were stacked at the far end of the table. My dad was only sixty-eight but he'd aged a decade in the two years between my mother's diagnosis for colon cancer and her death. His hair was now fully gray and falling over his eyes. His shoulders, usually so sturdy and broad, were thin and tilted inward. I felt alarm sweep through me. It wasn't easy getting here every day now that school had started, so who would make sure he ate, showered, and got out every day?

"I brought you some biscotti that I made." I put the Tupperware container in front of him. He glanced at it and then went back to the letter he was reading. "Dad?"

"I'm sorry." He put the letter down and looked up at me. "Thank you, my dear. You know how much I love your biscotti."

But he didn't open the container. I shifted my feet and looked around the room. My mother's hospital bed, where she'd spent the last three months of her life, was no longer next to the windows. Also gone were the piles of blankets, sheets, extra chairs, medicine, throw-up pail, bedpan, and all other accoutrements of the sick and dying. And yet I still felt her heavy presence in this room. Watching him, I realized that it wasn't a coincidence, despite all the rooms in this big house, that he'd chosen to do his paperwork in here.

"Have you been out yet today?" I asked. "Or yesterday?"

My dad tilted his head, thinking. "No."

"Dad, you promised to get out every day, remember?"

He waved his hand at me. "I've simply got too

much to do. Look, we just received a letter from your mother's cousin, Oliver, who's coming to the service next week. You remember him?"

How could I forget? His gift, Ellie the stuffed elephant, was forever immortalized in my mind. And in *Listen*, of course. I nodded.

"We're going to have quite a gathering." And then he smiled, a genuine smile, one of the first I'd seen in a long time. "Look at some of these responses."

I sighed and sat next to him. My dad and several of my mother's writer friends had arranged this "memorial celebration in honor of her writing life" at the Vineyard home of one of the writers. Logan and Beth, his fiancée, were coming in for it. My dad's siblings, Aunt Denise and Uncle Richard and their spouses, were driving over from western Massachusetts. And, as my dad told me the other day, there would be a "famous writer or two. Which would have pleased your mother."

I'd finally started to feel as if I had my life back—the last year of her illness had been excruciating for everyone and then there was so much to do after she died—and I wasn't looking forward to making her the center of attention again. But my dad wanted it. He'd been too shattered to do anything but a small family service when she died a year ago last August. I supposed that holding a celebration where we

411

read from her work was an appropriate way to say goodbye.

I picked up a letter from Agnes Menendez, who said she wouldn't miss the service "for the world."

"Who's Agnes Menendez?" I asked. "That name sounds familiar."

"Don't you remember? She and your mother were two of only three women in the English department. She and your mom had quite a rivalry although she isn't a Miltonist. After your mom started publishing fiction, Agnes became humbler."

I glanced at the space in front of the window where the hospital bed had been. My mother had not gone gently into that good night. She'd gone literally kicking and screaming without a moment of peace or resignment or inevitability or remorse or questioning or acceptance or faith. Crippling fear of death eventually killed her, I believed, and it had been excruciating and exhausting to watch.

But my dad didn't want to talk about this.

"How was school today?" he asked.

"Fine."

"That's good."

My parents had been incredulous when I decided not to pursue a PhD but instead work as Kitty's intern in the fourth grade at Meadows. "That's babysitting," my mother had said. I'd defended my decision—I needed to make money and getting a PhD would take years—but I had a hard time looking her in the face when I did it. Not because the job was beneath me, it wasn't, but because I wasn't at all certain that this was what I wanted to do with my life. I still wasn't certain.

I waited to see if my dad would ask anything else and perhaps then I'd give more details about my day. Instead he picked up another letter and read. And then suddenly he sat up and reached across the table. "I almost forgot. I have two things for you. One is a letter which came this morning."

I recognized the handwriting. Lee. Her return address was Manhattan. Last year, Sarah had told me that she was living there again. She'd also said that Lee had gotten married. My dad was watching me, and so I said, "It's from Lee."

"Wonderful. I didn't realize you two were in touch again."

"We aren't." All I'd told my parents, after a bit of probing from them, was that Lee and I had had a falling out and had not recovered.

"Maybe this is a good time to get back in touch. Why not invite her up for the service next week?" He arranged a stack of letters and then rearranged it.

I'd wait to open Lee's letter at home. That way, if she yelled at me again or if I started to cry, I wouldn't have to explain this to my dad. "I don't think so."

And then he put his hand over mine and stared at me with so much concentration that I sucked in a sudden breath. He cleared his throat. "I found something else you might be interested in. It seems as if Lee is all around us today. Here, look at this. I'd say that this is a sign, if I believed in that kind of thing."

He handed me the *Globe,* folded over and squared. In the center was a short article about five documentaries from first-time filmmakers that were set to play at the MFA for a short run beginning tomorrow. Included would be Lee Sumner's documentary, *The Long Slide: A Tale from America's Decline,* about the closing of an automotive plastics factory in Indiana and the "devastating effects this had on the county." I felt my mouth fall open. She'd done it. Lee had made a documentary.

The films, selected out of more than a hundred submitted, were experimental and designed to give an audience to "up-and-coming filmmakers under the age of thirty-five." The program was made possible by grants from several established documentary filmmakers, including Academy Award nominee Patricia Graceson.

Patricia Graceson. Of course. I looked up at my dad.

"Isn't that something?" he asked.

"How did she make a documentary in only four years?" I asked.

"It only took your mother four years to write *Listen*," he said.

"I know, but she was much older," I said. "We're only twenty-nine."

"Well, I can't say that I'm surprised. She was ambitious and although I'd never seen her work, I always had a good feeling about her."

I felt a sudden crush of emotions—jealousy and envy and confusion and despair. Awe, too. How had she come back from Thailand, supported herself, gotten married, and made a documentary that was good enough to be selected? Maybe it wasn't good. Maybe Patricia *had* to include it because she felt indebted to Lee, who dropped her entire life to go to Thailand with her. But that didn't seem right. Other filmmakers were involved in the selection process. You had to have talent and discipline to get something like this done. You had to know what you wanted.

I turned the letter over in my hand. Maybe she wrote to tell me about her film. Maybe she wanted me to see it.

"I tell you what," he said, adjusting his glasses on his nose. "Instead of going to the Public Garden tomorrow, as we planned, let's go see the film."

"I don't know," I said.

"Come on. It'll be fun."

And what could I say? He needed to get out

of the house and I was curious and there was no way Ben would be able to go with me. And so I nodded and made plans to pick him up the next morning at ten.

CHAPTER 22

The theater, tucked into a corner in the museum, was practically empty. An older couple sat in the second row and a young guy, maybe just out of college, a few seats away. When the door opened behind us, I turned and felt my heartbeat leap. But it was only an older man who nodded to us as he walked toward the front. I settled back into my seat. I hadn't realized until then that I was waiting for Lee. I didn't know if I was happy or sad that she wasn't here.

Last night I'd opened her letter when I got home.

> Hi Clare,
>
> Hope you and Ben are well. Things here are good. I got married last year, I'm not sure if you know that or not. Wallace and I met when I got back from Thailand. He's a wonderful guy and I'm very happy.
>
> It's been so long since we last spoke. I feel terrible about how out of touch we are. And so I'm writing for two reasons. First, I want to tell you that I've learned things over the last year that have given me some peace about all that happened, and I thought it might be helpful to you

to hear about it. Second, I have a favor to ask. I need your help with something. Do you think we might be able to get together to talk? I'm not interested in blaming or yelling or anything like that. I just want to talk. I can drive up to see you or maybe we could meet halfway?

I'm sorry, again, about your mom. I hope you're okay. Did you get the card I sent after she died?

It's been so long and I miss the good things about us. Please write back or call. This is really important for both of us.

Lee

For God's sake, what favor did she want to ask? What could I possibly do to help her? Surely she hadn't forgotten what I'd done. Just thinking about this again—which I tried so hard not to do anymore—caused sharp, hot stings to break out across the back of my neck. And what peace had she found?

"This is quite something." My dad leaned over and whispered in my ear. "Not many people get to make movies and have them actually shown in a real theater."

"I know."

"Your mother and I liked her quite a bit," he said.

"I know."

My parents met Lee when she visited the Vineyard for a weekend after freshman year. My mother hadn't wanted overnight guests. She was revising her new book and kept a strict schedule. But I'd talked so much about Lee that she and my dad were intrigued, especially when I said that there might not be another opportunity for her to visit (her aunt had a conference in Boston and Lee was driving out with her). And so it was agreed.

I met Lee in Boston and we took the ferry to the Vineyard. By the time we got to our house, my parents were asleep. The next morning, I woke late and the twin bed next to me was empty. I checked the house but couldn't find Lee. I looked out the window and saw my mother at the picnic table, her typewriter in front of her. When Lee came around the corner of the house and stood next to her, I hurried out.

"Lee was telling me about her farm." My mother kept her eyes on Lee as she spoke. Her opinions, her mood, her well-being, her reason for living, the affection she had for others—even Betsy, the woman in Oak Bluffs who cut her hair—depended on one thing. How she felt about her writing. And it had been a rough summer.

"Did you get some coffee, Lee?" I nodded toward the kitchen.

Lee, dressed in her Army fatigue cutoffs and white T-shirt, with a red bandana tied pirate style around her head, said, "Not yet."

My mother frowned as she looked Lee up and down, and I felt the obvious snub rip through me. I imagined what happened. Lee interrupted her and now my mother would make her pay, make *me* pay, for this infraction. How unfair.

"We're going to the beach." I spit the words.

"I'll change," Lee said. My mother glanced at Lee's shorts as she passed by the table on her way into the house.

"I told you, she doesn't have much money," I hissed through clenched teeth.

"Ah, yes, of course." She nodded slightly.

"Don't be so judgmental! God!" I stomped into the house.

After I changed and we packed a lunch, we walked by my mother on our way to the car. It was sunny and hot and the crushed stones on the driveway crunched beneath our flip-flops. I was still angry but Lee hadn't seemed to let my mother's condescension bother her. Nor did she seem intimidated. She'd talked nonstop as we made sandwiches. *You have so many flowers in your garden. It's so beautiful here! I've never seen anywhere like this. Why don't people paint their houses? Where did all of the stone walls come from? How many people live here year-round?*

As we put our cooler and towels into the trunk, my mother called to us. "The Donahues are coming for dinner tonight. Will you be joining us?"

No way. But Lee slowly smiled and nodded at me. I'd told her about the crazy novels that Mr. Donahue wrote, and that his wife was a painter, and of course she remembered. Of course she was intrigued.

"I thought we'd get lobsters." Was my mother offering an apology? Because certainly she remembered that lobsters were my favorite.

"I've never had lobster," Lee said.

"You're joking," she said. Lee shook her head. "They'll be here at seven."

"We'll be back by then, right?" Lee looked at me and then at my mother. "Maybe I could help with the lobsters. You know, see how you make them."

Not since I was little had anyone been excited to make lobsters with my mother. She kept her head tilted as she stared at Lee and then she nodded. Was she thawing? As we drove away, I wanted to stay angry. But as I watched her slump over her typewriter, her elbows on the table and her head in her hands, I felt that familiar pull toward her. I wanted to tell her that she didn't have to write today. She could work in the garden or go into town. No one would take away her legacy. No one would be angry if she took another two years to finish her new novel.

We were back from the beach by five, and when we walked into the kitchen my mother, standing at the counter, turned and smiled. She'd had a good writing day, I could tell, and that meant we might have a nice evening.

I was right. The lobsters were great—Lee had watched dutifully as my mother explained how to cook them—and we talked at the table for hours. My dad kept opening bottles of wine and my mother kept insisting that the Donahues stay. Lee didn't want to leave, either. She loved the lobster. She loved the salad. She said that she hadn't ever had that kind of wine but she loved that, too. We all felt her excitement, even my mother although she wasn't quite won over yet.

"But don't cornfields have their own sense of beauty?" my mother asked. We'd been talking about the stone walls along Middle Road, and Lee said it was the most beautiful stretch of road she'd ever seen. *In my entire life.*

Lee put her elbows on the table and leaned forward. "Maybe when you grow up with something, when you're around it every day, you don't see it anymore."

"Maybe you never really see it to begin with," Mr. Donahue said. He was a lawyer who wrote crime novels on the side and was probably my dad's closest friend. Mrs. Donahue, a landscape painter, sat across from him. She was nice but never said much, which was part of the reason why I thought my mother liked her.

"How can you not see something right in front of you?" Dad asked.

"It happens to people who aren't paying attention," my mother said.

"Maybe it takes something really unusual in your everyday life to get your attention," Lee said. "I remember one time last year when the sun was going down and I looked across the cornfields and the sky was the most unusual red that I'd *ever* seen. It was so beautiful that it hurt to look at it. It hurt everywhere. I almost couldn't breathe. I started to cry. I just sat there and kept crying."

"Our natural world can do that to a person, can't it?" Mrs. Donahue asked.

I knew for certain that I'd never felt pain or was unable to breathe when I looked at the sky or the stone walls on Middle Road or really anything in nature. I wasn't sure that I *wanted* to feel that way. But then looking at the smile on Lee's face and the way everyone was nodding, I felt as if I were missing something.

"A beautiful sunset or stone wall should make you feel good, happy. Isn't there enough pain in our world?" I asked.

"She's got a point." My dad grinned. "Practical Clare!"

Everyone laughed except my mother. She stared at Lee as if trying to decide something about her. I sucked in a breath and held it.

"The question is," my mother said to Lee as everyone turned to her, "what do you do with all that raw emotion you experienced watching the sunset?"

I looked at my mother. I didn't think I'd ever heard her utter the words "raw" or "emotion" and certainly never in the same sentence.

"You soak it in, the good and bad, and feel it, I guess," Lee said. "Eventually you use it in your work. Think about what you did in 'The Confidences.' Lieutenant McCalister and the others in the trench are great characters. They try to be brave but underneath they're terrified of death. Right? That's using raw emotion."

I expected my mother to recoil at this, but instead, she sat back in her chair and nodded slightly. Maybe this was because most people didn't talk to her about her short story, published in a literary magazine not long after *Listen* came out. Most people wanted to talk about her novel and how they had family members who had returned damaged from war. Or they wanted to tell her that they, too, had loved ones who had killed themselves.

I was proud, suddenly, that Lee could talk to these adults about things like raw emotion and documentaries and that we were so close. My high school friends had always been so weird around my mother. Shy. Intimidated. Or overly aggressive as they tried to impress her. Lee was none of these. She was unique and independent, the type of person people looked up to. And out of all the girls in our dorm, and at our school, she'd chosen me for a friend. *Me!* And this was before she even knew who my mother was. I blurted, grinning, "Lee's going to be a filmmaker."

"A filmmaker!" Mr. Donahue said. "Off to Hollywood, I imagine."

Lee shook her head. "I don't want to go to California because I don't want to make those kinds of movies."

I tried not to smile. If ever there was a way to get on my mother's good side, it was to be anti-Hollywood although Lee didn't know this.

My mother was still staring at Lee but she no longer looked as if she wanted to skewer her. She asked, "What kinds of films do you like?"

"All kinds," she said. "Sometimes my aunt and I spend weekends watching the same movie, over and over. But I want to make documentaries. Because I think it's interesting to try to get at the real truth behind actual people and events."

"You don't think a Hollywood film can get at real truth?" my mother asked.

"Maybe," Lee said. "But I think those kinds of films try to be entertaining more than anything else."

My mother licked her bottom lip and nodded slightly and I could tell that she was thinking about this, not dismissing it as she so easily did with information she didn't believe or care about. I grinned at Lee—wasn't this terrific?—because I liked that she wasn't intimidated. I liked that my mother was intrigued.

"So, where are you going to do this film-making?" Mr. Donahue asked.

"Well, this is the *most* beautiful place I've ever seen." Lee sat up, her voice high-pitched and excited. The wine and reflection from the candles had turned her cheeks shiny and red. "I can hardly take my eyes off everything, all these stone walls and the ocean. And the houses are so old. It has such a great feel! But I want to move to New York. I just think that's the place for me. I *have* to do this."

"Your joie de vivre is infectious." My mother chuckled.

"Amen," my dad said.

Lee grinned although I didn't think she had any idea what my mother meant. I raised my glass to her and we both took long drinks from our wine.

After that my mother was looser, laughing at Dad's description of the old whaling boat and Mr. Donahue's story about his law partner. I hadn't seen her like this in a long time and wouldn't see her like this again for a while. It was Lee, the wine, her writing day. I wasn't sure what else.

"Eleanor, I've been meaning to ask you," Mr. Donahue said. "Did you ever read that article I left for you? The interview with the South American writer?"

My mother began nodding vigorously. "Yes, yes, very interesting."

Mr. Donahue leaned forward as he glanced around the table. "This article was about a very successful writer although I'd never read anything by her. Anyway, she told the interviewer that her 'well of creativity' had dried up. All gone. Vanished. Vamoose! She blamed it on her eight years in psychoanalysis."

"Can the well really dry up or does it just go into hiding?" Dad asked.

"What happened?" Mrs. Donahue asked. "She conquered her demons?"

"That's nonsense," my mother said. "I never found therapy particularly helpful. The drugs they put me on made me an automaton. And what was the point of unearthing the mundane and the miserable? Wasn't it bad enough experiencing them the first time?"

Everyone laughed. Mr. Donahue kept nodding.

My mother didn't talk much about her childhood. The only miserable things she'd ever told me about happened to her parents and grandparents, not to her. For example, before she was born, her parents—stoic, no-nonsense New Englanders—had had a three-month-old girl who'd died in her crib, and they never spoke about it. And my mother's grandfather had killed himself behind his barn in Vermont, of course. To this day, I still didn't know what she meant by miserable.

I glanced at Lee, who seemed to be sitting on the edge of her seat, listening. And then she said, "Speaking of writing, can you talk about your new book?"

My mother waved her hand and laughed. She was a little drunk. "Let's just say that I'm in Saigon tackling issues associated with the South Vietnamese in the days before the fall. It's a bit of a love story but mostly a tragedy. My honorable American corporal has suffered greatly in the jungle. And that's all I care to say."

"Bravo!" Mrs. Donahue said.

"Your fans will expect a war story, to be sure," Mr. Donahue said. "It's an important subject, that troops coming home often suffer emotionally. You were the first to write about this."

"No," my mother said. "Crane and Vonnegut, among others, wrote about this."

"Maugham, too," Mrs. Donahue said.

"But you really highlight, in a different way, what happens to loved ones," Dad said. "Because families always suffer, too."

"Do you think you'll ever get away from writing about war?" Lee asked.

The candles flickered and outside, I heard the steady groan of the bullfrog from the Hendersons' pond. No one dared look at my mother except Lee, who had no idea what she'd just asked. Finally, I snuck a look. My mother was frowning, her eyebrows arched in severe half circles above her eyes. I felt a rush of heat to my cheeks and opened my mouth to say something.

"Not until our government stops meddling in places we don't belong!" My dad pounded the table with his fist and everyone jumped. Mrs. Donahue's wineglass teetered and would have fallen if Lee hadn't reached for it. "It's too important of a subject. Sorry, Lee. We get carried away by politics here."

My dad smiled at Lee and then everyone laughed, including my mother, who raised her wineglass and said, "To Lee, the budding filmmaker, and her first time in New England. And to Clare, who's made such an interesting friend."

Everyone cheered with raised glasses.

Later, after the Donahues had gone and my parents were in bed, Lee and I cleaned up the kitchen. By this time, I was fairly sober although Lee was a little drunk. She must have told me a dozen times how much fun she'd had. "It was so great, you know, sitting at the table and talking about everything. Mr. and Mrs. Donahue were so nice and smart. Everyone is so smart here."

Finally, I said, "I'm sure your parents do that when their friends are over."

"My parents don't have friends over."

"Not ever?" I asked. She shook her head. "Not even for dinner?"

"My parents don't have friends. And they

don't talk about politics or books or movies or emotions. My mom doesn't have a job. She isn't cool like your mom."

This was a year before I visited her farm and realized how different our backgrounds truly were. Still, I remembered feeling a little annoyed. "My mom isn't always like what you saw tonight. Most of the time she's really moody."

I handed Lee a wineglass that she dried and placed on the shelf. And then she put one hand on her hip and the other on the counter and said, "Yeah, I guess it'd be really hard living with someone who was that dedicated to her work."

And I remembered turning to her as she concentrated on drying another wineglass and feeling as if that had been the perfect thing to say. Not how great my mother was or how famous or that she was a good writer. Those were all things junior high and high school friends had said to me over the years.

Would Lee have had the perfect thing to say if I'd called while my mother was dying? Her sympathy card to me afterward was short and to the point. *I'm sorry for your loss. Your mom was always so nice to me. I hope you're okay*. No traces of anger. No asking for favors. She'd been busy, I knew now. She was making a film.

I glanced at my dad as the theater lights dimmed. He nodded and said, "Good. Here we go."

I sat forward in my seat. We were in the dark until a faint light appeared on the screen. Slowly the scene came into view as the camera passed over a vast field with stunted, brittle cornstalks and swirls of snow. I gripped the seat in front of me with both hands. I remembered that weekend when we visited her farm and how everything looked so bleak, just like this.

I was suddenly hungry for something familiar, a snapshot of her farm, her house, the bar where we met her aunt, the long driveway with the fields on both sides. I scooted forward until my knees touched the empty seat in front of me. The camera panned to railroad tracks, and I realized that these were Lee's tracks, where she'd taken me that day the goose was run over. There was the clump of trees. And the ridge above the river. This was it! Then her voice filled the room— "There's a particular sound a train whistle makes on cold winter mornings . . ."

I startled—actually, it was more like a slap across the face, so sudden and sharp—and in my mind I saw her smile and how we sat in her theater in Bloomington on Sunday afternoons, our feet on the chairs in front of us, eating stale popcorn while watching whatever was showing. But this was *her* movie, the one we should have been talking about all these years, and yet we hadn't. Because I didn't have the courage to write back. Because I had ended our friendship.

What favor did she want to ask? What peace? *I miss all of the good things about us.* Oh, God, I missed that, too.

I saw images on the screen. People talking. Cornfields. Empty parking lots. And suddenly the movie was over. I had no idea how much time had passed. As the credits rolled, people around us began to leave but I watched until the screen went blank and the lights turned on.

"That was awfully short but good," my dad said. "Timely, too. The disappearance of small-town America is happening everywhere. Logan and I were talking about this yesterday. He's quite a capitalist these days. I think we've lost him to the Republicans. Did you like it?"

"Yes," I said, still staring at the screen. But I'd have a hard time telling anyone what I just saw. I needed to go home and think about it.

That night Ben was home early—around eight—and we ate dinner on the tiny back porch of our condo. We'd bought this place last year. On the top floor of a four-story brownstone in Brookline, it was bright and spacious with two large bedrooms, a new kitchen, and a living room with a fireplace. It was close to the T and my dad and so new to us that we were still a little giddy that it was ours.

"So, tell me about it," Ben said as he scooted to the table. He'd changed into shorts and a Red Sox T-shirt but he still had that disheveled look

I always associated with work. Maybe it was because his hair, longer now than in college, was sticking out haphazardly on his head, as if he'd literally been pulling it out all day. I stood at the table, holding bowls of a new recipe, coq au vin, and then put one in front of him. Ben pushed the frame of his wire-rimmed glasses higher on his nose and dug his fork into his bowl before I'd even pulled out my chair.

"Well, it was good." I sat and cradled my wineglass in my hands.

"Come on, give me details," he said, his mouth full.

I put down my glass and took a bite. The chicken practically melted in my mouth and the sauce was both sweet and rich. I'd been right to make this last night and let it sit in the refrigerator for twenty-four hours. Ben nodded as he ate, his eyes glossed over in gastronomical ecstasy. It was still such a joy to watch him eat.

I took another bite and then a long drink of wine. Because I still didn't know what to think about Lee's film. Had I not been paying attention? Maybe it was just that I didn't like talking to Ben about Lee. I still hadn't told him what happened between us, not any of it, and now this omission—these lies—seemed almost bigger than the original sin. I cringed. Had I committed a sin?

"It was about a factory closing in Indiana

near her hometown and the damage that did to people," I said, finally. She'd interviewed a man in overalls with a John Deere cap and a shoe store owner who went out of business. Now I remembered.

"Was it any good?" he asked. I nodded. "Maybe you should call or something. Tell her that you saw it. It might be a good way to break the ice between you."

I looked away because I hadn't told him about Lee's letter, either, and what she'd said. I hadn't told him about any of the letters. I felt this wedge between us and I imagined, suddenly, sitting on broken pieces of ice and drifting away from each other. Married couples shouldn't have secrets from each other. I had an ocean full.

But this wasn't completely true. Years ago I'd confessed to not loving tutoring and that I didn't want to go for a PhD. He knew I didn't want to teach fourth grade for the rest of my life, either. I'd told him these things. I'd fessed up and it hadn't been a disaster. He'd been only mildly disappointed.

"You know, if you call her, you don't have to talk about what happened in Florida," he said. "She probably doesn't want to be reminded of that, either. Just talk about regular stuff. Talk about her film. You know?"

Let her go, I'll stay.

I took another long drink of wine. Maybe Lee

434

wanted help piecing together the events of that night in Florida. Maybe she wanted to press charges against those guys. It was one thing to tell Ben that I didn't know what I wanted to do with my life. But this was different. What was it that my dad said about Watergate? The cover-up was worse than the crime. He and Ben were talking about this the other night.

"How was work?" My throat felt tight, constricted.

"Pretty intense right now." Ben's voice sped up. "Now that Patrick wants me to argue part of the McDougal case, he's got me working all aspects of it. I found some hilarious laws, though, when looking through the New York state books. Did you know that it's against the law to throw a ball at someone's head? And that a person can't walk around on Sundays with an ice-cream cone in his pocket?"

Ben laughed, took a drink from his wine, and continued.

I stared at my wineglass. How did Lee get those bumpy opening shots of the cornfield and the snow? Maybe she hung out the window of a car. Did her husband help? How did she meet him? Were they thinking about having children, too?

"Hey." Ben nudged my arm, and I startled and looked at him. "You're not listening. But I get it. I'm pretty swallowed up in the minutia." He chuckled.

"I'm sorry. I guess I'm a little distracted." I smiled at him. Ben wanted to make partner someday, and he was doing everything possible to make this happen. The least I could do was be supportive. "Go on."

"Nah, forget it." He grinned and sat up. "Hey, I got two tickets for the last regular season game at Fenway. I thought I'd take your dad."

Ben would much rather go to the game with Tommy, a friend from law school who'd moved here last year, or with one of his three brothers who all still lived where they'd grown up, near Baltimore, and would fly up in a moment. I felt the goodness of this—it would help my dad *and* me—settle heavy in my chest. "That's so nice."

"Hard to believe he wasn't a baseball fan until I moved up here." He smiled, proud that he'd converted my dad, who'd never watched an entire game in his life.

"It was such an escape for him last summer and fall," I said, recovering a bit.

Ben dropped his eyes as he mopped up the last of his dinner with a huge hunk of bread. Over the last year, he'd been so helpful with things like setting up the hospital bed and taking their cars for oil changes. He fixed their downspout, which sent water into the basement every time it rained, and went to the lawyer with my dad to straighten out their trust. So, who could blame him if he couldn't be in the same room with my mother,

436

that her pain and paranoia made him petrified and mute? Who could blame him if he could barely stand to listen to me fumble with the grief and confusion I felt when she died? Ben had many strengths. Sitting with extreme emotions wasn't one of them.

I stood and began stacking dishes. I hoped Sophie and Talia were having a sleepover tonight. I wondered how Paolo, who hadn't found his mitt, would deal with the wrath of his dad. And I thought of Lee, maybe having dinner with her husband tonight, too, and wondering if I'd write back. I felt a sob start up my throat.

Ben reached for my arm, put the dishes back on the table, and then lowered me into his lap. I wrapped my hands around his neck and buried my face into his shoulder. He felt warm and smelled faintly like coffee and a bit like he'd soon need a shower. He whispered, "What?"

"I don't know!" I sobbed. But oh, I certainly did. I knew.

"Are you thinking about your mom?" he asked.

I shrugged and kept my face against his shoulder.

"Know what I was thinking?" He nudged my head so that I sat up and looked at him. He had a tiny piece of chicken between his two front teeth and a cold sore in the corner of his mouth. I ran my finger over his bumpy dimple and then tightened my hands around his neck. "Maybe we should start trying again. It's been a rough year with your mom and my job but that's behind us now. Well, not my job. But anyway, what do you say? You ready to go at it again?"

He was talking about a baby. Before my mother died, we'd tried for a few months but stopped when she took a turn and had needed so much. He was right. That was behind us. But I didn't know if now was the right time. I didn't seem to know much about anything except that being a mother sounded terrifying. I didn't know how to take care of a baby. What if I made a mistake? But I nodded because I didn't want Ben to worry, and I needed time to think about this.

The next morning, Ben got up early, went for a run in the drizzle, and as he showered, promised that tomorrow morning he wouldn't go in to work until ten. I was still in my pajamas, a cup of coffee in my hand, as I sat on the side of the tub. It was a perfect rainy Saturday to stay in.

"Are you always going to work weekends?" I asked.

"No, of course not," he said, his wet dirty blond hair shiny under the bathroom lights. "This is just because of what's going on now."

I wasn't sure I believed him.

"I'm sorry, sweetie." He toweled off and combed his hair and then I followed him back into the bedroom. He kissed me on my lips and yanked a polo shirt over his head. "I won't be late. Promise. Wanna do something tonight?"

"Sure."

As I listened to him in the kitchen pouring cereal into a bowl, I imagined him standing at the counter, eating quickly, his mind already on the tasks for today. I thought about Kitty yesterday, surprised that Ben worked so many hours. But I'd met the spouses of many of the lawyers in his firm, and their husbands and a few wives worked just as much as Ben. Besides, I was used to it. This was how my mother worked, obsessively, continuously, until two months before she died.

I watched the rain flow in parallel tracks down the window. Had Lee and I passed the automobile plastics factory when we visited her farm? I couldn't remember what she said in the film about why it closed. Or what the unemployment and poverty rates were. But I remembered how she pronounced Chicago with that sharp emphasis on the first syllable and how her voice climbed, in that familiar way, to emphasize a point.

I hadn't paid enough attention to the film. Maybe if I saw it again, I'd be able to answer these questions. I put down my coffee and headed for the shower.

Two hours later, I sat in the empty theater. This time when the lights dimmed and the scene opened on the cornfield and snow and I heard Lee's voice, I tried to concentrate on

439

what she said. The automotive plastics factory had employed 347 people, making it the largest employer within fifty miles. The closing affected every business in the county. The poverty rate doubled. Unemployment skyrocketed.

Why had Lee chosen this topic? How long did it take her to make? Did it consume her? If so, who did the laundry? The shopping? Who made dinner?

When the film was over, I felt as unsettled as I had yesterday.

The next morning after Ben ran, showered, and ate his cereal standing at the counter, I told myself that I wouldn't go back to the theater. With school in session all week, I should spend today getting things in order for the memorial service next weekend. I needed to pick out an outfit and plan Friday night's dinner. Logan had called to say that he and Beth would arrive on the four o'clock ferry, earlier than planned. Oliver would be there for dinner as well.

Maybe I'd look through the recipes I'd started to collect. Or, while shopping for a new outfit, I'd stop at the bookstore and look through cookbooks. Would the Vineyard farms still have produce available? Should I bake a few loaves of bread? See, these were the things I needed to figure out.

Instead, I showered and took the T back to the MFA. Because I needed to be critical. This time,

I'd critique it as I would a novel. I'd been good at this as a student. It was the creative part that always stumped me. What kind of interesting, original point did I want to make about a text? I couldn't ever come up with anything.

At the theater, I took my regular seat in the second row. When the door opened and an older woman walked in, I frowned. But I had no claims on this film. When it started and Lee's voice filled the theater, I began to pick it apart. The music was too depressing. The man complaining about the food in the soup kitchen was too predictable. And wasn't it self-indulgent to think anyone would care about a small town in Indiana? How ironic that she'd returned to her hometown for her first professional film after she'd spent so much time plotting to leave.

But as the poor woman who'd lost everything talked into the camera, I felt myself sucked into the narrative. Just look at her! She lost her job, her house, and then her husband died of heart disease. Lee had done a noble service, calling attention to this. And she'd lived her dream.

When the film was over, I stayed seated while the woman left and the credits rolled. I didn't move when the lights came on, either. Because this was it. All next week, I'd be in school when this was shown, and the following weekend, I'd be on the Vineyard. I rubbed my temples. It was time to go.

I took the T back to Brookline, stopped at the market, and picked up a few groceries for my dad. On my way to his house, I saw a girl on the sidewalk in front of me, her long black hair shimmering in the sunlight. I sucked in a quick breath and stopped walking. When she turned, I saw that she wasn't Lee. But I'd been looking for her. Maybe that was why I'd gone back to the theater. Maybe I was looking for her so she could explain what favor she wanted from me.

CHAPTER 23

I found my dad asleep on the living room couch, his shoes on the floor next to him and the newspaper, open to the crossword puzzle, across his chest. I tiptoed back into the kitchen, put away the ice cream, milk, and other groceries and then stood at the counter. I could clean although the kitchen was spotless. Instead, I walked into my mother's office.

A small room, it had most likely been a large pantry or the maid's room back when the house was built. Floor-to-ceiling bookcases covered two walls. A small window, on a third wall, looked out into the backyard. My mother's desk, a wood behemoth she'd bought from the widow of a Shakespearean, floated in the middle of the room. I sat in the leather chair and pulled myself up to the desk.

Growing up, I hadn't come in here much. It wasn't interesting in the way that some of my high school friends' parents' offices were. There were no pictures on the wall, no snacks in the drawers, no surprises (we found a bag of pot in Mr. Kepler's drawer). Just books. Her typewriter. A box of typewriter paper. Pens. And because she threw nothing out, stacks of manuscripts and correspondence. Which were now conspicuously missing. We'd gone through most everything, giving much of it to the university library for its Eleanor Michaels collection.

All that was left to go through were these drawers.

Not long after my mother died, my dad told me that he'd finally read over what she'd been working on for the last five years. It was about a ground patrol company in Europe during the latter part of the Second World War. Did I want to see it? No, I'd said. I was tired of her war stories. And I needed space from her.

When my mother became terminal at the beginning of last summer, I came here every day. I stayed with her while my dad ran errands or rested. I went with them to appointments at Dana Farber. I made meals and read to her. Occasionally my dad and I were alone together while she slept or the visiting nurse was with her. During those times, he never complained or criticized her. He was so crushed by what was happening that I didn't have the heart to complain or criticize, either.

But it was unbearable. A hospice nurse once said to me that "passing" was sometimes graceful, even peaceful. Not for my mother. Her fear of death was palpable in her shrieks and moans and dry heaves and shakes. She had bedsores, bleeding skin, terrible hallucinations, and a face constantly contorted with pain and fear. She had only twenty-four hours of unconsciousness before she died. It was hard to remember that day. Mostly I remembered her misery. And that there was absolutely nothing I could do to save her. Was there any wonder why I felt ready to move on when she finally died?

Under the desk and to the right were three large drawers, each stuffed. I'd tried to go at them before, but my dad had been adamant about leaving this for last. I pulled open the bottom drawer as far as it would go and lifted out a stack of papers. There were a few letters from Janice, a bunch of envelopes tied together with a rubber band, a box of pencils (unsharpened), a dry cleaning receipt, and a large manuscript in a blue binder. I opened to the first page. It was a draft of the ground patrol story. I glanced at the note she'd scrawled at the top of the page. *Draft #1.*

This would have to go to the library with the other drafts. I closed the cover and when I lifted it again, a paper slipped out and fell to the floor. It wasn't part of the manuscript. It was a letter. From Lucy. I sat back in my seat. I'd often thought of her over the years, especially toward the end of my mother's life when she lay in bed, thumbing through her copy of *Listen*, and I sat silent and baffled, unable (because she was dying? Because I was a coward?) to confront her with my understanding of what she'd done to this poor woman. I picked up the letter and began to read.

Dear Eleanor,

I have written you three times, all delivered to your publisher, without a response, and so I don't imagine you'll write me back this time. But I hope you will because I'm sure that I deserve answers.

I was a vulnerable sophomore when I met you. I used to sit in your Milton class, admiring you. You were so confident and smart! Soon afterward, we began having meaningful office hour conversations. Remember how you clapped after I recited that memorized part of Book One from *Paradise Lost*? You said you'd never had a student do that before. Never. I was the first and only.

We talked about my family, and you listened and smiled and gave me that extension on my first paper. That was so nice! But then something changed. Something always changes. And it wasn't because I didn't have "boundaries," like you said, or that I needed "real help." I was okay when you said we couldn't go out to dinner or coffee. I was! Here's what I think: You were so interested when I said my brother had come back, unhappy, from Vietnam. I think you were planning on stealing my story about him all along.

But you messed it up. My brother didn't kill himself. He wasn't ashamed of what he did over there. He didn't have mental problems. Nobody in our family has mental problems! He was a hero, even if he never got the medals he deserved. And the Phoebe character you created wasn't me, either. I wasn't some weird kid who "listened" and could only talk to adults. I had friends. People liked me. They did. You can ask anyone. And my brother liked me, too. But now he won't even let me in his house. He won't let me near his three children! And the reason is because of that book. It's because of you.

You owe me an explanation. You owe me part of the royalty money, too.

These years have been very hard. Because of this. I can't work because I have terrible migraines. My roommate is forcing me to leave our apartment. And my family refuses to help me. I'm not asking for much. (I know you've made millions. I've done research. You've sold hundreds and hundreds of thousands of books.) All I'm asking is for $15,000. I don't think this is too much to ask.

I scanned the rest of the letter, which was more of the same, and left it on the desk as I hurried from the room. I stopped in the kitchen and dropped into a chair. Lucy was emotionally unstable. How had I not seen that? Or maybe I had seen it but ultimately chose to believe her, anyway?

The letter made things clearer. My mother may have gotten the idea for Phoebe and Whit from Lucy, but there hadn't been an actual story to steal. My mother's version of the characters, and the suicide, weren't Lucy's, either. And yet I'd believed Lucy. For years, I'd been angry with my mother because I thought she'd been in the wrong.

"Hello? Who's there?" My dad's voice was shaky, full of confusion.

In the living room, I found him sitting on the couch, hair askew and his face in his hands as if he were crying. I knelt in front of him. "Are you okay?"

He dropped his hands. "I heard something. I didn't know it was you."

"I'm sorry. You were sleeping and I didn't want to wake you."

"I was having the most vivid dream," he said. "Your mother and I were walking on Middle Road and we'd stopped to admire a bunch of wildflowers and she'd turned to me, her face lit up and alive. Just like she used to be!"

I sat back on my heels. There it was on his face and in his voice; he'd like nothing more than to have her back with us. He stared at me for confirmation, for agreement, and I nodded even though I wasn't sure. Despite what I'd just learned, my mother still confused me. And I wasn't ready to forgive her.

CHAPTER 24

One dish!

That was all Logan brought in from the dining room. And now he leaned against the screen doorframe, arms folded across the front of his button-down, spouting off about politics while Ben and I washed the dishes. Beth, who was in the living room looking through our mother's books—Ben and I weren't sure she ever read anything, especially novels—hadn't even pretended to help.

"Mark my words," Logan said. "It was a big mistake not to follow Saddam Hussein back to Baghdad and annihilate him and that entire piece of shit country. I don't know why Bush didn't do that. It makes us look weak. And we can't afford to look weak in that part of the world. It's just too important. Oil is too important. Dad doesn't get that. He doesn't understand how oil rules the world."

"That's not very nice, Logan, he can hear you." I glanced out the window above the sink at Dad, who was in the driveway saying goodbye to Oliver.

Logan shrugged and took a long drink from his wine.

I looked at Ben, who was scrubbing a pot,

451

his expression unchanged. That Logan was a Republican was only part of the problem. "The Prince is a pompous ass," according to Ben, who tried never to engage with him. This drove Logan so crazy that it often made him more belligerent. Sometimes this cycle was too much. That we'd all had many bottles of wine made things even worse.

"I suppose you and Clare vote exactly like our parents," Logan said.

Ben stopped scrubbing and looked up. He'd begun to sweat, just a thin line running down his temple, and the vein in his neck—the one that pulsed so noticeably when he was stressed or angry—had begun to throb. But his voice was neutral, casual. "Can you check the table to make sure all the dishes are off?"

Logan sighed, turned, and disappeared into the dining room. Ben rolled his eyes at me, and I grinned as I wrapped my arms around his waist and buried my head in his chest. He smelled familiar, like dirt and the wind, and I felt his heart beating slowly, steadily against my cheek. Then I let go, picked up a dishcloth and started drying wineglasses.

Dinner had been a success. The menu I'd finally decided on—grilled salmon with sautéed new potatoes with fresh dill, salad, and apple cobbler with homemade vanilla-maple ice cream—turned out great. We'd sat around the table, Aunt Denise and Uncle Phil, Aunt Diane and Uncle Richard and Oliver, too, until nearly eleven. Now they were on their way back to the inn and I was exhausted. The memorial service was to begin at ten tomorrow morning. It would be a big day.

"What did you think of Oliver?" I asked.

Ben shrugged. "Seemed okay. Smart. Quiet. Nice to finally meet someone from your mom's side of the family."

"Did you hear Logan tell him that he has a cook now?" I whispered. "What was Oliver supposed to think? Why does Logan need all of that help?"

Logan and Beth's Manhattan apartment took up an entire floor. A cook, in addition to two maids, now meant that the staff outnumbered my brother and his fiancée. Logan worked hard for his money. But it was his attitude that bothered me.

"It's the money, Clare," Ben said. "I've seen it make even the most level-headed people crazy."

"Well, I wouldn't want it," I said.

"Really? I wouldn't mind having that house in the Hamptons." Ben grinned and nodded toward the door. "Or her."

I shoved him. "Right. Have you forgotten what you said about her? That she's drawn so tight the wind could snap her in half?"

Ben laughed.

Logan walked back into the kitchen, set two plates on the counter, and then filled his glass, and Ben's, with more wine. Ben kept on washing.

They were such a contrast; Ben in sneakers, jeans, and his favorite blue polo shirt, faded from so many washings, and Logan in tan chinos, loafers, and white button-down that looked so new and stiff that I imagined it could stand on its own.

I wondered, as I sometimes did, what it would have been like had Logan married Elise (I never did write to her). Maybe nights like tonight would have been more fun. Maybe Logan and I would have been closer.

Our five-year age difference never allowed for an overlap of friends or interests. Still, I remembered a time—I couldn't have been older than nine or ten—when Logan and I seemed connected. He'd often walk into whatever room I was in, pick me up, spin me around, and dump me on the floor, both of us laughing. Or he'd put me on his bike handlebars and ride into town for ice cream. We'd take the T to meet Dad for lunch, too. We always rode the waves together at Lucy Vincent.

And then everything changed. Seemingly overnight, he turned into an angry, distant grouch. He called our parents socialists and argued with them about everything from politics to the color of his bedroom. He spent most of his time with friends. He cut his hair and dressed in Lacoste polo shirts and argyle sweaters. And once he went off to Dartmouth, he rarely came home again. As I watched him lean against the counter, I thought that there was so much about him that I didn't know. Did he have a best friend? Had he ever done something he was ashamed of? Did he truly love Beth? Did he miss Elise?

And then Dad was back in the kitchen. His shoulders seemed to swim in his button-down and his face was drawn and tired. Logan had talked my parents into a major renovation of the house just before my mother got sick. Now we had a new kitchen with more counter space, a porcelain sink, and shiny, new appliances. We expanded the dining room and built a guest bedroom and bath around the corner from the living room. We added a new bathroom upstairs and a high-quality outdoor shower. It was lovely and more comfortable, although I couldn't help but feel that we'd sacrificed charm for resale value.

"Well, Clare, you outdid yourself," my dad said. "Dinner was delicious. Everyone loved it. Thank you."

"You're welcome," I said. "How are you feeling? Are you tired?"

"Yes, I'm quite exhausted. Do you mind if I turn in?"

"No, no, go ahead," Ben and I said together.

My dad gripped Ben's arm with one hand and patted him on the back with the other. He kissed my forehead and then stopped in front of Logan. "Well, son, I want you to think about something.

You don't ever want to invade another country unless it's absolutely necessary. We got the Iraqis out of Kuwait, where they didn't belong, but we didn't have the moral authority or the support from allies to follow them back to Baghdad. War is a terrible, terrible thing. You must never enter into it lightly. Now, good night. See you in the morning."

He patted Logan's cheek and turned for the living room.

Logan snorted and opened his mouth, no doubt to say something smartass.

"Can we lay off politics and war?" I asked. "I'm sick of both of them."

Logan shrugged and dropped into a chair. When he spoke again, his voice was softer, less confrontational. "He seems okay, Clare? Yes?"

How irritating. Couldn't he tell for himself whether Dad was okay or not? Couldn't he ask *him* how he was? But I also felt proud that he looked to me for the answer. It was an acknowledgment of who I'd been and what I'd done, especially these last couple of years when I helped our dad and sat by our mother's bedside while he was off in New York, Hong Kong, and God knows where else.

"It's day to day," I said. "He misses her, terribly."

I almost added that we all missed her terribly, but I knew that wasn't true. Even before she got sick, Logan had barely been around and I was still very much confused. I hadn't told anyone, not even Ben, that the first emotion I felt after she passed was relief. How awful did that sound?

But it was true. Sitting with Dad and the visiting nurse as my mother took labored breaths, I kept asking myself questions. How much would her agony increase if she pulled through? How would Dad manage? How would I manage? And yet how would we survive her passing? But when my mother finally stopped breathing and the nurse leaned over her and said to us, *she's gone now,* I felt a sudden lightness that made me cringe with guilt. I was relieved because I no longer had to take care of her.

I turned to the counter, picked up a small cutting board and brushed off bread crumbs into the sink. Then I studied the board. The tan wood was stained black and brown from so much use and the edges were chipped and ragged. When I made it during Girl Scouts in grade school, I hadn't been convinced that this was the project I wanted to pursue. We could choose only one, and I wanted to make a necklace for myself out of pink and white shells.

But I'd wanted confirmation that this wasn't selfish, that it was okay to think of myself. And so I asked my mother, the cutting board or the necklace for myself?

"Oh! I think a cutting board would be lovely," she said.

I remembered eyeing the half dozen cutting boards on the counter. Big, small, new, old, round, and rectangular. All I had to do was tell her that I *really* wanted the necklace. But I couldn't form the words. I didn't know why. "The shells are from the Bahamas. It probably won't be a very good cutting board."

"But it would be special for me," she said.

Yes, it'd be special. For her. I turned the cutting board over and saw my name burned into the lower right corner. *To Mom, love Clare*. Did she consider it special? Why didn't I tell her that I wanted the necklace? I searched my mind for things I'd asked her for over the years. And that she'd given me. I started to feel a little panicked when I couldn't come up with anything.

"How are you doing, sis?" he asked. "Holding up okay?"

I could tell by the way both sides of his mouth turned up and how he looked directly into my eyes that this question was sincere. But how could I trust him after his warmongering and obnoxious behavior at dinner?

"I'm okay," I said, trying to buy time to figure out what to say. "And you?"

"Sure, okay." He shrugged. "He's pulling out all of the stops tomorrow, huh? Bringing in heavy hitters to read from her work?"

I nodded. Mom's friends had promised a few superstars. Maybe even Mailer.

"Well, she's finally getting her due," Logan said. "The literary recognition that slipped through her fingers in life!"

"That's *terrible,* Logan." I leaned into the counter, the sharp edge cutting into my hip. I felt distressed, suddenly, that I was still defending her. When Ben handed me a plate, he held on to it a bit longer than necessary, but I wouldn't look at him. I knew he was trying to tell me to stop engaging with him. But I couldn't.

"It's true," he said. "She was a one-hit wonder. And it did her in."

"Her one-hit wonder is considered a classic," I said. "Dad still gets letters about it. And it's taught in high schools across the country."

"Good ole Phoebe and Whit," Logan said. "Our cash cow."

"Could you be a little more cynical?" But I dropped my eyes because my heart was only half in this.

He shrugged again, stood, and shoved the chair up to the table. "I see you're still the keeper of the flame. It's okay, little sis. Maybe someday you'll be able to see our mum more clearly."

"*You* see her clearly? You were never around long enough to see anything!"

"Anyone want more ice cream?" Ben pulled the Tupperware container filled with homemade ice cream out of the freezer and put it on the counter. He dug into the pale yellow mound and scooped out a spoonful. Then he shoved it into his mouth, smacked his lips, and smiled. But I saw the message in his eyes: *Stop arguing with him!*

"I like this guy! He never lets things get too serious." Logan grinned as he turned for the living room. "Well, we should be going."

I was so angry that I wanted to stomp out of the room, but Ben grabbed my hand and practically dragged me with him into the living room. Somewhere between here and the kitchen, Logan seemed to have forgotten our discussion because he suddenly pulled me in for a hug and told me that he'd see me tomorrow. Then he added, "Thanks for dinner, sis. You're a good cook, you know that? And believe me, I know good food. When you're ready to open a restaurant, I'll fund it."

As if nothing had happened in the kitchen. As if he hadn't just accused me of being the flamethrower or whatever he'd said.

Beth, who towered over me with her long legs and torso, suddenly came alive now that they were leaving. She had a mouth full of shockingly white teeth, giant green eyes, long, silky blond hair, and cheekbones so pronounced that they looked like miniature shelves. When she stretched out her arms for a loose hug, the silver and gold bangles on her wrists slid nearly to her elbows. "Lovely evening. Would you two like to come back with us? Stefan gave us the keys to his wine cellar."

Stefan was their friend from Manhattan who owned a house in Edgartown, on the water, where they were staying this weekend.

"Thanks, but it's late." I glanced at Ben, who nodded.

Neither Logan nor Beth tried to talk us into it. We followed them to the door and then waved as they drove away.

"I can't believe him," I groaned as I watched the car's taillights, sharp and red, slowly fade. "He's so cynical and condescending."

"Let it go," Ben said. "It's not worth the energy."

"But—"

"Don't make it so complicated, Clare, when it doesn't have to be. He likes to pull your chain. After tomorrow, you won't see him for what, another year?"

I sighed and looked through the screen to the sky. The moon, round and silvery, hung low over the trees and cast gray shadows across the yard.

"Let's go to bed," Ben said.

"I'll come soon," I said. "I'm just going to close up."

He kissed me on the cheek and started across the living room. I opened the screen door and walked onto the flagstone patio. The lawn

461

furniture had been replaced, too, but in my mind I saw the old picnic table where my mother sat writing. Tap, tap, tap, *zing!* That sound often woke me.

Logan tried to get her to use a computer but she refused and continued to write on her typewriter, just as she had every day for as long as I could remember. I thought about the morning I woke and saw Lee standing here on the patio. I had forgotten to tell her that no one, under any circumstances, should interrupt my mother while she was writing. But Lee hadn't let my mother intimidate her.

Had Lee been here tonight, we'd have rehashed everything. She'd have noticed how Logan and Beth wouldn't clean up. How funny Uncle Richard was about riding the ferry. How Oliver had been so quiet. She'd have had something to say about all of it, too. She wouldn't have minded things being so complicated.

But I was thinking of the Lee from before Florida, not the Lee from after.

When Sarah called after my mother died—I hadn't spoken to her in nearly a year—she asked, again, why Lee and I weren't speaking. But she was less argumentative than she'd been in the four previous years when she'd tried multiple times to broker a rapprochement between us.

"I don't get it." Her voice was gentle. "You two were best friends and now you don't even talk.

And you've basically disappeared. No one sees Lee anymore, either."

I remembered gripping the phone so tightly that my hand began to sweat and feeling that familiar, sick sensation in my stomach. Disappointment. Anxiety. And guilt, too. "I'm sorry. I don't know why I'm not in better touch with everyone."

"It's about that night in Florida, isn't it?" She didn't wait for my response. "You know, Ducky and I were there, too. We all feel guilty about this."

I didn't say anything.

She sighed. "I work with rape victims in my emergency room, and I see the toll it takes on them. We should have insisted that Lee get help that night. It would have helped her to address the physical and psychological trauma. Actually, it would have helped all of us."

Maybe. But you can't undo what's done. You can't change what happened just because you want to or because you wish you'd behaved differently. As my mother used to say, you can't *wallow* in it. You move forward. You get married, find a career, and eventually have children. You try to do your best. You try to be a good person.

I didn't know where Lee was with all of this. Because if she'd learned something about that night that had given her peace, that might give me peace, too, then that meant she'd been thinking and maybe talking about it. Did she tell her husband? Had she been to a therapist? And did she tell both of them what I did?

Without Lee around, without the job of taking care of her, without that constant reminder of what I'd done, I'd been happier. Ben and I were good now and had had so many great times over the last couple of years. On vacation in the Caribbean. At his Christmas party in the hotel downtown when we drank champagne on the rooftop in the snow. The night we moved into our condo and sat on the living room floor, laughing as we celebrated. Not once during any of those times did I dwell on what had happened.

But now I had that letter and her request and I didn't know what to do.

A cool breeze rushed across the lawn and blew the hair off my face. The air smelled like rotten leaves and decay—fall was approaching—and I shivered although I wasn't cold. I moved the wrought iron chairs so they were neatly aligned against the side of the house, and then I reached up and put my hand flat against the window. The glass felt cold and smooth beneath my palm. I thought about one of the last lucid conversations I had with my mother, before the pain became unbearable and the morphine was increased and she began hallucinating about naked people in the bushes with guns.

"What ever happened to Lee?" she asked one Saturday in early August. She was lying in the hospital bed in the dining room, the windows open and a warm breeze blowing through the screens. Her bald head was wrapped in a flowered scarf and her skin had a sallow, almost translucent sheen to it. She was chilled and had blankets piled on her, but she wouldn't let me close the windows. She hadn't been able to work for days. I didn't know it at the time, but she'd never work again.

"What do you mean?" I'd been reading to her from her heavily marked-up copy of *Paradise Lost*. My mother thought this poem showed Milton's supreme command as a writer and it was filled with the contrasts she loved—Satan and Christ, heaven and hell, light and dark, good and evil, love and hate, humility and pride. I'd forgotten how much of this poem was about war.

"You were such thick friends during college and right afterward, and now you rarely speak of her," she said. "Do you still see her?"

Over the years my parents had both said to me, why don't you have Lee come up to the Vineyard? Why don't we see her anymore? *Where's Lee?* I hadn't wanted to get into it with them. When I finally said that we'd had a falling-out and that over time I was sure we'd be fine, my mother seemed satisfied and didn't ask me to elaborate. But that day in the dining room she seemed to want something more.

"We grew apart," I said. What I'd done was so

un-Phoebe-like. And so unlike anything her war heroes had done, either.

"So, there was no argument?"

I shifted in my seat. "Why do you want to know?"

My mother closed her eyes and I thought that was the end of it. But then they shot open, and she tilted her head toward me and said, "Except for your father, I never had a best friend. I'm afraid I wasn't very good at all of that. But I was always impressed with you and Lee. You let her in, didn't you?"

I was so surprised that I nearly fell off my chair. I'd never heard her admit that she wasn't good at anything nor had I thought she'd given Lee or our friendship much thought. And it made me angry although I didn't know why. Soon afterward, she fell into a restless sleep and I left and we never came back to this conversation.

But I'd thought about it a lot over the last year and knew why I was angry. Why didn't we have more conversations like it? I thought about the cutting board and how I'd been unable to ask for, and tell her, what I needed and wanted. I'd always been hesitant like this with her. So, was our lack of communication my fault?

But she hadn't made it easy. She was unknowable. Protective and secretive. Maybe if she'd been more open, more accessible, more— what was the word? *Vulnerable*. Maybe then she wouldn't have been so confusing to me and to Logan although he'd never admit it. How much better would our lives have been if she'd allowed me, or anyone, *in?*

Lee once said that I had trouble being open and vulnerable, too.

But I'd tried. I'd let Lee in. Intimacy hadn't been easy for her, either. I remembered what her aunt said that day in the bar while Lee was in the bathroom. *She protected herself by not having many close friends.* I protected myself, too. From people who wanted at my mother through me. And maybe for other reasons, too, although at the moment I wasn't sure what they were.

I pulled my sweater across my stomach and looked up. Millions of stars dotted the dark, silent sky. I remembered a summer night years ago when Lee and I stretched out on the driveway, still warm from the afternoon sun, and counted shooting stars. Where was she right now? Did she think much about me anymore?

I shivered again and glanced at the house. Tomorrow morning would come quickly. While Ben was out running, I'd make oatmeal for him. I'd make sure that my dad ate it, too. They'd both be grateful for this.

I stared at the empty space where the picnic table had been and felt a sudden, familiar twinge of guilt. Why hadn't I done more to help my mother? Maybe if I'd worked harder, probed more, circled back to the conversation about friends, I could have gotten her to open up. Instead, I'd sat at her bedside, day after day, reading, taking care of her, at times silently seething at something I couldn't quite identify.

I glanced back at the house.

"Lycidas."

Of course. It should be acknowledged at tomorrow's service. I turned and started toward the door, certain that there was a copy on the shelf in the living room. And I felt a little better because this was something I could do for her.

CHAPTER 25

Mailer didn't show up and neither did Louise Glück. But Janice, my mother's editor, was here and so were a few other writers, such as the poet Melinda Stauder, who read the long passage in *Listen, Before You Go* when Whit describes the oppressive jungle heat to Phoebe. Margaret Ogilvy, also a poet, talked about my mother's unofficial role as the Mother of Minimalism. My dad, who loved my idea of reading from "Lycidas," wanted me to do it although no way would I get up in front of everyone. So, Uncle Richard read it.

We sat in wood chairs in Margaret's backyard, flowers bursting in vases on the tables near the house, in the gardens surrounding the shed, at the edge of the yard, and along the walkway. The sun, which should have been forgiving now that it was September, seared into my skin every time it peeked through the tree leaves. Birds perched along the stone wall chirped and sang and the air was fragrant with freshly cut grass. Everything was so alive and vibrant, yet we were here to say goodbye to my mother. The scene felt surreal and I imagined her appearing from around the shed, basking in the attention, deciding that she wasn't dead, after all.

As Janice made her way to the podium, I glanced at my dad, dressed in a new blue suit with an extra starched white shirt, and sitting forward in the seat next to me as if wanting to make sure he heard every word. On my other side, Ben kept crossing his legs, shifting in his seat, and taking a napkin across the sweat that dotted his upper lip and ran in a steady stream down the sides of his face. This morning, he'd been on the phone with Patrick and got a late start on his run. He hadn't completely cooled off before showering and dressing.

"Take off your blazer," I whispered.

"You don't think that's disrespectful?" he asked. I shook my head. He sighed, relieved, as he pulled off the blazer and draped it across the back of his seat.

"It's lovely to be here today to celebrate a wonderful writer." Janice placed her palms on the podium and looked over the crowd. I glanced at Logan, across the aisle, as he lowered his eyes and stared at his hands in his lap. Next to him, Beth, dressed in a loud pink and green flowered sundress, white-framed sunglasses as large as dinner plates, stared at Janice with a forced smile that made me wonder if she was even listening.

"Winning the North American Book Award for *Listen, Before You Go* not only changed Eleanor's life but changed mine, as well," Janice began. "Before this, I was an assistant editor, working on mid-list novels. But I knew Eleanor was something special. She worked harder than any writer I've ever known. Writing was in her bones and blood and gut."

People in the crowd murmured and nodded. My dad sat so still that he didn't appear to be breathing.

"It was a privilege to work on something so meaningful," she said. "Eleanor was a woman full of intellect and conviction. But writing, I believe, served a deeper purpose. Some people write for the thrill of publishing. Some write because they enjoy putting words together. Some write because they have to; their lives depend on it. A sense of fear or anxiety leaves them no choice. This, I believe, was Eleanor."

Logan and I turned our heads at the same moment to look at each other. That writing was something over which she had no control was a thought I was sure neither of us had ever had.

Then Janice began to talk about the early stages of *Listen*, but I kept repeating a word that she'd just said. Fear. *Fear.* When my mother was first diagnosed with stage four colon cancer, Ben and I had been incredulous that she'd never had a colonoscopy and only sporadically been to a doctor. It made no sense. Only later did I realize that she was afraid of doctors and what they might find.

Were these the same kinds of fears that made my mother write?

"I want to introduce you to someone," my dad said as he reached for my arm. The service was over and I was making my way through the crowd, trying to say hello to everyone. My dad stood next to an older man and woman, both short, bespectacled, gray-haired, and dressed in clothes that I imagined weren't even fashionable in the 1960s when they were purchased. I knew immediately that they were academics. "This is Agnes Menendez and her husband, Thomas LaFleur."

"Nice to meet you." I reached out my hand. "Thank you for coming."

Agnes, who must have been sweltering in her nubby, yellow wool skirt and matching jacket, had a limp handshake. But Thomas's hand was strong and firm, despite his slight frame.

"So, you're the famous Phoebe," Agnes said, raising her eyebrows.

I felt my cheeks warm and glanced at my dad.

"No, no," he said. "This is Clare. Phoebe was a novel character."

"She knew that." Thomas laughed, nervous, and when he raised his hand to scratch his nose, I saw a long, brown string hanging from the elbow of his mud-colored blazer. Agnes simply nodded, her way of apologizing, I imagined. How could

I get out of this? I looked around and saw Oliver alone by the birch tree.

"Agnes is a Victorian," my dad said. "She just published a very well-received book on Tennyson's poetry."

"Oh." I felt off balance in a way that I didn't like. "Congratulations."

"Thank you," she said. "My book is nothing like what Eleanor published. Of course, they were intended for different audiences. Mine required ten years of research."

Agnes turned away when a woman I didn't know tapped her on the shoulder.

Thomas leaned toward my dad and me and whispered, "Don't let her fool you. Eleanor achieved the grand triumvirate. Academia, novel publishing, and having children. *And* she was a female Miltonist, to boot! Agnes never got over any of it."

This was ridiculous. Why were they even here? When a waiter came by with a tray of champagne, I reached for two glasses, excused myself, and walked over to Oliver. It had been awkward at the house last night; we barely knew him, and Logan, having had too much to drink, dominated the conversation through most of dinner. Oliver smiled and thanked me when I handed him a glass.

"It's nice of you to come," I said. "I imagine you don't know anyone but us?"

He shrugged. "I'm happy to be here. When I got the invitation from your dad, I thought it'd be a nice way to say goodbye. I was already coming east on business."

I nodded and sipped my champagne. A cellist and flutist were playing over near the house. Servers were passing mini crab cakes and smoked salmon. Logan and Beth were talking with Uncle Richard and Aunt Denise near the garden. Ben was with the Donahues. And Dad was still enmeshed with the academics.

I glanced at Oliver. He wasn't much taller than I was. He wore a blue suit, a white button-down, and a red bowtie. His hair was thinning across the top and his glasses were too big for his face. He drained his champagne glass in one long drink. I tried to remember the day and circumstances when he gave me Ellie but couldn't. Why hadn't we seen more of him over the years?

"When was the last time you spoke to my mother?" I asked. Although she rarely talked about her family, she'd told me multiple times that Oliver was her favorite cousin. And then I suddenly remembered him at the apartment on Dean Street, long before *Listen* was published, sitting in the kitchen with us.

"Ages ago," he said.

Last night, he told us that he was a lawyer who worked for several wineries in Oregon. The wine he'd brought was so good that even Logan praised it. He told us that his wife had died several years ago and that his children were scattered all over the west. Other than that, he hadn't said much. He was one of those people who blended into the group; pleasant but not vocal, friendly but not too friendly, confident but not pompous. He felt trustworthy. I liked him.

"It's too bad you two didn't stay in touch." I'd only had one glass of champagne but it had gone to my head and made me dizzy. "My mother always said her family was so small."

Oliver stared at me, barely seeming to blink. "I called several times, especially after *Listen, Before You Go* was published, but she never called back."

I lowered my glass. He stared at me so intently over the top of his glasses that I felt as if he wanted to tell me something and was waiting for a sign from me to continue. I nodded and asked, "Why wouldn't she call you back?"

"It was hard for her, I think, to talk to me."

"Why?"

He took his fingers and thumb over the corners of his mouth. "So little was talked about in those days, when we were kids. I listen to talk shows today and think, my goodness. The things people say. And reveal! But then I read her novel and, well, art imitates life, doesn't it?"

I tilted my head as I looked at him. My mother had such little patience for memoirs and autobiographies and was so dismissive of confessional poets. But I also knew that writers wrote about what they knew. "Sure, to a certain degree."

"Are you a writer, too?" he asked.

"I'm a teacher and I was an English major in college, but I'm severely lacking in creativity. My mother had the monopoly on that."

"Did she ever talk about our grandfather?"

I wasn't sure where he was going with this but I nodded. "I know he liked to be outside and that he was quiet and loved poetry. He introduced her to Milton. She also told me that people said he was different when he returned from the war. He was suffering from post-traumatic stress although no one called it this back then. And I know he shot himself."

Oliver nodded.

"She liked visiting your grandparents' farm in Vermont every summer," I continued. "You were there, too, right?"

"Yes, for a number of years all the cousins went there every summer," he said. "Did she say anything else about our grandfather's suicide?"

I shook my head. "Nothing that I really remember."

"We come from a long line of silent sufferers, that's for sure," he said. "In her book, she wrote about it so eloquently. And fluently."

Now I was certain that he was trying to tell me

something. I let a server fill my champagne glass.

"There was always speculation that she was there." His voice grew stronger. "That she saw it. The rest of us were down at the pond, swimming. But your mom always had a hard time with my sisters. They weren't nice to her. Your mom was so smart and so loved by our grandfather, and I think they were jealous of her. Well, *that's* another story. Anyway, we assumed she was reading in her room. But then . . ."

I felt the hairs stand up on the back of my neck.

"Well, our grandmother, Gram, heard the shot and went looking for him. We heard the shot, too, but we didn't think much at first. We were in the country, after all. When we came up from the pond we found Gram cradling Grandfather in the mud behind the barn. After the sheriff arrived, I went looking for your mom. I found her in the attic of the house, standing in a corner and staring at the wall. She had fresh mud on her shoes. A bit of blood, too, although it was too dark to know for sure. Anyway, we think she was there when he did it."

Something cold began to drain down the back of my head and into my neck.

"It was quite chilling when I read the last scene between Whit and Phoebe," he said. "The details were so similar to Grandfather's death. Even the blood and mud on Phoebe's shoes. Your mother wouldn't ever talk about it with me. Or anyone.

Am I to understand that she didn't talk to any of you, either?"

None of this made sense. "Why didn't she tell anyone?"

"Why do most families keep secrets from each other? It was twenty years after the event when someone finally told me that my aunt—your mother's mother—had a child die at three months." He shook his head. "Maybe your mom didn't quite remember being there when Grandfather shot himself. Maybe it lived in her unconscious. That happens sometimes with trauma, you know. Or maybe, like Phoebe, she felt shame or guilt that she didn't, or couldn't, stop him."

Unconscious or not, if she wrote about it, then she must have remembered. That she'd chosen to keep this from us—I was fairly certain Logan didn't know, otherwise he'd have told me—felt cruel. It would have told us something about her. It would have helped us see her. My voice felt hot and sharp in my throat as I spit out the words, "I don't understand why it had to be a big secret."

"Ah, but it wasn't a secret. She put it on paper for the whole world to see. It was hiding in plain sight. Wasn't it?" He sighed. "I've often wondered over the years if writing was her way of self-medicating. Know what I mean?"

I choked and coughed into my hand and suddenly felt so overwhelmed by all I had to do—help clean up, answer my mother's fan mail, and write thank-you notes to everyone who was here today. How many people, seventy? Eighty? And then there was Max and his essay problems and Sophia and Talia and the science lesson plan that I hadn't finished. I began twisting the stem of my empty champagne glass. When had I drunk the rest of it? "Why didn't you tell us this last night?"

"I assumed you knew. But when your mom's editor mentioned her fear, I wondered. I thought it might be helpful for you to know. I'm sorry if I've upset you."

"No, of course not," I said. "Thank you for this."

I heard my name and looked across the crowd to Ben, his arm around my dad. By the time I reached them, he'd lowered my dad into a chair. Several people stood over him, worried.

"What's wrong?" I asked.

"He's feeling so dizzy," Ben said. "What should we do?"

"Dad? Are you okay? What's wrong?"

He held his head in his hands and wouldn't answer.

I scooted a chair next to him and sat. I put one hand on the back of his neck, damp with sweat, and another on his cold and clammy hand. "Can you hear me?"

"Just feeling a little weak," he mumbled.

I looked up at Ben. "Will you get him something to eat and drink, something sweet? Maybe a soda, too." Ben nodded and hurried off.

"You didn't eat anything, did you?" I asked. He scrunched his nose and shook his head. He'd been such a good host, wandering from group to group, making sure he'd said hello to everyone. Why hadn't I paid more attention?

Then Ben was back with a glass of soda and a plate of fruit, cookies, and smoked salmon. My dad took a long drink and started in on the salmon. Within minutes, the color was back in his cheeks, and the people who'd been standing over us, satisfied that he was okay, turned away. Ben, who sat on the other side of him, kept glancing at me over my dad's bent head.

Finally, my dad handed his plate to me. He'd eaten most of the salmon, all of the cookies but left the fruit. He sighed and put his hands on his thighs. "Those cookies weren't nearly as good as yours but they did the trick. Thank you, my dear. You're always taking care of me. You take care of both of us. Isn't that right, Ben?"

"Certainly is," he said.

I sat back in my chair, exhausted but glad he was all right. We were quiet for a few minutes. When I looked over the crowd, at people who'd known my mother in one capacity or another, I wondered how many thought they really knew her.

"Time to mingle," my dad said. "Maybe I'll wait here a few more minutes?"

"I'll stay with him," Ben said.

I nodded and stood. There were still hands to shake, people to thank, and questions to answer. I made my way through the crowd. Yes, we missed her. Yes, we were grateful that she was no longer in pain. Yes, we knew her books would live on. Several times, Oliver and I looked at each other across the lawn and he smiled, invitingly, but I always turned away. I didn't know what to do with what he told me. Later, when he said goodbye, he thanked me and said that I knew where to find him. He left with the first group headed to the Vineyard Haven ferry.

It wasn't until much later, after everyone had gone and we'd cleaned up at Margaret's and were pulling into our driveway at the house, that I said I had something to share. Logan, who'd driven us to the ceremony in his new Land Rover, turned to look at me in the back seat, where I was sitting between Ben and Dad. Beth, in the passenger seat, looked out the window. The sun had set and the lights from the house cast streaks of white across the lawn in front of us.

I told them about the swimming pond, the jealous cousins, the gunshot, Gram holding Grandfather in the mud, and our mother, standing in the attic corner with mud and possibly blood on her shoes. My dad sat very still next to me, hands in his lap, the shadows in the car obscuring his face. Still, I tried to find him in the dark as I asked, "Did you know this, Dad? Did she tell you?"

He hesitated and then said, "No."

Logan snorted. "How do we know it's even true? Just because Oliver, who until last night none of us ever spent more than one night with, tells us so?"

We all looked at Dad, even Beth, who'd turned in her seat.

"He could very well be telling the truth," Dad said from the shadow.

"*Please!* You mean to tell me that you two never had a discussion about this?" Logan said. "I find that hard to believe."

"And you're completely honest with Beth about every little thing you've ever done?" I asked.

Ben jerked his head to look at me again. Beth stared at Logan.

"This is no little thing!" Logan glanced back at Dad, his voice suddenly softer. "So, let's say that it's true. What do you make of it? Why didn't she tell anyone?"

"I don't know." Dad's voice was weak, fragile. He needed to rest. This was too much for him. I squeezed his arm.

Logan raised his eyebrows at me. Over the years he'd accused me, among other things, of protecting our mother too much (her Claretaker), being her muse, not seeing her clearly. Was he wondering how I failed to see this part of her?

"Maybe it was too traumatic and painful," I said, thinking about what Oliver told me. "Maybe she didn't tell us because she couldn't truly remember it."

"But she had to know because she wrote about the same kind of suicide in *Listen, Before You Go*," Ben said.

No one said anything for a moment.

"Maybe this was why she got depressed sometimes," I said. Logan shrugged, turned, and looked out the windshield. "Right, Dad? She was depressed?"

"Maybe, I guess, from time to time, but—"

"Don't you want to know the truth?" I blurted.

"And what good would it do?" he asked. "Your mother was far from perfect. Why rummage around for things that you'll never know for sure? Can't I have my memories as they are?"

"Sure." I sighed. He was still protecting her, even in death. But then I cringed because this was exactly what Logan had accused me of doing. I leaned back against the seat. Years ago, I'd been so quick to believe that my mother stole *Listen* from Lucy. I didn't want to unequivocally believe Oliver's version, either, and yet it made sense. I rubbed my forehead. Why did I care so much about this stupid novel, anyway? And yet I felt a stab of disappointment that I couldn't explain.

Beth lowered her window and the night air, cool and breezy, so unlike the heat today, blew through the car. I shivered.

"Well, it's late," Logan said.

The three of us slid out of the back seat and I shut the door. Logan lowered his window and leaned toward me. In the lights from the house, I saw how his hair had begun to thin along his forehead. I thought back to that awful dinner in Chicago when he'd come to the restaurant, drunk, his shirt wet from the rain, his long hair hanging in his face. A few years ago he apologized with a quick, *Sorry, sis, had too much to drink that night.* But when I questioned him about the things he'd said, he hadn't wanted to talk about any of it.

"I'm awfully tired," Dad said. "Good night, son. Thanks for coming. And thank you, too, Beth. I think I'll make a cup of tea before turning in."

"Good night," they both chimed.

"I'll go with you." Ben steered him toward the door.

When Logan moved to put the Land Rover in gear, I reached into the car and placed my hand on his shoulder. I didn't want him to go and yet I didn't really know what I wanted from him, either. He looked up, surprised.

"She was confusing, don't you think?" I asked.

"Eleanor?" He shook his head when I nodded.

484

"No, not to me. Eleanor was always about Eleanor. Ever since I could remember. She was irrelevant in my life."

"That's terrible, Logan, and not true. You were upset when she died. And I've seen you angry with her and hurt. That's hardly irrelevant."

He snorted and shook his head.

"You were furious with her that night in Chicago at the restaurant," I said. "But maybe you were too drunk to remember what you said."

Beth looked at her watch and then out the window. I wanted to slap her.

"You accused Mom of leaving you to die when we went to New York," I said. "You know, when you had the appendicitis."

Logan frowned and then nodded slowly. "I don't know why I brought up that whole thing at dinner. But I will tell you that I didn't know that I'd ruptured my appendix that day. I thought I was dying. I thought I was having a heart attack. That's what my coach yelled when I collapsed on the side of the pool, clutching my chest. 'Call an ambulance, we can't have him dying in the pool!'"

"That sounds like his fault, not our mother's," I said.

"You're right. He was a dick. But does that matter? The point is, I thought I was dying and she left me to go to New York for her award. You *both* went."

"Please don't say that you're blaming me," I said. "I was eleven."

"I know, I know, you're right." He sighed as he placed both hands on the steering wheel. "Look, we had different relationships with her, that's all. And I meant it when I said that that book did her in. But you know what I thought about today? Even if she'd gone on to publish dozens of successful books, that wouldn't have changed who she was. She's always been an unhappy, selfish person."

"No, not always. She was better when we were younger. Before *Listen*." I swallowed. The urge to defend her was relentless.

Logan chuckled and shook his head. "Okay, Clare, let's talk about the award ceremony. Do you remember what she promised if we went with her? The zoo and a ride in a horse-drawn carriage for you. I think that was what you wanted. I know she promised me a Knicks game. We'd make a family vacation out of it. A little something for everyone, she said. Remember? But did she follow through? Did you do the things she promised? I know you didn't. Because Eleanor never followed through with that kind of thing. Am I right?"

He was. I hadn't wanted to think about this—I'd put it out of my mind—but now I couldn't stop. I remembered sitting on the hotel bed the morning after the award ceremony and watching as she worked the phones, signed additional books that had been delivered, conducted interviews, and met with her agent and editor.

When can we go to the zoo? And the carriage ride? How many times did I ask this between interviews and phone calls?

"Soon," she answered. And then, "Later."

And finally, "Can't you see I'm busy?"

I raised my hand to my forehead, shielding my face as I wondered how to answer my brother. Sitting on the hotel bed that day, feeling so small and insignificant, I'd realized that I was invisible to the most important person in my life. But I hadn't wanted to accept it. I lowered my hand. I wasn't ready to admit this, especially to him. "Don't you feel sympathy for her after what Oliver told us?"

Logan straightened as a sly grin crept onto his lips. Had he seen through me? Maybe he was just done with our conversation. He put the Land Rover into gear and then spoke in a high-pitched accent. "If you figure this out, Dr. Freud, be sure to give me a shout."

"Bye!" Beth said.

I wrapped my arms around my waist and shivered as I watched them pull away, the gravel crunching under the wheels.

"Aren't you coming in?"

The screen door squeaked and then my dad stood next to me, slightly stooped, his hands in his blazer pockets. He was sad—I could feel it—that the day was over. That we'd said our goodbyes. He waved but Logan was already too far down the driveway. I felt so angry with him and with my mother.

"Logan always makes a joke of everything," I snapped.

"Ah, Logan is just Logan," Dad said.

How many meaningful conversations had my brother and I ever had? Once after our mother died when he arrived on the red-eye from Los Angeles, exhausted and teary. Last year when he called to tell me that he'd run into Elise in London and that she had two (*good God, two!*) children. *We had different relationships with her.* Maybe so. But why was I the only one confused by our mother?

Next to me, Dad sighed. The sky was a brilliant mix of bright stars and wispy clouds. I listened to the faint, gentle ocean waves mixing with the evening sounds—the cicadas, the crickets, and a bullfrog from over near the Hendersons' pond. It couldn't be the same bullfrog that Lee pointed out years ago, could it? I felt an ache in my heart for her, for my mother, for something I couldn't identify.

"It was a lovely day," my dad said. "Your mother would've been happy. The 'Lycidas' poem was a nice touch. Thank you for thinking of it."

" 'Yet once more, O ye laurels, and once more, ye myrtles brown, with ivy never sere, I come to pluck your berries harsh and crude, and with forced fingers rude, shatter your leaves before the mellowing year.' " I cleared my throat. "That's all I memorized. I don't really understand 'Lycidas,' to tell you the truth."

I was hoping for a smile, but he only nodded. He was grieving so deeply that sometimes I wondered if what I felt was grief at all.

"Your mother was interested in the structure of the poem, whether it should be viewed in two or three movements, as well as the pastoral elements," he said. "But when Richard read the poem today, all I kept thinking was that Milton wrote it about his friend, Edward King, who died much too young. Before his time. And how sad that was for him."

I nodded. He thought my mother died before her time, too.

"You miss her, too, don't you?" he asked, hopeful, maybe even desperate.

"Of course, I do." But truth was I didn't know what I felt. Because in addition to that lingering feeling of relief that kept crowding my mind, I also felt sadness, confusion, anger, regret, longing—and yes, I missed the best parts of her, too.

I glanced at him. We'd spent so much time together over these last few years. Sometimes we talked about the letters we opened from fans. Often he brought up happy memories he had of her. But I wished that we could have a real conversation and that maybe he'd tell me that he had felt ambivalent and confused. Maybe he'd admit that it wasn't easy being in her shadow, taking care of everything, taking care of her. Maybe he felt angry and relieved now, too.

"She made me so angry sometimes," I said, my voice careful. "I used to think that all she cared about was her writing and her books."

When can we go to the zoo?

"But that's not true," he said. "She loved us. In her way."

I shifted my feet. "Do you believe what Oliver said?"

"Why would he make it up?"

"But does it upset you that you never knew this?"

He tilted his head as he thought and then finally shook it. "We all have crosses to bear. It's what you do with them that matters, Clare. Your mother didn't like to dwell. I still admire that about her. Besides, do you ever truly know everything about another person? And isn't that okay?"

I felt my cheeks flush and looked away. Maybe my dad was more like my mother than I'd realized. Maybe people could be split into two groups, those who were doers, who moved forward without looking back, and those who dwelled. My dad, my mother, my brother, and Ben were doers. Who was I?

CHAPTER 26

In December, the parent organization at Meadows put on its annual holiday lunch for teachers and staff in the upper school's library. Tables were decorated with pinecones, garland, and snowmen that some enterprising parents made out of papier-mâché and cotton balls. Nonreligious holiday music (*Frosty the snowman, was a jolly happy soul* . . .) played loud enough over the speakers to hear but not overwhelm.

"A few years ago Candy Cosgrove spiked the punch and everyone got hammered," Kitty told me as we stood in the doorway to the library. I laughed, even though she'd told me this last year. School had ended for the holiday a half hour earlier and wouldn't resume for nearly three weeks. There was nothing quite like the frenetic energy of three hundred children, all anticipating Christmas and winter break, for weeks on end. The fact that Hanukkah coincided this year made their collective anticipation almost unbearable. We were all exhausted.

"Let's see what the troops brought in." Kitty started for the food table.

"I'll catch up with you in a few minutes," I said, eyeing something on the library counter. It wasn't often that I came up here. Our building down the

493

hill housed everything we needed, all classrooms, a small library and cafeteria. The administration prided itself on keeping the middle schoolers away from our easily influenced younger kids.

I said hello to several middle-school teachers—we got together as a large group often enough for me to know almost everyone—and stopped in front of the counter. Standing up and facing out between the card catalogue boxes was a copy of *Listen, Before You Go*.

How did this get here? It was much too old for middle-school students. I reached to take it down, to hide it, but stopped and put my hand in my pocket. I didn't want anyone to see me with it, to think I was the one who put it here.

I opened the card catalogue, to give me something to do. Although only a few people here ever asked about my mother, I had a feeling that everyone knew our connection. I glanced at the book again. The plastic cover was new, the edges not yet abused, and the spine wasn't broken. Maybe no one had ever checked it out. Maybe the librarian put it out today. I glanced around but no one was paying attention to me. Maybe I could just push until it fell behind the counter?

I began flipping through the cards. I hadn't looked at the cover in a while. Certainly my dad had copies all over the place, but I treated them as I would the refrigerator and water faucet—

just part of the fabric of the house. On the cover Whit and Phoebe stood with backs to the camera, Whit leaning on his crutches, Phoebe holding her brother's forearm with both hands as if afraid she'd lose him if she let go. The blue sky above them faded into the white edges of the book so that Whit and Phoebe always looked as if they were floating. At the time it was published, reviewers mentioned how innovative this cover was. Now it looked old-fashioned.

I stared at Phoebe with her shoulder-length brown hair and stick-figure legs. Toward the end of the novel, Whit told her that everyone had a gift and the trick in life was to find it and that hers was to "help people." As readers, we knew this was true because she'd kept Whit alive and she'd kept the family together and as one reviewer wrote, "She's the Virgin Mary, Mother Teresa, and Holden's Phoebe all wrapped up in one." This was my mother's favorite review, not only because she liked being in Salinger's company but also because it was the only time anyone compared Phoebe to Mother Teresa. I always thought that comparison was over-the-top. But now, thinking about what Oliver had told me at the memorial service months ago, I wondered if it had some kind of other meaning for my mother.

"Thinking of doing some reading instead of eating?"

I turned to see Justine Meachem, an eighth-grade English teacher, behind me. She had a cup of punch in one hand and a plate filled with food in the other.

"Oh, no, I don't know." I glanced over her shoulder at the people hovering over the food table. "How is it? Worth fighting the crowd?"

She put her punch on the counter, stabbed a piece of turkey with her fork, and put it in her mouth. She smiled, chewing. "Most definitely. Although I'd say that about anyone who cooks for me. I'm lousy in the kitchen but my husband's a good sport about it. What about you? Are you a good cook?"

I thought about Logan's offer to fund a restaurant and my desire long ago to make scones and cookies to sell at Lorenzo's coffeehouse. Yes, at one time I'd thought about doing something with this interest, but I hadn't had enough confidence to pursue it. But Justine didn't need to know this. I smiled. "I get by."

She stabbed another hunk of turkey and swooped up some salad with it. Justine was tall with short blond hair, thick eyebrows, and big green eyes. She always dressed in long, flowing skirts and wispy peasant shirts, even in the winter, which made her the resident hippie. She and I were two of just a handful of teachers that didn't live in the suburbs, and I liked her even if I didn't know her well.

"You've dropped out of book group?" she asked. I nodded and looked away. I felt bad about this and that I'd only been to one meeting. "It's okay. It's not everyone's cup of tea. You probably read more compelling books, anyway. I know I do. But it's fun to be with everyone, you know, just hanging out."

"Everyone's so nice," I said. And they were. The novel we'd read was compelling enough, too. I didn't know why I couldn't go to the group and hang out. It was only one night a month.

"Should I read that one next?" She nodded at *Listen*. I felt a little flustered as I glanced at Phoebe but then she laughed. "I'm kidding. I know your mom wrote it. I read it a long time ago. My question is, why is it in a middle-school library?"

"That's what I was wondering," I said. "The ending is so bleak."

"The book's language makes it accessible to eighth graders and it certainly addresses important topics." Her voice was slow and thoughtful. "But that doesn't mean it's appropriate. I worry that if kids read certain novels before they're ready, it might turn them off reading. Or scare them unnecessarily. I don't know. I think I'm just annoyed at these parents in our school who push and push. So what if a kid wants to read comic books. At least they're reading?"

"So, do you see your job as cultivating happy readers or making sure they're prepared as critical thinkers for the next grade?" I asked.

With her fork, she poked at the remaining turkey on her plate. "Honestly? Sometimes it's all I can do just to get them through the day with their little self-esteems intact."

We laughed. Maybe she worried about her students' friendships, too, and whether she was a good enough teacher. It had been a while since I talked to anyone like this. With the lower school teachers, our conversations were mostly about lesson plans, benchmarks, misbehaving kids, and lately about the new gym teacher. I heard a burst of laughter and we turned to watch Kitty and some of the others who had formed a tight circle around him. He was too young for them and a little too sporty, but he was good looking. I could see the attraction.

"What are you doing over vacation?" Justine asked.

"My husband and I are going to New York this afternoon for a few days."

"Lucky!" She smiled. "For fun?"

I wasn't looking forward to going, despite the promise of an amazing meal at the Christmas party tonight and the fancy hotel where we were staying, all expenses paid. "Ben, my husband, has a work party. The New York office of his law firm invited us down for it. For the rest of vacation, we'll be here. He has to work through the holidays. Unfortunately."

She rolled her eyes. "I know the feeling. My husband will spend this vacation trying to finish his dissertation. I'll be so happy when it's over. Hey, I was going to suggest that we get together for dinner with our husbands. But maybe just you and me for coffee sometime over break? To commiserate?"

I startled. What did she want? It was one thing to work together and talk, but to have coffee? To do something together out of school? That meant something more, like a friendship, and I wasn't at all sure I wanted to go there. I didn't really know her. She didn't know me, either. She didn't know anything about me.

I saw the corners of her smile droop, and I tried to recover by saying, "Okay. Sure. That'd be nice."

But it was too late. She'd seen my hesitation.

"Have you guys tried the lasagna yet? It's awesome." Kitty was beside me, thrusting her heaping plate between Justine and me. The lasagna was stacked nearly two inches high and oozing with cheese, spinach, and a garlic red sauce. And then two middle-school teachers walked up, also with plates of lasagna, and soon I lost Justine in the crowd.

After a while, I helped myself to some food, although I didn't feel hungry. I tried to catch

Justine's eye several times but she wouldn't look at me. I couldn't tell if that was because she was hurt or if she'd simply written me off. Not long after this, I left. I had to go home before picking up Ben at the office. We needed to be on the road by three in order to get to New York, settle into our hotel, change clothes, and make our way to the Manhattan partners' Christmas party.

At home, I found a message on the answering machine from Ben, who said he was running late. If I picked him up at four o'clock, he promised to be ready. I sat at the kitchen table, still in my winter coat, and felt irritated in a way I usually didn't. Most likely we wouldn't leave until at least four thirty and then what were we supposed to do, change clothes in the car on the way to the party? Why did he work so much? Why did we have to go to this party? I didn't want to go to Manhattan. Ben wasn't friends with the lawyers he worked with. He liked to keep these two parts of his life separate. That was what he always told me.

That was what I'd done with Justine today, too. But I cringed because this wasn't completely true. I put my elbow on the table and sunk my head into my hand. I didn't want to go to coffee and then maybe a movie and then after that to dinner with our husbands because eventually we'd talk about ourselves and our lives and at some point she'd realize I wasn't the person she thought I was. I'd disappoint her.

But wasn't I being ridiculous? After all, I tried so hard to be a good person now. I could be a good friend, too. But as I looked out the window at the bare brown tree branches, like spider legs across the pale blue sky, I felt such longing pull at me. Could I name my close friends? Did I even *have* any? Instead, I counted coworkers and acquaintances and people I saw at the gym and while waiting in line at Dunkin' Donuts and the supermarket.

"You had so many friends when we were in college," Ben said to me one morning several months ago as he headed off for another fourteen-hour day. "Why don't you call someone? You know, get together for dinner or something?"

Would I call Diana, whom I hadn't seen in five years, since I quit working at the coffeehouse? Lorenzo, whom I had nothing in common with now that we no longer worked together? Friends from high school, most of whom I didn't know anymore? I barely even talked to college friends. I didn't know why.

Of course I knew why.

I was a coward.

I stood and went into our bedroom, pausing in the doorway. We'd recently had the walls painted dark beige that matched the new comforter cover. Antique wood nightstands stood on either side of the bed. Our condo was beginning to resemble the distinct parts of our personalities.

Clean, modern, and neat (Ben). Antiques and books (me).

What was Lee's apartment like? And what about her husband? Did she want children? Was she trying to conceive and not having luck, either? I imagined tomorrow, out for a walk in midtown, and running into her. What would we say? How would I defend not calling or writing after receiving her letter months ago? Although I'd put it away in my nightstand drawer and hadn't looked at it in a while, I knew it by heart. *I've learned some things that have given me some peace with all that has happened. Maybe it would give you some peace, too. I have a favor. I need your help.* And below that her address and phone number in Manhattan.

I walked to the nightstand table, opened the drawer, and took out the letter. Maybe it was because I felt bad about Justine or because I couldn't get rid of the longing in my heart or maybe because I just wanted some peace, after all, but I put the letter in my pocket. And then I turned out the light and went back to the kitchen to wait for Ben's call.

CHAPTER 27

Ben threw open the curtains. The hotel window was massive and the shockingly bright sunlight made me flinch. I pulled the down comforter over my head. After a few moments, I peeked out and groaned, "What time is it?"

"It's late, seven forty-five." Ben, showered and dressed, stood in front of the mirror knotting his tie. Usually I never slept this late but last night Ben had been so keyed up when he came back from his dinner that we'd talked until two. He'd even skipped his run this morning.

"Are you sure you're okay alone again today?" he asked.

I bunched the pillow under my head, turned away from the window, and nodded. This wasn't how it was supposed to be. We were supposed to have time together. But at the Christmas party two nights ago, one of the partners asked him to come into the office and so yesterday he worked all day—and through last night's dinner—and now was working again today. But there was an upside, he said. The New York office was going to lobby for him to be made partner sooner than anticipated. Ben was so excited that he'd jumped on the bed when he got back to the room. It was hard to be disappointed when there was so much good news.

"I'm sorry," he said. "I'll make it up to you."

"No, you won't," I said. We'd been trying to get away together since June. Each time—and there were two others, in addition to this trip—work got in the way. That was what happened when you wanted to make partner, he'd said. Everything in our lives had to revolve around work.

He turned from the mirror and frowned. "Yes, I will. I promise."

"I'm kidding." Was I?

"I'm doing this for us," he said. "So we can have a good life."

"*And* because you don't know anything else," I said. "You're a workaholic."

"I know," he said, his voice a little defensive, a little proud.

A good life meant money, a lovely new condo, and a fulfilling career. I looked back out the window and thought about Meadows and the math lesson I'd botched last week. And how frustrated Max was with his writing. And that I had no answer for Abby's parents, who wanted to know why their precocious daughter didn't like to read. What a relief to be on vacation for a few weeks. But I shouldn't complain. I was lucky to have a job. It was my own damn fault that I was so ambivalent about it.

Ben put on his suit coat, draped his dress coat over his arm, and picked up his briefcase. "What are you going to do today?"

"I don't know." I sighed, pulling the blankets down to my waist. Yesterday I'd gone to the Met and walked through Central Park. Last night I had room service and watched a movie. I felt a nervous rumbling in my stomach and rolled onto my side.

I was nervous because I couldn't stop thinking about Lee. All day yesterday, I carried her letter in my pocketbook, and every time I passed a telephone booth I thought about calling her. Now it was our last day in Manhattan and I had to make a decision. But I'd waited so long that I wasn't sure I'd even be able to reach her.

Ben walked over and stood at the side of the bed. His cheeks were red from shaving and he'd missed a clump of hair in the middle of his dimple. He reached out and rubbed my shoulder with the knuckles of his right hand.

"I just thought we'd spend more time together, that's all," I said.

"I know, I'm sorry." He shook his head. "But it's something else, too. You've been edgy ever since we got here. I thought you liked New York."

"I do."

"Is it because we haven't been able to get pregnant?" he asked.

I shook my head.

He stared at me with his little green eyes not blinking, and I knew he was totally present and trying to figure out what he'd missed, what was wrong. I brought my knees to my chest in a fetal position and suddenly felt so small as he loomed over me that I reached for his hand. It wasn't fair to keep him guessing. And it wasn't his fault, either, that I kept secrets from him.

"I'm thinking about calling Lee," I said.

He squeezed my hand. "You should. That's a great idea. Do it, Clare."

"I don't know."

"Why not? It's been such a long time. It'll be okay, I bet." He dropped my hand and readjusted his tie. "I won't be late. I'll be back by five and we'll grab a quick dinner, okay? Before we leave?"

"Okay," I said as he started for the door. "Ben?"

He turned but I saw in his face that he was already gone. He was thinking about the case on which he was working and the New York partners. And I realized that he'd never make it back by five. I was looking at another day and evening alone. I felt nervousness grip me again, as if my stomach were in a vise.

"Good luck," I said.

He smiled, relieved. "Thanks. Have fun!" And then he was gone.

I turned my head and looked out the window.

I thought about a morning during junior year of college when Lee and I went running together. She had long, muscular legs and moved so fast, so efficiently, that she barely seemed to break a sweat. I, on the other hand, struggled just to put one foot in front of the other. It was a joke, the idea that I could keep up with her, and we didn't run together often.

"I just can't believe it!" she said as we started up the hill toward the library. "It had an amazing cast. Twelve nominations. It took a year to shoot in five different countries. It chronicled the Russian Revolution. What's more important than that?"

She was talking about the Academy Awards, broadcast the week before, and *Reds,* directed by Warren Beatty, her favorite *mainstream* movie of the year. It had lost the best picture honor as well as best actor and actress. She'd seen it three times, no small feat as it was more than three hours long, and I'd gone with her to one of the showings. I liked it. I just didn't feel as strongly about it as she did.

"Instead, they honor sappy sentimental bullshit? Who votes for these things? I'll tell you who. The establishment. They should know better. *Reds* wasn't an easy film. It was maddening, at times, and too long. But think of what it was trying to do!"

Halfway up the hill, I was trying not to die from

lack of oxygen. Lee had turned around so that she was running backward. Her long hair bounced on her back and her breathing was steady and easy.

"You know. That all these. Awards things. Are fickle. Right?" I sucked in breaths and thought about my mother, complaining over the years about the book awards that didn't go to her. I didn't like that Lee was so focused on winning, too.

She began shaking her head. "When that first witness came on the screen, I nearly launched out of my seat. How did Warren Beatty think to do that? The lighting was what made it. Did you see that? How the people seemed to bounce off the screen with that black background? It was ingenious."

We'd talked about this for hours already. She wanted to do the same thing in her film about Patricia. Witnesses talking to the camera. Bold lights. A black background. Just light and black. Black and light. I started to relax, even though the run was killing me, because I realized that talking about the awards was simply a segue to what really interested her. Technique. Substance. How films are made. Those were always the kinds of things about which she liked to talk.

We were only twenty-nine years old but of course she'd already made a documentary. Lee was the real deal, as my dad liked to say, and I was sure there would be more documentaries and what could she possibly want from me? What had she learned?

I reached up and turned off my bedside lamp. Out the window and across the street, an office building was waking up. Lights popped on. People moved in and out of cubicles. The window was at least eight feet tall by six feet wide. Had I been able to open it, had we not been on the fortieth floor, I imagined it was a window that a person—no, two people, easily, side by side—could walk through. Maybe run through.

I felt a sob rise through my chest and into my throat and I thought of that terrible abduction I saw on the news last night. A ten-year-old boy, the same age as my students, was taken as he walked to school. How horrible for him and his parents. And what the *hell* were they doing when this happened? I squeezed my eyes closed so tightly that I saw wispy white stars.

She hadn't yelled at me in her letter, not this time. She said she'd learned some things that had given her some peace. And she had a favor to ask.

I stood and went to the window. I put my palm on the thick, cold glass and leaned closer. I tried to see down to the street, but I was too far up and the angle wasn't right. I'd done everything that I wanted to do yesterday. I'd begun Christmas shopping and had lunch at the Vietnamese restaurant on Fifty-Eighth Street. After Central Park and the Met, I'd taken my time in the bookstore on Madison and found a great present for my dad: a hardback collection of World War I photographs. The store had all my mother's books, too, including the new reissue of *Listen, Before You Go.*

I picked up my pocketbook and took out Lee's letter. I didn't have to call. I could go home and that would be that. But Ben would ask later today about it, and what would I say? That I'd been too afraid to call? That I was a coward? Would I lie and say that I'd called but she didn't call me back?

When was I going to stop lying to him?

I picked up the phone and punched in the numbers before I could change my mind.

Lee answered on the first ring. "Hello?"

"Lee," I croaked. "It's Clare."

She sucked in a breath, I heard it so clearly, and said, "I'm *so* glad you called!"

Her voice—so full of excitement and optimism—was as I remembered it from the early days, before everything changed. I felt that rush of longing pull at my chest.

"Are you paying attention to traffic lights?" I blurted.

She paused and then laughed. "Yes, yes, of course."

"I'm here in Manhattan with Ben. And I just wanted to call. I'm sorry it's taken me so long. You know, after your letter." I was so unsteady, so nervous, that I was afraid I might faint. I sat on the edge of the bed.

"It's okay," she said. "Look, I have to switch some things around, but do you have time to meet for coffee?"

After that, we talked just long enough to make plans to meet. Later, she had an appointment that she couldn't cancel. My hand shook as I wrote the address to the café on the hotel notepad. After we hung up, I turned on the TV. Voices of local newscasters, strangers to me, filled the room.

I stood and went back to the window.

Once on a visit not long after Lee moved here, we were on Fifth or Madison or maybe Park when she stepped into the street after the light had changed. She wasn't paying attention—she was still in such a fog—and I pulled her back onto the sidewalk just as a cab barreled toward us.

For the next couple of months, whenever I talked to her, I often asked, "Are you paying attention to traffic lights?" Most of the time she laughed and I felt better. That was what I always tried to do in those days. Get her to laugh. Get her to forget.

Now we were going to meet for the first time in five years, and she would tell me the story of what she'd learned about peace, and we were going to have to talk about what had happened in Florida. What would we say? How would we start?

On TV the weatherman was telling me that

it would be warm in New York today. Record warmth for December. Shirtsleeve warmth.

I'd walk downtown to meet Lee. The hotel concierge would direct me and this would give me time, hours really, to think and remember and put together my own story of what I'd learned and what I'd been doing all these years.

I would start at the beginning, when I was eleven and came here with my mother when she collected her North American Book Award prize. But I didn't meet Lee until I was eighteen and a freshman in college.

I became more and more unsure as I showered, dressed, and rode the elevator to the lobby. It was quite easy, the concierge showed me on a map, to get downtown. I clutched the map in my hand and walked outside. The air was brisk and cool and the sun was hidden behind the buildings. People hurried by me. Cars and cabs zoomed up to stoplights. I began to sweat as I walked.

Finally, I stopped and stared at my reflection in a jewelry store window. I tried to see the color of my eyes and the whiteness of my teeth but the reflection wasn't clear. It was more like an old-fashioned black-and-white photo. But then I saw my shoulders sink and realized that I didn't have much of a story to tell—beyond the superficial—about what I'd learned and what I'd done these past five years.

I turned away and kept walking.

CHAPTER 28

The coffeehouse, which also functioned as a bar, was small and intimate and reminded me of Lorenzo's place. Lee and I met at a table in the back corner. She was still thin but her long black hair was cut to shoulder length. She wore jeans and loafers—no more clogs—a black peacoat that fit snug through the waist, small, tasteful silver hoop earrings, and no makeup. She looked completely familiar and yet utterly different. My heart pounded and my palms were damp. It was painful to look at her and yet I couldn't look away, either.

"It's so nice to see you," she said as she took off her coat.

"It's nice to see you, too."

Was she *truly* happy to see me? I shifted in my seat, trying to get comfortable, trying to find balance. My damp hands had turned cold despite how warm it was in the room. She smiled. She didn't seem as nervous as I was.

"How long have you been living back here?" I asked.

"A couple of years." She told me that she and Wallace met at a film festival and had been married for two years. I watched how her mouth moved and saw that the scar on her lip was still visible and thought how strange it was to be familiar with someone and yet know so little about her last five years.

"Is Wallace a filmmaker, too?" I asked.

"He's a producer. He finds the money and makes sure people get paid."

A waitress came by to deliver our drinks, cappuccinos for both of us, and I remembered the first time Lee had one. We were on the Vineyard and my parents had taken us to dinner. I was also with her the first time she tried Brie and lobster and drank Chateau Montelena chardonnay and now look at her. A documentary shown all over the country. A husband. An apartment in the city. I felt that familiar ping in my chest. Maybe it was envy. Or fear. Or that I suddenly missed her. Maybe it was all or none of the above. I began bouncing my leg under the table.

"I'm sorry about your mom," she said.

"Thanks. And thanks for your card. I'm sorry I didn't write you back."

She shook her head. "It's okay. How are you doing about it?"

I sighed. "Oh, okay."

I told her about the diagnosis, the chemotherapy, and the rough last couple of months. I told her about how sad my dad felt and how lovely the memorial service was on the Vineyard. I thought, suddenly, that I might share what Oliver had said. But it felt like such a long story and besides, it had been three months and I still didn't know what I thought about it. It was hard to be curious about what he told me when no one else around me felt the same way.

She leaned across the table. "But how are *you* feeling about it?"

I glanced at her and then down into my cappuccino. Lee seemed so steady and I felt so unsteady. "It's a loss. I guess I feel what you're supposed to feel."

I looked up. Lee was staring at me, her eyes not blinking and her face so still. She'd changed. She was calmer, somehow, and more mature. Marriage did that to a person. I was more mature and changed, too, although at the moment I felt off balance in a way that I hadn't in a long time. I didn't like it.

"Your parents were always very welcoming to me," she said.

"They liked you," I said.

She nodded and I shifted in my seat again. I was hot—my flushed cheeks had begun to throb—and my hands were so clammy. Did she feel how awkward this was, too? So much had happened in five years. How did a person explain those years? I couldn't decide if I was happy or scared. If I wanted to leave or stay.

"How's Ben?" she asked.

I told her about his job, my school, and the condo we'd bought. She told me that her parents and The Miracles were still on the farm. Her aunt, with whom she was estranged, moved to Tennessee. Lee had made the decision not to talk to or see her anymore.

"That's a shame," I said. "She was such a role model for you."

"Well, she certainly introduced me to the world beyond the farm." She nodded. "I'm grateful for that. It took me years to figure out the other stuff, the sibling rivalry that I was caught in the middle of. And the narcissism, of course."

Narcissism?

I began turning my spoon over on the table. In the years after we graduated, I had worked so hard to make everything okay, to see that she was happy and not thinking about Florida. But now I felt as if that night was alive and well and sitting here at the table, demanding attention, and I had absolutely no defenses to fight it.

Maybe I could tell her about the renovations to my parents' Vineyard cottage. Maybe I could tell her about the antique tables I found at an estate sale in Weston.

"Clare?" Lee folded her hands on the table and leaned toward me. "Can we talk about what happened?"

"Are you going to yell at me?" I blurted. Then I laughed but not because this was funny but because I was terrified. What happened was the source of so many problems for me and for us.

Why go through the pain of rehashing it? And yet that was why we were here, right?

She watched me—she was certainly not laughing—and shook her head. "It was too bad that we argued at Amy's wedding, but I think it was necessary. I was in a bad place in those years after college. I was depressed and confused and ashamed. I blamed myself for what happened with those guys, and I leaned way, way too much on you. It wasn't fair to either of us. Especially you."

"Oh."

"I wasn't my own person," she continued. "I lost myself. I looked to you to take care of me and underneath I was angry. Do you know why I was mad at you about Florida? Do you know why I yelled at you at Amy's wedding?"

I sucked in a breath and held it. *Let her go, I'll stay.* I nodded. "I left you."

"No." She shook her head and then took a deep breath. "I was angry with what you said while we put down our sleeping bags. Before Charlie and the guys came over to us. Do you remember what you said?"

Was it too early to have a glass of wine? I glanced at the bar behind me. The early afternoon sun was just creeping into the room. The window that looked out on the street was clear, no smudges or scratches. I turned to Lee again. "I'm not sure."

"I told you that you were the only person who knew me, the only one I'd ever really talked to." Her voice grew softer. "And you said that that was too goddam much responsibility and you didn't want it."

I cringed and squeezed my eyes closed. Had I said that? I couldn't remember. At the same time, something felt familiar about it. I opened my eyes. "I'm sorry!"

"It's okay, I'm not angry now. I've learned a lot about myself over the last couple of years and I want to tell you about it. Okay?" she asked. I nodded and stuck my cold hands under my thighs. She continued, "I've always had this sense that my parents, after the twins were born, abandoned me, emotionally, and left me way too much alone. Then when my aunt flaked out and wouldn't talk to me, which echoed what they'd done, it created this neurotic worry that scared me to my bones. I was miserable but I didn't know why. So much of it was unconscious. Anyway, I transferred this worry onto you. I worried that you were going to leave me, too. Remember how I had those dreams that you were ignoring me? Leaving me behind? It wasn't fair. It wasn't really about you. And I drove us both crazy."

"But I *did* end up leaving you."

Lee nodded. "Yes, but my worries were about you leaving me emotionally. I think I'd made you into a kind of mother figure. I wanted you to take care of me. Anyway, I told you to leave that night, remember? I think I wanted to do this altruistic thing to save you because you were my best friend. I'd been having sex since I was fifteen and thought I could handle it. But to be honest, I think I was also trying to make you feel bad for what you'd said. I knew you'd feel guilty or maybe even indebted to me if I gave myself up. But I got in way, way too far over my head. What a messed up thought process, huh?"

So she *had* wanted to be a martyr. But my relief was short-lived because I was confused and a bit shocked that she could admit this. I felt as if I were stumbling and spinning as I tried to understand. Did she really believe this? Was she really not angry? And how had she figured this out? But then I saw Charlie's face in my mind and sputtered, "I hate thinking about that night. It changed everything."

"I don't like talking about it much, either." Her voice became soft again, almost a whisper. "But maybe it might help to hear exactly what happened?"

She'd never told me the details. My sour stomach began to churn again. I looked down into my cappuccino—I'd barely touched it—and nodded slightly.

"So, first Owen took his turn and then Charlie." Her voice was suddenly stiff and tinged with anger. "Those two bastards were, well, they were quick. But then it was Mikey's turn and he couldn't get it up. He was tripping and too high, I think. Somehow this was my fault and he punched me and split my lip. And then. Well, then. Well, this next part is always hard. To think about. And say."

She looked down at her cappuccino. Her words felt measured and detached, as if she were reading from a script she'd rehearsed. The longer she paused, the harder this was. I sucked in a breath, feeling as if these details and now this silence, this waiting, were nearly as excruciating as the night everything happened.

She looked up at me. "Mikey was crazy. Or maybe it was the drugs. I don't know. But he scared me after he punched me, there was so much blood and my lip hurt so much, and I started to cry really hard. I think this freaked him out because he became so, well, disturbed. He ripped the shade off the floor lamp, took the lamp by the stand and kept thrusting the hot bulb at me. Then he began talking about something he'd seen on TV, about a kid who went blind when he stared too long at the sun. He thought they should do that to me. He said they should blind me with the lamp so I couldn't identify them to the police."

I felt a huge sob start from my chest and rush into my throat.

She began rubbing her cheek. "They went back

and forth about this but Mikey wouldn't let it go. He had it all planned out in his warped, pathetic little mind. He said they should tie me down and hold open my eyelids and sear my eyeballs with the light bulb from the floor lamp. Then he lunged at me and pressed the bulb to my cheek until Charlie shoved him."

I pushed away from the table, my cappuccino sloshing over the rim of the mug and onto the wood, and cried, "But I saw them! I could identify them!"

The waitress behind the bar looked over her shoulder at us.

"Well, of course you could," she said. "It was an idiotic plan. Because *he* was an idiot. After that, everything is mixed up. They argued a lot. I remember that. Somehow I got dressed. Charlie helped me, I'm pretty sure. They talked about killing me, too. Or maybe I imagined that. There was an explosion of glass. Then suddenly you were there. I remember that. You were standing on the step. It was like magic. Or a miracle. So, you see? You did save me, after all."

I burst into tears and dropped my head into my hands.

"Oh, God, the burn mark! On your face! It was from the lamp," I sobbed. She wasn't crying, but her eyes seemed tired and heavy and I didn't understand how she'd gotten here, to this point, where she could talk about this horrible thing.

She nodded slightly, and I dropped my head again, sobbing.

"Hey, hey," Lee said. "It's okay now. Clare? Look at me, Clare."

"I'm so, so sorry," I blubbered as I lifted my eyes. "This is awful. I'm so upset. I'm so *angry!* I didn't know this!"

"How could you?" she whispered. "I barely let myself know it."

"I hate those fucking guys!"

She nodded and looked down again. "I hate them, too."

I reached for a napkin and cleaned the tears off my face. I felt as if I were on a merry-go-round, spinning out of control and emotions—disgust, anger, panic—slapping me with every turn. Sweat began to pool under my arms.

"I want you to listen to this, okay?" she said, more control in her voice. "I barely remember the end of senior year and even parts of the years after. I was so full of shame and denial and fear. I was a wreck when I got to Thailand and almost bombed it like I did the internship. But one night, Patricia took me for a walk and asked what had happened to me—she said she felt it—and I told her everything about Florida and the lamp. About my track coach and my family, too.

"I hadn't been able to tell anyone about this. Actually, it was a shocking relief to talk about it. So, for months Patricia and I kept talking—she was a good listener, as I'm sure you can imagine. And when we got back, she gave me the name of a therapist. I started going to this woman four times a week. For years. I'm still going."

So, Lee had been to therapy. Was that what made her seem so different from how she was after Florida?

"I realize now that it wasn't my fault what those guys did," she said. "And no one was going to blind me now. Or ever. And I'm working on something else with my therapist although I can't seem to stay with it for long. But it's this. What if Florida wasn't the *source* or the beginning of my problems? Maybe they were more about growing up with no money, feeling dropped by my parents, being taken advantage of by my track coach, and not being able to count on people. Maybe that was what led me to my decisions, including the one in Florida."

I shook my head. "You're not minimizing what happened, are you?"

"Hardly," she whispered. "It still keeps me up at night. Sometimes I'm gripped with so much fear that I can't function. I'll always hate what those guys did, and I feel terrible that I put so much pressure on you. I didn't mean to do this. It wasn't fair to you. But I'm not ashamed anymore. Of anything. That's what I want you to know."

I picked up my cappuccino and drank, even though my stomach was still churning. My hands shook so much that when I set my mug down coffee sloshed over the side again and onto the table.

With a napkin she mopped it up. "Remember back in college when we watched Patricia's documentary and I asked for advice? She said that the unexamined life is not worth living. Then she said something like, 'For your life, sanity, and art, you must learn about yourself.' That's what I'm trying to do."

I hadn't lived that kind of life. I often didn't know why I did the things I did.

"Does any of this make sense to you?" she asked.

If I examined my life, what would I find? Fear and doubt. Compromises and mistakes. But also good, too. I'd tried to be good. I nodded. But then I remembered what Mr. Donahue had said years ago about the South American writer who suffered from writer's block after years of therapy. That was the danger with this kind of thing. It was bad for creativity. It made a person too self-focused. It was better to work hard and move forward. Life should not be spent wallowing over the past.

And yet her words were swimming around in my head. *What if Florida wasn't the source of my problems?* How could this be? Everything changed after that night.

The floor lamp.

I remembered. It was tall, the shade covered with different colored racing cars. Something thick and powerful rushed through me and I sucked in a breath and looked for anything to push it away. Oh, God, poor Lee. I blurted, "I liked your film."

She sat up. "You saw it? At the MFA?"

"It was good." I felt the tension inside me ease. "And fun to see Indiana again. But I did wonder what happened to your plans of finding a great person in history."

She smiled slightly and leaned back in her seat. "Remember how obsessed I was with that? It's so funny how your unconscious works. All those years of wanting to find a great person to film. I had no idea that I was really looking for my benefactor, to feature him, you know, to thank him."

Wait, what?

She shook her head and chuckled.

I felt a little lost. "Well, did you ever figure out who it was?"

"Not officially. Although, I'm pretty sure it was someone in the Meaghan family. You know, the ones who owned the automotive plastics company."

"So, you were able to thank him, after all."

She nodded. "I hope the film was about more than that. It took me a while to figure out what kind of filmmaker I wanted to be. It threw me off being in Thailand with Patricia. She was trying to change the world. I thought I had to do that, too."

"How did you figure out what to do?" This felt more comfortable and familiar now, me asking questions and Lee explaining.

"Process of elimination, I guess," she said. "Some filmmakers set out to expose something to the world. Others just try to make sense of their own worlds. I guess I'm in the second camp."

I knew only too well what my mother would say about this. With *Listen*, she always insisted that she was writing a novel to expose the dangers and hypocritical nature of war. She'd put herself firmly in Lee's first camp. But if what Oliver said was true, then wasn't she also trying to make sense of her world?

"Clare?"

They were going to try to blind her with the floor lamp.

I felt sour juices roil in my stomach and kept swallowing to keep them from rising into my throat. The muscles tightened across my upper back and tears sprang into my eyes again. No wonder she couldn't function after this. No wonder she'd been a wreck. "I feel so awful. I don't know what to say."

She sat very still now. "Sometimes I think that I could kill each of them if I ever saw them again. I really think I could do it. Maybe with my bare hands. When I'm feeling like this, it helps to remember the Rat Man case."

The Rat Man case was somewhere in the back of my mind. Before Florida. When I was a different person. Or maybe the same person. I didn't know.

"Remember how we talked about the torturer, that he had to have experienced something like that in order to do what he did?" she asked. "It helps to think about those guys that way. That they were troubled. Neglected. Somehow repeating their own abuse. Otherwise, how do you explain what they did? Especially Mikey?"

I wasn't ready to forgive them. Or maybe that wasn't what she meant. She stared at me with that faraway look in her eyes again, and I knew she was floating, drifting. But then she straightened and rubbed the back of her neck with her hand and said, "Sometimes I think that I want to find them. Or at least find out, for sure, what made them do what they did."

"They're probably all in prison by now," I said. "Or maybe dead."

We were quiet for a few moments. I took another napkin across my face.

"What do you think about what happened to us?" she asked.

I remembered how happy I felt when we sat outside the cold dorm and talked. And when we both realized that we felt the same way about so many things that were going on in our lives. I hadn't felt that kind of connection with anyone, not even Ben. "It's sad. We were so close."

"We connected on a very primal level. And when I was feeling so neurotic I think I scared you. Deeply. I'll always feel terrible about that. My therapist is really big on this transferring idea. She thinks people will repeat in the present a relationship that was important to them in their childhoods. I guess that sounds right in my case with you. But it makes me wonder. Are all relationships like that?"

I shrugged. I didn't know what to think about this. All I felt was sadness. About the lamp and all she'd gone through and what had happened to us.

"I'm so sorry!" I suddenly wanted to tell her every confusing emotion I felt about her, about my mother, and even about Ben. I would be vulnerable. Yes!

"It's okay," she said.

"But it's not!"

"It will be okay. I think. Maybe." She bit her lower lip. "Anyway, I have something I want to ask you, Clare. A favor."

I nodded.

"I want you to go back to Daytona with me."

"What?" I gasped.

"That night in Florida has taken up too much space in our lives. We let it have too much power.

If what my therapist said is true, that that night isn't the source of the problem, then let's face it. Let's go down there and tell that city to go fuck itself."

"I don't want to see those guys again."

She shook her head. "I don't want to see them, either, not really. I just want to drive through town. Maybe find both houses. I haven't been back since that night. Maybe it'll give me some closure. Or shift something in my head. I don't know."

I couldn't speak. I couldn't do this.

"I think it would be helpful and maybe for you, too," she said. "It might be healing. I don't think I can do it alone."

"But what about your husband!" I blurted.

She nodded. "Yes, he could go with me. But he wasn't there that night. You were. I need help putting all the events together."

"But I don't remember where the house is!" My breath felt shallow in my throat and I put my hand to my chest again. Why do this? Why go back and relive it?

"We could figure it out." She crossed her arms and rested them on the table. "I think it would be good for you, too, Clare. It might help you, you know, forgive yourself. Don't you think it's time you forgave yourself?"

Was that what had been wrong with me? I couldn't forgive myself? I shook my head. "I don't know if I can do it."

"I know it's a lot to ask."

"No, it's not just that." But I stopped because it *was* too much to ask, and I couldn't do it. Not only did I not want to relive that night, but how awkward would it be, traveling together after we hadn't seen each other in so long? And yet she'd put herself out there by asking this, and it suddenly felt dismissive, and a bit cruel, to rule it out so adamantly. "Maybe we can talk about it after Christmas?"

"Sure," she said. But I could tell by the way the sides of her mouth fell that she knew I didn't mean it. I tried to hold her gaze but eventually dropped my eyes and drank the rest of my cappuccino.

After that, we made small talk about the unusual weather and New York and then she glanced at her watch. She had to leave for a meeting. She said, "It was so nice seeing you. I don't know where this leaves us, but I'd sure like to keep talking."

"So would I." And I meant it. "We could write to each other. And phone, too."

"Yes, that sounds good."

We paid the bill and walked out to the street. It was mild, near sixty, and the sun, shining through a sliver of space between two buildings, was strong and warm. How could this be? It felt like late spring instead of the beginning of winter. Lee turned and smiled at me. And suddenly I felt so sad that our time was over and we were going back into worlds that didn't include each other. I had this terrible sense that I'd lost something, a part of who I was or wanted to be or could have been. Or maybe it was just that when I was with Lee I was somebody I used to know.

We hugged and said goodbye. And then I cried as I walked back to our hotel in midtown.

CHAPTER 29

"Just look at him." Kitty, a furry scarf wrapped tightly around her neck, pointed a gloved finger at a boy with curly brown hair who was bossing around a group of kids on the snow-covered blacktop. "He's gonna grow up to be a mass murderer. Mark my words, ladies."

"Kitty!" one of the third-grade teachers said. "That's a horrible thing to say."

"Okay, so I'm exaggerating," she said. "But it's been a long time since we've had a bully of his caliber in the school."

The other teachers murmured in agreement as we watched the boy. We were six altogether, huddled against the brick wall next to the playground, bouncing to keep the circulation moving, scanning the kids for any signs of imminent snowball throwing. Since we'd returned from break six days before, we'd had nothing but frigid temperatures and bouts of snow. So far, a foot was on the ground. But I didn't mind playground duty in the cold. It beat sitting in my classroom by myself, stewing as I waited for the kids to return. And I liked watching them play.

Today I was watching Sophia and Talia, who were each with different groups. Sophia was on the play structure, playing an elaborate game of house while Talia was with the boys, playing tag. Before break they'd been inseparable and exclusive, both on the playground and in the classroom, but since we'd been back, I'd only seen them together at random times. And so I watched, I knew, to see if I could determine what had happened. Was one snubbing the other? Had they had an argument?

"Hello, earth to Clare, hello?" a third-grade teacher said. I turned back into the circle. Everyone was staring at me, our white breaths forming a collective, malleable cloud in front of us. "Are you looking for something?"

"Well," I began.

"That's Clare!" Kitty laughed. "So attached to her kiddies. You're too invested, Clare. You gotta know how to let them sink or swim on their own."

"Kitty, *please*," Lindsey, a second-grade teacher, said. "Sometimes I think you'd be better suited as a prison guard."

"Hey," Kitty protested. They laughed. Then someone brought up the hot new gym teacher, and that started another flurry of conversation.

Stung with being discovered, I forced myself to listen to their cooing. We were all attached to our students—even Kitty—but I had a sense that maybe my attachment was different although I didn't know what that meant. No matter what, I wasn't going to look for Sophia and Talia. But when Talia ran by me, so close that her jacket brushed against mine, I turned and watched as she jumped onto the swings, only a few feet away from Sophia. Neither girl paid a bit of attention to the other. How could they go from being so tight to barely speaking?

I turned back to the group and when Kitty grinned at me, slyly, I jumped in before she could accuse me of anything else.

"How was Arizona, Lindsey?" I asked. "How is your grandmother?"

"It was good and she's better," Lindsey said. "Thanks for asking. My God, you have a good memory. I told you about my grandmother like a hundred years ago."

"No, just at the holiday lunch," I said. Everyone laughed and that started another round of comments, this time about the food served and whose parents were responsible for the cotton ball snowmen.

It was safe to peek at the playground again. Several boys were trying to make a giant snowball. Two others pulled icicles off the chain-link fence. Abby and the hangers-on were talking by the swings. And still Sophia and Talia were separate. But neither appeared to be looking for the other and neither seemed unhappy, either.

Later, as I saw them talking by their wood

cubbies after lunch, I chided myself for being so overly involved. My job was to teach them to write better, to understand math and science enough to pass fourth-grade benchmarks, not to obsess over friendships. My God, what was wrong with me?

When it was time for read-aloud, I gathered everyone on the rug. We'd finished *Matilda,* but the kids had become so invested in Roald Dahl that they demanded another book by him. Max had wanted me to read *The Witches,* but I thought that might be too nightmare inducing for some. We settled on *The BFG,* which also had some scary parts although when I examined the drawings they'd made about the book, nothing alarmed me.

"No, no." I pointed to Jonah, who was nettling Paolo with the toe of his sneaker. "Now you have to come sit next to me. Come on."

Jonah sighed, scooted next to me, and sunk his head in dramatic fashion.

I glanced at Sophia, who'd settled in front of me with her legs crossed and her hands folded in her lap. Talia walked by her without looking and plopped down next to Vanessa. Before break, Sophia and Talia always sat together during read-aloud. Something had most certainly happened. Or maybe their connection wasn't as close as I thought. I glanced at the window, now covered with so much condensation that I couldn't see out. It was their sweaty bodies and tiny, little breaths that did this.

The kids were seated now and staring at me with eager eyes.

Forgive yourself.

That was what Lee had said. It was time to forgive myself. For what? The list was lengthy.

I began to feel so irritated that when reading was over and the kids were working quietly at their tables on their vacation essays, I sat at my desk and stared at that fucking window and decided that I had to do something. I had to make a decision. If I was going to stay in teaching, I needed to get my master's degree in education. Then I'd have the credentials and knowledge to teach these children. Maybe that would give me the confidence, too.

I began calling them up, one by one, to talk about their essays. I left Max for last. Vanessa, I pointed out, needed more details about frosting Christmas cookies with her cousins and Abby didn't have a thesis. Then it was Sophia's turn. She hurried up to my desk, her essay clutched in her hand. She wore black leggings and a long, blue sweatshirt, and when she sat in the chair next to my desk, her brown bangs bounced before settling back against her forehead.

I read her essay about her vacation at her grandmother's house on Cape Cod. It was awfully good and I had little to offer in terms of improving it.

"You had a wonderful time." I smiled.

She giggled and nodded. She'd gone sledding and ice-skating with her cousins, aunts, and uncles, and it sounded like a big party, a week of celebrating. I smiled at her and then looked at the essay again.

"But then I had to come back here." Her smile turned into a cringe.

"Is something wrong?"

She shrugged and looked down into her hands, folded in her lap, as she whispered, "I have to go to the dentist today. I *hate* the dentist!"

"Me, too," I said. "Anything else wrong? Maybe here at school?"

Her eyebrows wrinkled in concern. "Like what do you mean?"

"Well, I noticed that you and Talia were really close before break and now you aren't together as much, and I wondered if everything was okay."

"Why wouldn't it be okay?"

"Well, you weren't playing on the playground today."

She smiled. "That was because she doesn't like to play house and I don't like to play tag."

Just like that. So matter of fact and to the point.

"We're still best friends," she said. "We both have lots of best friends."

I nodded and sent her on her way. Because

really? A ten-year-old had just made complete sense of something I'd bungled for months.

That night when I got home, the sun had already gone down and the streetlights were on. Flipping on the kitchen lights, I watched how the black and white floor tiles showed the clusters of dust bunnies and how the windows reflected and distorted the refrigerator, the stove, the counter, and me. People transfer things onto each other, Lee had told me. As I stood there in my boots and coat and saw Sophia's doe-like eyes in my mind, I thought, oh, God, *of course*.

How embarrassing, how obvious? Part of me knew what I'd done—I worried about Lee and me as I watched Talia and Sophia—but I couldn't, for whatever reason, stop myself. No wonder Sophia didn't understand what I was asking.

Oh, Lee.

That weekend in college when I visited her farm, we went to the river so she could film the train tracks. It was cold and windy and overnight snow had covered the fields and the small clump of trees next to the tracks. Lee was on her stomach, filming, when we heard tire squeals and a man's voice. We ran back through the trees to the road. About twenty yards from Lee's car, a man stood next to a different car. He turned to us, distraught, and said, "They came out of nowhere."

Up ahead, two geese were on the side of the road, one sitting, the other honking and strutting. Lee ran past the man, slowed, and dropped to her knees. I followed and saw that the smaller goose wasn't sitting but lying on the pavement, half of its body crushed. The other, bigger goose, his breast cream colored, his colored feathers dull in the gray light, honked at his friend, then at us, as he strutted. Why had they been in the road? Why hadn't he taken better care of his friend?

Lee started to sob, uncontrollably. And I soon became more worried about her reaction—I'd never seen her cry like that—than I was with the goose.

The man shrugged at us as he got in his car and drove away. I didn't want to stay and watch this, either. "Come on, Lee. There's nothing we can do."

Lee wouldn't move until finally I reached down and pulled her up. When I asked for the keys, she gave them to me and climbed into the passenger seat. Tears running down her cheeks, she watched out the back window as I drove away. At the time I remembered thinking that this was sad, but inevitable. Geese could survive the cold, avoid coyotes and foxes, and find food in the winter, but how could they defend themselves against cars? They'd let their guard down. They weren't paying attention. And now look. Their lives changed forever in an instant.

"I bet the goose is in shock and so maybe it's not in so much pain," I said.

She turned and stared out the windshield. "That poor goose."

"It must be awful to die like that."

She shook her head, violently. "No! The other goose! Did you see him pacing? He didn't understand what happened. What will he do, stay there? For how long? *Forever?* All alone? He's all alone! That was the saddest thing I've ever seen!"

I glanced at Lee, worried again. I hadn't thought to feel sorry for the other goose. Nothing I said seemed to help until finally, an hour into our drive back to school, she fell asleep against the car window. By that time, the intensity of her emotions and how undone she was by this had made me angry. I didn't like this feeling one bit. And I remembered being frustrated with Ben when, after telling him about it, he said, "But why were *you* mad at *her?* It sounds like she was really upset."

I was angry because it felt like too much. It felt familiar. It felt like my mother.

I leaned against the counter and put my hand across my heart. We repeat important relationships from our childhood, Lee said. When she was feeling so neurotic and needy, she reminded me of my mother. And I resented it. Why hadn't I ever realized this? Maybe because on the surface Lee and my mother didn't appear *that* much alike. Lee was more outgoing, thoughtful, and not as selfish. But like my mother, she had the capacity for big feelings that could be overwhelming. And like my mother, she looked to me to take care of her.

I watched the snow melt from my boots and form puddles on the tiles. It had been four weeks since Lee and I talked in Manhattan and in that time I'd gone over our conversation hundreds of times. I always came to the same conclusions. I was too afraid to go back to Florida. I didn't know if I had the courage to live an examined life. I wasn't ready to forgive myself.

I glanced back out the window.

Mikey. Jittery Man's name was Mikey. All this time, all these many years later, I finally learned his name. But did it matter? Because Lee said that Florida wasn't the source of her problems. And what I'd said to her wasn't the problem, either. *Growing up with no money, feeling dropped by my parents, being taken advantage of by my track coach, and not being able to trust anyone.* Those were the real problems. How she grew up. The things that happened to her as a child.

Why didn't I ever talk about this kind of thing anymore?

I tossed my coat onto a kitchen chair and hurried into the living room where we had a large, antique bookcase. I wanted to read something by

542

Freud. I searched the shelves, my fingers tracing the bindings, but the only college books I found were from my literature classes. *Sons and Lovers* and *Lady Chatterley's Lover. The Catcher in the Rye, Wuthering Heights* and *Middlemarch*. I let my fingers linger on a first edition of *Listen, Before You Go* and pulled it off the shelf.

The first time I read it, I was surprised that people liked it so much. The long conversations between Whit and Phoebe were boring and nothing seemed to happen. And how could this book be about war when there wasn't a single battle or army? The second—and last time—I read it was in high school and I better understood the subtleties, symbolism, and foreshadowing. I understood that I had to read between the lines. But I was still terribly upset by Whit's suicide.

I turned to that section, when he and Phoebe were behind the garage and Whit put the gun in his mouth. But I was so surprised that I lowered myself to the floor. There was an entire page after the suicide that I didn't remember.

I started to read.

Phoebe stared at the red specks stuck to the garage wall. She heard the faint gurgling of blood as it left the hole in Whit's head and seeped into the mud. She felt herself falling and falling and the sky darkening and the air thickening. And then she was in a hole, black and stifling, the walls crushing her thin chest.

She had watched as he slowly raised the gun, put it in his mouth, and pulled the trigger. She had watched as if this were a show on television.

Something terrible had happened to her brother.

And she would live in this hole forever because she had been his keeper, the chosen one, and yet she was no better at helping him than the Army or the doctors at the hospital or the pink-faced, sweating lieutenant who had stood in their living room and told Whit about all he had to look forward to. If only he'd let go.

He couldn't let go. Because he was dead but alive, he'd told her. And now she finally understood what that meant. Shame burned into her cheeks.

But then she saw light in the corners of her eyes and suddenly the room was flush with it, and she was in the house and staring at the wall. How had she gotten here? She looked down at her shoes, caked in mud and splattered with tiny flecks of blood and bone. She hadn't wanted these ugly black and white saddle shoes. She'd ached for penny loafers, like her stylish cousins, but her mother had refused.

This memory, this desire, filled her with relief. Because how could she be dead but alive if she felt desire? She wouldn't live like that. She didn't have to live like that. So she decided never to tell anyone what she saw and how she'd failed. She'd work, yes, work was the way to do it, at keeping this day at bay. At always keeping this day at bay.

Years later she wouldn't remember this rationality. Or the hole. Or the decision she'd made. In fact, she wouldn't remember much about this day at all.

There was nothing minimalistic about this passage. It was about as explicit as could be. Had I missed it? Or did I just not remember it?

All these years I thought I was supposed to be Phoebe, that my mother had wanted me to take care of her as Phoebe had taken care of Whit. But really, *she* was Phoebe, the little girl who'd witnessed her grandfather's suicide and felt traumatized and ashamed at not being able to save him. She'd been writing about herself, all along. Was she trying to make sense of what had happened? Was she trying to explain herself? Apologize?

Had my mother lived an examined life, had

she talked through this terrible event, would she have had an easier time? Would she have been happier? Would she have not needed to write a book that seemed to give her more anxiety than joy?

Maybe if I'd known all this, she wouldn't have seemed so confusing. Maybe if I'd known her better, I wouldn't have believed Lucy over her.

I was ashamed, too. I abandoned Lee that night. I said those awful words to her. And now I refused to help her by going back to Daytona. I'd let that terrible night in Florida—all of it— hang like a noose around my neck. But if it was true that that night wasn't the source of trouble for her, then did that mean it wasn't the source of trouble for me, either? How could this be?

I looked at the snow piled on the sill outside the living room window and thought about recess a few days ago when I'd tried to roll a giant snowball toward the snowman that the kids had made. But it was too big and impossible to budge. So, I left it there because it would have been too much work to take it apart and carry it to them in pieces.

What was the point of taking your life apart, unearthing it, examining it, carrying it around in pieces, anyway? You can't change the past. Can you?

My mother was Phoebe and Phoebe was my mother.

Where did that leave me?

Maybe I'd wanted to believe that I was Phoebe because I was looking for a way, any way, to connect with my mother. And if I could be Phoebe and take care of my mother, save her, then she'd feel connected to me, too. I'd be important to her.

I felt a bit sick, thinking that my mother hadn't had me in mind when she wrote about Phoebe. And yet, another feeling was starting to grow. I thought about how present I tried to be for my students, how careful I was with their feelings, how hard I tried. I wasn't a great or even good teacher. But I wasn't a bad person. Maybe I was a good person who just made a couple of bad decisions.

I'd always felt that I'd lost something that night in Florida, a confidence or clarity about who I was and what I should do with my life. After all, how could I be the lifeline in the middle of the night if I'd failed so miserably with Lee? But if I was never intended to be that person in the first place, if this identification with Phoebe was a fantasy that I, and others, created, then how could I lose something I'd never really had? Maybe this night wasn't the source of my problems, after all, either.

Lee had looked to me as a mother figure, she'd said, and blamed herself for what happened to our friendship. But I had a responsibility in this, too, didn't I? I'd taken on the role of caretaker.

I'd encouraged the attachment. What would our friendship look like if I no longer had to take care of her in that same way?

I thought of that ten-year-old boy in New York, abducted on his way to school, and how critical I'd been of his parents. But maybe they'd done everything right. Maybe it was just horrendous luck. Maybe there was a difference between saving people and taking care of them. Because it suddenly seemed to me that there were things in life that happened—sickness, death, choices made based on events that happened in childhood, being at the wrong place at the wrong time—that no amount of "saving" could prevent.

What a terrible thing for my mother, as a child, to have witnessed. Maybe Logan was right, after all. The writing and publishing of *Listen, Before You Go* aggravated our mother's insecurity and egocentricity. But that book didn't create her problems.

My poor mother. Maybe it was time to mourn the good parts of her and let go of the bad. Maybe it was time to forgive her.

I closed my eyes. And suddenly, I saw myself on the porch of our sorority house, a book on my lap, others around me. I was young, maybe only a sophomore, and I remembered looking up as Lee started up the hill toward us. When I stood and waved to her, she burst into a smile and ran, her backpack slapping her shoulders and her long black hair blowing behind her. It was warm that day, the sun high in the sky, the green grass bright and fragrant. She had something important to tell me. Maybe it was a realization she'd had in film class or a new take on the book she was reading for English. And I remembered feeling happy for this and that I'd never met anyone like her and that this kind of friendship was rare. It might happen only once or twice in a lifetime.

Lee wasn't my mother and my mother wasn't Lee.

How ironic that for so many years I thought I was supposed to help Lee but instead she ended up helping me. It was time to move on, just as she'd moved on. And it was time to forgive myself, too.

I closed *Listen, Before You Go* and put it back on the shelf.

And then I reached for the phone. I was going to call Lee and say yes, I'll go to Florida with you. Just name the date and time and I'd be there.

Books are produced in the United States using U.S.-based materials

Books are printed using a revolutionary new process called THINKtech™ that lowers energy usage by 70% and increases overall quality

Books are durable and flexible because of smythe-sewing

Paper is sourced using environmentally responsible foresting methods and the paper is acid-free

Center Point Large Print
600 Brooks Road / PO Box 1
Thorndike, ME 04986-0001 USA

(207) 568-3717

US & Canada:
1 800 929-9108
www.centerpointlargeprint.com